PRAISE

'As tightly constructed ar                                    ıs

'Bold, biting, and blood-soaked in wit, *Seven Reasons to Murder Your Dinner Guests* is an all-you-can-eat feast for readers, and no doubt I'll be coming back for seconds.'

**Mallory Arnold**

'Deviously plotted and utterly entertaining—KJ Whittle proves you can't trust anyone at the table. A genuine delight to read.'

**Lauren North**

'A mystery to die for. Agatha Christie would be proud of this perfectly constructed whodunnit. RSVP to *Seven Reasons to Murder Your Dinner Guests* immediately!'

**L M Chilton**

'Every guest has a secret, and every secret is deadly...clever, engaging, and enjoyable.'

**Stacy Johns**

'Twisty, surprising, and impossible to put down, *Seven Reasons to Murder Your Dinner Guests* is a deliciously sinister tale of fate, fear, and the price of knowing too much.'

**Tom Ryan**

'A gourmet dish that crime aficionados will devour with relish. Hugely entertaining.'

**Martin Edwards**

**Seven guests. Three courses.
One deadly evening.**

# SEVEN REASONS TO MURDER YOUR DINNER GUESTS

*K. J. Whittle*

HarperCollins*Publishers*

HarperNorth
Windmill Green
24 Mount Street
Manchester M2 3NX

A division of
HarperCollins*Publishers*
1 London Bridge Street
London SE1 9GF

www.harpercollins.co.uk

HarperCollins*Publishers*
Macken House,
39/40 Mayor Street Upper,
Dublin 1, D01 C9W8, Ireland

First published by HarperCollins*Publishers* Ltd 2025
1

A catalogue record for this book is available from the British Library.

ISBN: 978-0-00-873871-6

This novel is entirely a work of fiction. The names, characters and incidents portrayed in it are the work of the author's imagination. Any resemblance to actual persons, living or dead, events or localities is entirely coincidental.

Set in Adobe Caslon by Amnet.

Printed and bound in the UK using 100% Renewable Electricity by CPI Group (UK) Ltd

MIX
Paper | Supporting
responsible forestry
FSC™ C007454

This book is produced from independently certified FSC paper to ensure responsible forest management.
For more information visit: www.harpercollins.co.uk/green

*In memory of my incomparable mum Christine Harden
who taught me everything I know about love.*

'Let us never know what old age is.
Let us know the happiness time brings, not count the years.'
— *Ausonius*

# The Dinner Party
## *November 2015*

**Vivienne**

Stepping out of the taxi, Vivienne squints at the dark street for any sign of the restaurant.

'I can't seem to find it…' she says, but her voice is lost in the roar of the engine as the taxi speeds off.

'Idiot,' Vivienne mutters. She glances at the loose change in her gloved palm and drops it into her handbag. She has never agreed with tipping taxi drivers, especially those who talk incessantly about their kids.

Light rain is falling, the sort that soaks you before you even feel it, and Vivienne's dry hair is prone to frizzing at the mere mention of moisture. Searching her bag for an umbrella, she groans as she realises she's left it in the taxi. Then her hand lands on the invitation. She doesn't need to read the gold words again.

*Serendipity's, 13 Salvation Road…*

This isn't quite what she'd pictured. The street reeks of disappointment. Every building a failed enterprise someone had invested their hopes in. A trendy cupcake café, a retro clothing boutique, a themed bar… all with weather-beaten 'for sale' signs attached. A young woman pushing a buggy bows her head to the rain and marches by, nearly knocking into Vivienne. An elderly man moves slowly on the other side of the road, leaning heavily on his stick, scowling at the pavement. Vivienne thinks better of asking either of them for directions, and searches for numbers on the worn-out shop fronts: 7, 9, 11 … but then the road ends.

*A waste of time.* She pulls her mobile from her bag to ring another taxi. A few more minutes in this rain and her make-up will landslide down her face, her hair panicking and heading in the other direction. If she hurries, she'll still make her 6.28 p.m. train home and her feet will be happily nestled in her sheepskin slippers with a Poirot mystery on the telly.

'Looking for Serendipity's?' A soft voice seems to slide straight into her ear, making her jump, her Clarks heels echoing on the wet pavement.

'Oh sorry, I didn't mean to startle you,' the man says as Vivienne spins towards him. *Perhaps 'boy' is closer to the truth*, she thinks as she takes him in. His eyes are magnified as he peers through rain-streaked glasses, giving the impression of a baby owl. His long hair is sodden, and hangs in ropes down to the collar of his denim jacket. In fact, his whole body seems to have been dragged down with the rain. A drowned baby owl.

Then she catches sight of her own reflection in the boy's glasses. Crepey skin, frizz-ball hair, downturned mouth. This boy might be unappealing, but at least he still has youth on his side. As she marches well past middle-age, Vivienne feels herself becoming more invisible. She wouldn't be surprised to look into a mirror one day soon and find no reflection at all. Anger flares, fighting her rising hopelessness.

'Yes,' Vivienne snaps. 'Why?'

'I-I'm looking for it, too,' he says, his voice barely more than a whisper, then she notices he's clutching a familiar envelope. Thick, black card and expensive lettering. It had looked so different to any other mail she received, yet a week earlier, she'd chucked it straight into the bin.

'Some naff PR event,' she'd muttered to her colleague, Cat, rolling her eyes. 'Cheap wine, beige canapés, and a presentation about a new air freshener.'

But Cat had already retrieved the invitation from the bin and was scrutinising the lettering.

'Looks like it could be a posh dinner party,' she'd said, raising a perfectly arched eyebrow. 'If you don't want it, do you mind if I go? Bit short of cash this month…'

'It's addressed to the Deputy Editor, *not* the junior writer,' Vivienne had snapped, snatching the invitation back.

Cat had turned away, blinking at her screen. Vivienne knows what the girls in the office think of her. A nasty old spinster with no life, but she has more talent in her little finger than most of them have in their whole fake-tanned, gym-sculpted bodies. Some days she could happily strangle the lot of them.

When Vivienne had started out at the magazine, a wide-eyed twenty-three-year-old, she'd been one of only two women in the place. Through sheer hard work she'd eventually made it to Deputy Editor, but then she'd got stuck. Vivienne had become part of the furniture while the house around her had been reno-vated. All of a sudden, the work-experience girls were lecturing her about Facebook and Instagram. One of them – with skin so flawless Vivienne could hardly bear to look at her – had even offered to read through her copy to give it a 'younger vibe'. Let's just say, *she* didn't last long.

During her time in the deputy role, the publisher had intro-duced five different (always male and always younger than her) editors to do the top job.

Last week, the latest incarnation, a thirty-eight-year-old former teen magazine editor called Damian, with a bald spot shining through his spiky hair and a very loose grip on the basic rules of grammar, had asked for 'a quick conflab' in his office. Vivienne had been shaken to hear that magazine sales had dropped further in the last six months and there was real risk of closure. The editor himself had seemed unfazed as he'd pasted on his most sympathetic face, whilst glancing at his watch. Perhaps he was already in receipt of another job offer. Vivienne could only imagine having the kind of bulletproof confidence that requires no evidentiary talent to sustain it.

Back at her desk, she'd picked up the envelope again, turning the thick card over in her hands. Her name was spelt out in the intricate gold writing, but it didn't say who was holding the dinner and there wasn't even an email address to RSVP. For the next two days, it had stayed propped up behind her keyboard, and her eyes had regularly drifted towards the ornate lettering.

That morning, as she'd pulled on her reliable black shift dress from M&S, she'd seen those letters again in her mind's eye. Dragging a brush through her greying hair, she'd frowned at her ageing reflection, lifted her chin to see two loose folds of skin starting to form underneath. *Jowls.* What an utterly depressing word. She'd mouthed it at the mirror and the folds had wobbled as if in acknowledgment. *Ageing is a privilege denied to many*, she'd told herself, then turned away from her reflection. Picking up her handbag, she'd wondered about the other dinner-party guests. Perhaps she could make some new contacts who might come in handy if the magazine did close, or maybe there would be a mature male journalist on the lookout for an intelligent, like-minded partner. Over a nice glass of wine, she'd astonish him with the news that today was in fact her sixtieth birthday. *'You don't look a day over forty-five!'* he'd gush. Well, fifty-five, maybe…

Now, watching this man-boy wipe his nose with his grubby denim jacket sleeve, Vivienne wonders if she's made a mistake in coming tonight. She'd assumed it was a PR event for senior journalists, but he didn't look the part at all. Vivienne wonders what would have induced the dinner-party host to invite them both along. She looks down the street, considers making her excuses.

'I'm Tristan, freelance computer programmer,' he says, offering a weightless excuse for a handshake.

'Vivienne, magazine editor,' she snaps back, no need to mention the 'deputy' bit. 'I'm off home now, looks like the place doesn't even exist…'

'You're a magazine editor? Wow, that's a cool job.' He beams at her.

'Well, it has its moments,' she says, a smile pulling at the corners of her mouth. She looks down at Tristan's trainers. They have Velcro straps (surely, he's learned to tie his shoelaces by now?) and have turned a dishwater grey thanks to the rain. His socks must be soaked through, too…

'Look, you really must get out of this rain…'

'Hang on, I didn't notice this door before,' Tristan says, his attention on an alleyway set back from the road.

Vivienne looks up and sees a black doorway. She blinks and two gold numbers glisten in the rain.

'Thirteen! This must be it,' Tristan cries, a childish triumph to his voice. Despite herself, Vivienne feels a spark of excitement in her chest. She has always loved a good mystery, finds comfort in revisiting her favourites, *Prime Suspect* and *Poirot*, and reading anything by Agatha Christie. They step down the alleyway and Tristan pushes the door open to let Vivienne through.

The door snaps shut behind them, cutting off the sound of the city's early-evening traffic. Vivienne can hear only her footsteps on the tiled floor and Tristan's breath behind her.

'I can't see a thing,' she whispers, taking tiny steps forward.

'Look, there's a sign,' Tristan murmurs.

As Vivienne's eyes adjust to the darkness, a large gold plaque appears on the wall ahead of them. The word 'Serendipity's' is written in stern capitals, just above a staircase leading down. Vivienne's heart is galloping, but she doesn't want to come across as a scared older woman, so she takes a deep breath and walks towards the steps. She reaches out for the smooth wooden banister as her toes tentatively feel for each step.

'Here we go.' She tries to give her voice a sing-song quality, as if attending creepy dinner parties in hidden underground restaurants is something she does every day.

At the bottom of the stairs, they're greeted by a heavy, dark wood door, with a huge gold handle in the centre. Muffled voices, then a screeching laugh, emanate from the other side. Vivienne's racing heart slows a smidgeon at the sound of other people. Even though her conscious mind is telling her that she's in central London, with thousands of people just metres away from her, she had started to feel like she and Tristan had entered a different world. She pushes the door open and gasps. It is the most splendid dining room she's ever seen, with its roaring fire framed by an elaborate marble fireplace, dark wood panels, and enormous oil paintings hanging from the walls. Vivienne had always dreamed of living in a grand house with rooms like these. She'd been glued to *Downton Abbey* imagining herself right at home alongside the well-bred ladies. Vivienne puts her hand on the smooth marble fireplace and looks up at the image above. Unlike the other paintings, which depict generic landscapes and plump, dreamy women, this is a black-and-white inked drawing. A devilish face pokes through the centre of the circular image, which features a series of animals dressed as humans. At the top is a peacock wearing a top hat and tails; then an eagle holding up weighing scales; two brawling dogs in white shirts; a pig in a suit digging into a roast chicken; a bow-tied lizard peering at a scroll; a pipe-smoking cat; and a top-hatted sheep gazing at a well-dressed ewe. Could this be a clue to tonight's event? If so, then Vivienne is impressed. This is a cut above the usual lacklustre marketing tricks. Stepping closer, Vivienne gazes into the eyes of the devil, who seems to be looking right at her. She leans forward and notices that the image is slightly coming away at the corner. She reaches her hand to it.

'Look at that table,' Tristan says, standing a little too close behind her, like a nervous toddler.

She reluctantly turns from the picture and takes in the circular table, with its white tablecloth, in the centre of the room. Above it hangs a silver chandelier, with white tapered candles burning brightly. From the chandelier, long green vines hang down to the table and wind around a series of silver candelabras, like an octopus's tentacles. Seven places are set, with silver cutlery and crystal wine glasses. Once again, she's reminded of a period drama. Vivienne wonders if she's meant to be the old dowager countess of the group.

'Well, hello there,' a booming male voice calls from across the table. 'Come and sit down.'

Vivienne squints at the dark silhouette behind a candelabra. Walking towards the table, she spots two empty spaces, both with small black cards between the cutlery. As she gets closer, she sees her own name, written in the same style as the invitation. Peering at the card, she sees the eagle with weighing scales once again. To her right sits a lean man wearing a fitted grey suit and an arrogant expression; he nods at Vivienne. To her left is Tristan's setting. They both sit down.

## Matthew

Leaning back in his chair, Matthew watches the old lady and drippy (literally – the floor around him is soaked) bloke make their way to the table, taking the last two seats. Well, now he really is confused. The woman is the same genre of dried-up spinster you find in every office across London. A couple of cats at home and a freezer full of ready meals no doubt. As for the drip: too-long hair, smudged glasses, a fan of outdated rock music (judging by his T-shirt). Adding all this together, Matthew would surmise that he has a badly paid job involving computers. Already seated are the Botoxed lingerie boss with huge knockers, the old Welsh police officer who clearly loves a drink-or-ten, the too-skinny

7

YouTuber frowning at her phone, and the dull TV doctor desperately waiting to be recognised. Glancing around the table, Matthew flicks his glossy hair and wonders who has brought this random wedge of humanity together – and why.

'Welcome to London's most mysterious dinner party.' The old copper jumps up, offering his spade-like hand to the two new arrivals. Matthew's own knuckles still ache a little from his bone-crushing greeting.

'I'm Melvin. No sign of our host yet,' he adds.

'My name's Vivienne … it took us a while to find the restaurant…' the older woman babbles, trying to smooth down her hair as she takes Melvin's hand.

'Tristan,' the geek mutters, shaking the proffered hand but staying in his seat. He removes his glasses and wipes them with a napkin. Without the specs, he looks more vulnerable. He has the spots of a teenager, an unexpected boomerang-shaped scar running along his cheekbone, as well as a receding hairline. He's a good ten years older than him, Matthew reckons, probably late thirties.

'Good to meet you both, I'm Matthew,' he nods from the other side of Melvin, flashing his most winning smile, but stays seated so that he doesn't have to shake Tristan's hand. As the two new arrivals take off their coats and Melvin introduces the other guests, Matthew notices with satisfaction that they're both squinting a little. He has dazzled them, just as he does with everyone he meets. He takes a languid sip of his wine and doesn't need to look up to know that six pairs of eyes are on him. It's the same wherever he goes. Women, men, everyone, can't help but stare.

'Well, the wine's certainly good,' he says, raising an eyebrow at the lingerie boss to his left, who'd introduced herself as Janet.

'Delicious,' she responds, beaming and flashing her cat-like, amber eyes.

It's clear to Matthew that Janet had been stunning in her twenties, but now, in her early forties, at a guess, she's past her prime. Sure, the wonders of Botox have ironed out her forehead, but the lines around her eyes and mouth cruelly betray her. And Matthew would hedge a bet that she's put on a few stone in the last five years. Great boobs, but she's 'paying the ass-tax', as his colleagues at the investment bank would say. Noticing Matthew's appraising eye, a blotchy, pink rash spreads unattractively across Janet's mighty cleavage, which bounces heavily as she lifts her wine glass and takes three large gulps.

'Malbec, Argentinian, at a guess.' Janet grins at him, her lips already turning inky thanks to the tannins.

'Ah, a woman who knows her wine,' Matthew purrs, casually hooking his left arm over the back of her chair.

And, just like that, the daft cow is all his. Despite the multiple rings on her wedding finger, despite the obvious disparity in their ages, despite the fact that she's been in his company for all of ten minutes, he knows without doubt that he could take her home right now. He doesn't want her, of course (he's already decided that the young YouTuber, Stella, will be the lucky lady) but it's always fun to practise.

As if reading his thoughts, Matthew's mobile buzzes to life in his jacket pocket, right next to his heart. Probably Robyn, or maybe Charmaine. God, it could be any of five or six pretty yet vulnerable women he'd plucked from various dating websites. Occasionally, he slums it and heads to one of those cheesy night-clubs at around 1 a.m., when he can guarantee some easy targets. Bowled over by Matthew's expensive looks and cheap charm, they happily oblige his darker fantasies, stay at home waiting for his calls, and cancel plans with their friends (who eventually give up inviting them) until they become totally reliant on him. By that point, he could do anything – *anything* – to them and they'd accept it. That's when he performs his signature U-turn and just stops calling. Some of them take it worse than others, like this one girl, Eleanor, who wouldn't accept it was over. You'd think she'd be grateful for the few weeks of the high life he'd shown her, but she'd messaged and called him incessantly. Matthew had worried that he'd have to take matters into his own hands and find a way to silence her for good, but thankfully she'd got the message in the end.

Shaking his head to shoo the thought away, Matthew's mind returns to the dinner party. When the black invitation had appeared in the mailbox at his flat on the Brompton Road, he'd presumed it was some sort of elite, singles mixer. Ever since he'd agreed to that mortifying article in the free paper, 'London's Hottest Bachelors' or whatever, he'd been overrun with invitations. Most had ended up in either the literal or digital bin. But there had been something about this one, the luxurious paper, the hint of mystery, that had piqued his interest. He'd hoped it might bring him some fresh meat, some new challenges. It's all getting a bit easy.

'You can keep your fancy wine.' Melvin is addressing the group now. 'Beer's my tipple, always has been.'

*And your body isn't thanking you for it*, Matthew muses, taking in Melvin's bulging stomach pushing against the table. Matthew's personal trainer, Felicity, keeps his body in perfect shape. She's worth every penny – and never charges for those delightful extras.

'Is that a Welsh accent I detect?' dull Dr Gordon pipes up. 'There can't be many like you in the Valleys.'

And the table goes quiet. Janet rolls her eyes at Matthew, Vivienne clears her throat, and Stella glares at the doctor. But Melvin just lets out a laugh, straight from his sizeable middle.

'No Gordon, there aren't many black people in Wales, but that makes us all the more special,' he chuckles. And just like that, the tension is defused. Matthew imagines that Melvin is a good police officer, equally capable of taming flying fists and providing comfort when needed. It's not the sort of life that would appeal to Matthew, though. His more subtle skills are better suited amongst the traders. In fact, when he thinks about it, he approaches his work life in much the same way as his personal life. He befriends new, inexperienced traders so that they confide in him when it all inevitably goes wrong. He offers to help and then swoops their clients away before the poor kids know what's happening. The turnover is so high in his company that no one seems to notice Matthew's predatory approach, except perhaps his boss who simply gives him a look of admiration when he turns in impressive monthly figures.

'So, who do you think the mystery host is?' Janet asks, directing her question straight at Matthew.

He decides to indulge her with his attention once again.

'Simon Cowell, Ryan Gosling, Prince Charles?' he grins, giving a wink.

'Sounds more like that game, Snog, Marry, Kill,' guffaws Janet, not letting her gaze stray from Matthew's. He notes with satisfaction that the other guests have fallen quiet as they listen in.

'Go on, then,' he dares, slowly passing the tip of his tongue across his upper lip.

Janet leans back in her chair, clearly loving the spotlight. Matthew's eyes travel from her face to her neck. Her jugular vein is gently pulsating, sending lascivious blood from her brain to her heart.

'Marry Cowell. I'd never have to work again,' she squeals. 'Kill Ryan; nice guy but not much fun. And snog Prince Charles; he might appear like Mr Sensible with his grey suits and cufflinks, but I bet he knows how to please a lady.'

'What would your husband say?' Melvin comments with a laugh but Matthew hears an undercurrent of disapproval. He's probably the type who doesn't like women talking about sex, Matthew imagines.

'Who cares?' she snorts, turning back to Matthew. 'Your go: Beyonce, Hillary Clinton and Nicole Kidman?'

He puts his finger to his lips as if considering her question carefully. He lets a few seconds pass and the table falls silent waiting for his answer.

'Could I kill them all?' he says, sending Janet into hysterics.

A door on the opposite side to the entrance swings open, and a clutch of bow-tied waiters file in, each holding a small gold tray bearing fresh jugs of red wine.

'Water for me, please,' Gordon pipes up, and Janet again rolls her eyes at Matthew, who winks in response.

'Do you know if the host is on his way?' Melvin asks one of the waiters, receiving a small shrug in response, before they all disappear back through the door – presumably leading to the kitchen.

'Looks like we'll have to make our own entertainment,' Matthew says, glancing around the table. It's time to sprinkle some of his magic around…

'What about you, Vivienne, was it?' He draws the old bag in, deliberately excluding Stella, the YouTuber. 'Does Prince Charles do it for you?

'Oh God, no. Benedict Cumberbatch is more my type…' says Vivienne, taking a sip of her wine, briefly closing her eyes as the rich taste hits her.

'Ew, he's ancient,' Stella suddenly pipes up, her voice much more refined than Matthew had anticipated.

'Is Justin Bieber more your bag, then?' he asks, finally looking at her, dipping his chin and flashing a stern look.

'Hardly. I like Michael B. Jordan, great actor and so stylish,' Stella says, and Matthew turns away as if she hadn't spoken.

'I wonder if they're bringing my water. It's getting a little warm in here,' Dr Gordon cuts in, dabbing at his forehead with a napkin.

'Who needs water when the wine tastes so good,' Matthew says, reaching for the carafe and turning back to Janet. As he does so, his place setting catches his eye. Underneath his name is a drawing of a sheep wearing a top hat and monocle, looking down at a ewe. Shrugging, he pushes it to one side and proffers the carafe to Janet.

'Don't mind if I do,' she says, beaming as Matthew carefully pours the dark red liquid into her glass.

Red wine has always reminded him of blood. And in the brooding light of Serendipity's, even more so.

### Stella

Stella looks from gorgeous Matthew to past-it Janet and back again. *WT actual F.* Why is he bothering with her? Sure, she's got huge boobs, but she's big all over, and old enough to be his mother – probably. Stella's eyes glide over Matthew's sculpted cheekbones, his long eyelashes, and she realises she's seen him somewhere before. Then it comes to her: he'd featured in an article she'd recently read, 'London's Most Eligible Hotties' – or something equally lame. But one bachelor, with impossibly dark eyes, had stood out. The writer had clearly been taken with Matthew, too, describing him as 'devastatingly dishy' (*please!*). The article had featured the net worth of each 'hottie', and Matthew's was nowhere near her father's, from what she can recall, but he was definitely going in the right direction. She takes in his Savile Row suit, the gold signet glinting on his pinkie finger. She'd sworn off dating for a while, but perhaps she can make an exception for this Matthew. After all, her father has been threatening to cut her off again, and she could really use a back-up. Matthew had definite potential. And yet he'd barely looked her way since she'd walked in…

Sighing, Stella wonders if she'd made a mistake coming along today. The invitation had looked expensive, she'd anticipated some luxury freebies, a few glasses of champers and perhaps some exclusive content for her channel. When all she got was a dreary dinner party with gross red wine and a load of weirdos. Not to mention a racist thrown in. She's still fuming over what that doctor said to

Melvin about being black and Welsh. With a mum from Ghana and a white dad, she'd heard it all before she was twelve. Melvin should have torn a strip off that weedy man, but instead he'd just laughed. Infuriating!

She picks her mobile back up and logs on to her YouTube page. Just before heading out tonight, she'd uploaded a new video all about where and when to wear cowboy boots and how to find the perfect pair without paying hundreds of pounds. Already, she had dozens of comments from her teen followers thanking her for her insight. Her subscribers are escalating at a faster rate than her rival, Highstreet Heroine's, and she's had two recent offers of sponsorship, which are what actually matter to her, not finding affordable fashion for skint teenagers. God knows what makes them think the high street can compare to designer, but they lap up any old nonsense she spouts, and who is she to tell them otherwise? Looking down at her own Versace cowboy boots, a treat from her dad for her twenty-second birthday, she thanks her lucky stars she doesn't have to bother with cheap knock-offs.

You could say she'd fallen into fashion vlogging. After being kicked out of school (as *if* she'd steal from those stuck-up bitches!), her dad had lined her up work experience at various places, but she'd hated every tea-making, photocopying second, and they weren't even paying her. Then, one day a few years ago, Stella had started her YouTube page. What had begun as a bit of a hobby had quickly escalated to a phenomenon (to quote the *Daily Mirror*) as her views and subscription numbers soared. Within months, she was being invited to showbiz parties and blogger events, often asked to give presentations about her incredible success. She'd had all kinds of freebies, thanks to the offer of association with her YouTube page, clothes, accessories, beauty products, slap-up meals in Michelin-starred restaurants, bottles of champers and so on. Of course, Stella could easily have paid for it all, but that isn't the point.

Her thumb moving quickly, Stella logs out of her StellaStylez account and into the other one. She smiles to herself as she sees the comments she's clocked up on there, the shouty capital letters, the exclamation marks. She pictures the tears, the hurt, even the fear that her words have caused, and, instantly, she's exhilarated, as if she can feel the blood racing around her body, she feels so … alive.

'So, you're in fashion?' the old lady suddenly asks Stella, talking across Dr Gordon.

'Yeah,' Stella murmurs, reluctantly putting her phone face-down on the table. 'I've got a YouTube channel with nearly half-a-million subscribers.'

Stella glances around the table and sees that the other guests are impressed, apart from geeky Tristan who appears to be choking on his wine.

'Oh excellent, yes I think my daughter Louisa watches those sorts of things. She's fourteen,' Gordon cuts in.

*Please don't talk to me about your boring teenage daughter…*

'And you're a doctor?' Stella asks, trying to sound like she gives a flying F. Her boarding school had drilled into her the importance of small talk, along with other useful skills like using the correct cutlery and how to foxtrot.

'You might recognise me.' He clears his throat and touches his powder blue tie. 'I regularly appear on *The Morning Show*…'

'Oh right, well I'm not much of an early riser.' Stella shrugs, reaching for her phone again. Why had no one told this man that skinny ties are only acceptable at fancy dress parties?

'Not to worry.' He shrinks back into his chair. 'I'm a doctor of nutrition and appear quite regularly on television to discuss the latest fad diets, that sort of thing.'

'Oh, darling, now I know where I've seen you,' Janet calls from the other side of Stella. 'You were on the other day, labelling some poor celeb as bonkers for her maple-syrup diet. And there I was, just about to stock up.'

'Well I'm not sure I called her "bonkers"…' Dr Gordon splutters, picking up his fork and wiping it with his napkin.

'Perhaps it'll help slim down her thighs,' Stella mutters, but finds herself royally ignored as Janet is now gazing at the doctor who's sitting a little straighter in his chair. No doubt she's hoping to get a few tips on how to lose a bit of weight herself. The dress is definitely designer, but she's spilling out of it. Nice rings, though, Stella has to admit: the woman's engagement rock looks to be three carats maybe even four.

'There's no solid scientific evidence to support it,' Gordon is saying to Janet, putting the now sparkling fork down and warming to his topic. 'In fact, it could cause problems with blood sugar and insulin levels. And the short-term weight loss will only be reversed when the person returns to solid foods.'

'Oh, I don't know who I was kidding, anyway. As if I could live without red meat,' Janet chuckles, cutting short Dr Gordon just as he's getting going.

Stella rolls her eyes, zoning out of this lame chat. With no bubbles in sight, she decides she might as well give the red wine a go. She leans forward to push her place setting (which weirdly features a lizard reading a scroll) aside and picks up her glass. The blackcurrant-y wine tastes bitter on her tongue but then slips easily down her throat, sending a pleasurable warmth through her.

'Not your usual tipple?' Matthew asks, his dark eyes on her from across the table. Surely, they're dark brown, though they appear black in this light.

She shakes her head. 'I prefer champagne.'

'Do you know how to tell if it's a good wine?' he asks, his voice almost a whisper beneath Dr Gordon and Janet's rising crescendo ('… and what about the baby food diet?').

She swallows and shakes her head again, pushing her poker-straight hair behind her ear and frowning at her deep red fingernails.

Matthew picks up his wine glass by its stem and slowly swills it round and round, the scarlet fluid spinning then starting to climb up the sides in tiny tidal waves.

'See, it's got legs,' he murmurs, keeping his eyes on the glass. Stella sees how the waves slowly ebb down, giving the appearance of long legs.

'Oh, yes, I see them.' She beams at him. He mirrors her smile for a second, flashing pointy white incisors, then it's gone and he's turned to his right to top up the policeman's glass. She has been dismissed and finds herself still grinning gormlessly at the side of Matthew's face.

Feeling foolish, Stella turns back to her own glass and attempts to emulate the wine swilling but it splashes over the rim and leaves red spots on her white napkin.

Sighing, she finishes off her wine, then pours herself a second glass, takes a large sip. This one is going down much easier.

Already the edges of the room have a hazy quality, like the old photos in her mum's photo albums from the 80s. It's quite a pleasant feeling and Stella leans back in her chair, suddenly finding Janet's flirting amusing, rather than irritating.

'So, are you single, Matthew?' Janet is asking. 'Or is there a lucky lady at home?'

'Still searching,' he tells her. 'If you know anyone?'

As Janet guffaws, throwing back her blonde blow-dry, Matthew catches Stella's eye and gives her a split-second wink. A frisson of excitement sparks through her. Maybe tonight will bring some distraction after all.

## Tristan

Staring down at his gnawed fingernails, Tristan listens carefully to the conversation going on around him. Chatter weaves in and out, certain words hanging in the air, like cartoon speech bubbles.

*Mysterious … Serendipity's … celebrity…* The truth is, Tristan can't remember the last time he'd been to a dinner party. Perhaps it had been back when he was a student, sharing pizza with some like-minded computer-science undergrads. Counting on his fingers, it dawns on him that he hasn't even spoken to anyone face-to-face for five days. The number of people in this room, their loud voices, their different personalities, their range of opinions, it is all hurting Tristan's head. All he wants to do is run out of this place, jump on the tube and get home, return to the safety of his little flat in Manor House.

'God, no, they ruin your body and spoil all your fun,' Janet bellows across the table after Matthew asks if she has children. Her painted red lips are stretched wide, her strange yellow-green eyes bright with humour. It all seems so forced, and Tristan wonders if this is true. He glances at the journalist, Vivienne, sitting on his right, her sharp profile is pointing towards Janet with a look of open disgust. She is a person whose thoughts are projected straight onto her face, and right now her face is showing that she's not impressed with Janet – or any of the other dinner party guests, it seems.

When he'd bumped into her in the street, he'd watched her take in his unappealing appearance, his soaking wet hair, and his old denim jacket. She'd instantly written him off as insignificant; she'd probably even considered pretending she knew nothing about the dinner party. But the invitation had been clear to see in her hand, so she had no choice but to admit she was looking for the restaurant, too. When he pointed out the door, she'd swept past him and marched down the stairs as if she owned the place and he was merely a doorman. When they'd entered the dining room, she'd immediately distanced herself from him, her eyes scanning the room for anyone more interesting, more dynamic, more altogether *palatable* than Tristan.

His hand instinctively reaches up to touch the scar on his cheekbone; the tip of his forefinger fits perfectly into the hollow left by that thug's boot. The wound has healed, but the dent will always be there to remind him of that night. He looks down at his old Metallica T-shirt and thinks he probably should have made more of an effort. Janet appears to be wearing a ballgown of some sort; Matthew and Gordon are in suits; Stella is wearing a tight black dress and cowboy boots, diamonds sparkling in her ears. Tristan rarely thinks about his appearance these days, but today, before he'd got dressed to come out, he'd stood naked in front of his bathroom mirror and had wondered where this nearly-forty-year-old had come from. It had felt like mere months ago he was a nowhere-near-twenty-year-old with an exciting and possibly lucrative future at his stretched fingertips. Lately he'd grown his hair longer, brushing it across his forehead so it just about hid the worst of his widow's peak. It doesn't seem fair that his hair is disappearing and he still suffers from acne… Then his eyes had fallen to his sad-sack belly, which has surprisingly inherited the hair he's lost from his head. Lately, he finds himself patting it protectively, like you see pregnant women doing.

Just as he'd been about to leave, his landline had rung. It could only be one person and he'd hesitated before deciding it was easier to get it out of the way.

'Why did you take so long to answer? You scared me half to death,' his mother had shrieked.

'I was just on my way out.'

'Oh, are you seeing Ellie?'

'No Mum, it's over, remember?' he'd sighed.

'It's such a shame. You never did tell me what you did to chase her away…'

'Mum, I have to go. I'll call you tomorrow,' he'd told her, hopping from one foot to the other.

'OK, you go. Have you been taking those vitamins I sent? Muriel next door said they helped her son's acne. He's eighteen now and just started a medical degree at Edinburgh.'

'Yes Mum, I've been taking them,' he'd muttered, teeth gritted together. *Please go.*

'And don't forget, your father is driving over tomorrow to look at your boiler…'

As he'd made his way to the restaurant, he'd reflected on the months he'd spent living back at home over the summer. His mother had insisted, keen to 'look after' him following the break-up. It hadn't been so bad at first; she'd filled him up with all his childhood favourites, shepherd's pie, lasagne, home-made chips and pale sausages. He'd spent whole days in his old bedroom, his laptop on his knee as he'd sat up in bed, wrapped in his single duvet, like a large receding Baby Jesus. But, one Sunday morning when his parents were at church, boredom had led him to poke around in their bedroom. Tucked under their bed he'd found a box. Why hadn't he just left it where it was? Why had he chosen to release those secrets?

Now, sitting at the table amongst these loud and rude people, he thinks wistfully of his quiet flat, even his parents' cosy semi. Still, he forces himself to tune into the chatter. They're all trying to work out who has planned the dinner party, but Tristan can't think about that now, his mind is already overloaded. He hasn't spoken a word since he' sat down. He should say *something*.

'It reminds me of a murder-mystery night,' he mumbles. He'd gone to one with Ellie, had hated every second. His teeth push together, his jaw clenches at the memory. His words drift across the table and disperse like cigarette smoke as the other guests watch Matthew and Janet resume their excruciating flirting. Looking at Matthew, Tristan notices how the candlelight creates a halo effect around his thick chestnut hair, his eyes as dark as a well. Vivienne had at least acknowledged Tristan before dismissing him, whereas Matthew's gaze had hopped over him, stopping only briefly on Vivienne to flash his luminescent teeth. The older chap Melvin had greeted them both enthusiastically and introduced Janet, who hadn't taken her eyes off Matthew; then Stella, briefly glancing up from her phone to give him a reluctant wave. As for Dr Gordon, Tristan had earned a curt nod of the head.

As Matthew laughs and Janet grins back at him, Tristan lets out a controlled sigh and turns away. His eyes fix on the name card in front of him, which has on it a picture of a bulldog in a white shirt, its arm raised, paw balled into a fist. He focuses on the human-like fingers of the fist  and counts. Two, three, five, seven, eleven, thirteen…

'Oh goody, I'm *starving*,' Janet squeals, as the smartly dressed waiters file back into the room and stand elegantly poised behind each seat. In one synchronised movement, they place seven plates in front of the guests.

'*Foie gras* – my favourite,' Matthew says, beaming at Janet, who grins back.

'Could you confirm there are no sesame seeds in this, as I'm allergic?' Dr Gordon asks his waiter and gets a brief nod in response.

'Anyone going to tell us what this is all in aid of?' Vivienne queries, but the waiters are already  marching out of the room.

'And they say there's no such thing as a free lunch,' Janet chuckles, picking up her cutlery.

Tristan gazes down at the sticky, beige square in front of him, the wafer-thin crackers. He hasn't eaten since breakfast, but the sight of this food isn't exactly tingling his tastebuds. He watches Janet expertly smear the sticky substance onto a cracker and land it on her pink tongue. She closes her eyes in apparent ecstasy. He tentatively picks up his own knife and scoops up some *foie gras*. But, as soon as his knife touches the cracker, it instantly crumbles into an unappetising heap on his plate.

'Bit tricky, that?' Melvin asks, smiling at Tristan.

'I've never eaten anything like this before. Not used to fancy restaurants,' Tristan replies.

'Me neither, so let's make the most of it,' Melvin says, picking up a dessert spoon and scooping up some foie gras and broken crackers from his own plate.

'Good idea,' Tristan chuckles, copying him. He looks up to see Janet staring at them in disgust, before turning her ravenous eyes back to Matthew to grill him about his dating experiences.

Despite its unappealing appearance – and dubious ethics – the *foie gras* is utterly delicious, and Tristan's plate is cleared in no time. His tastebuds are celebrating. Poor things are more familiar with beans on toast.

'I'd have thought a young man like you would be out on the town every night?' Melvin says, taking a large gulp of red wine.

'I prefer a takeaway at home with friends,' Tristan replies, which is only a half-lie. He has a takeaway most Friday and Saturday nights, but never with friends.

'My wife and I used to go out lots when we first married but not so much these days… She's recovering from chemo…' For the first time, Melvin's voice is low, almost a whisper. A strange expression on his face.

'Oh, I'm sorry to hear that. My dad had prostate cancer a few years ago. He's doing great now…' says Tristan.

'That's good,' Melvin cuts in. 'I'm sure she'll be fine. She's a very strong lady, my Mary. More wine?'

Tristan nods and watches Melvin wave over the waiter to request another bottle. He's smiling again, filled with bonhomie. Clearly, he doesn't want to talk about his wife's illness, and his expression hadn't been one of sadness, more like guilt. Odd.

### Gordon

Gordon finds he cannot tear his eyes away from Janet as she hungrily smears thick, sticky *foie gras* on to the cracker. She doesn't seem to notice that she has also coated her thumb; her focus is totally taken with the food carefully balanced on the tips of her fingers. As if in slow motion, she raises the cracker, her blood-red lips parting – Gordon can see her expensive dental work – and it is devoured. Then she finally spots the blob of beige on her thumbnail and that too disappears into the red cavern. He tries to ignore the twitch in his groin.

Looking down at his own plate, Gordon scrapes a modest amount of the *foie gras* on to his knife and carefully spreads it around the cracker. Made up mostly of duck fat, *foie gras* is certainly calorific, but, in actual fact, in small quantities, the monosaturated and polyunsaturated fats can be a beneficial part of a healthy diet. Then he picks up his wine glass and takes a small sip of the red wine, allows the liquid to swill around his mouth, one, two, three times and then swallows. With its links to lowering heart disease, Gordon allows his wife Elizabeth to pour them a glass of red wine each once or twice a week. Elizabeth inevitably tries to persuade Gordon into a second glass, but then he reminds her the health benefits most likely stop after just one. As he's always telling his wife, it's all about moderation, a principle this Janet woman clearly doesn't live by.

As he watches her repeat the process with a second cracker, it takes everything Gordon has to maintain an impassive expression on his face. Inside, he is screaming at this woman: *you are disgusting!* He thinks back to medical school and the autopsies they all had to partake in. About half of his class had rushed off to vomit, a couple fainted right there and then. But Gordon, he'd loved every second. He'd relished the feel of the scalpel pushing through the skin, the beauty of the organs fitting together just so. His tutor had been amazed by Gordon's focus at such a young age. The thought still makes him smile. Looking up at Janet now, he pictures the layer of fat he'd find if he cut through her skin with his scalpel. Yellow and bulbous. Perhaps, if she saw that, she'd change her ways.

Slowly chewing his modest portion of *foie gras* (exactly thirty-two times to aid the digestion process), he briefly closes his eyes with pleasure. It is truly delicious. A small voice inside his head is saying: *'Go on Gordon, eat it all up. Worry about it later.'* He looks down at his plate and picks up a second cracker, smearing another thumbnail of foie gras on top. Again, he slowly chews and swallows before pushing the plate away from him, away from temptation. He leaves the last three crackers and barely touched *foie gras.* As he does so, he notices his place setting. Pleasingly, it reads, *Dr Gordon MacMillan,'* and underneath there's a tiny drawing of a peacock in a top hat. He peers more closely at it: the peacock looks rather distinguished. Perhaps it is the emblem for some sort of high-profile guest-speaker society. Gordon allows himself a moment of excitement.

'Pass that over if you don't want it,' Janet calls, her fingers wriggling as she reaches across the table for Gordon's plate.

'Oh, I might have more later,' he responds, a little quicker than he'd intended, pulling the plate back out of her reach. Gordon suppresses a smile as Janet visibly huffs and turns back to gazing at Matthew. She's got no idea what a fool she's making of herself. As if that young athletic chap would want an over-weight middle-aged woman!

'Get it down you, Gordo,' Melvin calls across the table, as if he's shouting at a rugby referee. 'You could do with a bit more meat on those bones.'

'Thank you, Melvin, perhaps I will have a bit more,' Gordon says and gingerly picks up his knife once again. He takes a sidelong glance at Melvin who is now leaning back in his chair, his unsightly stomach shaking as he laughs at something Matthew has said. It's really no wonder that the police force is in such a state, with men like Melvin in their camp.

'You look like you'd make a good winger. There's no sport better than rugby,' Melvin bellows.

Gordon inwardly rolls his eyes. His dad had loved rugby too, a die-hard Edinburgh Rugby fan, couldn't understand Gordon's preference for his bedroom and books over the muddy sports field. Another niggle of his: how the world is obsessed with sporting 'heroes' over scientists who really do save lives and make a difference.

'So sorry to hear about your wife,' Gordon says now, fed up with this mindless sports chat.

Melvin's smile quickly disappears, and he nods solemnly at Gordon.

'Did you know that a healthy diet can reduce your risk of cancer? In fact, obesity is a cause of thirteen different types of cancer,' he says.

'Well, Mary certainly isn't obese,' Melvin snaps, putting his cutlery down rather abruptly, causing a loud clatter and silencing the table.

'Oh no, that's not what I was implying.' Gordon gives the police officer a reassuring smile.

'It's all about eating plenty of fruit and vegetables, wholegrains and proteins. Avoiding red meat, alcohol, and sugary foods.'

'So tonight isn't helping our chances of living long lives, then,' Vivienne cuts in from Gordon's left. He looks up to see her cool blue eyes staring hard into his. It's a look that Elizabeth sometimes throws him when she feels he's 'going on a bit'.

'Well, everything in moderation, I always say,' he splutters, looking quickly towards Janet.

Elizabeth has warned him before about his over-zealous 'lecturing' on healthy eating. But what does she expect? Conversation at dinner parties naturally turns to food and drink, and he can't miss the opportunity to educate others.

Gordon goes back to his plate, as conversation around the table turns to the recent christening of the royal baby, Princess something-or-other. He sighs into his starter at the inexplicable interest that people have in these entitled little children who just happened to be born into the right family.

God, this *foie gras* is *delicious*, he can't deny it. At home, he made sure that he, Elizabeth, and Louisa followed a strict and balanced diet.

'It's like a diet camp,' Louisa would sulk, and he'd started to wonder if she was supplementing her meals with high-sugar snacks when she wasn't at home. He could see her body filling out. Her derrière rounding off, her upper arms starting to wobble.

'She's a teenage girl going through puberty, don't say a word,' Elizabeth had warned when he'd mentioned his concerns to her. But really, what would it look like for a respected *high-profile* doctor of nutrition and dietetics to have an overweight daughter? Hypocrisy, that's what. When Elizabeth was out of the room, he'd occasionally mention to his daughter the impact of fatty foods on the body, causing cellulite and acne. He was proud that he could talk in a language that teenagers would understand. He'd learned that through his television work. And goodness, he loves every second of it. When that camera is on him, he feels like a superhero, a world leader, royalty. Finally, his chance to educate the common man! Unfortunately, he's only asked on every few weeks, so, when the invitation for tonight's dinner party had appeared on his desk, he'd hoped to meet some media types to whom he could slip his new business card. The peacock on his place setting had made him wonder about a speakers' gathering. But the more he hears from his fellow dinner guests, the less likely this seems.

Then he looks down at his plate and realises with horror that it is scraped clean. Had he really eaten that huge portion himself? It didn't seem possible, yet everyone else was either chatting or finishing off their own starters, so it had to be him. Suddenly, the heat from the open fire is unbearable, his suit jacket nipping under his arms.

'Excuse me, I won't be a moment,' he mumbles, turning to Stella on his right and then Vivienne on his left, but neither respond nor even show they've heard.

Gordon skirts the table and pushes open the heavy door they'd walked through just an hour before. Opposite him are the stairs heading up and, to his right, another wooden door marked *'WC'*. He pushes it open and finds a rather elegant restroom inside, complete with chaise longue, an enormous mirror with an ornate silver frame, huge porcelain sinks and a neat pile of individual towels. He walks straight to the single cubicle and locks himself inside. Spinning around to face the toilet, he leans against the door and allows his body to slide down on to his haunches. The toilet bowl is perfectly clean, not a mark or spot of dust to be seen. Just how he likes it. He takes a deep breath and leans forward on to his knees. The trousers of his slim-fitting suit pulling a little on his thighs.

Then he hears something. A creak of a door, a footstep. Someone is coming. They can't hear this, they can't smell it, they just can't. If it got out, his burgeoning television career would be over. Quickly, he gets to his feet and flushes the toilet. Stepping back into the restroom, he glances at himself in the mirror. Sweat glimmers off his forehead, his cheeks are faintly pink. He grabs a towel and mops his brow, throwing it in the bin and then pushes through the door. Glancing left and right, he sees the corridor is empty. He lets out a long sigh and walks back into the dining room.

### Janet

Gazing at the gorgeous young banker to her right, Janet feels alive for the first time in months. When her PA had handed her a pile of post last week, she'd been drawn to the thick black envelope right away. As the MD of Sophia's Whisper lingerie company, she receives all manner of invitations every day, but when she'd opened the envelope, read over the words, she'd found herself pulled in by the air of mystery, as well as the promise of a proper sit-down dinner rather than those fiddly canapés. God knows, she needs some intrigue in her life right now. This morning, she'd spent yet another breakfast in silence. Her husband, Bill, had flicked through the *Financial Times* with his left hand while shovelling bacon, fried eggs, and buttered toast into his mouth with his right. Cheerful yellow egg yolk had dripped down his chin, but he hadn't noticed, just carried on flicking and chewing, flicking and chewing.

'There's a bit of egg on your tie, dear,' Janet had said, but even that didn't make him look up or acknowledge his wife's low-cut dress, which she'd picked up especially for the dinner party.

'Oh crumbs, it's my best one,' he'd muttered, grabbing a napkin. Watching Bill's vain attempts to wipe the yolk away, Janet had tried to remember a time when they'd talked late into the night, a time when they'd danced with their hips pushed together in a crowded club. But those memories escaped her, like darting fish. Had they ever been like that?

'I'll be late home tonight,' she'd told him. 'Work party. Don't wait up.'

'OK, dear,' he'd mumbled, his focus now returned to his paper and half-eaten – but never forgotten – full English breakfast.

As she'd walked away from the table, Janet had briefly wondered if Bill had his own plans, a secret passion he kept hidden from her, gambling, drugs, women? Glancing back to see him merrily munching away, with yolk still smeared over his chin, not unlike a weaning baby, she found the latter option hard to believe.

'Did you get a chance to ring Caroline yet?' Bill had suddenly called over to her, finally looking at her. 'She wants to speak to you about the christening.'

'Erm ... not yet, I'll see if I have time this afternoon,' she'd responded, caught off-guard.

'You can't ignore that baby forever,' Bill had said. 'She's absolutely gorgeous and our only niece.'

'I'm not ignoring her, Bill,' Janet had snapped back. 'I've just been busy.'

Grabbing her favourite Chanel tote, Janet had glared at her reflection in the hallway mirror. Trust Bill to bring the baby up just when she'd been in such a good mood. Janet had supposed it was bad form not to meet your sister's baby, and she'd be, what, eight weeks old now. Bill had never understood. It didn't matter how many years passed, the aching sadness still raised its head at the sight of a baby, especially a newborn.

'New dress?' Bill had commented, getting up and coming towards her, his chin cleaned of egg yolk.

'Yes, what do you think?'

'A little on the tight side,' he'd commented, appraising her. 'Perhaps it's time to size up. Or think about utilising that extortionate gym membership.'

Janet had fumed silently as she'd watched him *waddle* off. How dare he comment about her size? She'd closed her eyes and brought up the image that had comforted her lately: Bill cold and dead in bed next to her. She'd be sad for a while, of course, but she'd got over worse. Yes, she could picture herself as a sexy young widow. Then she'd taken a deep breath, slicked on some of her favourite chilli-red lipstick, and crossed her fingers for an adventure tonight.

With hungry eyes on Matthew, she wonders now if her adventure will come in the form of a younger man. She is sure there's lots she could teach him about the world, about women. It wouldn't be the first time she'd sought passion elsewhere. Or the second, or third…

'My God, that *foie gras* was amazing,' Matthew sighs. 'Even better than at The Magnolia Room.'

Janet beams. Matthew recognises her as a woman of class who knows her haute cuisine.

'Agreed,' she says, nodding trying to ignore the single drip of sweat snaking down between her shoulder blades.

'Still no sign of our host,' Vivienne pipes up. 'At first I thought this was an elaborate PR promotion, but surely they'd have got to the point by now.'

'Not sure why an old copper like me would be invited to a fancy PR event,' Melvin responds. 'Maybe we're taking part in a new reality TV show. Mary used to watch that one, *Married at First Sight*. Not my sort of thing, but you do get sucked in.'

'Oh God, do you think they're filming right now?' Vivienne says, glancing around the dark corners of the room. Janet notes that her eyes stop and linger on Matthew a little too long. She's old enough to be his mother – or even grandmother – for goodness' sake.

'Well, I doubt tonight's events would make for compulsive viewing,' Janet guffaws, whilst inwardly congratulating herself on wearing her new red dress. If they are being filmed, she's sure it would look great on camera. 'Could be some form of performance art?'

As Janet speaks, she leans over and holds her glass out towards Matthew.

He obliges, fills it to the top. She notes, with pleasure, that his eyes are gazing admiringly at her chest. So what if she's put a few extra pounds on her bottom and tummy over the last five or so years, her greatest assets are as magnificent as ever.

'Chateaubriand,' Janet's waiter says, gently placing a plate in front of her. She hadn't even noticed the starter plates being cleared away, and now the stealthy waiters are back, serving up their latest delectable offering.

'Thank you, my dear,' Janet replies, taking in the finest steak, beautifully sliced showing its obscenely pink insides. Nestled next to the meat are delicately roasted potatoes, bright green asparagus, and a small jug of yellow béarnaise sauce. She wonders how anyone could even consider vegetarianism. Why deny yourself life's greatest pleasures?

Everyone else has been distracted by the food, but that pesky journalist Vivienne is digging her (low, sensible) heels in.

'Excuse me,' she barks at her waiter. 'Do you think we could speak to your boss? We're due some sort of explanation…'

'Let it go, Vivienne, love,' Melvin says. 'They'll get to it soon enough. Let's just enjoy this marvellous food.'

Thankfully, Vivienne seems to accept Melvin's advice and the waiter scuttles off. 'Marvellous' is certainly the right word for this steak, thinks Janet. She picks up her cutlery and feels her knife slip through the beef without resistance, it's so tender. She balances a piece of potato on her fork with the steak and closes her eyes as the flavours explode in her mouth. Was there really anything better in life than a plate of exquisite food? Except an afternoon in bed with a young man, perhaps, she thinks, drinking in Matthew's endless dark lashes, his long fingers tapping away at his phone. As she reaches for her glass, her eyes fall on her place setting. Under her name is an intricate drawing of a pig eating a roast dinner. Janet holds back a gasp, quickly glances over at Matthew, relieved that he hasn't seen it, then pushes the card into her tote. Looking around the table, she notices that Melvin the copper is tucking his white linen napkin into his shirt collar, the IT boy is fiddling nervously with his cutlery, and skinny Stella is poking at her steak and frowning. A motley crew, if ever there was one. What on earth does Janet have in common with that miserable old journalist or the rugby-loving police officer? And don't even get her started on the sanctimonious TV doctor trying to spoil all her fun. Thank goodness their mysterious host had thought to invite Matthew. He is obviously interested. Taking another bite of her steak, Janet decides to stop concerning herself with why she's here, and just enjoy the evening.

'I think we've met before,' Vivienne abruptly says, her sharp voice cutting through Janet's thoughts.

Janet looks up at the older woman and raises an eyebrow. She'd said she was a journalist, but it's unlikely she works on a fashion publication, going by her shapeless black dress and frumpy shoes – and Janet would be shocked if she were wearing underwear from her high-end brand – Vivienne looks more like an M&S white-cotton-granny-knickers sort.

'I don't think so…'

'Yes, I interviewed you, a few years ago. It was a profile piece for our *Women in Business* page.'

Janet narrows her eyes. Actually, that did ring a bell… It was about three months after she'd sold her company and just started at Sophia's Whisper. She'd been busy getting to grips with the new job, but this woman kept emailing and phoning her office until Janet had finally agreed to spend a miserable hour with her at a coffee shop near work. Vivienne had started off quite pleasant, complimenting her on the highly lucrative sale of her clothing app, and her new heels, but then she'd ambushed her, asking about the 'loyal staff' she'd fired. God knows why the woman was so bothered about them: a couple of barely literate graduates Janet had got to write the press releases; a faceless, computer chap who'd dealt with the technical side of things; a few savvy girls whom she'd sent out to scour charity shops for designer clothes and jewellery that she could sell on as 'vintage'. I mean, she *had* told a tiny lie when she'd encouraged them to invest in the company, but you can't make an omelette without breaking a few eggs, and this had been one hell of an omelette (it had paid for their summer house in Greece, a new place down in Cornwall, and new cars for her and Bill). Besides, those freelancers would surely have benefitted just from having the company's name on their CVs.

When the article came out, this journalist woman had referenced the 'ruthless' sale of the company, but the worst bit for Janet had been the rather cutting comments about Sophia's Whisper's latest catwalk show. Her boss had thought the article was great publicity, but Janet had seethed at the writer's implication that she was letting the side down, 'a female boss reinforcing the male gaze', she'd put. Janet had even rung the magazine editor to give him a piece of her mind.

'Oh yes, I remember now,' she mutters. 'You said our models stomped all over the feminist dream, or something.'

'I'm so pleased you read it.' Vivienne smiles tightly.

'Of course I did. You know, we have plus-size models now,' she says.

'And by plus-size, I'm guessing you mean size ten, maybe a twelve at a push?' Vivienne parries.

Janet isn't in the mood for this tonight. She's spent hours in boardrooms having the same argument with her – mostly male – shareholders. Just this afternoon, she'd patiently explained to the CEO why every model doesn't need to be 'at least a C-cup', but she's not about to tell Vivienne that. She's come to Serendipity's to have fun, not to be grilled by a withered old harpy.

'Let's be honest, Vivienne, who wants to look at big girls in their bras?' Janet chuckles. 'Am I right, Matthew?'

'Oh, I don't know, I've always had a soft spot for a curvy girl.' Matthew looks up from his phone and raises his eyebrows suggestively at her.

Silence falls across the table. Vivienne purses her lips and Stella nearly chokes on her steak. Janet instinctively beams back at Matthew, but then a cold realisation hits her. He's talking about her. Janet knows she's no 90s supermodel, but surely not a 'curvy girl' either, despite Bill's hints.

Six pairs of eyes are on Janet, waiting for her reaction.

### Melvin

Melvin nearly spits out his wine as Matthew's 'curvy girl' comment reverberates around the room. He can see from the pink blush climbing up Janet's neck that she has never thought of herself in this way. The woman's a stunner, no denying it. She's one of those women who carries her looks around like a queen wearing her mantle; she'd swept into the restaurant, surveying her property and her subjects. Those yellow-green eyes had flashed around all the chaps, landing first on Matthew, then Gordon, and finally Melvin, weighing up their worth. Young Tristan, with his smudged glasses and old T-shirt, hadn't got a look-in, poor kid. But her low-cut dress, her unladylike comments about sex, her flippant attitude towards her own marriage just aren't to Melvin's taste. He thinks of Mary. Despite everything she's been through, all the needles, the pain, the hair loss, she's retained her dignity. Mary is a lady, unlike Juicy Janet. Still, the last thing he wants is for Janet to get upset, she'd been having such a good night. He holds his breath as he waits to see how she'll handle this unwitting insult. Should he say something?

'Well, the whole world *is* talking about Kim Kardashian's bottom,' she eventually splutters, the thumb of her left hand absent-mindedly spinning her eternity ring round and round her finger, sending flashes of light across the table.

*Good save, fair play.* Melvin shoots her an encouraging smile. But really, at her age, she should know better than chasing after a young man like that. It's clear that she's a good twenty years too old for this Matthew. As he watches Janet wave at a passing waiter, demanding more wine, Melvin wonders about her husband: where is he tonight? Does he have any idea she's spending the evening flirting so obviously with another man? Then he thinks of a 999 call he'd answered a month or so before. There had been a reported domestic disturbance on a nice road in Belgravia. He'd been sent to have a quiet word and had pictured a tipsy well-to-do couple falling out over which Farrow & Ball shade to paint the drawing room. But, when he'd rung the bell, a man had come straight to the door, tears of blood streaming down his face.

'I did it, I'm sorry,' he'd confessed as Melvin had pushed past to get into the house. The poor woman had been lying in a bloody heap on the kitchen floor, a spatula still clutched in her hand. When Melvin had touched her neck, she was already cold.

'I just couldn't take it anymore,' the husband had said to Melvin as he'd been guided to the patrol car. On the way to the station, he'd talked incessantly about day-to-day pettiness, passive-aggressive battles over bin day, and forgotten anniversaries. The man's words had been doused in sorrow but also in relief. Worse, Melvin understood. He understood how a marriage, even a good marriage, could become suffocating, and how close one – or both – sides come to snapping.

He'd usually tell Mary the details of his day, and surely she would have been horrified by that tale, but he couldn't do it. He was filled with shame at the sympathy he felt for the man who had murdered his wife.

Melvin looks from Janet to Matthew. It strikes him just how different young men are these days. When he himself was in his twenties, living in a small village just outside Cardiff, you were deemed 'well-groomed' if you had regular haircuts and wore clean shoes for a date. These days, young men have *manicures*, wax their chests, and spend hours honing their muscles at the gym. He'd even heard that some wear make-up! Mind you, Matthew looks pretty good on it. His dark brown eyes and high cheekbones remind Melvin of Christian, his new colleague at the station, and then he's wondering what Christian is up to right now...

*Stop it!*

During his fifty-eight years, Melvin has often wondered about certain men who have crossed his path. It was to be expected, he'd told himself. He'd spent his teen years on a rugby pitch – and in the communal baths afterwards – then joined the police force, working predominantly with men, spending weekends watching rugby or football and drinking in the pub with his male friends. But the appearance of Christian has ramped this up. Now Melvin's 'wonderings' last for hours, epic daydreams whilst he sits next to Mary watching the *Antiques Road Show*, tortuous nightmares that leave him drenched in sweat and shaking all over with an all-consuming ache for this man. Christian's earnest brown eyes are the backdrop to his every waking moment.

'Oh, yummy.' Janet's voice cuts through his daydream.

Melvin looks up to see the waiters reappear, presenting their plates of something chocolatey, sending Janet into apparent ecstasy.

'Not sure my belly can take much more,' Melvin says, but picks up his spoon anyway. As he digs into the sponge, dark shiny chocolate sauce comes oozing out, mixing with the vanilla ice cream, reminding him of the Yin-Yang sign. Years ago, Mary had taught him what it meant – a little bit of good in every bad person, and a bit of bad in every good person. Right now, Melvin feels all bad because his daydreams about Christian are teetering on the edge of reality. Yes, unbelievably, Melvin has started to think that Christian might have feelings for him, too. The way he holds his gaze for a second too long, the casual touch to his knee as they sit side by side in their patrol car, the charged air between them.

And so, every nice thing that Mary does for him is now infused with guilt, his home no longer the refuge it was. Melvin pictures himself balancing on the edge of a cliff, filled with paralysing fear. In order to avoid both his guilt and his temptation, he's been hiding out at the Dog and Partridge boozer every day after work. Five pints at the pub, getting home after Mary has gone to bed, then wrestling a hangover to be up at 6 a.m. and in the office by 7 a.m.

Last week, when the black envelope had appeared on his desk, he'd tossed it on top of the ever growing pile of paperwork that he never got around to looking at. It was only that afternoon, as he'd sat at his desk fighting his heavy eyelids, that he'd actually opened the envelope and decided to go along. Leaning back in his comfy office chair, Melvin had pictured Christian excitedly pointing out restaurants as they'd patrolled the streets together, asking Melvin about the sorts of food he liked. As daydreams gave way to real life, Melvin had smiled to himself as he'd wondered if Christian had planned an intimate date for them, disguised as a dinner party.

Now he sees how ludicrous that thought was, and reflects that he might have been better off in the pub after all. At least he'd just have himself to put up with. This is a mixed bunch, that's for sure. As well as handsome Matthew and sex-obsessed Janet, Vivienne is a lady of around his age and seems to have elected herself the headmistress of the group, looking offended at every turn. Melvin finds there's always someone who makes a daft comment about his colour, and tonight that award has gone to uptight Dr Gordon. If looks could kill, the Scottish doctor would have dropped dead thanks to young Stella, but Melvin just laughs these things off. He'd heard it all on the rugby pitches around Cardiff and found humour was the best reaction. The younger generation don't see it this way, you just needed to look at Stella's face to know that.

Now that Melvin thinks of it, he realises he's met Stella before. Over the summer, he'd been called to a nice flat in Kensington to a report of burglary. He'd got there and found a very well-dressed, well-spoken, middle-aged chap in a three-piece suit, who introduced himself as a barrister (putting Melvin firmly in his place) and announced that some 'extraordinarily expensive jewellery' had been stolen from his daughter's flat. When Melvin had started to take down the details, it had become clear that Stella was too inebriated to give a statement, telling her father to 'just buy me another one'. Melvin had then acted as a referee, as father and daughter had yelled at each other about the diamond-encrusted necklace. Watching them, Melvin had felt an almost overwhelming urge to put his hands around both their necks and squeeze the life out of them. He'd had enough of privileged people wasting police time. At least Stella is more composed tonight. Not only that, she appears to be wearing a diamond necklace, just like the one they'd described. Good job he'd never got around to filing that police report.

After polishing off his dessert, Melvin picks up his glass and downs the lot. Then he forces himself to tune back into the conversational tennis flying over the table. The guests, now a little worse for wear, are sending balls in all directions.

'Oh, come on, you can't beat snogging a stranger on a sweaty dancefloor,' Janet screeches.

'It's just not an efficient method,' Matthew replies, his tie now slightly askew. Melvin can also detect a bluntness to his vowels that hadn't been there earlier. Surely, perfectly polished Matthew couldn't be northern?

'I wouldn't be surprised if you had a harem on the go, with all their attributes written up on a spreadsheet,' Vivienne says.

Melvin notices that Matthew starts at the mention of 'harem'. Has tipsy Vivienne stumbled across a truth?

'As if I'd be so disrespectful, Vivienne! I'm a gentleman,' he cries.

'I have to agree with the ladies,' Melvin cuts in. 'I met my wife Mary at a wedding and our first kiss was to *Dancing Queen* at midnight. We've been married for more than thirty years.'

Janet and Vivienne grin, and Matthew shrugs his shoulders in defeat. Then a lull falls over the table. Vivienne turns to Tristan to ask about his IT work, and Matthew talks over Janet's head to young Stella.

'What's this?' Janet suddenly cries, clutching a tiny black envelope, a mini version of the one which had contained the dinner party invitations. Melvin glances around the table and sees that they all have identical envelopes by their wine glasses. Where on earth had *they* appeared from?

Conversation at the table grinds to a halt as the other guests watch Janet open the envelope. Clearly enjoying the attention, she slowly peels it open, pulls out a small black card using the tips of her painted red nails and looks at it. Then her smile freezes.

'Is this some sort of joke?' she splutters, the card in her hand shaking.

'What is it?' Vivienne snaps, her recent comradery with Janet now apparently forgotten.

'*Is* someone filming us?' Janet cries, looking frantically around the room.

'What are you talking about?' asks Gordon. 'What does it say?'

'Get it away from me,' she yelps, throwing it to the centre of the table.

'Take it easy, Janet, love,' Melvin says.

Vivienne reaches across and picks up the card. She pulls her glasses from her handbag and squints as she reads the letters in the dim light.

'It says: *"You will die aged forty-four".*' She gasps and, drops the card as if it's on fire. The guests all look at each other. In an instant, the atmosphere in the room turns from warm and pleasantly tipsy to suffocating and disorientating.

'Take no notice. It's probably just a silly PR stunt,' Matthew says, putting his hand on Janet's.

'It's not silly, it's downright cruel,' snaps Vivienne, standing up. 'I'm going to speak to someone about this.'

'Hold up, Vivienne,' Melvin calls but, before he can do anything, Vivienne has marched towards the door through which the waiters had disappeared. They all watch as she abruptly stops, her hands pushing in vain against the solid wood.

'It's locked,' she says. She bangs her flat palms against the door but there's no answer.

Vivienne goes back to her chair, as they all watch Janet sob quietly.

'First thing tomorrow, I'll find out which PR company planned this dinner party...' Vivienne mutters, though her voice has lost some of its power.

'Let's see,' Gordon says, quickly ripping open his own envelope. 'Mine says fifty-three. That's three years from now.'

'You shouldn't have opened it,' Vivienne scalds. 'I'm certainly not opening mine.'

'Me neither,' Tristan mutters, pushing his own envelope away.

'I feel sick,' Janet sobs and Melvin notices her skin has paled. 'I knew there was something strange about this dinner party.'

'Calm down everyone,' says Melvin, picking up Janet's card from the table. 'I tell you what, I'll take this to the station tomorrow and see if I can find anything out.'

'No wonder the host didn't make an appearance, if they were planning to pull this stunt,' Vivienne says.

'I'm sure it's nothing to worry about,' Matthew says, taking a glug of his wine.

'It would be interesting if the ages were correct, though, wouldn't it?' Gordon mutters, turning over his own card as if hunting for clues.

'Interesting?' Janet snaps. 'I'm already forty-four, it's my birthday in July! That card is a death sentence!'

A chuckle bursts from Stella. They all look over as she starts to cough.

'Something funny?' Janet snarls.

'Sorry – wine went down the wrong way,' she splutters. Matthew takes his hand off Janet's and reaches across the table to give Stella his napkin.

'We've all had a bit too much to drink,' he says. 'We'll be laughing about this in the morning.'

'I doubt that,' Janet snaps, dabbing at her eyes with her own napkin and looking forlornly up at Matthew.

'It's time we all call it a night,' Melvin says. 'Give me your contact details, everyone. I'll look into this and let you know what I find out.'

They each pass him a business card, with Stella scrawling her email address on a napkin. Melvin notices that Vivienne pushes her own black envelope into her bag before wishing them all a brusque goodbye and marching unsteadily out of the room. Minutes later, Tristan follows her out, tucking his envelope into his back pocket. Matthew and Stella move across to the fireplace for a whispered conversation. Gordon stays sitting at the table, frowning at his mobile phone.

Melvin looks over at Janet, whose smeared make-up reminds him of a tired clown. She glances gloomily at Matthew and Stella as she pulls on her coat. Melvin pushes the business cards and napkin into his pocket. He notices that two unopened envelopes are still on the table but leaves them be. He isn't sure how his name ended up on the guest list for this odd dinner party – maybe it's one of his colleagues winding him up. Truthfully, he doesn't care. He has no real interest in unmasking the dinner-party host. But, as a police officer, he should be seen to make an effort, to take control of upsetting situations. He'll make a few calls tomorrow, hopefully settle the ladies' concerns. Glancing at his watch, he sees it's just before 11 p.m. Bit early to head home, Mary might still be up. He just wants to get as drunk as possible and try to forget about his problems for a few more hours.

'One for the road, to calm your nerves?' he asks Janet, and she nods.

# The Wine Bar
## *December 2015 –*
## *two weeks later*

**Vivienne**

A single tear trickles down Cat's flushed cheek and lands on the paper in front of her, leaving a muddy mascara splodge. Slowly letting out a sigh, Vivienne wonders when Cat will realise that the waterworks have no effect on her. Oh yes, Cat's tears are like liquid kryptonite to the editor, leaving him falling over himself, contorting his portly frame into whatever shape might stop the flow. The chief sub editor had been powerless when Cat had sobbed after being pulled up for spelling a celebrity's name wrong. He'd ended up dashing over the road to get her a fancy latte which he'd delivered with a flourish, and one of those tiny chocolate brownies. Vivienne had been working with the old sod for fifteen years and he'd barely thrown her a kind word, let alone an overpriced coffee-shop snack. Vivienne sees Cat's crying for what it is: a desperate attempt to get herself out of a tough spot. A pathetic show of weakness that reminds her male colleagues that she isn't quite up to the job, but she is pretty and makes a decent brew.

When Vivienne had started on the magazine, the only other woman in the office had been the high-heeled, tight-skirted secretary. The then-editor had made it abundantly clear that Vivienne was lucky to be given the chance to write. He'd knotted his unruly eyebrows and warned her she'd have to work 'even harder than the boys'. And by God, she'd done that. At her desk a full hour before her colleagues, compiling long lists of features ideas. When an interview came her way, she'd fill her notebook with spidery short-hand notes and carefully craft the article together, like an artist painting a masterpiece. Yet she'd repeatedly been overlooked and talked over. Every Friday lunchtime, the editor rounded up the (male) writers for a 'quick loosener' in the Golden Eagle pub on the corner. Two hours later, they'd roll back into the office, chuckling about some in-joke and raving about a feature idea that, to Vivienne, sounded utterly unoriginal and undeniably misogynistic.

Cat's sniffles cut through her thoughts.

'Here,' she snaps, handing her a tissue. Cat takes it but doesn't look up, just continues to stare with dismay at the paper, which is covered in red crossings-out and angry exclamation marks. Cat should be grateful to have *her* as a boss, instead of that caterpillar-eyebrowed bully, Peter Patten. In fact, it was in this very room he'd witnessed the one and only time that Vivienne had let her emotions get the better of her at work. She'd spent the morning waiting to present her features ideas to the department. The editor and her colleagues had enjoyed a particularly lengthy liquid lunch that day and it hadn't taken long for the meeting to descend into an old boys' club. Every idea of Vivienne's had been greeted with silence, barely-concealed sniggers and, once, an audible yawn. By the end, Vivienne had felt her cheeks burn as a single tear had rolled down her cheek.

'She's crying,' the deputy editor had spat out.

'No, she's not,' Patten had snapped back and quickly concluded the meeting.

As the others filed out, he'd laid a hand on Vivienne's shoulder and closed the office door.

'Don't make me regret hiring you,' he'd muttered through clenched teeth. 'I want to see ten workable ideas by the morning and don't let me ever see you crying again. This is a place of work.'

Vivienne had stepped out of that meeting knowing that emotion equalled weakness and must be avoided at all costs. She'd never cried at work again. Instead, she'd let her tears – of frustration, sadness, loneliness, and occasionally joy – flow while she lay in the bath at home. They'd roll freely and abundantly down her face and plop into the soapy water. But never, never at work.

Now, here was this young woman, around the same age Vivienne had been when she'd started. Cat had everything on her side, an equal-opportunities employer, a university degree no doubt bankrolled by wealthy parents, and (let's not pretend it doesn't help) a beautiful face. And yet here she is, crying *again*. Time to wrap this meeting up.

'You've worked here for two years now, Cat,' she sighs, her words heavy with disappointment. 'I expect better than this.'

'I'm so sorry, Vivienne,' Cat splutters. 'I started a bar job last week, and I've had to stay until 2 a.m. to clean up.'

Vivienne has to admit, Cat's usually porcelain skin has an unhealthy grey sheen today, and she looks like she'd got dressed in the dark. But we all have busy lives – and we've all had to get on with the terrible pay that media jobs bring. Hell, Vivienne has lived in the same poky cottage in Teddington for twenty years now.

'Read through my notes carefully. I want this rewritten by first thing tomorrow. If it's no better, I'll have to pass the travel section on to Lauren,' she barks, standing up.

A surge of wicked joy shoots through Vivienne as she observes Cat's look of horror. Lauren is the office intern, has made it abundantly clear she has ambitions to write and has already started a charm offensive on the editor.

'Yes, of course. I'm working again tonight, but I'll find the time.'

'Remember, in this industry, there's a queue of people after our jobs, younger, with more enthusiasm and less expectation,' Vivienne says.

With that dark warning, she marches out of the office back to her desk. Cat doesn't need to know that the article deadline isn't for another week. Vivienne just wants to teach her a valuable lesson and make her feel some of the pressure that she herself is always under. Cat should consider herself lucky to have such an experienced mentor.

Sitting down, Vivienne brings up her emails. She flicks past the spam messages, some PRs trying to promote their inane products, news agencies sending their story ideas, then one email catches her eye. She frowns at the sender's name: Melvin Williams, and its from a Met Police email address. It's vaguely familiar. Then she remembers: Melvin the police officer from that odd dinner party two weeks ago.

She hesitates before clicking on the message.

**From: Melvin Williams**
**To: Serendipity's group**
**Subject: Some sad news**
**Hello everyone,**
**Following the dinner party of 26th November 2015, I ran some searches through Land Registry and discovered that a Serendipity's restaurant is not registered on Salvation Road or anywhere else in London. So we can only assume that we dined at a pop-up restaurant as part of a PR stunt, or practical joke, and put that night behind us.**

**On a separate note, a report came into the station late last night of the passing of a young woman after she accidentally fell in front of a London Underground train. I'm sorry to inform you that the woman was Stella Cooke, whom we all had the pleasure of meeting at the dinner party.**

**I have added below a news report about the accident in case this is of interest.**

**Kind regards,**

**Melvin**

Vivienne clicks on the link to a news website.

## *YouTube Sensation StellaStylez – Dead at 23*

*Popular fashion vlogger, Stella Cooke has tragically died after falling in front of a London Underground train on Friday night.*

*Twenty-three-year-old Stella had been attending a celebrity-studded fashion label launch earlier that evening – from where she posted a series of videos and pictures – before leaving around 10 pm and falling in front of the train at Sloane Square station.*

*Tributes have flooded in for the young fashionista, known online as StellaStylez, who was famed for her YouTube videos advising teenagers on affordable alternatives to designer clothes and accessories.*

*One tribute, from JBFan98, reads: 'RIP StellaStylez!! I'll always love you and will never take off my pink cowboy boots in your memory.'*

*Stella's father is the controversial barrister Lord Arthur Cooke, who has a reputation for helping celebrities dodge speeding fines. He has yet to comment on his daughter's passing.*

*In the past, Stella has spoken out about her 'inhumane experience' attending a £30,000-a-year Sussex boarding school and swore that she would never send her own children away.*

*Stella's funeral will be held at Our Lady's Church in Kensington on Saturday. Family have requested donations to the Lambeth Homeless Shelter in lieu of flowers.*

Vivienne hits reply and types:

**To: Serendipity's group**
**From: Vivienne Holmes**
**Re: Some sad news**
**Hello Melvin,**
**This is very tragic news about Stella. She was a very beautiful and apparently successful young woman. It strikes me as odd that she fell in front of a tube train, given how often she must have travelled on the underground and didn't appear to be a big drinker (from what we saw at the dinner party). Were there any witnesses?**

**Thank you for consulting Land Registry about Serendipity's. Who is listed as the owner of that building, incidentally?**
**Best wishes,**
**Vivienne**

Seconds later, an email pops up from Janet Tilsbury. The lingerie boss in the too-tight red dress, Vivienne remembers.

**To: Serendipity's group**
**From: Janet Tilsbury**
**Re: Some sad news**
**Oh my God! What was Stella's number? Was it 23? I've had nightmares ever since that horrid dinner party. I've hardly slept. Does anyone want to put money towards a private investigator? We need to get to the bottom of this before it's too late!**

Then a message pops up from Dr Gordon, with a university email address.

**To: Serendipity's group**
**From: Dr Gordon Macmillan**
**Re: Some sad news**

**Dear Melvin,**

**I appreciate you passing on the details of Stella Cooke's demise.**

**I am compelled to inform the group that I hold some information that is significant in light of Miss Cooke's death.**

**I propose that we congregate at the location of the aforementioned funeral to discuss this matter.**

**Regards,**

**Dr Gordon Macmillan**

**Author of *The Clean Eater* and *You Are What You Eat*, published by Blue Sky Books, available in all good bookstores.**

Vivienne rolls her eyes at Gordon's email and then clicks back on to the article, zooming in on the accompanying photo of Stella. Her short curly hair framing her beautiful face. Vivienne's mind wanders back to the last time she'd seen her at Serendipity's.

Once the furore over Janet's envelope had died down, Vivienne had taken her leave as quickly as possible. The room had become unbearably warm and airless, she'd craved fresh air and space to think. As she'd walked away from the table, her heel had caught on the corner of the huge Victorian rug, and she'd stumbled. Back outside, she'd been surprised to find her whole body felt sluggish, her usually sharp mind filled with cotton wool and soaked in honey. She'd felt oddly helpless when she realised her phone was out of battery. Her jittery hands had fumbled with her bag, spilling its contents all over the wet pavement. Thankfully, Tristan had appeared, had helped her gather her things and then walked her to the nearest tube station. They'd had a nice chat, had laughed about Janet's flirting and Gordon's many faux pas. Vivienne had been grateful that Tristan hadn't brought up the envelopes. Rather, he'd asked insightful questions about her job and been most concerned when she'd told him about the magazine's latest downturn in sales.

That night, her sleep had been filled with gold lettering, penguin waiters, and a non-specific sense of unease. She'd woken up with the words in Janet's message swimming through her mind. When Vivienne had left Serendipity's, she'd planned to leave the evening behind, but the mystery just wouldn't let her go, it trailed behind her like a ghost over the following week. She hadn't taken the little black envelope out of her handbag, which went everywhere with her. Often, she'd thought of it, wondered about the number inside. Yet Vivienne's instinct at Serendipity's had been to leave the envelope sealed and the memory of Janet's terrified face, the suffocating atmosphere of that room, had stayed with her, casting an oddly superstitious spell over it.

Then, last Friday, she'd set off for home after work, walked down the steps at Oxford Circus tube station. The next thing she knew, Vivienne was sitting on a train heading to Heathrow Airport. She'd glanced at her watch, almost 11 p.m. She'd lost five hours. Her legs and shoulders ached, her head throbbed. Thankfully, her handbag was still on her shoulder, with her purse and phone still inside. She'd managed to get a taxi at Hounslow station, which took her safely home where she'd dropped gratefully into bed. But, the following morning, she'd woken feeling shaken and exhausted. Luckily, it was a Saturday, so she'd stayed in bed and let her mind drift back to the last time she'd experienced a fugue state, at just eighteen years old, when she'd endured the most traumatic moments of her life. It was no wonder that her brain decided to check out. Vivienne had rolled on her side, clutched the loose skin of her tummy and allowed the tears to come. She'd never discussed that time with anyone, not even her mother who had witnessed it all. Her mum had died twenty years ago so it was only Vivienne who held the memory now.

Trying to find rest in her old queen-sized bed, the questions hadn't stopped: why on earth had a fugue state happened again after all these years? Had something about Serendipity's sparked it off? At that, Vivienne's eyes had sprung open, she'd pushed off her covers and walked on wobbly feet across her bedroom floor to the pile of clothes she'd tossed aside the night before. Picking up her trusty old handbag, she'd thrown her phone, her purse, tissues, her notebook and pens onto the bed. Her hands had circled the lining of her bag. She'd sat back down next to her things as the realisation hit her. Her envelope was gone.

Now, looking at Stella's perfect smile, frozen in time, Vivienne thinks of her standing by the fireplace at Serendipity's, her eyes sparkling as she'd basked in Matthew's attention, and she shivers despite the heat of her office. When Vivienne had left that place, she'd never expected to see those people again, and yet something irresistible has taken hold. Despite a dark sense of foreboding, Vivienne decides to go along to Stella's funeral the following Saturday.

### Matthew

Stepping back on to the pavement, Matthew curses as his patent leather shoes are splashed by a huge black limousine gliding towards the church. Then he's jostled by a pair of teenage girls who giggle as he glares at them. He grips his umbrella and wipes at a trickle of sweat on his forehead. This isn't what he'd expected at all. People – actually, mostly teenage girls – are standing on either side of the road, some clutching teddy bears, which in turn hold red love-hearts; others have single red roses; many are wearing cowboy boots. A gaggle of photographers have set up their huge cameras in a semi-circle around the church entrance. The arrival of the car sends a surge of energy through the pack as they strain to see who will emerge from it. The smartly dressed driver gets out, walks around to the back of the car and opens the door. One long, bronzed leg and a spiked heel appear, followed by another, and a tall woman with cropped blonde hair totters out wearing an incredibly short dress with barely-there straps.

'Matthew – you came!' Janet cries, suddenly appearing in front of him, practically falling into his arms.

'Where did *you* spring from?' he says, reluctantly returning the hug. Janet's floral perfume fills his nostrils, making him feel light-headed.

'Can you believe this has happened?' Janet gasps, stepping back and almost tripping up a photographer, who is rushing towards the stunning woman holding his camera up, as if it's a weapon.

Matthew conjures up his best mourning face. It takes more concentration than it should.

'What a tragedy, poor Stella,' he says.

'She was twenty-three, wasn't she? I wonder if that was her number. Did you see if she opened her envelope? I know you two left together,' Janet prattles, pulling down her own umbrella and stepping under Matthew's.

Suddenly Matthew is struggling to breathe, his lungs seem to have filled with Janet's overpowering perfume and there's no air. He turns his head, forces himself to take a deep breath, to will his galloping heart rate to slow. Thankfully Janet hasn't noticed his panic.

'No, I didn't see her open it,' he manages to say. 'Didn't you read the news report? It was an accident. It has nothing to do with the envelopes.'

'Do you really think so?' Janet looks up at him with pleading eyes.

Matthew nods and thinks back to that night. He'd thought none of the others had heard him invite Stella back to his for 'coffee'. Clearly, he hadn't been as discreet as he'd hoped. None of it had gone as he'd hoped, come to think of it. Stella had seemed pleased enough at the invitation but had gone quiet as they'd walked up the stairs to his penthouse apartment, seemed nonplussed when he'd opened one of his most expensive bottles of wine, had even looked a bit bored when he'd described his latest million-pound deal at work. When he'd asked about her background, she'd talked for a good ten minutes about her barrister father's peerage, her boarding school where students compared diamond-encrusted gifts from home, and her own 2,000-foot apartment in Kensington, and he'd realised she wasn't his usual type. They'd had sex in the end, but it had been a depressingly lacklustre event and she'd called a taxi ten minutes later. Just before she'd walked out of the door, she'd turned, given him an apologetic little smile and said, 'Maybe we can catch up again soon – unless my number's correct.' He'd laughed and heard her chuckle as she'd made her way down the stairs and out to her waiting cab.

Matthew is silent as they watch a second limo arrive. The photographers burst to life again as the presenters of *The Morning Show* step out and walk solemnly towards the church. He vaguely remembers Janet and Gordon talking about one of them at the dinner party. God, it seems like months ago, not just two weeks.

'So, what about you and Melvin?' he says, keen to change the subject. 'I saw you two leaving arm in arm.'

'I was barking up the wrong tree with that one,' she guffaws, an hysterical tone to her voice, causing some nearby mourners to turn and stare.

'You've got lipstick on your teeth,' he tells her and then tries not to cringe at the squeaky sound she makes as she rubs at her teeth with her finger.

'Who'd have thought it, the macho copper with a wonderful wife has an eye for the boys,' she chuckles, weaving a hand into the crook of Matthew's arm.

'Oh look, here comes Vivienne and – what's-he-called, Trevor or something,' Matthew says, relieved to escape the suffocating umbrella bubble.

Janet shrugs but steps forward to greet them.

'Such a tragedy,' Vivienne says, raising her head to brush her cheek against Janet's.

'Poor Stella,' Janet responds.

'Incredible turn-out though,' Matthew says, kissing Vivienne's dry cheek and nodding at the bespeckled bloke. Tristan, that's his name.

'Looks like she had lots of fans,' Tristan says. Is he really wearing a *Stairway to Heaven* T-shirt?

'Where's Gordon?' Janet says. 'I wonder what his *important information* is…'

Then a shiny black Land Rover drives quickly down the road, causing an errant photographer to jump out of its way. It screeches to a halt in front of the church.

'How *dare* you,' a woman screams as she bursts from the car. She has Stella's heart-shaped face and wears a fitted black dress, cut low at the front, huge sunglasses and a black scarf wrapped around her head. Stella's mother, has to be.

'Naomi,' a tall man in a well-fitted charcoal suit calls, exiting the car on the other side and marching after her. Presumably Stella's father – Lord Cooke.

'Wait,' he pleads, in a voice that is clearly unused to pleading. 'You misunderstood me. Remember, I loved her, too.'

'Oh yes, you showered her with gifts, sent her off to that ridiculous boarding school, but you never *showed* her love, never *told* her you were proud of her. She lived for your approval and all you did was criticise,' Stella's mother snaps back, walking a few steps ahead.

'You never told me that. Why did you never tell me that?' he yells at her back, grief fuelling his anger.

As they both disappear into the church, Matthew recalls Stella talking about her father that night, with a curious mixture of sarcasm and pride.

'Perhaps going inside would be an intrusion too far?' Vivienne says quietly. 'There's a nice wine bar around the corner…'

'Yes – I need a drink,' Janet says, nodding effusively.

'Did someone say "drink"?' Melvin says, suddenly appearing next to them, with Dr Gordon trotting behind.

'This way,' Vivienne calls, once she's greeted Melvin and Gordon.

As they walk, Matthew notices that the rain has finally abated, so he takes down his umbrella and gives it a little shake. He'll be happy to get a whisky to steady his nerves. It hasn't been the best week for him.

The day after the dinner party, he'd met Robyn in town. They'd been dating for a few months, and she hadn't yet refused any of his requests. He'd had something particularly depraved in mind for that night. Three Mojitos in and Robyn was giggling as his hand slowly worked its way up her long leg when … he'd heard it… The name he thought he'd consigned to history.

'Matty Mucus?' the voice said, for a second time. 'Is that really you?'

*Think, think, how to get out of it…* But he found his brain strangely sluggish.

'You've got the wrong person,' was the best he could come up with, turning away from the bloke with slicked-back hair and a familiar toothy grin.

'It's me, Gareth Atkinson, we were at St Mary's together,' the man persisted. 'You look so different. No mucus, or jam-jar bottom glasses now. Mate, we were so horrible to you in school…'

For once, Matthew had been lost for words, all he could do was stare dumbly between Gareth and Robyn. From Gareth's faux-leather biker jacket to Robyn's vintage Louboutin heels. Two worlds he'd never imagined would collide. Finally, Gareth had got the hint and sidled off, but the damage had been done.

'Matty Mucus?' Robyn had chuckled.

'Erm … I had allergy problems as a kid…'

'I thought you'd be the bully at school, not the *bullied*,' Robyn had cried, her eyes wide with astonishment. 'And I didn't know you were *northern*. Did you used to talk like him?'

And just like that, Matthew's power over her had seeped away. It no longer mattered that he was an investment banker with a two-million-pound flat, that his eyesight was perfect thanks to laser surgery, that his body was a sculpted masterpiece and his accent as artificially smooth as his chest. Now, every time she looked at him, Robyn would see the bullied kid at school, snotty and short-sighted. The evening should have ended with Matthew bending Robyn over his coffee table for a spank. Instead, she'd mumbled something about an early-morning meeting and they'd gone their separate ways.

That night, his sleep had been haunted by characters from his childhood he thought he'd forgotten, moments that he'd hoped he'd left behind forever. Acne-ridden bullies chanting 'Matty Mucus' every time he put his hand up in a lesson. Sweating under his bed-covers, the sound of his bedroom door creaking open, his mother's unnaturally sweet tone.

'Matthew dear, Uncle Nigel's come to see you…'

Every weekend she'd introduce a new 'uncle', each bringing their own particular horrors.

At sixteen, he'd escaped his mother's house for a tiny bedsit and began an accountancy course at the local college. His GP had sorted out his sinus problems, he'd got contact lenses, and he opened his eyes to the possibility of reinvention. So Matty Mucus had walked away from his past and become smooth sophisticated Matthew. So far, his new life had been perfect, just as he'd designed it. And now this, this … resurfacing of his past.

The following morning, he'd felt like hell so had called in sick to work. Usually, his weekends were back-to-back with dates, but predictably Robyn had gone quiet and he couldn't face the date he'd planned with a new girl whose profile picture had been promisingly sexy.

On Monday morning, he'd forced himself back into the office.

'You look awful.' His boss had chuckled, giving Matthew a wink. 'Busy weekend?'

'You could say that.' Matthew had attempted his cat-that-got-the-cream grin but feared it was more of a hyena-with-a-hernia grimace.

While his computer was starting up, he'd pulled out his phone and opened up Facebook. That's where he contacted his dates before he felt ready to upgrade them to swapping mobile numbers. That name again: Gareth Atkinson. He'd swallowed and clicked on the message:

**Sorry we didn't get to talk properly the other night. Let's meet up for a drink to discuss old times. Don't say no, Matty, I've got an old class photo here and would hate your colleagues to see it… Followed by two laughing emojis.**

Matthew had breathed deeply. What did he mean? Was it a threat? In a daze, he'd typed a reply.

**Sounds good, how about next Wednesday?**

Seeing Gareth again was the last thing he'd wanted to do but he couldn't risk ignoring him.

He'd tucked his phone back in his pocket and then logged on to his email account. That's when he'd seen Melvin's message about Stella.

Beautiful young Stella. Dead.

He'd thought of the last time he'd seen her, standing in front of his apartment door, saying those words: '*We can catch up again soon. Unless my number's correct.*' There could only be one explanation. Stella knew her number. And it was twenty-three.

Suddenly, sweat was dripping down his face, down his back, drenching his crisp white shirt. He'd squeezed his eyes shut and all he could see was Stella lying on the tube tracks, blood pouring from a wound on her head. He'd stumbled through his office, into the lift, blindly pressing the buttons until he arrived on the top floor. He made his way to the back right-hand corner of the roof, where he couldn't be seen. Leaned against the railing and forced himself to look out over the London skyline, trying to calm himself down. His gaze followed the line of the Thames, snaking through the city. It had always brought him comfort, that continuous movement of water, watched by Londoners for centuries, always there and yet always moving and changing. But it brought no comfort then. Because all he could think of was his own number. Ticking ever closer.

Somehow Matthew had made it through the rest of the week, enduring phone calls and meetings on autopilot. He'd read over Melvin's email several times and made the decision not to attend Stella's funeral. Yet, that Saturday afternoon, he'd found himself marching along a rain-drenched Kensington High Street, pulled along by a force he didn't understand.

Matthew focuses on Vivienne's frizzy-haired head as they weave their way through the crowds of shoppers on the high street and finally file into the wine bar. Vivienne sits down at a large circular table by the window. The others take their places around her.

### Tristan

Tristan waits patiently as the pretty waitress moves around the table to take their orders. Predictably, she starts with Matthew (double whisky), then works her way around the table to Janet (white wine), Melvin (draft beer), Gordon (sparkling mineral water), Vivienne (also white wine – 'let's just get a bottle': Janet, 'of course') and finally himself (Guinness, *let's see if she gets it right*). As he looks around the group, Tristan realises that they have unwittingly sat in the same formation as at the dinner party. There's even an empty chair between Janet and Gordon, where Stella would have been. He looks from Matthew to Janet and remembers their teeth-gritting, embarrassing flirting two weeks ago. Then, Matthew had lain his arm casually across the back of Janet's chair while she had leant towards him, lapping up the attention. Today, though, Matthew's arms are crossed, he's looking gloomily down at the table, his body slightly angled away from Janet while she keeps sneaking a side look at him between nervously rubbing her teeth with her forefinger.

'Well, I wish we were meeting up under better circumstances,' Melvin says, his large hands planted heavily on the table, as if he's chairing a board meeting.

'Poor Stella, what a tragic accident. Were there any witnesses, other people on the platform?' Vivienne asks as she fishes around in her handbag, finally pulling out a notebook with silver hummingbirds on the front, then a pen.

'Spot the journalist!' Janet guffaws – a strangely hollow sound – while her eyes move eagerly to Melvin.

'No one else was down that end of the platform, it seems,' Melvin says. Vivienne makes a note in her book.

'Did anyone happen to speak to Stella at the end of the dinner party?' Vivienne asks, raising her journalist eyebrows at the others.

Janet clears her throat and gives Matthew a meaningful look.

'Erm yes. We had another drink but went our separate ways afterwards,' he says, looking down as he spins the bezel on his silver watch. Tristan notices the dark shadows under his eyes, the stubble on his chin and thinks back to the dinner party where shiny Matthew's attention had moved hungrily from Janet to

Stella, even Vivienne, vying for their attention, their admiration. Today's Matthew is like a poor imitation, a second-rate tribute act.

'What about all that trolling stuff?' Janet blurts out. 'Maybe she annoyed the wrong person and they came after her.'

'She was clearly a very mixed-up girl,' says Vivienne. 'We saw what her parents were like. She's had everything except love.'

'You know what they say, a man's life does not consist of the abundance of his possessions,' mumbles Tristan.

In the days since Stella's death, social media had exploded with the story of Stella's secret trolling. She'd targeted her rival YouTubers in a string of disgusting and hate-ridden messages. The shocking discovery had overshadowed the tragedy of her death and sparked off a wave of criticism, from MPs to reality-TV stars to the run-of-the-mill average troll. Stella's father had even appeared on that women-only chat show to defend his daughter.

The table goes quiet as the waitress returns with a tray of their drinks, passing them around, leaving Tristan till last. He watches her place a pint of cider in front of him. Closing his eyes, his jaw clenches painfully. He forces himself to go through his numbers: one to fifty, then odd numbers, then evens, then prime numbers… Finally, he's able to pick up his drink.

Vivienne continues to scribble away in her notebook.

'Are you doing your own investigations now, Miss Marple?' Melvin asks, looking at her notebook. He's smiling, but there's irritation in his tone.

'Seems like you might need some help on that front, darling!' Janet pipes up, patting Melvin on his splayed fingers.

Melvin's smile tightens and his large chest rises as he takes a deep breath.

'*Did* you get any closer to finding out who planned the dinner party?' Vivienne asks.

'It's a bit of a mystery,' Melvin says, shaking his head. 'The building used to be a restaurant, years back. Now it seems the landlord lets it out for events. I've been ringing the landline, left a few messages, but haven't heard back. I was planning on popping round there but then *this* happened…'

'I had a search online, and rang around a few PR agencies we deal with, but no one knew about an event at Serendipity's,' Vivienne says, scrawling another note in her book.

'I'll get the next round in.' Melvin jumps to his feet and strides towards the bar. There's a bounce in his step that had been absent at Serendipity's.

'Water for me, please, Melvin,' Gordon calls to his back.

As Tristan watches Melvin, he remembers him and Janet whispering together at the end of the dinner party. He wonders what they'd been discussing. Perhaps they'd argued: they don't seem on the friendliest terms today. The night had fizzled out by then, Vivienne had just left, and Tristan had suddenly been overcome with tiredness, so he'd made his way upstairs. Outside, he'd found Vivienne standing over the spilt contents of her handbag, staring blindly at her mobile, apparently disorientated.

'My phone seems to be out of battery,' she'd told him. 'I need to call a taxi.'

'The tube station isn't far,' he'd assured her. Once he'd helped her pick up her things, they'd walked the twenty minutes together. They'd talked a bit about the other dinner-party guests, and then Vivienne had opened up about her magazine's struggling sales figures, her inexperienced boss, and hopeless colleagues. He'd listened, asked a few questions, and then, outside the station, she'd blushingly thanked him before stomping off towards the escalators.

Gazing into the bright station, he'd decided he'd had enough of people and noise for one night, so he'd turned away and made his way home by foot. He'd marched through London, with his thoughts about the dinner-party guests similarly marching through his mind. Janet's red lips, Matthew's impossibly black eyes, Melvin's bassline voice. Then Janet's horrified face when she'd opened her envelope…

Tristan had been surprised to find himself already standing in front of his block of flats. Going inside his flat, he saw that everything was just as he'd left it. His small kitchen clean and tidy, his laptop closed on the desk, the sheets on his double bed perfectly ironed. Everything was the same, but he felt different. It was as if he was fully charged, having spent years on low battery. His fingers and toes had tingled with energy. He tried to sit down on his sofa, but his body wouldn't let him rest. He paced around his little flat, up and down, circling his small kitchen table.

Finally, he'd sat down at his little desk, opened up his laptop and clicked on to Facebook. He'd gone straight to Ellie's page and immediately noticed two changes. Firstly, the blue button that usually came up saying 'friends' now said 'send friend request'. She had 'unfriended' him.

'What?' he'd shouted at her smiling profile picture.

She must have known he'd looked on her page, must have known he would see this right away. He knew she'd dated someone shortly after him. It had nearly broken Tristan when he'd seen her tag a man alongside a series of pictures showing menus from posh restaurants, two hands (one clearly masculine, a chunky silver watch on his wrist) clutching champagne cocktails and other shots of theatre tickets and a private ride on the London Eye. Then it had gone quiet and she'd even deleted the pictures. A friend had written a comment.

*What happened?*

Ellie had replied with a broken-heart emoji. But that was all months ago and there had been no mention of him since. Why would she suddenly unfriend Tristan? They hadn't spoken in months. The only thing he could think was that she had started seeing someone new, someone serious. Staring hard at the pixels that made up the word 'friend', Tristan had forced himself to count. The numbers, those lovely reliable numbers were the only things that had stopped him from throwing his laptop against the wall.

'These should help with the shock,' Melvin says, proudly bearing a silver tray with six shot glasses filled to the brim. Melvin is grinning broadly as he hands the glasses around, like the best man on his first ever stag do. It strikes Tristan that, while Matthew is a sadder version of himself from the dinner party, Melvin appears to be a happier version. Matthew grabs a glass and knocks back the transparent fluid. He closes his eyes as the alcohol rolls down his throat, clearly enjoying the sensation. To Tristan's surprise, Vivienne quickly follows suit.

'Bottoms up,' Melvin says, lifting a glass and clinking it against Tristan's.

'To Stella,' Tristan says, putting the glass to his lips. The overwhelming taste of aniseed fills his senses. It takes all his willpower not to spit it straight out. Squeezing his eyes shut, he forces the burning liquid down, convinced his stomach will quickly give it its marching orders. But no, it settles and then a warm feeling washes through Tristan and he slowly opens his eyes.

### Gordon

Gordon clutches the small shot glass in front of him. The transparent fluid inside looks innocent enough, but he knows it contains around forty per cent alcohol and none of the anti-oxidant properties of a nice glass of Malbec. Of course, Janet had knocked hers back immediately, but he'd waited for Vivienne to push hers away, or Tristan to abstain, but, to his amazement, they'd both thrown back the disgusting drink. Gordon lifts it to his mouth, takes the smallest of sips and then hides it behind an empty pint glass on the table. Thankfully, no one notices and he breathes out a controlled sigh. After what happened following the dinner party two weeks ago, he has no intention of over-indulging this afternoon.

'Can you believe we were having dinner with Stella just two weeks ago, and now she's gone?' Vivienne is saying, both hands clutching the handbag on her knee, as if it is a wayward baby likely to throw itself on to the ground at any moment. 'You just don't know when your number's up.'

Gordon's hand goes to his jacket pocket. It's time.

'Aren't you going to ask about my information?' he says, and five pairs of eyes turn to him.

'Oh yes, Gordon, you said you knew something about Stella's death?' Janet responds.

'Before we get to that, I wondered if Stella's passing has made any of you give further thought to *your* numbers?' he says.

'Gordon, I really don't think it's appropriate to discuss this on the day of Stella's funeral,' Melvin says.

'Well, I happen to believe this is the perfect time…' Gordon says.

'I haven't stopped thinking about it, if you must know,' Janet cries, her voice cracking.

'Now, now, Gordon,' Melvin says, in his most calming police-officer tone. 'Didn't we agree that we wouldn't take those envelopes seriously? Stella's death was a tragic accident, no one could possibly have known it would happen.'

'I watched her leave her envelope on the table,' Vivienne says. 'There's no point discussing it when we'll never know the truth.'

'Won't we?' Gordon says and then pulls a tiny black envelope from his pocket, tossing it into the centre of the table like a magician performing a trick.

Janet lets out a melodramatic gasp as all eyes turn from Gordon to the envelope, clearly bearing Stella's name on the front.

After the dinner party, Gordon had watched the other guests leave. As he'd pulled on his jacket, he'd noticed Stella and Melvin's envelopes still lying by their place settings. Instinctively, he'd picked them up and pushed them into the side pocket of his briefcase. Out on the street, he'd followed Janet and Melvin as they'd swayed along the road together. When they'd entered a hotel bar, he'd stood in the shadows outside and watched them take a seat by the window, Janet clutching Melvin's hands across the table, wagging her ludicrous chest in his face. He'd found he couldn't stop watching her, that strange combination of disgust and interest had stirred in him again. Later, he'd flagged down a black cab and must have dozed a little on the way home, as it felt like only minutes later that the taxi stopped with a jolt outside his green gates on their quiet road in Wandsworth. He'd paid the man quickly and then tiptoed his way inside and up the stairs to their bedroom. Elizabeth had been fast asleep, and he'd gazed enviously at her; his body ached with tiredness, but he knew he couldn't go to bed just yet. He'd known he had to do something about all the food – and wine – he'd consumed. Sitting down on the bed, he'd pulled off his clothes and laid down next to Elizabeth, just for a minute.

But he'd woken hours later, morning light seeping through the wooden shutters and no sign of Elizabeth. He'd assumed she'd set out on her morning run. Gordon's mouth and tongue had the texture of felt, his head heavy. He couldn't stop thinking of the food working its way through his body, his perfectly balanced digestive system screaming out in horror. He'd leapt up from the bed and crouched down in front of the toilet in their en suite. Quickly, he'd pulled his spare toothbrush from under the sink and felt relief wash over him as his steak dinner, red wine, and the gluey, digested potatoes filled the toilet bowl.

'Gordon, what are you doing?' Elizabeth had suddenly appeared behind him, glancing from the toothbrush still in his hand to the contents of the toilet.

When they'd first met at university in Edinburgh, he'd confided in her about the bulimia that had beleaguered his teenage years. 'But I'm over it now,' he'd assured her, and she'd squeezed his hand, telling him some totally unrelated story of how she'd stopped eating for three days when her first boyfriend had dumped her. When his problem had re-emerged during a stressful time at work, Gordon had put it down as a one-off and never mentioned it to Elizabeth. But, gradually, over the last three years, gorging and then purging had become part of his routine.

Still staring at the toilet bowl, Elizabeth had been furious.

'Why didn't you tell me?' she yelled over and over, not listening to his perfectly reasoned explanation. Eventually, he promised it wouldn't happen again, and she'd agreed not to tell their daughter, or anyone else.

'After all that lecturing you do about nutrition and looking after your body?' she said, with an almost smug edge to her voice.

That comment had stung, and, a few days later, as he'd faced the cameras on *The Morning Show*, he'd heard it again. When asked about the apple-cider-vinegar diet, he'd faltered, started to answer then stopped, doubting himself. Silence had filled the air, that loud oppressive silence that you only get on live television or radio. The presenter had stared at him, her perfect eyebrows raised in anticipation. The seconds had stretched out, painfully, agonisingly. His heart had started to beat loudly between his temples as his anxiety spiralled before flatlining. Finally, he'd mumbled something about lack of scientific evidence, and they'd cut to an advert. Afterwards, the producers played it down, but he could tell they weren't impressed.

The following week, Gordon had been in the middle of typing an email to a producer on the show, stating his availability, when Melvin's message had popped up on the email group. That young woman Stella was dead. He'd pictured her rudely turning away from him at the table, diamonds glistening in her ears. *She got what she deserved.* The words were in his mind in an instant. He'd read over Melvin's message, along with the news article. That's when he'd remembered the envelopes in his briefcase. Pulling them out, he'd read over the names on the front: Stella and Melvin. At the dinner party, Gordon had been bemused by Janet's dramatic reaction to her envelope, by Vivienne's over-zealous questioning of the waiting staff. Clearly, the event had been an orchestrated PR prank, certainly nothing to concern himself with. But now Stella had died, and he had her envelope in his possession. He'd pushed Melvin's envelope into his desk drawer and focused his attention on Stella's. Turning it over, he'd noticed that it had already been opened. He'd had a quick look then typed out his reply to Melvin's email.

In the days running up to Stella's funeral, Gordon had regularly cast his mind back to that night at Serendipity's. At the time, he'd dismissed it as a frivolous event by a misguided media company, but another theory was percolating. A theory that excited him, that energised him and perhaps would prove to be his making. He wasn't sure how much he'd reveal to the other guests, but he'd wanted to entice them to gather once more with his hint about more information, specifically the envelope. He'd expected them to thank him for his quick thinking in picking it up. But, oddly enough, they all looked horrified. No one had even tried to touch the envelope.

'It's been opened,' Janet gasps, narrowing her eyes at him.

'It was like that when I picked it up,' Gordon says, holding up his hands. 'Matthew, you're the last one of us to see Stella. Did she mention that she'd opened her envelope?'

Matthew shakes his head.

Gordon reaches over and picks up Stella's envelope. He wasn't going to let Janet or Melvin steal his big moment.

'Don't you dare,' Janet cries, slapping at his arm.

'What do you mean?' he asks, genuinely confused. 'If we open it and it says twenty-three, then we'll know that the predictions are correct.'

'You should have left it there,' Vivienne says. 'What benefit is there in knowing the number inside?'

All Gordon can do is stare at her. Does he really need to state the obvious? Vivienne is an experienced journalist – albeit on a women's magazine – and he'd taken her for having a bit more intelligence than this.

'Perhaps we should leave it alone, and Melvin could take it to the police station, look into it for us,' Tristan says, looking at the police officer, who is nonchalantly tapping at his mobile phone.

Gordon can't fathom it. *What is wrong with these people?*

### Janet

Janet stares at the black envelope in the middle of the table, Stella's name written in perfect cursive script. Her right hand is pressed against her chest, where she can feel her heart galloping underneath. She closes her eyes and sees her own envelope on the night of the dinner party, bearing those unforgettable words – *You will die aged 44.* She'd been enjoying the evening, the delectable food and wine, the company of a gorgeous young man, the amusing conversation. In an instant, it had felt like the air had been sucked from the room, sucked from her very lungs, as if Death himself had appeared and pointed directly at her. She'd done her best to pull herself together afterwards, to tell herself that it had been the work of a rogue PR company. It hadn't helped that the light of Matthew's attentions had turned to shine on that young girl Stella, but thankfully Melvin had swooped in, offering to take her for another drink, and she'd been relieved to leave that suffocating place on his arm. But when they'd settled into the hotel bar, got to work on a bottle of whisky, the truth about Melvin had come spilling out.

'I think I'm falling in love,' he'd admitted, referring to a *male* colleague. 'I can't stop thinking about him.'

'You have to be honest with yourself. And honest with Mary,' Janet had counselled. As the minutes had ticked by, Melvin had become more drunk and melancholy, while Janet had grown antsy, in need of something more distracting to wipe that number from her mind.

Finally, once they'd polished off the bottle, she'd persuaded Melvin to get a taxi home and make plans to come clean to his poor unsuspecting wife, whilst also ordering her own cab to take her to Giles's place. He'd been her lover for six months, until she'd called it off a few weeks ago. That spoilsport emotion, guilt, had raised its ugly head. Yet, in that moment, she'd needed *something*.

'I thought you said our little liaisons were over?' Giles had beamed, appearing in his doorway with adorably ruffled hair.

'I missed you,' she told him. He'd satisfied her as he always had and cleared her mind for a good hour or so, but, afterwards, with him snoring beside her, she'd found sleep impossible. Once she'd recovered her red dress from the kitchen floor, she called a taxi to take her home just before 2 a.m. Crawling into her own bed, she'd found Bill disappointingly still breathing and spread-eagled right in the centre. In the end, she'd marched into the spare room where she'd finally drifted off but had slept fitfully, tormented by dreams of dinner parties with farm animals wearing tuxedoes and numbers scrawled in blood on the walls.

She'd woken with Bill standing over her, squinting unattractively without his glasses on.

'Don't you have a meeting this morning, dear?' he asked, scratching at his pyjamaed crotch.

'*Shit!*' she'd yelled when she'd realised it was nearly 8 a.m. and the shareholders' meeting was due to start at 8.30.

It had been nearly midnight by the time she'd got home that night. All she wanted was a nice long soak in the bath and then to climb into bed, but Bill had pulled out his diary and tiny golf pencil for their monthly 'scheduling meeting'. Watching him peer through the glasses perched on the end of his nose (from whence hair abundantly sprouted), she'd wondered where this old man had sprung from. She'd met Bill when she was twenty-five; he'd been a charismatic forty-year-old with a teenager's sex drive, a sprinkling of salt-and-pepper hair, and a muscular frame thanks to a life-time of sports, but now, at nearly sixty, he was an old overweight man with barely enough energy to climb the stairs, let alone anything else, whilst Janet was only just reaching her prime.

'The baby's christening, May 16th?' he'd asked.

'Fine,' she mumbled. Plenty of time to think up a last-minute meeting and get out of it.

'August at the villa?'

'Yes, Bill, just like every year. Do we really need a meeting about this?' she snapped.

'Then there's your birthday – your forty-fifth – rather a big one,' he'd said. 'What shall it be this year, a spa weekend with your friends, a city break, or shall I plan a surprise?'

Bill, for all his faults, had always made a fuss of her birthday. In the early years of their marriage, he'd taken her to Paris, Rome, even Bali once. He'd smiled benignly at her then, waiting for his instructions, but the mention of her birthday had sent instant cramps across her middle and she'd been forced to dash straight to the loo.

'Must have been a dodgy oyster at dinner,' she'd told him afterwards. 'Let's talk about my birthday another day.'

'OK, dear, but don't leave it too long. It's your big day and we wouldn't want you to be disappointed.'

Janet had plodded upstairs and drawn herself a bath, with Bill's words still in her ears. *'Your forty-fifth … rather a big one.'* She'd wanted to scream at him: what if I don't live that long? Just to see the look on his stupid face. Lately, she'd been picturing her life after Bill's death, but perhaps fate had other ideas and it would be Bill who was left behind. As she'd soaked in the warm water, popping the bubbles with her toes, Janet's mind drifted again back to Serendipity's, to those words – *You will die aged 44*. The other guests had dismissed it as a PR stunt but, when she thinks back, the evening had been so vivid, the flames from the fire reflected in Matthew's dark eyes, the rich flavours of the food and wine, the scent of the burning candles, dripping their wax down the candelabras. There had been nothing fake or contrived about any of it. And the number on that card had instantly felt real to her. She'd hoped the panic she'd felt at the dinner party would pass but it hadn't. Rather, it had settled in her body like a rumbling volcano, heat slowly rising up, waiting for the right moment to erupt. As she'd patted herself dry, pulled on her favourite silk pyjamas, Janet had told herself she was being silly. She just needed a good night's sleep and to throw herself into preparing for the big Sophia's Whisper show the following week. She'd always loved the event, her models splashed across the papers, online sales soaring and the baskets of champagne and expensive chocolates that always landed on her desk. *That's* what's real, she'd told herself. Not some random number at a tacky dinner party.

Unfortunately, the show hadn't exactly gone to plan. Just before the grand finale, the director Marcel had lost track of the real gold bustier that the singer, Lila Daze, was supposed to wear. He'd been screeching Janet's name backstage but she'd been otherwise engaged. Poor Marcel had got the shock of his life when he'd opened a storage cupboard to find Janet on her knees in front of the Financial Director. She'd just about managed to keep her job. The worst of it was, she'd only got herself in that situation after she'd gone overboard on her expenses one too many times and the FD had made it clear he would brush them under the carpet in return for certain favours.

Janet's blushes were only just fading when Melvin's message had popped up. She'd rolled her eyes as she'd skimmed over his hopeless attempts at investigating the dinner party but then gasped when she'd read about Stella. Her hands shook as she clicked on the news website and scanned the report. Janet thought of the last time she'd seen the girl at Serendipity's, standing so close to Matthew. Stella had met her eye for the briefest of moments, *'I won'* her look had said. And now she was dead, and Janet had felt the sweetness of revenge washing through her. The girl had fallen under a tube train at a station near Janet's office. It could have happened to anyone, she'd supposed.

Then the volcano inside her had rumbled. *The numbers.* She couldn't remember Stella opening her envelope at the dinner party but what if her number had been twenty-three? Quickly, she typed a response to Melvin's message. She *had* to know what Stella's number was. Because, if it was twenty-three, then forty-four might indeed be hers. She'd scanned over Gordon's message, doubted he had anything useful to tell them, but nodded to herself at his suggestion of meeting up again. From then, she'd counted the days down to the funeral. When news of Stella's trolling had broken, she'd read it over with only mild interest. So there had been more to Stella than a beautiful face and an eye for fashion. Janet wouldn't have admitted it out loud, but the trolling had actually made her like Stella a bit more.

When Janet had bumped into Matthew outside the church, she hoped he'd put her mind at rest about the numbers but he'd behaved so strangely. He hadn't met her eye as he half-heartedly reassured her, became jittery when she'd spoken of Stella. Honestly, he'd been all over Janet at the dinner party, but today he'd seemed to recoil when she merely linked his arm with hers.

In front of the others, Janet had done her best to play down her panic. But then that smug doctor had tossed Stella's envelope on the table. Now, looking at Stella's name, that overpowering nausea is creeping up on her again.

'Janet, are you OK? You've gone very pale,' Vivienne says.

'I need a minute,' she gasps, standing up. 'Don't anyone touch that envelope while I'm gone.'

## Melvin

Melvin registers only the odd word from the conversation going on around him. 'Melodramatic' from a sighing Matthew, 'illogical' from a frustrated Gordon, a muttered 'upset' from quiet Tristan. He's focusing instead on the message that has just popped up on his phone. `Can't wait for tomorrow. Our first date! X`

Beaming despite himself, Melvin sends a quick response then puts his phone back in his pocket.

'What's made you smile?' Vivienne asks him.

'Sorry, just a text from a friend,' he says, pushing the smile away.

*Come on, Melvin.* It's the day of Stella's funeral, for goodness' sake, and you're a police officer: you should know how to act in the face of grief. And that means not grinning like an idiot. That poor girl was just twenty-three, barely an adult, only just making her way in the world, perhaps marriage or children in front of her, and it's all been snatched away. While he is an old man in comparison, nearing retirement, and yet incredibly about to embark on a whole new life. That dinner party, just two weeks ago, had been the catalyst for this change.

'Did you do it? Did you tell her?' Janet asks, suddenly standing too close to him, leaning over to whisper in his ear.

'Erm…' he mumbles, aware of Vivienne's head turning incrementally towards them, ears twitching. 'Tonight, all being well.'

Mercifully, she doesn't say any more and goes to sit back down. When he'd suggested going for another drink with Janet, he hadn't planned to spill his guts, but the whisky had loosened his tongue, and all his woes had come tumbling out, right at Janet's feet. Melvin suddenly feels his hands sweat as he remembers the things he'd said to her. It had felt safe, confessing it all to a stranger in a strange bar. He pictures Janet's leonine eyes looking earnestly into his own.

'You must tell Mary,' she'd insisted. 'She deserves your honesty. And you deserve to start living your life. Who knows how long any of us have?'

Stella had less than two weeks…

That conversation had carved a path out of the hell Melvin had been enduring. Before then, he'd seen himself as stuck. But Janet had spelled it out to him – he just had to be honest. And so last week he'd casually suggested a post-work drink to Christian, who had nodded happily. Melvin had taken his courage in both hands, opened his mouth to let his feelings out, but then Christian had jumped in. First apologising in case Melvin might find his words 'inappropriate' (he'd looked so adorably vulnerable when he'd said that) and told him that he'd had feelings for Melvin for months. Melvin had been elated, and hadn't even needed to broach the awkward subject himself. Together, they'd planned out tonight. Melvin would cook Mary his legendary lasagne, pour them both a large glass of red and serve up the truth to his wife: their marriage cannot continue because he is gay. Last night, he'd called Christian once Mary had gone to bed to go over the final details.

'I'm taking you out on Sunday,' Christian had cried, his voice thick with happy tears. Melvin had hung up the phone and slumped back on their old sofa. His whole body was starting to feel lighter as if shackles on his wrists and ankles were starting to slowly loosen. Soon, he'd be free of his old life. Free to be with Christian. He hadn't felt this happy in years.

He just wishes he hadn't had to see Janet again; she clearly isn't the most discreet sort.

'Here we are, ladies and gentlemen.' The waitress appears with two bottles of champagne, shadowed by a waiter carrying six champagne flutes.

'I thought we should say goodbye to Stella in style,' Janet says. 'After all, she was *dead* stylish.'

Melvin's eyes meet Vivienne's as the comment hits home, whilst Janet just smirks and holds her glass up until it's filled to the top. She downs half of the contents in one go and lifts it up again for a top-up.

Once all the glasses are filled and the waiters step away, silence settles across the table once more. Stella's envelope is still there, daring one of them to open it. Gordon hasn't even looked at his champagne, he's just fidgeting in his seat; Matthew has finished his drink quickly and is now staring into his empty glass; Vivienne is taking small eager sips from hers while reading from her notebook; Tristan holds his drink in his left hand and chews the fingernail of his right thumb; and Janet's lipstick-stained glass sits between her and Stella's envelope.

'Let's look at the facts,' Gordon says, in full lecture mode now. 'Janet opened her envelope at the dinner party, which explicitly stated she would die at forty-four. And what age are you now, Janet?'

She clears her throat and looks from Gordon to Matthew and then Melvin, who shrugs his shoulders.

'As you know, I'm forty-four,' she says, her voice croaky. She clears her throat and adds: 'It's my birthday in July.'

'Gordon, I'm not sure this is helping anyone…' Melvin says when he notices Janet's glass shaking in her hand.

'Mine was fifty-three,' Gordon says, holding his palm up towards Melvin. 'Did anyone else open theirs?'

'My envelope's gone missing,' Vivienne admits. 'It was in my bag after the dinner party, but I seem to have mislaid it since then.'

'Mine's probably still in my jeans pocket at home. I haven't opened it,' says Tristan. 'Forgot all about it, to be honest.'

'No idea where mine got to,' Melvin says, with a shrug.

They all look at Matthew, who is glaring at his empty champagne flute.

'I must have left it at Serendipity's. I didn't open it.' He shrugs then reaches for the second bottle and tops up everyone's glasses. Melvin notices that it shakes slightly in his hand and some wine spills on to the table.

'Sorry, it's an emotional day,' Matthew says, colour rising in his cheeks. 'Anyway, here's to beautiful, stylish, mischievous Stella.'

They clink glasses, lost in their own thoughts.

Gordon clears his throat, keen to get back to business.

'So, if the number inside Stella's envelope is twenty-three, then we'll know for sure…'

'We'll know what for sure?' Janet cuts in. 'What exactly are you implying, Gordon? That some God-like figure has seen into our futures and knows when we'll all die?'

'No, I'm a scientist,' Gordon huffs. 'I do not believe in God – or God-like figures as you put it.'

'Then what?' Vivienne snaps. 'A serial killer giving us all fair warning of our murders?'

'Now, stop right there, everyone. I've read the police report. The girl fell in front of a tube train. It was an accident. There's no suggestion at all of foul play,' says Melvin.

'But there were no witnesses, no CCTV…' Vivienne mutters.

'Even if the card does say twenty-three, it could still be a coincidence,' Matthew mutters, his voice strained.

'He's right,' says Tristan.

The table falls quiet as six pairs of eyes rest on the envelope.

'Let's see, shall we?' Gordon says and, quick as a whip, he grabs the envelope and yanks the card out.

Janet gasps and covers her eyes. Gordon peers at the card and then he looks up at Janet and blinks slowly.

'For goodness' sake,' Matthew snaps and snatches the card out of Gordon's hand.

'What does it say?' Vivienne asks.

Matthew reads the words and then drops the card on to the table.

**You will die aged 23.**

'I suppose one correct number could be a coincidence but not two… So, we just wait and see if it happens again,' says Gordon, taking his glasses off to clean them.

'If *what* happens again?' Matthew snaps, turning quickly to Gordon.

'If another prediction comes true, we'll know that this is no PR stunt.'

Janet's head drops into her hands and lets out a muffled yelp.

'I'm going to faint,' she cries.

'You're all right, Janet!' Melvin calls, dashing around the table. While Tristan fetches a glass of water and a shot of tequila from the bar, Matthew fans Janet with a wine menu and Melvin clutches her hands, keeping up a stream of reassurances.

After twenty minutes, she has some colour back in her cheeks and her hysterical crying has finally abated.

'I was thinking about what Janet said earlier, about Stella's trolling,' Vivienne says, flicking through her notebook. 'Perhaps the dinner party *was* an act of revenge by one of Stella's trolling victims. And we have been unlucky enough to get caught in the crossfire.'

'That does add up,' says Tristan, nodding.

'Like I say, I haven't seen any evidence of murder,' says Melvin, glancing at his watch. 'But I'll have a word at the station on Monday, see if my colleagues can look into those bloggers Stella offended.'

'Yes, please do,' nods Vivienne.

'I have another theory…' Gordon starts.

'Gordon, please,' Melvin cuts in, his deep voice raised a little. 'Today is Stella's funeral, and it's just not respectful to be tossing daft theories around. Let's all agree right now to throw the envelopes away.'

'But what if Vivienne's wrong and there is a killer on the loose?' Janet cries, downing the last of her drink and glaring across at Gordon.

'Janet, love, there's no murderer out there. I promise you. You'll be dancing at your forty-fifth birthday party before you know it,' Melvin tells her, but she's already standing up and turning away from the table.

'Let's hope so,' she snaps and then marches towards the exit without looking back.

'I'd better be going, too. Elizabeth and I have tickets for the theatre tonight,' Gordon announces to the table then abruptly turns and marches out.

'And it's time I headed off,' Vivienne says, pulling her coat on. 'Melvin, do email us with any news.'

'I'll walk to the tube station with you,' Tristan offers, and they both say goodbye.

As the door swings shut behind them, Melvin looks over at Matthew. He thinks back to the dinner party once again and remembers how confident and charismatic he had been. Janet had been putty in his hands, even Vivienne had shone when he'd deigned to throw some attention her way. And, Melvin had to admit, his own gaze had been drawn to Matthew's dark eyes and the broad shoulders straining through his shirt. But today Matthew's shoulders are slack, as if his body is falling in on itself, his face wears an expression of downright grief, and he keeps fiddling with his watch. Surely this isn't the result of Stella's death – he barely knew her.

'Are you all right, bud? You're very quiet,' Melvin asks.

'I'm fine, thank you for asking. It's not been a great week, I must admit. Pressure at work,' Matthew mumbles.

'I was just wondering,' Melvin begins, gently. 'Why did you lie about your envelope? I saw you open it at the dinner party.'

Melvin can picture him, confidently tearing a corner of the envelope and yanking the card out. His dark eyes had flashed across the number, he'd shrugged and then tucked it into his jacket pocket.

'What if—' Matthew's voice wobbles and he stops, then tries again. 'My number is twenty-nine. I turn thirty in three months. What if Gordon's right and I'm next?' he says, the words becoming gradually quieter, so that by the end of the sentence, Melvin is leaning in and the word 'next' is hardly uttered, just mouthed, Matthew's straight white teeth bared as his lips pull wide.

'Matthew, you're a fit young man, you've got years ahead of you…' Melvin says.

But Matthew isn't listening, he's lost in a maze of fear.

'Stella's number was twenty-three and look what's happened to her!' Matthew cries, streams of sweat rolling down his face now. 'If my number's correct then I've got three months, max. This whole thing has made me realise how much time I've wasted. I thought I'd have years to, you know, get serious about life…'

Melvin sees that the cocky character from the dinner party had been a persona, hiding someone else – someone vulnerable – underneath.

'Listen, we've had a bit too much to drink. Stella's death was simply a tragic accident, I really believe that. It is just a coincidence that her number was twenty-three,' Melvin tells Matthew, using the practised voice-of-authority tone that has proved effective with raucous teenagers and over-excited football fans.

Matthew's hands drop from his face, and Melvin sees he's getting through to him.

'Do you really think so?' he says, just like a child asking to be reassured that Father Christmas does exist.

'I really do. Now get yourself home, have an early night and maybe take a lovely lady out for lunch tomorrow.'

They say goodbye at the doors of the wine bar. As he walks away, Melvin pulls his phone from his pocket, writes a message to Mary – On my way – and presses send.

# The Restaurant
## *March 2015 –*
## *three months later*

**Vivienne**

'Weeeee…' A blur of red and blue shoots past Vivienne as she peruses the rail of blouses.

'Careful!' she calls after the speeding child, who is dressed in a Spider-Man outfit, nimbly swerving around the clothing rails on a Batman scooter.

Shaking her head, she wonders when children were suddenly allowed to ride scooters around M&S – and wearing fancy dress, no less. As a child, she'd been expected to walk sensibly alongside her mother around the shops, warned to keep her shoes clean and make as little noise as possible.

'Bam, bam, bam,' the tiny terror cries, now shooting Vivienne from his wrist and then laughing hysterically while he leaps behind the twinsets.

*Honestly, where are his parents?* All Vivienne had wanted was to pop into town and pick up something to wear for her interview next week. After the month she's had, is it really too much to ask? The last thing she needs is to be terrorised by a knee-high super-hero whose parents have apparently abandoned him – perhaps in the hope that a kindly older lady will take him off their hands.

'Charlie, where are you?' the voice of a frazzled mother calls out. A familiar voice. Vivienne is stuck to the spot, her eyes wide as if she's been caught out. Just in time, she ducks behind some turtlenecks.

'There you are, you silly billy. Why are you always running away from Mummy?' The relief in Cat's voice is evident. She scoops up the little blond-haired boy and rains kisses down on his curls. Despite her aching knees, Vivienne's heart throbs at the sight of a love she'll never know.

'Bam, bam, bam,' he giggles.

'Oh no, you got me,' Cat laughs. 'Now, would Spider-Man like a slice of chocolate cake at the café?'

'Yay,' he cheers.

As the pair walk off, Cat awkwardly carrying Charlie in her right arm, and the scooter in her left, Vivienne can hear their happy chatter fade away. Standing up, she frowns as her bones creak and complain. Lately, every movement feels like an effort. As a young woman, she'd taken her supple body for granted. Now, with every twist and shift, she is painfully aware of her joints, her muscles, her ageing bones. God, it's depressing getting older. Vivienne leaves the store without an interview blouse, makes her way back to the tube station, and onward to Teddington with the image of Cat and Charlie framed in her mind. There is no mistaking that he is her son, not a nephew or friend's child: she'd referred to herself as 'Mummy'. And they had matching dimples, like brackets around their mouths. Cat has worked for Vivienne for two years and never once mentioned that she has a son. Charlie looked to be around three, so he can only have been a baby when she'd started at the magazine. Vivienne can't make sense of it. *Why wouldn't Cat tell her?* Did Cat think that she would treat her differently if she knew she was a mother? Was it because Vivienne was childless herself and Cat felt she wouldn't understand? Suddenly, she starts to spot clues that she'd blindly missed in the last two years. The time when Cat had interviewed a woman whose young son had leukaemia and Cat had sobbed her way through the phone call. Vivienne had given her a right rollicking afterwards, lecturing her on professionalism. The times Cat had dashed off with her mobile and told Vivienne her friend was going through a rough patch with a difficult boyfriend. Those mornings she'd turned up with dark circles under her eyes and Vivienne had presumed she'd been out partying late with her friends.

And last week, when the editor had announced that the magazine would be closing in a month's time, Vivienne had seen Cat's crumbling face as a typical over-emotional reaction.

'What are we going to do? I need this job,' Cat had cried, and Vivienne had dismissed her concerns. Cat was in her twenties, had her whole career ahead of her. It was Vivienne herself who was bound to struggle, at her age and having worked at the same place for years. Now Vivienne sees that Cat has a little boy who's dependent on her, while Vivienne just has her two cats who mostly ignore her anyway. Plus, the mortgage on her cottage was paid off years ago.

Closing her front door behind her, Vivienne is greeted by piles of papers on her living room floor. Despite her meticulous system, she has managed to accumulate an extortionate amount of paperwork over her many years on the magazine. Perching on the end of her old sofa, she grabs a handful of papers and pulls them on to her knee. As she flicks through, a yellowing photo floats to the floor. Bending over to pick it up, she catches her breath at the image of the impossibly young version of herself, James's tanned arm draped casually over her shoulder, the leftovers of calamari and chips on the table in front of them. Closing her eyes, she can almost taste that moment again, the lemony, salty seafood and the start of something new, the hope that she may have found her forever. Then she remembers the tears, the physical pain of a broken heart, of a broken body, and the catalyst for her first fugue state. Pushing the picture to the bottom of the pile, she continues her search and finally finds what she's looking for. An article Cat had written not long after she'd started at the magazine. It is covered in Vivienne's signature red pen, tattooed with crossings and capital letters saying things like *'WATCH YOUR SPELLING!'* and *'THIS MAKES NO SENSE!'*. Vivienne's comments remind her of something. Then she realises – Stella's parents arguing outside the church, her furious mother shouting: *'She lived for your approval and all you did was criticise.'* Regardless of the wealth her father bestowed on her, Stella had only heard his disapproval. She'd ended up feeling inadequate and had turned that negativity on to her rival vloggers. Which – in turn – had ended in her death. Reading over her notes, Vivienne sees that in her own way she's been 'trolling' Cat. She looks now at Cat's writing and sees a certain flourish, an effortless style that makes for easy reading. But Vivienne's comments hadn't referred to that – or said anything positive at all. Slumping down on the sofa, Vivienne feels ashamed. She'd seen herself as an inspiring mentor; yes, she'd been tough, but only because she'd wanted Cat to improve. Now she sees she'd been overly critical at every turn, passing on her own feelings of inadequacy to Cat and hammering down the girl's confidence. Cat must have been miserable at work, and then gone home to look after her young son alone.

\* \* \*

The next day, Vivienne sits at her desk watching her colleagues moving with purpose around her, filling cardboard boxes with old magazines for new portfolios, freebie beauty products and handfuls of pens.

'Could you look at this *feature* for me?' the editor asks, dropping a sheet of paper on her desk then winking with all the subtlety of an early-90s boyband ballad.

'Sure,' she says, giving him a small smile.

She flips over the CV he'd dropped and works her way through correcting spelling and punctuation mistakes.

Never in her wildest dreams did she expect to be helping Damian get a new job but when she'd caught him mid-panic attack one night after work last week, she'd unexpectedly felt sympathy for him.

He'd explained that a rival publisher had asked to see his CV, but his undiagnosed dyslexia meant he struggled with the formal format. His 'creative mind' (as he put it) had no trouble with mood boards and layouts for the magazine, but struggled with a simple CV. Vivienne had surprised herself by offering to help. She'd waited for the inevitable trill of jealousy, of bitterness, to follow since she herself had had no response from the speculative CVs she'd sent around, but those feelings didn't come. In fact, she'd started to wonder if the magazine closing might be an opportunity for her to try something new. And really, what harm could helping a colleague do?

Once she'd returned the CV to Damian – receiving a second wink for her trouble – she walks past Cat's desk. As the rest of the team are busying themselves with packing up their desks and printing off their cover letters, having already sent their rushed last jobs over, Cat is so still at the centre of the storm, totally focused on her screen, methodically typing away at her final article.

'Cat, could I have a word?' Vivienne asks.

'I'm nearly finished,' Cat says, eyes not leaving her screen. 'I know I said I'd have it done this morning, but would one o'clock this afternoon be OK?'

'That's fine. It's not about the article. Shall we go to the café and get some fresh air?' Vivienne suggests.

In the café, Vivienne pays for her own tea, Cat's coffee, and a large slice of chocolate cake to share.

'Is everything OK?' Cat asks, her hands clutched together on her lap, not touching her coffee or cake.

'Fine, well – as good as it can be,' Vivienne says, picking up a knife and cutting the cake carefully in half. 'Did you get up to much at the weekend?'

'Not really. Had a look around the shops yesterday.'

'Actually, I saw you … with Charlie,' Vivienne says evenly.

'Charlie?' Cat splutters, taken off-guard. 'He's … he's … I'm sure you realise, Vivienne. He's my son.'

Despite being caught in a two-year-old lie, Cat can't help the pride shining out of her face at the word 'son.' And Vivienne can't help smiling back. Cat should be proud, he is perfect. Albeit a reckless rider and ruthless web-slinger.

'I'm so sorry I didn't tell you about him,' Cat says. 'I didn't expect to get the job, then I swore I'd mention it on my first day, but the opportunity never seemed to come up because—'

'Because I was such an evil cow,' Vivienne finishes.

'I wasn't going to say that,' Cat gasps, her hand rushing to her mouth.

'Well, it's true,' Vivienne sighs. 'I'm the one who should be sorry. I've treated you terribly these two years.'

'You don't need to apologise,' says Cat. 'You've taught me so much. I just hope I can find another job soon.'

A look of such concern crosses Cat's face that Vivienne finds herself reaching across and touching her hand.

'Do you have any help with Charlie?' A question that feels two years too late in the asking.

Then tears are rolling down Cat's cheeks and something strange happens. Vivienne doesn't feel the usual combination of frustration and anger. She just feels sad. Pulling a tissue from her bag, she hands it to Cat.

'My mum passed away just before Charlie was born. His dad lives in Australia. I've got a friend with a little girl who takes him when I'm at work, but she's moving away, too, and I'm already behind on my rent…'

'Deep breaths,' Vivienne coaches.

'I'm so sorry, I know you hate tears at work,' splutters Cat.

'We're not at work, though, are we? And this really is something worth crying over. Never mind a tired old magazine closing down.'

Cat looks up at Vivienne and smiles.

\* \* \*

'Two years she's worked for me and never once mentioned that she's a mother,' Vivienne says as she marches along the pavement.

'Hmm, that's strange,' Tristan mumbles, trotting along beside her.

'Is there something else you'd like to add?' Vivienne asks, suddenly stopping and turning to face him.

'Well… I must admit… when we first met, you didn't strike me as the warmest of people – although I know differently now,' Tristan says, looking down at his feet. 'I can understand Cat perhaps not feeling that she could confide in you.'

Following Stella's funeral, Vivienne had asked Tristan about his area of expertise and whether he knew much about creating blogs. He admitted he did, and she'd persuaded him to meet her the following Sunday in a lovely little café near Waterloo. Admittedly, she'd been hoping to pick his brains without paying for IT consultation fees, but she'd got more than she'd bargained for.

When he'd shuffled into Café Bleu wearing a stained T-shirt and pushing back unwashed hair from his face, the group of elegantly dressed ladies on the next table had openly stared and Vivienne had wondered if she'd done the right thing. But, once they'd ordered their drinks and he'd started talking, her doubts had begun to fade. His instructions were intelligent and clear, he'd answered her questions patiently without a hint of condescension. Two hours had flashed by, and, when Vivienne had commented that she had to get home for *Downton Abbey*, they'd chatted for another half hour about which series had been the best (the second one, they agreed, although Vivienne has a soft spot for the current series – six – *'especially if Edith gets her happy ending'*). They'd ended up meeting every Sunday for the last three months. Tristan had even visited Vivienne's cottage to give her computer a 'spring-clean' after she'd complained of its snail-like loading times. Thanks to Tristan's tutorage, Vivienne's new blog has been taking shape.

Vivienne opens her mouth to object but then closes it again, shakes her head, and continues marching along.

'Where are we going?' Tristan asks, but she's still thinking of Cat.

'I found an old article she'd written. I'd torn it apart, thinking I was being helpful, but perhaps she didn't see it that way,' she admits.

'Well, there's time to make it up to her.'

Vivienne crosses the road in front of one of the towering buildings and then turns left, skirting around its shiny side. She stops in front of a metal door, glancing all around her then reaches for the handle.

'Vivienne!' Tristan cries. 'I don't think you're supposed to go in there.'

'Shh, and I think you mean *we're* not supposed to go in here. Come on.'

Tristan looks shocked but follows her anyway. Just as she thought, the door opens up on to the emergency staircase at the side of the building. She looks up and sees at least twenty staircases up above. Good job she's worn her flats today.

'Are we going all the way up?' Tristan whispers.

She doesn't answer, just leads the way, up and up. At the fifteenth floor, her legs are aching and a stitch cuts into her side.

'Just need a minute,' she says to Tristan, leaning against the railing. His cheeks are red and trickles of sweat are rolling down his temples.

'This is Matthew's office building, isn't it?' he splutters, between heavy breaths.

'I just had to see it for myself,' she says, nodding.

'Might be easier if I wasn't wearing this today,' Tristan mutters, tugging at the collar on his new white shirt.

'I noticed you've made an effort,' she says. He's also wearing navy trousers and brown shoes in place of his customary jeans and trainers.

'Well, I couldn't miss your not-so-subtle hints,' Tristan says, rolling his eyes.

'Matthew would approve, I think. He did always wear the sharpest of suits,' she says, suddenly feeling tears threaten.

\* \* \*

Vivienne had been daydreaming at her desk last week when the email had come through. She'd just taken two paracetamol for a throbbing headache, the remnant of a fugue state from the previous day. It hadn't lasted so long this time, she'd popped out of work on her lunch hour to take a parcel to the post office, had come round at just after 6 p.m., sitting on her train home. She'd had to ring the editor to tell him she'd taken ill. Her weak and shaky voice sounded convincing, at least. Vivienne had tried to find reassurance in the fact that this fugue state hadn't felt so violent, hadn't lasted so long. She'd hoped it meant they'd ease off now. But the message from Melvin only made her head pound more.

**From: Melvin Williams**
**To: Serendipity's group**

**Subject: More bad news**
**Hello everyone,**
**I am so sorry to be the bearer of bad news once again. But I**
**feel obliged to let you know that this news story is about Matthew.**
**Please do not read too much into this. The stress of his job clearly**
**became too much. His company are hosting a memorial this**
**weekend. Details to follow. Hopefully see you all there.**
**Yours sincerely,**
**Melvin**

The news story had reported that a twenty-nine-year-old
banker had committed suicide by jumping off the thirty-second
floor of a Canary Wharf building. The piece included a list of
three other young male bankers who had died the same way in
the previous six months.

In a daze, Vivienne had read over Melvin's words and then
the news story. But no matter how many times she went over
them, the words didn't change. Matthew was dead. Handsome,
charismatic, young Matthew. Gone.

After half-an-hour Gordon had responded:

**From: Dr Gordon Macmillan**
**To: Serendipity's group**
**Subject: Re: More bad news**
**Dear Melvin,**
**Well, this news totally discredits Vivienne's theory that**
**Stella was killed as revenge for her trolling. While we cannot**
**confirm it, we can only presume that Matthew's number was**
**29 and thus his is the second prediction to come true. What**
**theory do you have now, Vivienne?**
**I will see you all at Matthew's memorial.**
**Regards,**
**Dr Gordon**

Vivienne's back teeth had crunched together at Gordon's flippancy over Matthew's death, but she'd refused to be drawn into an online debate and merely responded that she would see the four other guests (Janet had left the email group following Stella's funeral) at the memorial.

Over the next hour, she'd printed off all the news reports about both Stella and Matthew's deaths, as well as a naff article called 'London's Hottest Bachelors' Matthew had recently appeared in, and some profile pieces about Stella and pushed them into a plastic folder. That night, once she'd got home, she'd shifted her coffee table and armchairs against the wall of her little lounge and laid out all the articles across the floor. Vivienne had then carefully worked her way through each one, armed with her highlighter pen. Afterwards, she'd sat back on her heels and surveyed her work. An accident and a suicide, Melvin had insisted, but something hadn't felt right to Vivienne. If Matthew had been feeling that way, would he really do this in front of his colleagues, in the middle of a working day? The articles reported a 'suspected suicide' but surely his building, right in the middle of Canary Wharf, was covered in security cameras, even on the roof? Why was there any doubt about what happened that afternoon? That's when she'd decided to take a look for herself.

Once she'd updated her notebook with these latest suspicions, Vivienne had searched her bedroom again for her envelope. After pulling out all her drawers, checking behind them, then clearing out the bottom of her wardrobe, she'd flopped back on the bed, exhausted and defeated. Spotting her handbag on the back of her dressing-table chair, she'd been gripped with an idea. Using some nail scissors, she'd carefully picked apart the lining of her bag. Finally, there was space to wiggle her finger into it and then feel around for anything that had somehow fallen into that space. But there was nothing. She'd thrown her bag down in disgust. *Why* hadn't she opened her envelope when she had the chance?

All she could do now, she'd decided, was to pour her frustration into the investigation.

* * *

Vivienne sighs and then sets off again up the stairs.

'Which floor are we stopping at?' Tristan asks, trudging behind her.

'The top – thirty-two,' she calls over her shoulder and chuckles at Tristan's groaned response.

Finally, they make it to the roof where another metal door greets them. Vivienne's body is alive with adrenaline as she pushes the handle down. As she steps outside, the wind instantly lifts her hair straight up. She walks tentatively forward, taking in the incredible view across London. The Thames sweeping in an elegant 'S', the comical Gherkin and the futuristic Shard in the distance. A shiver of déja-vu dashes across her mind, gone before she can grab at it.

'From what I gleaned from the articles, he must have been on this side,' she says, walking over to one corner. A low railing runs around the edge, which could easily be stepped over without much effort. Vivienne pulls out her notebook and starts to scrawl out a floor plan of the area.

'There are cameras there and there,' she says, making small crosses on her map. 'But not here.'

'I can't imagine he was thinking about that,' Tristan says, hovering in the doorway, his fingers still clutching the handle.

'Are you OK?' Vivienne asks him.

'Fine. I'm just not that keen on heights,' he mumbles.

Vivienne catches sight of something on the floor, tucked behind the railings near where she believes Matthew went over. Some sort of black material.

She steps towards it then stops as she hears heavy footsteps coming from the door.

'What are you doing up here?' a voice bellows above the wind. A square-shaped man with a protruding forehead and one black eye strides towards them.

'Oh, I'm sorry.' Vivienne puts her hand to her chest, her face filled with horror. She drops her handbag to the floor, tipping it slightly so that her reading glasses and umbrella spill out. 'I think we got a bit lost,' she says. 'Thank you so much for finding us.'

'Yes, dear, you are certainly lost,' he snaps, but already the edges of his words have smoothed a little.

'Please could you direct us to the tube station?' she asks. 'I just need to pick up my handbag.'

'This way,' he responds gruffly.

As the man turns away with Tristan following, Vivienne stoops to pick up her things plus the mystery item from behind the railings. She shoves it all in her bag and follows the others out of the door.

Minutes later, they're unceremoniously deposited back on the pavement outside.

'Just in time,' Vivienne says, glancing at her watch.

'Was that really necessary?' Tristan frowns, following her to the memorial.

'Yes, I believe so,' she says, pleased to see that she's shocked him.

They walk along in silence. Vivienne thinks she probably shouldn't tell Tristan about her visit to Sloane Square tube station – the location of Stella's death – the night before. It had been interesting. Vivienne had ascertained that there were two staircases at the entrance, leading to the two ends of the platform. Stella had fallen on the far-left side, whilst most of the passengers boarded on the other side. Why, Vivienne wondered, had she been all alone at that end, which also happened to be the side without any CCTV coverage?

Within minutes, they're standing in front of the restaurant. Tristan holds the door open and Vivienne has a surge of pleasure at the novelty of entering a social gathering with someone by her side. For once, she doesn't have to endure those initial flailing minutes of searching for a familiar face.

They are ushered through the foyer into the main restaurant area where about fifty chairs have been lined up facing a large picture of Matthew, looking devastatingly handsome. The front row is already taken by a row of women and there are a few well-dressed men seated around but otherwise the turn-out is surprisingly sparse. Melvin waves over at them from his seat in the middle of a row towards the back so they shuffle along to sit next to him.

### Tristan

'Take a look at the weeping widows,' Melvin whispers, indicating the women on the front row. 'Do you think they're *all* Matthew's girlfriends?'

Tristan glances over at the beautiful women – eight of them, all wearing short black dresses and high heels, dabbing their eyes prettily with tissues, staring up at Matthew's picture. They send off a chorus of sniffles, sighs, and distraught feminine whispers.

'I wouldn't be surprised,' he mutters, his right hand clenching and unclenching on his knee.

'It's so tragic,' Vivienne whispers. 'He had *everything*…'

*You can't walk on hot coals and not expect to be burned.* The line pops into Tristan's head.

'Twenty-nine was his number, then,' Gordon announces from the row behind, pressing his long fingers on the back of Tristan's chair.

'Hello there, Gordon. Shall we talk about that later?' Vivienne snaps and Gordon sits back, huffing like a disgruntled teen. The sound of a door slamming shut makes Tristan turn, and he sees

93

Janet standing at the back. At least he *thinks* it's Janet. The woman is wearing a fitted black dress with a high neck, over towering heels, topped off with a wide-rimmed black hat and veil falling across her face. Tristan nudges Vivienne and nods his head towards Janet.

'Bit over the top…' she mumbles, and he stifles a laugh.

Vivienne lifts her hand to wave Janet over, but she's already found a place towards the back. Silence drifts across the room as a small, tanned man with a gold ring on his pinkie makes his way to the podium at the front and starts fiddling with the microphone. Noticing the man's pristine white shirt and perfectly fitted suit, Tristan's cheeks burn. Thanks to this morning's exertions with Vivienne, his underarms are damp with sweat and he has an unpleasant grey stain on the front of his shirt, from when he'd leaned on the railing in the stairwell. Compared to this man, Tristan feels like a grubby little schoolboy. He shakes his head: *why* had he allowed Vivienne to drag him up there?

'Thank you, everyone, for attending on this very sad day,' the man says. 'As I'm sure you all know, I'm Kenneth Wiseman; Matthew worked for me for the last five years.'

With thinly veiled jealousy, he talks about Matthew's 'effortless charm' when dealing with clients and colleagues alike. Then, with something verging on relish, he notes his own surprise that Matthew had been 'hiding a deep depression'.

*Deep depression, deep depression, deep depression.* The words drift into Tristan's ears and settle on to his tongue. He finds himself silently mouthing them at the back of his throat, his lips drumming out the 'd' over and over. It's like poetry, like a drumbeat. He can't seem to shake it. So he forces himself to look around the room, and his eyes settle on the 'weeping widows' on the front row. Eight women, 50 per cent blondes, 37.5 per cent brunettes and 12.5 per cent redheads. The maths pop into his head without any conscious effort. It's something he finds himself doing whenever he's in a room full of people (which isn't often): percentages of men and women, percentages wearing glasses, and so on. The simplicity of the numbers, the irrefutable truth of them always works to calm his racing thoughts.

'I believe the lovely Robyn would like to say a few words,' Matthew's boss announces, and it strikes Tristan that his tone is more like a chat-show host introducing the latest Hollywood starlet. One of the fifty-per-cent blondes stands and totters towards the microphone.

'Hello, everyone, and thank you for coming,' she breathes, holding a tissue to her throat like a character from an old French movie. 'I'm Robyn, Matthew's girlfriend.'

At the word 'girlfriend' a ripple of discontent travels along the front row.

'I just wanted to say, he really was the most thoughtful, generous, and wonderful boyfriend. I know he would have made a fantastic husband one day.' A pause as she takes an exaggerated breath, then: 'My heart is broken.'

Despite her apparent devastation, Robyn's words are clear and have the ring of rehearsal about them. Her eyes are perfectly made-up and look neither swollen nor bloodshot. She demurely bows her head as she clip-clops back to the front row. And then it's over. Matthew's boss is inviting everyone to stay on for champagne and canapés, and the mourners are picking up their coats and shuffling back down the rows of chairs. The whole thing has lasted no more than ten minutes.

'Right, then, champagne and canapés it is,' Vivienne says, standing up so that Tristan has no choice but to get to his feet and move down the aisle.

As they make their way back towards the bar area, they pass Janet sitting on the back row. Her elbows are propped on her knees, her head bent forward. Tristan glances at Vivienne, should they speak to her?

'Erm … Janet, are you all right?' Vivienne asks, hovering next to her seat while a tutting Gordon marches past.

'I just need a moment,' comes the voice from under the veil.

'We'll wait for you in the bar,' Melvin says, touching her shoulder and then gesturing at the others to follow him out.

Melvin leaves through the doors and heads to the high table near the bar where Gordon has sat down.

As Melvin balances his large frame on one of the tall bar stools, Tristan notices he looks different, slimmer definitely, younger somehow, and wearing a three-piece tweed suit. Tristan is certainly no style expert, but he feels that the bow tie might be a step too far.

'I must say, you're looking rather dapper,' Vivienne notes, once she's balanced her smaller frame on a stool.

'Is it OK?' Melvin asks, a hand on his trimmed-down middle.

'Very smart,' Gordon nods, sounding bored.

'Thank you. My colleague Christian has given me a bit of a makeover.' At the mention of the name 'Christian', Melvin's manner changes slightly, his chest pushes forward, his face brightens as if a light has switched on inside him.

'And how's Mary?' Vivienne asks.

'Oh, actually she's been unwell, had to have another round of chemo unfortunately but doing better now,' Melvin mumbles before excusing himself to go to the bathroom.

'Any sign of those canapés?' Vivienne asks.

Tristan watches her search the room. It's midday now, and he knows Vivienne has her breakfast at 6.30 a.m. – a bowl of granola with a handful of berries on top – so she'll be peckish (her word) by now. She looks up and gives him a proud smile, she's thinking about how smart he looks in his shirt and trousers, he can tell. Honestly, it's like he's picked up a second mother in these last few months. When Vivienne had asked him about blogs following Stella's funeral, he was sure she was only looking for a freebie

IT lesson. He'd opened his mouth to tell her he was too busy, but then she'd said something that had stopped him. *I fear the modern world is leaving me behind.* She'd been so cold when they'd first met in the street, all edges and ice, but she'd thawed a little before his eyes, and he'd glimpsed a side of her that he suspected she usually kept hidden. He'd handed over his card and, before he knew it, he was walking into a stuffy little café in Waterloo. A group of ladies had turned to sniff at him and Vivienne, sitting bolt upright at a small table in the corner, had looked a little disappointed. He'd have run right out of there if she hadn't already seen him. Yet, once they'd got going, something unexpected had happened – he'd started to enjoy himself. Vivienne was an eager and conscientious student; she'd asked insightful questions and picked up new ideas easily. And when he'd talked, she really listened, her pale blue eyes wide, absorbing each word. They'd met up every Sunday since, and now Tristan finds he looked forward to his afternoons with Vivienne.

'A little help if you don't mind?' Janet snaps, holding a silk-gloved hand out to Tristan who steps off his own stool. She hooks her heel over the bar at the bottom of the stool next to him and then attempts to pull herself up.

'Come on now, put your back into it,' she says, gripping his hand tightly as he bears the brunt of her weight. At this close proximity, Tristan can't help but notice that the woman is considerably larger than three months ago. He hears a grunt from Gordon's direction as Janet's hand starts to slip out of the glove that Tristan is clutching. He looks up to meet Vivienne's eyes, which are wide with mischief.

Then slowly Janet starts to keel sideways. Her hat flops to the floor, with the veil flailing in its wake.

'I've got you,' Melvin says, suddenly appearing on the other side of Janet and easily lifting her on to the stool and then retrieving her ludicrous hat.

'Thank you, Melvin,' Janet says. 'These damn slippery gloves! I wanted to wear my leather pair, but I could only find one.' She pushes the offending gloves into her bag and pulls out a small mirror in which she checks her hair.

At Janet's words, Vivienne's head snaps up. Her eyes are perfect circles as she stares at Tristan. *What?* he mouths in response.

But then two waiters appear; one holding a tray of smoked-salmon blinis, the other bearing a tray of tall champagne glasses.

'Don't mind if I do,' Janet says, helping herself to three blinis and two glasses. 'Be a darling,' she says to one of the waiters, 'and fetch some lunch menus, too?'

Gordon clears his throat.

'So, now we have more evidence,' he says, shaking his head at the waiters who turn from them and head over to the next table where the 'weeping widows' are sitting.

'Evidence? Are you referring to Matthew's tragic suicide?' Melvin booms.

'I am. So Stella's number was correct, and you have confirmed that Matthew's number was indeed twenty-nine…' Gordon says.

'I thought Matthew didn't open his envelope,' Vivienne says.

'That's what he told us at the wine bar, but after you all left, he admitted to me that he'd seen his number – and it was twenty-nine,' Melvin says gravely.

'I knew it!' Janet screeches, wobbling on her stool, not unlike a giant Weeble.

'What else did he say?' Vivienne asks.

'Poor kid was terrified,' Melvin says. 'I tried to reassure him, but it looked like the depression had already taken hold.'

'He must have been tortured by the thought,' Tristan murmurs, picturing Matthew up on the roof.

Tristan's eyes drift over to the table of weeping widows. Eight of them! Tristan isn't sure he's even spoken to eight beautiful women, let alone dated them. Why couldn't Matthew have been happy with just one? Tristan had been more than happy with Ellie, her gap-toothed smile, her wild curls, her cackling laugh. He'd given her everything. And yet it hadn't been enough.

He'd spent hours trying to answer his mother's question: 'What did you do to chase her away?'. The only answer he could find was that he'd loved her too much. When they first met, he'd read the books she loved, listened to her favourite folk bands, even let her pick out clothes for him, like linen shirts and one particularly loud tie-dye top.

When it was the two of them, it was perfect. It was just when other people got involved that things went wrong. Ellie's sister was chronically unwell, and she was forever in and out of hospital. Ellie's phone would ring and then she'd dash off at a moment's notice. And her colleagues at the school were constantly dragging her out for drinks after work. At first, she'd ask Tristan along, but he shudders even now when he pictures her teacher friends laughing at their in-jokes. The creepy way the headmaster had watched Ellie, even with his glamorous wife and young child in the room. After a while, Tristan had started to make excuses whenever she'd invited him out with her work friends.

'Don't you like them?' she'd finally asked, when he'd cited a migraine on the night of the headmaster's birthday party.

'I just don't trust them – and I don't think you should, either,' he'd admitted.

'I know you're just thinking of me, but sometimes you can be quite suffocating,' she'd told him. 'It's like you see the worst in everyone.'

Tristan had promised to step back, to give her friends another chance. They'd gone on a make-or-break holiday, which he thought had gone well, but Ellie had ended things the following week.

'I'll have the arancini balls for starters – actually make that two portions – followed by the burger and chips with a side of onion rings,' Janet tells the waiter. Vivienne and Melvin both order sandwiches and Gordon impatiently waves the waiter away.

'I wonder if any of Matthew's family are here,' Vivienne says, glancing around the room.

Tristan looks for an older couple, or a sibling who shares Matthew's dark eyes. But there's only the weeping widows, some smart-suited colleagues, and them.

'Perhaps they weren't close...' Gordon says, with a shrug.

'That's no excuse,' Vivienne snaps.

Then Tristan pictures his own parents attending their only child's funeral. His dad's stocky shoulders shoe-horned into an old suit that stopped fitting him years before. He couldn't imagine him crying; no, he'd be more likely to hit the bar and hope to drink his sorrow away. His mother would have bought a new dress especially – probably with a garish floral design – and the tears would be freely rolling down her face. But then Tristan cuts short this line of thought. After what he'd discovered in the box, perhaps they wouldn't react in that way at all. Perhaps they would just see his death as a blip and their lives would continue as before.

And what about Ellie? Tristan wonders whether his ex-girlfriend would turn up at his funeral. Perhaps that would be the shock she'd need to finally realise that she'd made a mistake to end things with him. That, like Robyn had said of Matthew, he would have made a fantastic husband. It would be too late then, though. Suddenly, Tristan's heart is racing. Adrenaline is rushing through his body. He can't sit there any longer.

'I'll just be a minute,' he mumbles, practically falling off the stool and heading for the door.

Outside, he turns right, nearly crashing into a large plant, its palm-like leaves spiking his shoulder but also hiding him from view. Crouching down, Tristan covers his eyes, starts to count.

'Are you all right?' a voice asks from the darkness. Tristan feels a hand on his shoulder.

'Get off,' he snaps, pushing it away, hard.

'All right, pal, take it easy,' the man says, apparently undeterred by the shove. Tristan detects a strong northern accent, a strange mix of Geordie and Lancashire. 'I'll just stay here until you feel a bit better.'

Tristan takes seven deep breaths and then reluctantly uncovers his eyes and glances at the man now crouching alongside him. He's not looking at Tristan, just staring ahead, apparently lost in his own thoughts. The man looks to be around Matthew's age, dressed in a suit, but it's too broad on the shoulders and made from a cheap-looking shiny material that would have horrified Matthew. His hair is slicked back from his face, giving it a plastic effect. Tristan has an irrational urge to reach out and touch it. The man's trousers have ridden up at the ankles, and Tristan notices that one sock is black, and one is navy blue.

'Thanks, I'm fine, really,' Tristan says. 'Sorry about that.'

'No worries,' the man says, flashing a row of small, pointy teeth. 'Gareth Atkinson.' He sticks out his hand. Tristan shakes it, trying not to turn away as a strong smell of beer hits him.

'Did you know Matty very well?' Gareth asks Tristan.

'Erm … not really,' Tristan mumbles, but it's clear that Gareth isn't listening, he's just looking for an opportunity to talk about 'Matty'.

'Actually, he hated being called Matty,' he goes on, his hands pressed together as if in prayer. 'We went to school together. Hadn't seen him in years, but then I bumped into him a few months ago. He wasn't pleased to see me, mind, can't blame him really.'

'How come?' Tristan's knees are starting to ache, so he shifts his weight slightly.

'I wasn't that nice to him at school. But you should have seen him back then, thick glasses, a constantly streaming nose,' Gareth says. 'It's no excuse for bullying, though, I know that now.'

'No, it isn't,' Tristan says, thinking of his own childhood.

'He had the worst possible start in life. His mother was … evil is the only word for it. God knows what she put him through behind closed doors. But he managed to get away from her, away from all of us. It's just sad it ended like this.'

'OK, Tristan?' a voice asks.

He looks up to see Vivienne standing over them. Nodding a quick goodbye to Gareth, Tristan follows her back inside.

### Gordon

Gordon watches Tristan return to the table, taking in his pink-rimmed eyes and paler than usual complexion. Elizabeth often accuses Gordon of lacking empathy, so he's pleased he can ascertain that Tristan is devastated about Matthew's death. Yet this, in itself, is puzzling. He hadn't realised they'd been close; in fact, he can't recall seeing the two men even speaking to each other at the dinner party, or the wine bar, three months ago. Gordon frowns, so many of his observations of human interactions are a mystery to him. Thank goodness he inhabits the world of science, where hard facts provide a firm foundation. Anyway, he's not here to wonder about Tristan's social skills or sexual orientation. He's got bigger fish to fry, as the metaphor goes.

'All right, bud?' Melvin asks, handing both Tristan and Vivienne a fresh glass of champagne.

That's five each they've had. Gordon is still nursing his first. True, champagne isn't as calorific as red wine, but its light and bubbly nature makes it easy to drink to excess, and Gordon must keep his wits about him this afternoon.

Clearly, Janet has no concerns of this nature, Gordon thinks, watching her take a large gulp of champagne and then a huge bite out of her burger. Surreptitiously glancing down her body, he sees how her derrière is practically swallowing the small stool. Honestly, she must have gained two stone in three months and her skin has that unhealthy sheen that one often sees on those who partake in alcohol a little – or a lot – too regularly.

'He's fine,' Vivienne is responding to Melvin. 'So, what were you saying?'

'Matthew is the fourth banker to die this way in the last six months. The pressure these fellas are under is unbelievable. I shouldn't tell you this, but we found out that he was taking antidepressants and seeing a counsellor every week,' Melvin says gravely. 'He did mention work problems to me when we spoke last time. It's just such a shame.'

'Yes, yes, it's very sad,' says Gordon. 'But I think the main point is that Matthew's number is the second one to come true. We can now safely presume all the numbers are correct.'

'But how could anyone have known Matthew would die this way?' Tristan asks.

'Perhaps he didn't jump. Perhaps he was pushed,' Vivienne says, pulling out that pesky notebook and some sheets of paper from her bag.

'You don't really believe that Stella and Matthew were murdered, do you?' Melvin asks.

'I've been looking into it and yes, I believe that could be one explanation,' Vivienne says. She clears her throat, apparently preparing to launch into a monologue.

'Who cares *how* it happens,' Janet cuts in, not looking up from her burger. 'It's happening, we just need to accept it now.'

'Well, I, for one, won't be going down without a fight,' says Gordon.

'Another theory could be, rather than warning about murders, the numbers actually pushed them towards their deaths,' Tristan says.

'Are you referring to some sort of self-fulfilling prophecy?' Gordon asks, leaning closer to Vivienne to see what she's drawn in her notebook. A map of some sort, with lots of Xs. She moves her hand to cover it from his view.

'That's interesting, Tristan. I can imagine, given that Matthew suffered from depression, then perhaps being told you only have so long to live might send you spiralling,' Vivienne says, nodding.

'He took matters into his own hands, you might say,' Gordon mutters, more to himself than the others.

'But what about Stella?' Melvin asks. 'There's no suggestion she jumped in front of the tube train.

'Isn't there? She clearly had her own mental-health challenges...' Tristan says.

Gordon sighs and shakes his head impatiently. He is continually amazed by the intellectual incompetency of this group. But, he supposes, that's what their dinner-party host was banking on.

'One theory I've been working on is that perhaps our host orchestrated a social experiment,' he says.

'Social experiment?' Janet repeats.

'Have you heard of the Stanford Prison experiment?' Gordon asks, speaking slowly and clearly so that the group will keep up. 'Back in 1971, a mock prison was set up and the participants were assigned roles as wardens and prisoners. Well, they took their positions far too seriously, the wardens were violent and cruel, the prisoners became depressed and the experiment had to be cut short.'

'What on earth has that got to do with us?' Janet snaps.

'That experiment asked the question: how would a certain situation affect behaviour? Perhaps Experiment Serendipity is asking the question: how do people react when they know their death age?' Gordon surmises, then bites his lip. He hadn't planned to reveal this much of his theory.

'And then kill us all off, one by one?' Vivienne cries. 'Talk about unethical! No one would approve an experiment like that, Gordon.'

'Ridiculous,' Janet says.

He takes a deep breath. There's no point trying to explain his theory to them any further. They are simply incapable of understanding. Vivienne does have a point about ethics. Such an experiment wouldn't be allowed by the science authorities. But Gordon believes this experiment is being conducted outside of their jurisdiction.

'It could be a psychic,' Janet suddenly pipes up, having now polished off her burger and chips.

'Be serious,' Gordon snaps.

'I am being serious,' Janet cries. 'I saw a psychic when I was a teenager. She knew so much without me saying a word; like that I had a younger sister and that my Auntie Margaret had recently died. She predicted I'd marry an older man whose name started with the letter W and that I would be a successful businesswoman...'

'She probably says that to everyone,' Vivienne says, with a sniff. 'We did a feature about fraudulent psychics. It's such a big business, they'll do anything for clues, go through your rubbish, search social media, ask around friends.'

'Well, like I said. I don't think it matters any more,' huffs Janet. 'I'm on the countdown now and I'm going to make the best of things.'

They fall silent for a moment. Then Vivienne shudders.

'I've been having disturbing dreams about the dinner party, that table with the vines coming down, the silent waiters and the strange pictures on the wall,' she says, her cheeks now pink, probably due to the champagne. She flips a few pages back in her notebook where Gordon sees some rough sketches.

'I was trying to remember exactly what was on that strange picture on the wall. It had a load of animals dressed as humans and matched our place settings: mine was an eagle, and I remember Tristan's showed two dogs fighting,' she says, flipping open her book and showing them drawings of an eagle holding up weighing scales and a dog in a shirt raising his fist.

'I'd forgotten about that,' Melvin says. 'Mine was a cat, smoking a pipe, I think.'

'I had a pig – bloody charming,' Janet snorts, pushing her empty plate away and taking a large glug of her champagne.

Vivienne scrawls in her notebook and looks expectantly at Gordon.

'I believe mine showed a peacock in a top hat but I'm quite sure it's not significant...' he says.

But now Melvin is talking to Janet about the steak and Vivienne is flicking through some papers on her knee. He'd never let on to the others, but the night of the dinner party had changed things for him. After Elizabeth found out his little secret, she'd made him promise to seek counselling. Gordon had recoiled at the thought. There was nothing some jumped-up busybody with an airy-fairy psychology degree could teach him. But Elizabeth wouldn't let it go, so he'd given her a name and told her he'd booked a weekly counselling session. Every Saturday morning, he'd say goodbye to his wife and spend a delightful hour working out at a gym in Richmond. That's all the self-improvement he needed, thank you very much. It had been the perfect arrangement until Elizabeth had done her own research and discovered that Dr Leonard McCoy was in fact a character in *Star Trek* and not a psychologist specialising in eating disorders. Gordon had spent the last three months sleeping in the spare room and being ignored by both his wife and daughter, who didn't know about the argument but just presumed Gordon was in the wrong.

This ostracisation had had the opposite effect that Elizabeth might have hoped. Gordon is enjoying the space to think, the lack of interference from his family in his routines. He is constantly striving to be a prime specimen, both physically and mentally and has started to wonder if certain elements of his life have been holding him back.

The only negative has been the cessation of his television appearances. It seems his momentary lapse had knocked the producers' confidence in him, and the calls have stopped coming.

He'd even phoned them up to offer his take on the 'cotton-wool diet' which some silly models had been swearing by lately. They'd promised to ring back, but, the following morning, Gordon had been horrified to see the smug face of Dr Beverley Booker explaining exactly why the cotton-wool diet is ineffective and also dangerous. Once his indignation had passed, Gordon had reached the conclusion that, in actual fact, the TV appearances had most likely been adding to the stress in his life and that he could use his time more wisely.

Last week, when Melvin had emailed with the news about Matthew, Gordon had been sitting on his bed in the spare room, his laptop balanced on his knees. He knew Matthew's office, he'd been in the area only recently himself to attend a seminar entitled, 'Multivitamins – the World's Greatest Scam'. He'd walked past the tower block on that day and remembered Matthew proudly telling him the name of his company at the dinner party. Gordon's mouth had curled into a smile as he'd read the email, thinking back to Vivienne's smug theory about Stella's death. She'd been so pleased with herself, but she was embarrassingly far off the mark. Gordon had stayed sitting on the bed for a good half hour afterwards, working his way through the problem. Until finally, he reached his conclusion. He'd agreed to come along to Matthew's memorial on the pretext of paying tribute to him, but actually it would be an information-gathering exercise. It was crucial he had all the facts at his disposal before he proceeded with his plans. For Gordon has become convinced that the dinner party was laid on by a secret scientific society. He'd heard whispers of them since university. You can only join their number by completing an intellectual challenge like no other. Serendipity's, the numbers, the envelopes, are Gordon's challenge. And he's going to rise to it. In fact, he's going to do better than that. He just needs to keep one eye on this group, track their numbers and their reactions to them, gather all the information he can. Then he will make his move.

He's about to ask Vivienne about her number again, when raised voices from the next table put a halt to the conversation. It's the table of Matthew's harem, as Gordon has come to think of them.

'What did you just say?' the woman, Robyn, who said she was Matthew's girlfriend, screeches.

'You don't care about him. You're just looking for sympathy – and another rich banker,' an auburn-haired woman responds, wiping a fat tear from her blotchy face.

'So what, you think he *loved* you?' Robyn hisses through clenched teeth.

'Yes,' the sobbing woman splutters, now dissolving in another torrent of tears.

'He told me he loved me, too,' a curly-haired woman says sadly, patting Robyn on the back.

'Come on, Natalia, you met him on Tinder, didn't you suspect he was dating other girls?' asks Robyn, indignation dripping from her every word.

'Oh, shut up, you've got no idea what Matthew and I had. We did *things* together I've never done with anyone else,' Natalia snaps before turning pink and rushing to the ladies' room.

'Don't worry, love, we all know about his tastes for the perverse,' Robyn calls to her back.

Gordon and the others turn their attention back to their own table as Matthew's boss scuttles over to 'comfort' dry-eyed Robyn.

'I do feel that the animal drawings could be a clue,' Vivienne says, looking over the scribblings in her notebook. 'I'm pretty sure the image on the wall had been papered on, and they were on each of our place settings…'

Gordon sighs heavily. He really must get this conversation back on course.

'So … I wonder who's next?' he asks, looking round the table.

'What do you mean, who's next?' Tristan snaps, turning surprisingly menacing blue eyes on him.

'Well, we know that my number is fifty-three, so that's at least a year away, two at the most. Janet's is up to four months.'

At the back of his mind, Gordon can hear Elizabeth's admonishing tone, but he can no longer concern himself with social faux pas, it's time to approach this as a scientist, with all the facts in place.

'Gordon,' Melvin snaps, glancing at Janet. 'I'm sure that Janet—'

'Oh, darling, you don't need to protect me. Clearly, I'm next. And I've decided I'm going to make the most of the time I have,' Janet slurs, standing up, grabbing her half-full bottle of champagne and marching over to a table of young bankers. Ridiculous woman.

'So, what about the rest of you?' He looks from Tristan to Vivienne.

'I opened mine,' Tristan pipes up. 'My number is forty-five, if you must know. I'm thirty-eight now.' He doesn't even look up at Gordon.

'Forty-five? Oh, you've got plenty of time...' Gordon says.

'You didn't tell me that,' cries Vivienne. 'I thought you'd lost your envelope, too.'

'I didn't want to worry you,' he tells her. 'It's years away – nearly twice what Stella had – and I'm not taking it seriously anyway.'

'Forty-five is no age to die,' Vivienne cries, grabbing Tristan's hand.

'Did you find yours, Vivienne?' Gordon cuts in.

'Unfortunately not,' she tells him but doesn't look away from Tristan. 'I searched the house again, but I think I need to accept it's gone.'

Gordon takes a deep breath and attempts to swallow his irritation.

'Maybe it's better you don't know. I haven't got mine either,' says Melvin. 'Must have left it at the restaurant.'

Gordon watches him and his hand moves to the envelope in his jacket pocket, with Melvin's name on the front. Should he reveal it?

'Personally, I like to have all the facts at my disposal,' he says, checking Melvin's reaction, but the man is as unperturbed as if he's watching some sort of reality-TV show, mildly entertained but ultimately unbothered. Then Melvin reaches into his pocket for his phone, grins inanely at it and starts tapping away. Decision made. He'll keep the secret for now.

'Well, I think I'll be off. I've got a busy weekend planned,' he says, shaking Tristan and Vivienne's hands and waving over at Melvin, who is still absorbed in his phone.

Gordon steps down from his stool and walks towards the doors. He has work to do.

### Janet

Janet has learned her lesson with the bar stools and doesn't even attempt to mount one again. Instead, she stands by the table, a smidgeon too close to the tallest banker there and places her bottle down in front of him.

'Do you mind if I hide out here for a minute?' she asks, tilting her head to one side when the man turns to face her. 'I'm rather bored of my companions this afternoon.'

'Of course we don't mind,' the man says, adjusting his spectacles as if to get a clearer look at her. 'I'm Jonathan.'

He introduces the other three men at the table. One is small, one is hairy and one is Matthew's boss. She doesn't take in their names, what's the point? Jonathan is the chosen one. She rarely stoops below six foot and he's a good six foot two inches by her estimation. Glasses and pockmarked skin, but still…

'So, I gather you worked with the gorgeous Matthew?' she asks the men, who happily lift their glasses for a top-up of champagne.

'We did,' Small tells her. 'He was gorgeous all right, and knew it. Pretty ruthless when it came to the stock market, too.'

'Is that so?' she purrs. 'Tell me more. The stock market has always fascinated me.' She's trying her best to flirt but, even to her own ears, she sounded disingenuous.

'Let's not talk shop,' Jonathan butts in, mercifully. 'So, how did you know our Matthew? I don't suppose you were one of his conquests?'

Janet opens her mouth to respond, but the other men burst out laughing. She grits her teeth and tries her best to chuckle along.

'You don't look like his type, to be honest,' Hairy rudely comments as he gazes over at the table of girlfriends.

'Mate, don't even bother. They're well out of your league,' Jonathan says.

'They're upset. I'm sure I can offer a shoulder to cry on,' he laughs, taking Janet's bottle and walking over to the table.

'This should be fun to watch,' Matthew's boss says, with a chuckle.

Janet doesn't have time for this. She decides to crank things up a notch with Jonathan.

'So, are all you bankers as naughty as Matthew?' she mutters to Jonathan, placing a hand on his.

'You must be joking,' Small cuts in. 'All Johnny talks about is his wife and kids. He's the best-behaved of us all.'

Janet tries to let her sigh out slowly. Trust her to pick the wrong one. And she's lost her drink... Looking over, she sees the banker pouring Robyn a drink of *her* bubbly and nodding sympathetically at whatever drivel she is talking.

'Here they are,' Jonathan says, showing her a picture on his phone of three red-haired children.

'Oh lovely,' she says. 'You must be very proud.'

'I am,' he replies, beaming at the picture, apparently not noticing her robotic response.

'Shall we order more champagne?' she suggests, but Jonathan is now flicking through his photo album with more shots of his Weasley-esque kids.

'Do you have children?' he asks. Ah, the question Janet has been batting away for more than twenty years... Which response should she plump for today: flippant, jokey, earnest, honest or just flirt and divert?

'No, I don't,' she says, short and sweet.

'Best thing I ever did,' he tells her. 'There's still time for you. You hear of women having babies in their fifties these days.'

Janet tries to blink away the insult.

'My wife's talking about a fourth,' Matthew's boss says, and the two start debating the merits of an even number of children.

*Janet has up to four months.'* Gordon's words swim through her mind. Definitely not long enough to make a baby. Even if she could. As soon as she'd married Bill, she'd been plagued with well-meaning friends and family quizzing her about pregnancy, raising eyebrows if she asked for a glass of water at a wine bar. At first, she'd laughed it off, she was still in her twenties and focused on her job. Bill had grown-up kids from his first marriage so wasn't pushing it. When she'd turned thirty-five, it wasn't exactly an overwhelming urge, but she'd felt it was 'now or never'. She was pregnant by thirty-six and didn't dwell too much on her growing bump – until she felt her baby girl kick just after twenty weeks. But just days later, the unthinkable happened, she went into labour early. Her cervix had ruptured, and everything had gone black. When she woke up, Bill had been leaning across her sore body, sobbing into her neck: 'Thank God you're alive, Janey!'. It took a midwife to tell her that things had got so bad that Bill had been forced to choose between her and the baby. 'He chose wrong,' she told the woman who shook her head sadly and then delivered the killer shot that, to stop her bleeding, the surgeon had been forced to perform an emergency hysterectomy. There would be no more children for Janet. She'd spent the next three days between wakefulness and sleep, trying to find a place where her baby had survived. Once, as she'd slowly started to wake, she heard Bill talking to a doctor.

'It's for the best,' he said. 'The baby was all her idea and life is much simpler with just the two of us.'

Janet had burned with fury at those words. She'd been filled with hatred ever since, and not just towards Bill, but towards the world and everyone who lived in it. If anything, that feeling had grown, not faded, with time.

'It was lovely to meet you, Janet, but it's time I headed home,' Jonathan says, putting his hand out to shake hers.

'And I might see if my colleague needs any help over there,' Small says, eyes back on the beauties on the next table.

'I suppose I should go back to my friends,' Janet responds but the men have already turned away, leaving her alone at the table. Glancing across at the others, she sees Melvin, Vivienne, and Tristan with their heads close together, serious expressions on their faces. She considers marching past them and heading home. Or at least straight to Giles's place. Their affair has really gained momentum lately. They see each other three or four nights a week. 'Insatiable' is what he calls her and that's how she feels right now. Funnily enough, Bill had used the same word the other day when he'd been going through the credit card bills: 'Your love of shopping is insatiable,' he'd said, and he hasn't even seen the rows and rows of clothes and boxes of shoes in their spare room, unworn, still with tags on. Sex, food, wine, clothes, she can't get enough, and, with her number constantly on her mind, Janet is no longer holding back. Her time is almost up, after all. Surely, there's no better way to go.

As she marches back to the table, Janet notices that conversation abruptly stops, and the three of them look guiltily up at her.

'Allow me,' Melvin offers and steps off his chair to help her back onto a stool.

She clutches the table to get her balance and then sees that her missing leather glove is lying in front of her.

'Where did *that* come from?' she asks, picking it up, turning it over, reassured by the soft leather and expensive label that it is indeed hers.

They each exchange awkward glances, and finally Vivienne clears her throat.

'I found it at Matthew's work,' she says.

A silence falls across the table as Vivienne's words sink in. It's broken by a roar of laughter from the weeping widows and beaming bankers.

'I've got nothing to hide,' Janet says, with a shrug. 'I had a meeting in Canary Wharf. I didn't realise he worked there, but I happened to see him standing outside his office.'

It is only a small lie. She hadn't exactly had a meeting in the area. That's what she'd told her colleagues too, but she'd been thinking about him and googled the company address, went over on her lunch hour hoping she'd see him. It had felt like they'd had unfinished business.

'He was arguing with a man wearing a sports cap. He looked upset, was shaking his head over and over again. Then I saw them go inside,' she tells them. 'I must have dropped my glove outside his office.'

'When was this?' Vivienne quizzes, in full journalist mode now, scribbling in her notebook.

'Last Thursday, the day he died,' she says, her voice breaking, betraying her.

'Janet, I found it on the roof,' Vivienne says. 'The roof that Matthew allegedly jumped off.'

'Well, that's impossible,' Janet responds, working hard to maintain nonchalance in her tone. 'I told you – I stayed outside. He never even saw me.'

The three of them look at her, waiting.

But she's determined not to crack. She pulls her lipstick from her handbag and paints on a fresh layer. It always makes her feel better, stronger.

'Is there something you want to say?' she asks, aiming her question at Vivienne.

'You do have a motive,' Vivienne says. 'You made it clear that you wanted Matthew that night and Stella got him in the end. I saw the way you looked at her. If looks could kill ... well, she was dead two weeks later.'

'Vivienne, that's enough!' Melvin booms.

'As if *I* could be a murderer,' laughs Janet.

'Then, with Stella out of the way, you went to Matthew's office to have another go at seducing him. He turned you down and you got angry,' Vivienne goes on.

'This is ridiculous,' Janet says, still chuckling. 'So how would you explain the numbers? Did I plan the whole thing in order to seduce Matthew? I'd never met him before. Wish I never had now.'

'You probably saw him in that hot-bachelors article, set your cap at him,' Vivienne says. 'Perhaps this was your PR stunt all along. Your company is no stranger to tacky stunts. It would explain why you were the first to notice your envelope and open it.'

Melvin groans and covers his eyes, while Tristan just looks on, his hand over his mouth in shock.

'I'm not sticking around to listen to this ... this *fiction*,' Janet says, stepping off her stool and facing up to Vivienne. 'You think you're so clever with your pathetic little notebook, but actually, who's to say you're not the killer? It's very *convenient* that you've lost your own envelope!'

'Are you serious?' Vivienne gasps.

'Just as serious as you,' Janet snaps. 'I'd think twice before throwing accusations around. Because your number's coming, too.'

As she walks away from the table, Janet pushes her fascinator into her bag... The cheek of that woman! She passes a waiter holding a tray of drinks, takes two glasses, downs them both then heads towards the door.

Janet had left the Serendipity's email group after Stella's funeral, so she hadn't seen Melvin's message about Matthew. She'd found out about his death when she was in a taxi back from Giles's place. She'd googled his name and a series of newspaper articles had popped up:

**Respected Banker Dies in Suicide Tragedy.**

That's when Janet had known Matthew's number had been twenty-nine. And that she had to be next. That's when she'd resolved to make the most of the time she has left.

'Janet, let me walk you out,' Melvin says, his heavy arm suddenly around her shoulder.

'It's OK, I'm just going to get a taxi,' she tells him.

They step outside and Melvin stops, his hands in his pockets, clearly with something to say.

'What you said in there ... don't give up, we don't know for sure...' he mumbles, looking down at his too-trendy brogues.

'Honestly, Melvin, I haven't given up. I'm going to enjoy every second of the time I have. Actually, I think it's an approach more people should adopt. Especially you, given what you told me after the dinner party...' Janet says, raising a knowing eyebrow.

'I'm not sure what you mean, Janet,' he snaps, looking right at her.

Janet hails a passing taxi, which slows down in front of them. She pulls the door open and suddenly feels pain in her elbow.

'Ouch,' she gasps.

Melvin grips her arm as he guides her into the car. Just as he's about to close the door, Janet grabs hold of his hand.

'So, we're still in the closet, then?' She chuckles.

Melvin looks down at her hand, quickly spins his arm around and squeezes her wrist, hard. He pulls her towards him. The fragile bones beneath her skin ache under his mighty grip.

'That's none of your business,' he spits into her ear. 'And, if you know what's good for you, you'll keep your mouth shut.'

Then he releases her. She sits back in the seat and looks down at the bruise already forming on her arm.

She swallows and turns back to him. She's not afraid now. Of anything.

'Oh, I won't say a thing, darling. I've embarked on enough affairs to spot one a mile off. Enjoy it. It won't end well...' she tells him with a smile.

She pulls the door closed and waves him off, bejewelled fingers wriggling.

'See you in hell,' she adds, with a smile.

## Melvin

Melvin makes his way slowly back to the table. He looks down at his hands, bewildered by what they've just done. *Where had that come from?* Despite his size, he'd never been a fighter. He'd always been the one breaking up fights, defusing situations. And to grab a woman like that, to threaten her? What had he been thinking? At his age, you'd think he'd know himself, but lately Melvin is surprised to find himself doing things he'd never imagined. His hands are a good example. Fresh from a manicure, he doesn't recognise them. When Christian had commented about his 'workman hands', Melvin had just laughed. Hands were for doing practical things with, driving, eating, fixing things, and so on. Mary had always admired how good he was with his hands. He'd never thought of them as decorative, something that should look nice. But Christian had kept dropping hints about male grooming, and in the end he'd gone ahead and booked Melvin in at a trendy salon and asked for 'the works'. Stepping out onto the street afterwards, Melvin had felt pleased with his new, shorter haircut, his all-over wax and mani-pedi (a term that – despite having the word 'man' in it – was possibly the least manly thing he'd heard in his life) but had also hoped he wouldn't bump into one of his colleagues, particularly not one of the old-school coppers.

What he'd said to Vivienne earlier wasn't a lie, but it wasn't the whole truth, either. Christian *was* his colleague and *had* given him a makeover, Mary *had* been poorly again. But that wasn't the whole story. After Stella's funeral, Melvin had had every intention of telling Mary the truth. He'd rustled up his signature lasagne, which controversially includes sliced boiled eggs and bacon, and got in some decent red wine (Argentinian, he'd remembered Janet's comment at the dinner party). Banoffee pie was chilling in the fridge. Once they'd polished that off, he'd planned to explain his feelings to Mary in the gentlest terms possible. But, halfway through the lasagne, Mary pushed her plate away, insisting she was full. For the first time in a while, Melvin had looked closely at his wife and noticed the purple crescents under her eyes, how pale she was.

'Do you feel OK?' he asked, a wave of dread creeping through him.

'Not really, Melvin,' she'd admitted. 'I haven't felt right for a while now, so I went to see Dr Kershaw last week. She did some tests, and it seems the cancer is back.'

'Why didn't you tell me? I always come to your appointments with you,' he'd cried, reaching across the table to hold her tiny hand.

'I didn't want to worry you if it was just a cold or something.' She'd sighed, flicking away the hair that had just recently grown back.

'What did Dr Kershaw say?'

As Mary explained about the chemo, to start as soon as possible, followed by radiotherapy, Melvin's mind had wandered to

Christian. He would be waiting for the call to say Melvin had come clean to Mary and to make plans for their first date. Then Melvin had looked at Mary, listened to her clear voice explaining treatment that would cause her more pain, more anxiety, more uncertainty. He knew for certain then that he couldn't do it to her. He couldn't leave her when she needed him most.

'I *knew* you wouldn't go through with it,' Christian had snapped when Melvin phoned him late that night after Mary had gone to bed.

'I'm so sorry, Christian. Once she recovers, I'll speak to her, I promise,' Melvin had babbled, but Christian, too angry to listen, had accused him of being a coward before hanging up. And that's where it should have ended. Melvin had resolved to speak to the station boss the following day, request a transfer to another department and focus entirely on looking after his poorly wife. But that's not how it had turned out. Christian had been waiting for him outside the station when he'd got to work the next morning, asking to talk. After work, they'd gone to the Dog and Partridge, a quick pint in the pub with his colleague, what was wrong with that? But one quick pint turned into several and Melvin had ended up back at Christian's modern flat in Brixton. They'd kissed for the first time and ended up having the best sex of Melvin's life. And so, Melvin had found himself having an affair with Christian, as his wife battled cancer for a second time.

Melvin's phone rings. He sees it's Christian calling so he hops off his stool and steps away from the table.

'Are you on your way? I've been waiting an hour for you already,' Christian says down the line.

'I'm still at the memorial,' Melvin admits. He glances at his watch and is shocked to see the time. He'd planned to meet Christian for an early tea in town before getting back to take Mary to the hospital for her support-group meeting. This will be the third time in a row that he's stood Christian up.

'Is it awful?' Christian asks. They'd talked about Matthew's suicide, the shocking rise in young men dying this way and how sad the day would be.

'Actually, there's quite a party atmosphere now,' Melvin reports, raising his voice above the roar of laughter coming from Matthew's now-merry widows.

'OK, well I hope Mary's meeting goes well later. Ring me tonight?' Christian asks. Melvin assures him he will, feeling that familiar wave of guilt. After his initial anger, Christian had been so understanding about Mary, kept reassuring Melvin that he was proud of the way he was looking after her. But Melvin can't help but wonder just how long Christian will wait around for him. The blissful snatched hours they get together are enough to sustain Melvin, but will they always be enough for Christian?

Melvin walks into the gents'. As he washes his hands, he gets a little shock when he faces his reflection in the mirror. He'd taken Christian's style advice on board without question, and Mary had been too ill to notice, but sometimes Melvin wonders if a police officer in his late fifties with Cristiano Ronaldo's eyebrows and a wax to match isn't a bit ridiculous, not to mention the *Toad of Toad Hall* suit. And the thought creeps into his mind without warning – what would his dad think? You'd imagine, by this age, he'd have stopped worrying about impressing his father, a father who had been dead for more than forty years, but actually Melvin finds he thinks of him more as he gets older. A huge but quiet and gently-spoken man, whose innate ability to fix anything made him a hero with his colleagues at the steelworks. Melvin never saw his dad happier than the day his son completed training and was accepted into the Met – their chance for a fresh start in London. Just a year later, Melvin Senior died suddenly from a heart attack. He was only fifty-four, younger then Melvin is now.

Frowning into the mirror, Melvin wonders what his proud and loyal father would have made of the life his only son is living now. What would he make of the lying, the cheating, the sneaking around behind his sick wife's back? In the mirror, he stares with disgust into his brown eyes and shakes his head at his souped-up image. Melvin knows that his dad would detest what he is doing, he knows he is not the son Dad would have wanted. Not ready to go back to the table, Melvin washes his hands again, turns them over under the tap and wonders what they are capable of: more than just cheating. Last night, as he'd been adjusting the pillows around Mary's sleeping head, an insidious thought had crept up on him. If she didn't survive cancer's latest onslaught, then Melvin would finally be free to love Christian openly and without guilt. Watching his wife's peaceful face, he'd looked down and realised he was holding a pillow between his hands, his fingers digging into its soft belly. He could end it for her now, end her suffering once and for all... And thus end his own feelings of guilt and frustration. He'd crept closer to her. She'd been so still, her incredibly thin body so fragile under the covers, her chest barely moving, almost like she was dead already. He'd lifted the pillow towards her face and then she'd suddenly let out a low moan, tilted her head to one side. As if waking from a dream, Melvin had jumped backwards, dropping the pillow on the floor before picking it back up and carefully laying it down on the bed. Of course he would never do such a thing. Never.

With one last look in the mirror, he pulls off his bow tie, stuffs it in his pocket and then takes off the jacket. As he walks back to the table, he glances over to see Matthew's boss having an animated conversation with Robyn who seems to have shaken off her heartbreak rather quickly. She knocks back some champagne and rests a hand on his pin-striped shoulder, which is actually lower than her own, so creates the odd image of an adult praising a child. He beams up at her, a proud son with five o'clock shadow. Melvin shakes his head and wonders once again how Matthew could have done this. At least at fifty-four, Melvin's dad had lived some life, but you could hardly say that about dying at twenty-nine. And then his mind drifts inevitably to Mary, who is fighting with everything she has to stay alive.

Walking back to the table, Melvin finds Vivienne and Tristan in a deep discussion, their two fair heads almost touching, opposite elbows on the table, like a mirror image.

'So, Vivienne, are you pleased with yourself?' Melvin asks. 'Janet was quite upset when I put her in the taxi.' He pours himself another glass of champagne. 'One more for the road.'

'No expense has been spared on the catering front,' Vivienne murmurs, as another two waiters appear from the kitchen, laden with trays of more smoked-salmon blinis and delicate vol-au-vents.

'Only the best for Matthew,' says Tristan, helping himself to a flaky hors d'oeuvre. The table goes quiet as the three disappear into their own thoughts.

'You know, before all of this, I never believed in destiny or "writings on the wall", I have always believed that we are in control of our lives,' says Vivienne.

'I don't know, Vivienne,' sighs Melvin, suddenly aware of how loud the room has become. 'Sometimes I feel that my life will continue on a certain track no matter what I do.'

'I can't help but wonder about my envelope. I'm so cross with myself for losing it! Sometimes I imagine the number is my age now, sometimes it's five or even ten years away,' Vivienne says. 'My death age wasn't something I'd ever thought about before, but lately it's on my mind all the time.'

'I'm sure it will turn up, and then you'll have to decide if you actually want to open it,' he says. 'I bet Matthew wished he hadn't.'

Then his phone beeps with a message. Mary.

Are you on your way? The meeting's at 6. x

'That's my cue,' Melvin says, standing up and throwing his jacket back on. His bow tie falls out of his pocket on to the floor, but he just steps over it and heads for the door.

# The Pub
## *August 2016 –*
## *six months later*

**Vivienne**

Pushing open the front door of her cottage, Vivienne's senses are immediately assaulted. Her nostrils are hit by a mixture of fried onion and garlic, with a pinch of char. Cat is 'cooking' again. Music is blaring from the direction of the kitchen accompanied by two out-of-tune backing singers. Stepping into her lounge, she can see the place is in chaos, Lego bricks scattered like confetti, several neon-coloured fancy-dress costumes just stepped out of, and miniature vehicles of every colour and size on every surface. Despite the mess, she smiles to herself and considers how her life has changed in the last few months. Since Cat and Charlie had moved in.

In the same week that the magazine closed its doors for the final time, Cat's landlord had increased her rent. Over the years, Vivienne had toyed with the idea of getting a lodger in her loft conversion. It has a large bedroom with an en suite shower and bath. She'd rather liked the idea of a young (male) Italian or Spanish student moving in, imagining she'd help him with his English, offer herself up as a London tour guide. It had all seemed like too much effort in the end, too little return at the cost of her privacy. Yet, there she was, suddenly offering up the loft to Cat, a co-worker who she'd only just really got to know. Following Matthew's memorial, the discussion of the numbers, Janet's words as she'd stormed out: *'Your number's coming'*, Vivienne had found herself looking at her life differently. What if her number was sixty? That would give her three months to live. Sixty-one would be fifteen months. Whatever her number, her time was ticking down with every second. She'd had years of living alone, years of sitting quietly reading her books, watching her detective programmes. Now was the time for a new phase in her life. Cat's immediate response had been, 'No thank you, we'll find somewhere.' But Vivienne had insisted that she at least come and look at the place. Once Cat had climbed up the steps into the airy attic room, scanned the large space, with Vivienne pointing out where Charlie's bed might go, it was clear that she'd been won over.

'Vavi!' a voice yells, and a bright orange dragon bursts out of the kitchen and charges towards her, hopping easily over the various obstacles and propelling itself into Vivienne's middle. She flops back on to the sofa, giving in to the bear hug. A bolt of pain shoots up her spine and spreads out to her shoulders, closely followed by a feeling of dread. She'd noticed these new aches in her back and hips lately: could they be a sign that her number has come knocking? She bites her lip until it passes.

'Well hello, Charles,' she says finally. 'I'm pleased to see you, too.'

Charlie turns his head and presses his ear against Vivienne's chest. Lately he's become interested in how the human body works and loves to 'check heartbeats'.

'Your heart is fast today, Vavi,' he whispers, his long blond lashes fluttering over eyes the exact, shiny brown of conkers. When they'd first met, the name 'Vivienne' was quite a mouthful for three-year-old Charlie, so instead he'd called her 'Vavi', which she'd come to like. She dips her nose into his soft hair and breathes in the combination of baby shampoo, garlic, and the toffee-apple essence of Charlie. Feeling his strong little arms squeezing her, she wonders yet again how she'd gone for so long without properly touching another human. There would be the odd handshake at meetings, a brief hug when she met old friends, but she hadn't held someone close in years. Within minutes of meeting her, Charlie had climbed on to her knee, handing her a worn copy of *That's Not My Lion*. The sudden closeness of him had disoriented her for a moment, but his own nonchalance brought her back and, by the end of the story, his weight was reassuring and his little moist hand on her dry older one felt right. She had been sorry when he'd climbed off and gone back to Cat.

Living with Charlie had been a crash-course in children. Up until then, they were something that Vivienne had craved for a number of years, before becoming a vague and general annoyance in shops, restaurants and at weddings and parties. But never a living, breathing, shouting and mess-creating reality, until now. Charlie had been an impatient teacher, demanding Vivienne understand his garbled words, to hold him when he needed it and entertain him with whatever whim held his attention in that moment. It was all at once draining and life-enhancing. He would throw his arms open and ask for a 'ruddle' over the smallest thing, like if she'd told him no, he couldn't have another biscuit, or if he'd watched something scary in a cartoon. Or just because he felt like it. She'd marvelled at the toddler's ability to express his emotions and tell her what he needed back from her.

'What's Mummy cooking?' she asks him, 'beeping' his freckled nose.

'She burned it,' he says, his eyes wide with horror and humour. 'It smells *ex-gusting*.'

Then he jumps off her knee, picks up a small red car and races back into the kitchen, announcing Vivienne's arrival to his mother. Vivienne chuckles to herself as she takes off her coat and throws it on to the sofa, adding to the chaos. Cat is always trying to help around the house, making dinner, doing some laundry, cleaning the bathroom, but she isn't naturally inclined towards domestic work, it must be said.

'Pizza tonight?' Cat says, emerging from the kitchen looking rather sheepish, with Charlie trailing behind.

'I'll throw together some green spaghetti.' Vivienne comforts. 'Won't take long.'

'Yummy,' cheers Charlie, who picks up the remote from the sofa and expertly switches on the telly.

Twenty minutes later, the three of them are sitting at the kitchen table, slurping on the pesto-covered pasta. In between mouthfuls, Charlie is telling them about the bit in Roald Dahl's *The Twits* where 'Mr Twit eats worms not spaghetti!' He can hardly finish the sentence, he throws his head back and opens his mouth wide revealing half-chewed spaghetti and a mouthful of tiny perfectly white teeth.

'Are you feeling better today?' Cat asks when Charlie's giggles die down long enough for them to have a conversation.

'Much, thank you,' Vivienne says, with a brisk nod. 'That'll teach me not to have that extra glass of wine.'

As well as these pains in her back and hips, she'd also experienced another fugue state. On Saturday she'd met an old friend in the West End. They'd seen a show and gone for a glass of wine afterwards. Vivienne had hailed a taxi at around 11.30 p.m. Poor Cat had such a shock when she'd heard knocking on the front door just after 2 a.m. and found a confused Vivienne on the doorstep. She hadn't wanted to make a fuss and have to explain about the fugue states, so she'd put it down to too much alcohol. But inwardly, this sudden resurgence of fugue states is a worry for her. Serendipity's seems to have started it. Those numbers again. Like seven little timebombs preparing to blow apart seven different lives. Though Vivienne had been distracted with her new flatmate, that dinner party still nagged at her. Those two young lives cut short. Most nights she'd sit in bed, flicking through her notebook and her piles of print-outs. *Had* she been right about Janet? If she had, then surely the deaths would stop now. At Matthew's memorial, Melvin had promised to look into her theory, but she hadn't heard a thing from him. The Serendipity's email group had gone quiet, too. So she'd sent him an email directly, asking him if he'd found out anything, to which she'd had no response. She makes a mental note to chase him again.

'How's Tristan?' Cat enquires as she wipes Charlie's green-stained chin.

'He's doing better, I think,' says Vivienne, nodding. 'The coun-sellor seems to be helping, and he meets up with his university friends every week now.'

After Matthew's memorial, Tristan had retreated. He'd cancelled their Sunday meeting and then tried to cancel a second one, but Vivienne was having none of it. She'd messaged him.

**I've got an interview for an online editing role, I need your help!**

Vivienne hated using exclamation marks, almost as much as she hated begging to see someone, but she'd sensed this was an emergency. She'd recalled his haunted expression at the memorial. He wouldn't say what had happened, but, from where Vivienne was standing, it had looked like a full-blown panic attack. He hadn't been friends with Matthew, yet his suicide seemed as though it had really affected Tristan. When he'd turned up at Café Bleu to meet her, he'd looked awful. He was hardly a vision of health at the best of times, but his skin had taken on a waxy tone and there was a subtle, unwashed odour emanating from him. Perhaps, she'd wondered, Tristan's number had been haunting him, as hers had been haunting her.

'Right so, when's your interview?' he'd asked, sitting down at their usual table, squinting over at Vivienne and bringing to mind a vampire who'd been forced to step into the sunlight.

'There's no interview,' Vivienne had told him bluntly. 'I needed to get you out. What's going on? You can talk to me. Did you have a panic attack?'

Tristan had let out a long, long sigh, his shoulders sagging and his head drooping towards the table, deflating like a bouncy castle after a raucous birthday party. When he'd looked up, his face was the colour of wax and the scar on his cheek an angry red, like a poker burn. Then he'd talked. The words spilled from him, gushing across their little circular table and filling the floor of the stuffy café. He'd admitted that, yes, he'd suffered from panic attacks since he was at school. Terrifying, overwhelming moments of anxiety which his mother had dismissed as 'Tristan's funny little turns', so he'd stopped telling her about them, but they'd increased in intensity and frequency as he'd got older. Two traumatic events he'd endured in the last year had escalated his anxiety: breaking up with his girlfriend Ellie last summer, closely followed by an horrendous attack by a gang on a night bus, leaving him badly injured, and not helped by the police officer who'd witnessed it doing nothing to catch the thugs. The thought of Matthew standing on top of that building had set it off this time.

'Every time I have an attack, it makes me scared to even leave the house again. I'm sorry if I've let you down,' he'd said.

Vivienne had been silent for a while, taking in his words, making her own calculations.

'You haven't let me down at all. Listen Tristan, you're not alone,' she told him finally, taking one of his hands. 'You need to let other people in, and they can help you.'

He had nodded, and she put a plan in place. Tristan promised to keep up with their Sunday meet-ups, no matter what. The following Monday, he went to see his doctor and told her about the panic attacks, afterwards ringing Vivienne to report back. The doctor had suggested anti-anxiety medication – which Tristan had refused – and a counsellor – which he'd reluctantly agreed to. Over the last few months, Tristan had opened up about his regrets over his relationship with Ellie, and how he'd ignored messages from his old university mates, so Vivienne had encouraged him to try and reconnect (as the young people say) with them; she had even invited Tristan over for rowdy dinners with Cat and Charlie. He still had his quiet moments, but, on the whole, he seemed happier. Vivienne had been tempted to discuss the numbers with him, but she'd kept quiet on that front, sensing that it could spark another panic attack.

Despite everything he was going through, Tristan had continued to help Vivienne with her blog, which had become a surprising success and spawned a website. It was a mixture of her own ponderings, news stories that interested her, real-life features about incredible women who happened to be over forty, as well as books and films that took Vivienne's fancy. Her following had soared, with regular emails from 'women of a certain age' who felt they'd found an outlet that really spoke to them. To her surprise, Vivienne had even been approached by advertisers and had started bringing in some money. For the first time in years, she was infused with purpose and her phone and inbox were constantly demanding her attention. She'd even ordered some fancy business cards, proudly declaring her the founder of the website, to give out at networking events. Every Sunday, she thanks Tristan for what he'd brought her. She also makes sure to hug him goodbye, knowing that human contact is something he needs now more than ever.

\* \* \*

Later, while Cat is putting Charlie to bed, Vivienne pours two glasses of wine – red for herself and rosé for Cat. She's still recovering from her latest fugue experience and could do with an early night, but she senses that Cat is in need of a chat about the new job.

'Join me?' she asks, when she comes back down.

'Thank you, I will,' Cat says, taking the wine and perching on the edge of the sofa.

'So, was she in a better mood today?' Vivienne asks, settling into the battered leather armchair opposite.

When Cat and Charlie had first moved in, Cat would put Charlie to bed and then scuttle away to hide in her loft room, terrified of invading Vivienne's space. So lately Vivienne had been encouraging her to chat. She found she wanted to know more about Cat and to hear about her new job on a magazine website, aimed at 'the thinking thirty-something child-free woman' (Vivienne couldn't help an eyeroll when she'd first heard that particular description). It turned out the editor was an old foe of Vivienne's. Sally Jenson-Bell was lazy, arrogant and prone to having favourites. And let's just say, Cat isn't one of the chosen ones.

'A bit,' Cat sighs, looking sorrowfully into her drink.

'Did I tell you about the time the publisher sent a crate of champagne to the office to congratulate the team on great sales figures?'

Cat shakes her head.

'Well, do you know what Sally did? She asked one of the writers to carry the box down to a taxi so she could take it all home for herself.'

Vivienne chooses not to tell her about the revenge she took on Sally. It had got a bit out of hand and the memory fills her with shame.

Then the doorbell rings. Vivienne glances at her watch. It's just after 9 p.m., late for anyone to call.

'I'll just go and check on Charlie,' Cat says, scooping up a Spider-Man costume and a handful of Lego bricks as she goes.

Vivienne opens the front door and is pleased to see Tristan standing there – until she notices the expression on his face.

'Have you heard?' he says, walking inside, holding his mobile phone in front of him with both hands.

'*Tributes paid as underwear chief dies suddenly,*' Vivienne reads aloud, then drops down on the sofa as the words sink in.

'So it looks like Janet is no longer a suspect,' Tristan says.

'Oh God,' Vivienne cries, covering her face with her hands. 'What happened?'

'She was knocked over by a taxi in Notting Hill,' says Tristan. 'Just three days before her forty-fifth birthday.'

Vivienne gazes up at Tristan and then tries to focus on breathing. But all she can see is Janet's envelope:

You will die aged 44.

\* \* \*

Later still, Vivienne is lying in bed but is unable to sleep. She can't help remembering her words to Janet at Matthew's memorial: '*You have a motive ... you got angry and pushed him*'. Janet had laughed it off, hadn't seemed to take anything seriously that afternoon, but Vivienne's words must have hurt. And now Janet is dead and Vivienne is no closer to finding the killer. Because now, no matter what Melvin says, she's sure their party host is a murderer and won't stop until they are all dead. Then she has a thought: that strange black-and-white picture on the wall at Serendipity's, their matching table settings. She grabs her notebook from her bedside table, pulls her laptop on to her knee and searches 'cat smoking a pipe'. Hundreds of cartoon drawings pop up – some trendy posters and apron designs – and gasps when she finds the very image from the wall of the dinner party. The devilish face peers at her once more, the seven anthropomorphic images around him. Underneath, there's a brief description.

'The seven deadly sins,' Vivienne reads.

She looks at the pig image, remembers Janet saying: '*Mine was a pig, charming!*' Next to the picture is the word 'gluttony'. Thinking of Janet stuffing her face with that greasy burger, downing the champagne, Vivienne realises that Janet *had* been gluttonous.

The leering sheep had been on Matthew's place setting, depicting lust. Well, *that* makes sense, too. Working her way around the image, she notes down that the pipe-smoking cat on Melvin's place setting is for sloth. Gordon's had been the peacock for pride. Tristan's was wrath and Vivienne's was envy. Which means Stella's must have been greed. So, if each of them represented a 'sin' then who was the 'devil' in the middle who was orchestrating it all? It dawns on Vivienne that perhaps she'd been looking in the wrong direction. Rather than pointing her finger inwards to the table of guests, she should turn her accusations outwards.

'Who is the devil?' she scribbles in her notebook.

\* \* \*

A week later, Tristan and Vivienne walk into the Royal Oak pub in High Holborn. Vivienne cringes as her heels stick to the carpet.

'Well, this isn't what I expected for Janet's wake,' she says, glancing at the '2-4-1 drinks on Sexy Saturdays' posters on the wall. The pub is dark and has a vague odour of stale beer mixed with old socks. Two tables are taken up with people of various ages, including an elderly lady in a wheelchair and a frazzled-looking mum rocking a baby. Presumably Janet's family. Then a couple more tables dotted around are taken up with mostly middle-aged, mostly red-faced and rotund men in suits. Janet's colleagues, Vivienne guesses.

'Me neither. I don't think Janet would be impressed,' Tristan says.

They walk to the bar where an older chap is leaning heavily on his elbows. The end of his tie is dangling into a puddle of spilled drink, which he seems oblivious to.

'You here for Janet's memorial?' he splutters, his cheap-whisky breath creeping into Vivienne's nostrils.

'Yes, we're so sorry…' Vivienne starts, but the man interrupts her.

'Worked with her for years. Bit of a ballbreaker, but all right, really,' he slurs, stuffing a piece of paper into her hand and swaying off in the direction of the gents. They both peer at the paper. A folded piece of A4 with a blurry picture of Janet on the front.

RIP Janet Tilsbury. 1972–2016

She skims over the brief bio and well-worn poems without enthusiasm.

'*Stop All the Clocks*? What a cliché!' she sighs, tossing the paper back on to the bar. 'Is this really what forty-four years of life adds up to?'

A loud guffaw bursts forth from across the bar, and Vivienne sees an overweight man in a waistcoat beaming at the auburn-haired barmaid. His large nose is an unnatural shade of red and trickles of sweat are snaking down his face.

'Bill?' she mouths to Tristan, and he shrugs his shoulders.

They order their drinks and sit down at the table near the window.

### Tristan

Tristan sips his Guinness and gazes around the pub. It is strangely silent. There's no music playing and everyone is speaking at a very low level. Then a baby starts to cry and its mother is standing up, rocking her sacred bundle back and forth. He glances at Vivienne, expecting to hear her usual complaint about 'children in adult spaces', but she's looking over with a benevolent smile on her face.

'Poor woman looks stressed,' she murmurs then digs into her handbag, pulls out her notebook and places it on the table between them.

'I wonder if she's related to Janet, looks a bit like her,' Tristan comments, watching the woman lower the now quiet baby into a pram.

'They must be devastated,' Vivienne says. 'She was young – and had such a lust for life.'

Tristan holds back a snort. That's one way of putting it. On the three occasions that Tristan had met Janet, they must have exchanged no more than twenty words. Her eyes had easily skipped over Tristan as if he wasn't even there. Janet had barely even registered his existence. He wasn't attractive or powerful, he wasn't competition, a conquest or a potential comrade. To her, he was nothing. And now, it is Janet who is nothing. Literally nothing. She is no longer on this earth. Ashes to ashes and all that.

'Well, hello there,' a deep voice booms out, cutting through Tristan's thoughts. Melvin is beaming as he plants a kiss on Vivienne's cheek, gives Tristan a heavy pat on the shoulder and then sits down with them.

'Melvin, how are you?' Vivienne asks. Tristan notices that Melvin's paisley shirt has a red wine stain on the sleeve; his eyes are bloodshot and sort of glazed. Has Melvin come to a wake straight from a night out?

'Good … well, saddened by the news, of course,' Melvin says but his smile only flickers for a second. 'I'll get another round in.'

'We've only just—' Vivienne starts to say, but Melvin has already rushed towards the bar, so she shrugs at Tristan.

'He seems … upbeat,' Tristan comments, watching Melvin laugh with the barmaid.

'I do wonder if it's time we made an official report to the police,' Vivienne says, her voice low.

'We agreed to wait and see what Melvin has to say,' Tristan reminds her.

Melvin appears with a tray bearing six brightly coloured cocktails complete with tiny umbrellas and pink straws.

'It's two-for-one on all cocktails – I couldn't resist,' he says, plonking the tray down in the middle of the table, right on top of Vivienne's notebook.

'Well, Janet might not have approved of this place, but she'd certainly approve of these cocktails,' Vivienne says, taking one.

'When the report came into the station and I realised who it was, honestly, it shook me,' Melvin says, taking a large slurp from a bright pink cocktail. 'She was a lovely, vibrant lady.'

A loud laugh suddenly echoes through the pub, and they look over to see Bill standing at the bar.

'I think that must be Janet's husband,' Vivienne says. 'He doesn't exactly look heartbroken.'

Tristan watches him and wonders if he had any idea of the way his wife carried on with other men. Perhaps it went both ways. Perhaps they had some sort of arrangement. Who knows what goes on in another person's relationship?

Tristan only knows that he'd found a rare love with Ellie. As more time passes from their break-up, this fact only becomes clearer. They were meant to be together. Until it had been snatched away – yes, partly by his own behaviour but also by her vindictive friends who he's sure pushed her into ending their relationship. He picks up a bright blue cocktail and takes a sip. *Urgh*, it's so sweet and syrupy, he can instantly feel the sugar coating his teeth. He pushes it away and reaches for his Guinness again. He thinks of Ellie's irresistible gap-toothed smile, bright clothes and wild curls, but then the image is suddenly replaced by a different one: hair pulled back into a harsh bun, grey trousers, a baggy black shirt and a deep scowl across her forehead.

Following Matthew's memorial, Tristan had been plagued by dreams of Ellie dressed in black at his funeral, of himself-as-Matthew standing on top of that office tower, his hair ruffled by the wind. He'd find himself wide awake in the early hours of the morning, so he'd get out of bed, endlessly check Ellie's social media or pull his coat on and walk the streets of London. Then, one night, he'd finally seen it. On Ellie's Facebook page, where it had previously stated 'single', it had changed to 'in a relationship'. Even though he'd been expecting it, a white-hot rage had surged through him, and he'd roared into the darkness of his little flat.

Three days later, Tristan had leaned against a bus shelter on a quiet street in Bermondsey, holding a Metro in front of his face. A bus had slowed down and he'd waved it on.

'For God's sake, Dale, hurry up.' A familiar voice, but harsher than he'd remembered. Although his eyes had been studiously trained on the paper, Tristan's every other sense had been alert to the house next door.

'You sound like a fishwife, yelling like that,' a man's voice had responded, then slammed the front door, hard.

'We'll be late for the appointment, then I need to get to work, and it's parents' evening tonight,' Ellie had answered, more gently this time, but her voice was dull with exhaustion.

'You're not the only one with a busy job, you know,' the man called Dale had said, and suddenly they'd appeared at the end of the driveway, walking quickly towards the bus stop. Tristan had bowed his head behind the paper and held his breath. He'd got a quick look at Dale, with his stocky frame, his self-assured walk, a few steps ahead, knowing without looking back that Ellie was following.

'But I am also lugging this around,' he'd heard Ellie say with a sigh. He'd peeped his head quickly around his paper to see her hand resting on a small bump in her middle.

'It's what you wanted, isn't it?' Dale had snapped, without stopping or even slowing his pace.

Tristan thought his gasp must have been loud enough for them to hear, but the bickering couple had continued their mismatched march.

When Tristan and Ellie were together, she had always spoken wistfully about having children. Whenever she'd brought it up, Tristan had changed the subject. He could just about look after himself let alone a demanding baby. He shakes his head now at how dismissive he'd been, how immature. Mind you, it didn't look like Ellie was exactly relishing the prospect of impending motherhood, like he'd thought she would. She'd seemed thoroughly miserable – as had her boyfriend. But they'd made a baby together and that could never be undone. They were joined together for life by a bond much stronger than any wedding vow. Tristan had wanted to see for himself if Ellie really had moved on, if he really had missed his chance. And what he saw confirmed that it was over. Regret and fury fuelled his walk home. As he'd marched along a well-to-do road just a mile from his flat, he'd taken aim at the wing mirror of an obnoxiously large Land Rover, landed a flying kick which sent the mirror shattering into the road. It made him feel better. So he'd done another, and another. By the time he'd got home, his foot was aching, his faced scratched when some splinters of mirror had rebounded back at him. Yet he felt a wonderful sense of release. But the next morning, he'd woken up filled with a festering fury once more. For the next few days, he'd locked himself away in his flat. It had been Vivienne who'd yanked him out of his hibernation, made him talk.

'You're not alone,' was what she'd said. And then she'd turned a new page on her notebook and started to make a list. He'd followed her plan to a tee – well almost. He'd seen his GP, mentioned panic attacks. He'd nodded along and walked out with a handful of leaflets, covering everything from medication to counselling. The leaflets had gone straight into his recycling bin. Vivienne's second demand had been to get back in touch with his old uni mates. The thought had made Tristan's stomach twist. As an eighteen-year-old, he'd bonded with Dave, Eddie, and Fergus during three years of shared frustrations over the opposite sex and all-night debates about the comparative merits of Sega and Nintendo. After graduating, Dave and Fergus had gone travelling, Eddie had taken a job in IT for one of the 'Big Four', and Tristan had signed up with a temping agency. Every few months they'd swap messages about their current jobs (Dave: now a university lecturer, Eddie: director at an accountancy firm, and Fergus: something vague to do with 'project management'), or gossip about former classmates. Tristan had allowed himself to drift away from them, making excuses when they'd tried to meet up. So, when he sent Dave a quick message apologising for not being in touch, asking if he was around for a pint soon, he'd been amazed when a response popped up within minutes.

**Friday 8pm, usual place?**

But, when Tristan had walked towards The George in Elephant and Castle a week later, a feeling of dread had started to work its way upwards from his toes. As he'd got closer to the door, he'd found his legs carrying him past the entrance. He'd quickly glanced through the window to see Dave sitting at their usual table, two pints of beer in front of him. Still tall, although no one would call him 'lanky' these days, and clearly finally able to grow a beard, but Tristan would have recognised him anywhere. Later, when Dave messaged to ask, What happened to you? I waited for an hour, Tristan had just deleted the message. The following Sunday, Vivienne had asked how it went, and he'd assured her they'd had a brilliant night and planned to see the other two the following week.

'The taxi driver said that Janet stepped out in front of him. He wasn't speeding or driving dangerously. No one else was involved,' Melvin is saying now.

'Any CCTV in the area?' Vivienne asks.

'Not on that road,' Melvin says, with a hint of irritation. 'It's not on every street in London, as a lot of people think.'

'So you're claiming it's another accident? But how could anyone have possibly known?' Vivienne queries.

But Melvin isn't listening, he's focused on the tray of cocktails and choosing a second. He takes his time before he finally picks up a bright green one with a yellow umbrella, takes a long sip from the twisty straw then pulls a face and coughs.

'Too sweet,' he splutters.

'Melvin?' Vivienne snaps. 'You told me you'd look into Janet's background after Matthew's memorial. And the CCTV on the street.'

'Not much point now, is there? With Janet dead, too,' Melvin says. 'You can't pin it on her anymore.'

'I do feel bad about accusing her,' Vivienne says. 'She did seem to be the most likely candidate but perhaps I was too quick to point the finger at one of the guests. These numbers are just getting to me, I think.'

'I understand,' says Melvin, reaching across to take Vivienne's hand. 'I've been thinking about it a lot, too.'

Then Melvin's mobile beeps, he drops Vivienne's hand and Tristan sees his expression switch in an instant from sympathy to frustration. He pulls the phone from his pocket, quickly reads the message then drops it roughly on to the table.

Vivienne meets Tristan's eye, then her gaze shifts to the window behind him. He watches her face suddenly freeze, her eyes wide with shock. She gasps, pointing at the window.

Melvin and Tristan spin around but there's nothing to see, just the usual Sunday afternoon shoppers marching by.

'What was it?' Tristan asks.

'A face looking through the window. Its mouth and head were covered. I just saw these menacing eyes staring at me,' Vivienne explains, taking a large sip of her cocktail.

'I wondered if I would find you three here.' A man wearing a bright white tracksuit with his hood pulled up and a white scarf wrapped tightly across his mouth is suddenly standing over them.

'It's you!' Vivienne cries.

'Gordon?' Tristan says, recognising his Edinburgh lilt.

'Yes, it's me,' Gordon replies, keeping his hood up but pulling his scarf down slightly to reveal red cracked lips and alarmingly sharp cheekbones. 'So that's three correct predictions now. How are you going to explain that, then, Melvin? Vivienne?'

Before either of them can respond, Bill ambles up to the table.

'I presume you're friends of my Janey?'

They all look up at him, and Tristan sees that his previous bonhomie was merely an act. Up close, Bill is cloaked in sadness, pulled down by it. As he shakes their hands, his movements are heavy and laboured. This is a man grieving.

'We'd only recently met Janet, actually,' Vivienne starts to explain, smoothing down her hair with her fingers, but Bill is ready to talk, not listen.

'Married for thirteen years, hardly said a cross word to each other,' he says, beginning a speech he'd apparently been performing all day. 'The key to a good marriage is to have your own interests, that's what I always say. My Janey, she loved to socialise, she was always at one works party or another, whereas I prefer a quiet whisky at home...'

'So, she'd been at a work party on the night of the accident?' Gordon asks. Vivienne sighs loudly and Melvin glares over at him, but it's clear Gordon is oblivious.

'Actually, I don't think so,' Bill mumbles, his sails suddenly empty, his hull momentarily unsteady. 'Her colleagues hadn't known about a party. She was in Notting Hill, but no one's sure why. Must have been visiting a new friend. She had so many I couldn't keep track.'

As Gordon glances around the others, Tristan sees his face change as the truth suddenly emerges. The tiny silver ball dropping into the hole on a pinball machine. *Oh.* Janet had been with another man on the night she died.

'We're so sorry for your loss, Mr Tilsbury.' Melvin stands up to shake Bill's hand. 'She was a lovely lady.'

Bill takes the larger man's hand, and he opens his mouth to respond – but then closes it again. He looks at Melvin and nods.

'I don't know what I'll do without her,' he says quietly.

'Bill, sorry to interrupt, but Auntie Maureen is leaving and…' says the woman holding the now awake baby in her arms.

As she looks over apologetically at the group, Tristan notices her familiar eyes. Amber, the exact shade of Janet's. In fact, she's just like Janet, only a more rumpled, shrunken-down version. This woman's blonde highlights make way for a couple of inches of dark roots, her black, long-sleeved dress accessorised with a milky stain on the shoulder.

'This is Caroline, Janet's sister,' says Bill, visibly pulling himself back together. 'And baby Tabitha, our niece, who sadly Janet hadn't met yet.'

'Hello everyone,' Caroline says as she distractedly bounces the grumbling little girl who has pink cheeks and a matching pink pacifier which twitches rhythmically under her furious sucking.

'She's beautiful,' says Vivienne.

'Thank you.' Caroline smiles, though the joy doesn't reach her eyes. 'She's not very happy today. The dummy seems to be the only thing to settle her.'

'Darling, Auntie Maureen needs to go to the restroom,' a man says, putting his hand on Caroline's shoulder, which she quickly brushes off.

'On my way, Giles,' she snaps. 'This is my husband.'

They watch the three of them walk away, Bill a few steps in front, Caroline gazing down at her baby who starts to cry again and Giles trotting behind.

'So, how are you, Gordon?' Vivienne asks, pointedly looking him up and down.

'In excellent health, Vivienne,' he says, pushing his hands into his pockets and hopping from one foot to the next. 'Clean living is agreeing with me, it seems.'

'Been for a run?' Melvin frowns when Gordon fails to offer an explanation.

'Not today,' he says. 'I just wanted to check in with you all following the news of Janet's demise. The email group has gone quiet. Vivienne, did you find your envelope in the end?'

## Gordon

Rather than answering his question in a timely manner, Vivienne turns to roll her eyes at the others and then takes a large sip from her repulsive-looking drink, no doubt laden with sugar and artificial colours. They all seem to be annoyed by his very presence, that much Gordon can perceive, but he really doesn't have time for this. Then he's distracted by a pile of coins that lie on the table in front of Melvin. Research has shown that coins can harbour pathogens like *E. coli* and salmonella. They're amongst the most bacteria-ridden things that people touch every day, including mobile phones, washing-up sponges and remote controls. He can practically see the little cucumber-shaped bacteria crawling over the coins and scuttling like centipedes across the table towards him. He takes a deep breath and forces his eyes up to Vivienne, who is now flipping through her notebook.

'So, *did* you find your envelope?' he asks again, ensuring he breathes through his nose, thus helping to protect him against any viruses his companions might unwittingly be sending his way. Vivienne slowly lowers her drink back to the filthy table and sighs loudly. Why can't she just answer his question with a straight yes or no?

'Sadly not, Gordon,' she says finally.

'It really was quite careless of you to lose such an important piece of evidence,' Gordon admonishes.

'Don't speak to her like that,' Tristan snaps, turning his cool blue eyes on Gordon.

'It's OK, Tristan,' Vivienne tells him, touching his elbow. 'I'm thoroughly annoyed with myself about it.'

'She's not one of your students, you know,' Tristan mutters, grabbing a green cocktail and taking a noisy sip from the straw.

Gordon watches Tristan and thinks how, despite his age and reasonable intelligence, his behaviour is reminiscent of Gordon's teenage daughter. In other words, he seems constantly on the brink of a tantrum.

Then he glances at the police officer, Melvin, who is merrily slurping on his own illuminous drink and then to Vivienne, who is frowning as she flips through her notebook. Sighing, he thinks of Elizabeth, who might have offered some advice in dealing with these people. But he hasn't spoken to his wife in three weeks, hasn't seen her in months.

On his train ride back home following Matthew's memorial, Gordon had started to put together his action plan. He had marched into the kitchen, where Elizabeth and Louisa had been sitting facing each other across their kitchen table, hands encasing large mugs of hot chocolate, with a number of pink and white marshmallows floating on top. They'd both looked up at him guiltily, and between them, like crime scene evidence, had been a canister of squirty cream and a little plastic tub of chocolate powder. He'd done a double-take; those items definitely had not been in the kitchen cupboards when he'd looked that morning. His wife and daughter must have hidden them away from him... No matter, he had more important things to discuss. Sending

Louisa off to her room still clutching her mug as if it was an extension of her hand, he'd told Elizabeth they needed to talk and had laid out his plans in the simplest, most concise manner. Unfortunately, his wife hadn't responded in kind, and had started sobbing before he could finish.

'So you're leaving me?' Elizabeth had spluttered, dabbing her cheeks with the tissue Gordon handed her.

'Well, yes, but I think it will be beneficial for all of us.' He attempted to reassure her with some statistics he had to hand but she hadn't been in the frame of mind to listen.

'Is there another woman?'

'Of course not,' he'd cried, genuinely horrified by the thought of adding yet another stressful element to his life.

'Be honest with me Gordon, do you want a divorce?' she asked once the flow of tears had eased off somewhat.

'Oh no, I think we should stay married,' he said, putting an arm around her shoulders as he knew it would provide her with some comfort and reassurance. His research had shown that divorced men are more likely to live shorter lives.

So, as Elizabeth watched, eyes ringed with make-up smudges, he'd packed up his little travel suitcase and walked away from the home he'd shared with his family for more than a decade. He'd looked back and seen Louisa's strawberry-blonde fringe poking out between her bedroom curtains. For a second, he'd pictured the five-year-old Louisa who had waved him off to work every day from that very spot. But teenage Louisa just glared and then was gone. Walking away from that house hadn't been easy for Gordon, but he'd been determined to stick to his plan and felt that, ultimately, the move would be beneficial to his longevity. After a few nights in a hotel (with the highest hygiene rating he could find), he'd managed to secure a furnished flat within walking distance of the university. It was in a new block, built just two years ago and the landlord had assured him that all the furniture was brand-new. He'd arrived at the flat armed with a cornucopia of cleaning products, along with new, white bedsheets, towels, and some essential consumables. He'd even bought one of those UV lights to check for stains on the mattress and carpets (all clear, thankfully). Elizabeth had filled their home with garish coloured rugs, cushions and various trinkets. She favoured reds, oranges, and purples (which, Gordon liked to joke, reminded him of the birth canal). Gordon himself had always liked the colour white or – to be more precise – the shade of white. It was clean and practical; you could see clearly if something was dirty. So he kept his new flat entirely white and even took to wearing a white boilersuit when he was at home or a white tracksuit on the rare occasion he went out. Unfortunately, he couldn't get away with this at work, where the accepted dress code for teaching staff was a suit, but, after work, he made sure to strip off in the doorway of his flat and pull on the boiler suit.

Then Gordon had set up the flat ready for work, with two brand-new whiteboards and two packs of whiteboard pens, one all black and one all red. Using a black marker, he'd written EXPERIMENT SERENDIPITY at the top of one board, and EXPERIMENT 54 with a red marker at the top of the second board. On the first board, he'd drawn a circle to replicate the dinner table, written: their seven names around it and their numbers next to each one. Just Vivienne's was missing. Next to Stella's name and number, he'd written: 'ignored'. Next to Matthew's, he wrote: 'took matters into his own hands'. And next to Janet's: 'overindulged'. Then he carefully drew a line across each of their names.

On the second board, he'd written the number 53 at the top. Underneath, he wrote his three commandments:

*I will take my number seriously.*
*I will fight my number.*
*I will not overindulge.*

Inspired by the findings of Experiment Serendipity, Gordon will write his own paper, using himself as his main research point, aiming to beat his number of 53. To make it to 54, and beyond. He'd reached the conclusion that the secret science group had selected him for their experiment, set him the challenge to beat his number. Not only would he do that, but he would use their findings to write a paper so extraordinary that it would gazump theirs and make himself a star in the science world. Then they'd be begging for him to join their group.

Gordon had already achieved his first commandment and now he was embarking on the second commandment. Fighting his number. Starting with the basics, he worked his way through the research, reading that women tended to live between five and ten more years than their male counterparts, with eighty-five per cent of the people living to 100 being women. This was partly due to the XX chromosome, which means women are less likely to suffer from diseases associated with genetic mutations such as haemophilia, as well as testosterone which causes aggressive behaviour in men and may lead to road accidents, fights, and the like. These elements were out of his control but there were other factors he could control: his risk of developing cardiovascular disease by eating a nutritious diet, taking regular exercise, and cutting down on alcohol consumption. This led very nicely into commandment number three. Unlike greedy Janet, he wouldn't be overindulging. He would do the opposite.

Back in 1935, a scientist found that rats with severely restricted diets lived up to thirty-three per cent longer than previously known possible. Similar experiments on other animals more recently backed up the theory. By restricting calorie intake by around fifty per cent, lifespans extended by up to 300 per cent, as a result of reducing metabolic rates and free-radical damage. In other words, the body is healthier when it's processing less food. For ethical reasons, this theory had not yet been tested on humans, but Gordon has the scientific knowledge plus the self-control to be the perfect candidate. His first step had been to reduce his calorie intake by fifty per cent, which he hopes will provide a range of benefits including a lowered risk of developing cancer, diabetes and heart problems. To keep it simple, he eats the same three meals every day, making up 1,300 calories. Breakfast is a boiled egg and single slice of toast; lunch is cheese, rye crackers and a sliced apple and for dinner he has salmon steak with steamed broccoli and a kiwi fruit.

His research had also shown the irrefutable health benefits of weight-training, so he'd invested in some weights and gym equipment for use in his flat. (He had concluded that the potential risk of an accident was outweighed by the physical benefits.) When he'd lived with Elizabeth, he'd cycled to the university every day. The thought of such a treacherous journey now makes him shudder. He finds he can gain the same benefits by setting his bike on a stand and never having to leave his flat. To make space for his new equipment, he'd asked his landlord to remove the dining table and he now eats standing by his kitchen counter. Every day after breakfast and after work, he embarks on a one-hour fitness programme, alternating cycling and weight-training. After ten minutes' rest, he then spends three minutes and thirty seconds performing a perfect headstand, which is known to alleviate stress as well as activate the pituitary gland and stimulate the lymphatic system.

And, so far, it is working wonders, he is sure. His skin and hair are shining, his stomach is never bloated, and he feels younger than he has in years. Admittedly, he does seem to have lost some weight, but he's enjoying the leaner look of his body, thanks to the strength training. He is starting to feel excited at the prospect of presenting his findings to Professor Goodacre, picturing the look of enlightenment on the man's face.

'I must admit, I never did warm to Janet,' Vivienne says now, as if this information is somehow significant. 'But I was impressed when I read about the campaigning she'd done from within the company, encouraging them to hire more diverse models.'

'Yes, it seems she had a lot more integrity than she perhaps let on,' Melvin says, nodding.

'Do you think?' Gordon asks, picturing her nearly toppling off her stool, burger oil rolling down her chin and flaunting her assets at Matthew and Melvin. *That* certainly didn't look like integrity to him.

Nor did stumbling out of some man's Notting Hill apartment in the early hours of the morning, strutting down the street in a skirt that barely covered her derrière, oblivious to anything except satisfying her own base needs...

Gordon isn't here for small talk. He doesn't want to hear about Janet's redeeming features, socialise in grubby public houses or listen to Vivienne's crank theories. He's here to keep track of his fellow dinner guests, to see how they are reacting to their numbers so he can keep up to date with the rival experiment. The dinner guests have thrown around all sorts of theories, from serial killers to psychics to self-fulfilling prophecy. Gordon doesn't know exactly how the secret science group has organised the deaths, but it's irrelevant. There's something much more important at play here. Sacrifices must be made in the name of scientific advancement.

Three months after he'd moved into his new flat, Gordon's boss Professor Linus Goodacre had knocked on his office door.

'All well with you, Gordon?' he'd asked, sitting down in the chair opposite Gordon's desk, without waiting for an invitation. Gordon had sighed and put down the paper he was reading. Professor Goodacre was an ambassador for informality, had never once used the title 'Dr' when speaking to him, as if he hadn't slaved for five years at medical school.

'Yes, thank you, Professor.' Gordon had nodded. He made sure to always give others their full title, hoping they would follow suit. In the past five years, this hadn't worked once, yet Gordon wasn't about to give up.

'Linus, please. I haven't seen you pop up on my television of a morning, lately. No longer doing your cameos?' Professor Goodacre had asked.

'Oh no. I felt my time was better served elsewhere,' Gordon responded, taken aback that his boss had ever watched *The Morning Show*.

Professor Goodacre nodded knowingly, adjusted his maroon tie, then he'd leaned across Gordon's desk (spotting ink on his thumb, Gordon wondered when he'd last washed his hands) and picked up the paper he'd been reading.

'*The Longevity Project*. Not your usual area of expertise.'

'No, but I've been considering how calorie intake and exercise might impact life expectancy,' Gordon had said, thinking on his feet.

'Oh, fascinating,' his boss said nodding. 'I could put this to the board, see if we can send some money your way.'

'That would be … most beneficial,' Gordon told him.

Watching Professor Goodacre walk out of his office, Gordon had been struck by the thought that perhaps *he* was part of the secret science group. He'd never once encouraged Gordon's research or shown any interest at all. Now here he was, offering up funding and support. Now Gordon thinks of it, had the maroon tie been a sign? Back in his university days, the tie had been a sign of membership to an elite group at the college, only accessible, by personal invitation, to the most intelligent and best-connected students. Despite his excellent grades and highly regarded research, Gordon had never once received the invitation. Professor Goodacre, then just Linus, had been a few years younger than him but had suddenly started wearing the maroon tie. Was the secret science society linked to this group? Gordon would just have to wait for explicit notification from them. It wouldn't be long, he was sure of that.

Though his experiment has been an unrivalled success up until now, there have been some slip-ups. He blames Elizabeth for those. Every week she phones him up, asking how he is, what he's working on, when he's planning on seeing Louisa next. He finds her never-ending questions wreak havoc on his clean and serene mind. As soon as he hangs up, he inevitably starts to doubt his new life, even thinking fondly of the warm double bed (with its ugly, purple bedspread) back in their bedroom in Wandsworth. Sometimes the only thing that wipes the slate clean is to splurge on some disgusting takeaway food from the twenty-four-hour burger place opposite his flat, or a large fruit pie from the bakery, depending on whether his savoury or sweet tooth kicks in that day. He stands in front of his white kitchen countertop, plants his feet squarely on the floor and focuses all his being on consuming every crumb of the food in front of him. He then allows himself ten minutes to lie on the sofa, stroking his bloated belly and picturing the food slowly working its way through his digestive system, unaware of where the journey will end. Then he makes his way to the toilet, retrieves his toothbrush from under the sink, and rids his body of the vile pollution. The guilt he feels immediately afterwards is fleeting. Once it passes, he's flooded with a feeling of renewal, of calm, ready to continue with his experiment the next day.

'How's your daughter getting on, Gordon? It's Louisa, isn't it?' Melvin suddenly asks, pulling him out of his thoughts.

For a few seconds, the question throws him. He can't remember telling this man his daughter's name.

'She's well, thank you,' he says. Just last week, they'd spent a particularly awkward hour sitting side by side at a coffee shop near Gordon's flat. After almost twelve minutes of silence, Louisa had stopped looking at her phone and had come out with something that had surprised him.

'So what's your new project about, then? Mum says it's ridiculous.'

'Well, your mother is no scientist,' he'd snapped but then he'd looked at his daughter and noticed she'd been waiting for an answer. It was possibly the first time she'd shown an interest in his work. Even when he was on *The Morning Show*, she wouldn't bother to watch it. So he'd taken a deep breath and told her. About the calorie cutting, the weight-training, the medical tests, and even the head-stands. Afterwards, two lines appeared above her nose (just like his, he'd realised). She started to speak, and then stopped herself.

'What is it?' he urged. He had to admit, he hadn't planned on giving her such depth of detail. But he hadn't told anyone about it and it had felt good to speak about his work.

'It's just, I was thinking, what's the point in living longer when you're on your own, away from me and Mum? What are you living for?'

Gordon had been initially stuck for a response, until he'd remembered that his paper was for the good of science, for the good of mankind. Louisa had seemed satisfied with the response and, at the very least, the meeting would keep Elizabeth off his back for a few weeks.

He reaches into his pocket for his antibacterial spray, but his hand goes to the envelope and the folded piece of paper he'd brought.

'Melvin, I picked this up at the dinner party,' Gordon says, placing the envelope down on the table. 'I suppose I should have given it to you before now, but you didn't seem interested in its contents. Anyway, it's your decision to make.'

'Oh, thank you, Gordon,' Melvin mumbles, glancing briefly at it.

'You had it all this time!' Vivienne cries.

'It wasn't *yours* to keep hold of,' Tristan snaps.

'Perhaps this will be of more interest,' Gordon says to Melvin, ignoring Vivienne and Tristan's uproar. He places a folded piece of paper on top of the envelope.

'What is it?' Tristan asks.

'It's something I'm working on. How a solitary existence, alongside a calorie-controlled diet and exercise can lead to a longer life,' Gordon says. 'It really has proven to be beneficial to my own situation. I haven't felt this healthy in a long time, let me tell you.'

Melvin picks up the paper and frowns as he skims the information that Gordon has carefully written down for him. Then he drops it back on to the table, right on top of the infested coins.

'I appreciate it, Gordo, but this isn't for me,' he says, with a shrug. 'If my number's coming up soon, then so be it.'

Gordon stares at Melvin, speechless for a moment. That information is the result of months of research and careful experimentation. It will soon be on the front page of every newspaper and make Gordon himself a big name in his field. And yet Melvin has barely bothered to look at it. For the first time today, he takes a closer look at the police officer. His shirt is stained on the sleeve, he's lounging in his chair, legs akimbo in front of him, head rocking back as if he can't be bothered to hold it up. The whites of his eyes are beginning to yellow – a sure sign of a regular drinker. This man does not deserve to benefit from Gordon's work. He is disgusting, just like that Janet woman. Weak Matthew and rude Stella weren't much better either.

'Don't you see? We need to learn from them,' he cries. 'I've given you a chance and you've blown it.'

Then he marches out of the café without a backward glance.

## Melvin

Melvin watches Gordon, in his ludicrous white tracksuit, flounce from the pub clutching the piece of paper in his hand.

'What was all that about?' he says, turning back to Vivienne and Tristan.

'No idea,' Vivienne says. 'Can you believe he had your envelope this whole time?'

'It doesn't matter,' Melvin says, with a shrug.

'You're not tempted to look?' Vivienne asks.

'I meant what I said to him,' Melvin says. 'I'm going to let life take me where it will. I'm just along for the ride.'

'You know what they say: "Evil exists when good people fail to act",' Tristan mumbles. Melvin just about makes out what he's saying.

'Well, that's a new one on me.'

'It seems like Dr Gordon is trying to fight his number with science,' Vivienne says. 'I suppose you can't blame him. We've lost three of the group now and his number isn't far off.'

'Perhaps you should have listened to him. He might be on to something,' Tristan says directly to Melvin, icy blue eyes aimed straight at him. He hadn't noticed the colour before, so pale they almost blend into the whites of his eyes.

Melvin shrugs and picks up Janet's tribute from the table, flicks through it. They'd used that lovely poem from *Four Weddings and a Funeral*. As his eyes bounce over the familiar words, he can't help but hear them in John Hannah's delicious Scottish brogue.

Then his phone beeps with a message. Christian.

**We're at the bistro. Where are you?**

He glances at his watch. Nearly midday, already. He'd felt brilliant at 10 a.m., when he'd decided to head straight to the pub, his body buzzing with Jägermeister and Red Bull. But now, as the sugary cocktails curdle in his stomach and he considers the prospect of eating lunch while hiding his inevitable hangover, he suddenly feels a touch nauseous. There's only one thing for it.

'Anyone up for a real drink, somewhere with a bit more atmosphere?' he says now, raising eyebrows at Vivienne and Tristan. 'I know a little place around the corner.'

'Sorry, I can't. Got some work to do,' Tristan says, pushing his chair back so quickly that it flips over on to the carpet.

'On a Saturday?' Vivienne asks quietly. A look passes between them. Melvin briefly wonders what they're silently conveying.

'Yep, big project beginning on Monday, I need to get a head start,' he says, giving Vivienne a quick kiss on the cheek and then raising a hand at Melvin before walking out of the door.

'What about it, Vivienne, say goodbye to Janet properly?' Melvin asks.

'Go on, then,' she says, standing up.

\* \* \*

Vivienne perches on a bench next to a small table by the door while Melvin gets their drinks. The barman greets him like an old friend and Melvin wonders if that's how he treats everyone, or if he remembers Melvin from a night out. He peers at the barman's bald head, semi-circle glasses with red frames, scarlet suit, and bright-yellow pocket square and tries to find a memory that matches this rather memorable image. He finds nothing and so nods politely and orders the drinks. His mobile starts to buzz in his pocket. Christian again. He quickly rejects the call but not before the barman spots it.

'Trying to avoid someone, are we?' the barman chuckles. 'Have you been a naughty boy?'

'Oh, nothing that exciting,' Melvin mutters, quickly passing the man a twenty-pound note and willing the conversation to end.

While the man counts out his change, Melvin types Christian a text.

**Still at Janet's wake. Everyone very upset! I'll ring when it's over.**

A reply pops up almost instantly.

**Poor you! Hang on in there. We'll see you later. Xx**

Melvin sighs, switches his phone off and puts it back in his pocket. He carries the drinks over to the table and finds Vivienne is giving him a curious look.

'A friend of yours?' she asks, tilting her head towards the barman who Melvin sees is wiping down the bar while gazing over at him.

'Never met him,' Melvin says, then lifts his glass. 'To fabulous Janet. Heaven just gained a very mischievous angel.'

They clink glasses, and Melvin takes a big gulp of his beer and sighs. No matter how many expensive and interesting wines Christian has persuaded him to try, he still feels you can't beat a good old pint.

'It's just tragic. Bill seemed devastated. He clearly had no idea what she was up to that night,' says Vivienne. 'Marriages really are a mystery to me.'

A moment of silence settles between them, then Melvin remembers something.

'Actually, I did hear something about Janet's death that struck me as odd,' he says.

'What was it?' Vivienne asks, putting her wine down and giving Melvin all her attention.

'Well, I was quite surprised by who was first on the scene…' he teases.

'Who?'

'Giles,' Melvin says, and then waits for Vivienne to put the pieces together.

She leans back on the bench and folds her arms across her chest. Then it hits her. She sits forward again.

'Not … her brother-in-law? Caroline's husband from the wake?' Vivienne cries.

'The very one,' Melvin tells her, trying but failing not to smile broadly at the revelation.

'So that's where she must have been. Oh, Janet, of all the men in London,' Vivienne says then reaches into her voluminous handbag to pull out her notebook and some sheets of paper.

'He was shocked, but I wouldn't say devastated exactly,' Melvin says, hoping this nugget of information will get Vivienne off his back for a bit.

'That actually fits in with a theory I've been working on,' she tells him, flicking through her book. 'I know it sounds odd, but I wonder if Janet's behaviour somehow led to her death.'

'All the evidence points to another accident,' Melvin says. 'She probably stormed off after a lovers' tiff and ran into the road.'

Vivienne purses her lips, sighs.

'I keep thinking about her drinking, her eating, her flirting – her gluttony.'

'OK…'

She flicks through the book and opens it to a circular sketch showing seven rough drawings of animals with a word written in red next to each one.

'You remember we talked about the black-and-white drawing on the wall of Serendipity's, with the same images on the place settings? Well, I found out that it's a very old portrayal of the seven deadly sins.'

'Like, pride, lust, gluttony, and all that?'

'There are seven images, and seven guests,' Vivienne points at each drawing in her book. 'Janet's showed a pig eating a roast dinner and that's the image for – guess what?'

'Gluttony?'

'Stella's was a lizard with a scroll, depicting greed; Matthew's was a male sheep leering at a ewe – lust. Gordon's is peacock, for pride, and Tristan's was two dogs fighting, that's wrath,' she says.

'What about mine? The cat smoking a pipe.'

'It's supposed to be sloth, Melvin,' Vivienne tells him, with a grimace.

'Well, I've never thought of myself as lazy,' Melvin says.

'No, you're not lazy at all,' Vivienne says. 'But I looked it up. Sloth can also refer to a lack of action, a person who just lets things happen.'

'Ha – well perhaps this party-planner knows me better than I know myself,' Melvin says, then rubs his eyes. He's too tired for this.

'I mean, they don't all add up,' Vivienne says. 'Was Stella really greedy, or just prideful? And I'd never describe Tristan as angry.'

Melvin thinks of the many glimpses of barely-contained anger he's seen from Tristan, the clenched fists and jaw, the venomous glances and withering comments, but he doesn't want to encourage another of Vivienne's wacky theories. Since Matthew's funeral, Vivienne has bombarded him with requests to help with her 'investigation'. To appease her, he'd told her he'd spoken to the Serendipity's landlord, who claimed he couldn't find the contact details of the person who hired the venue that night. After that, she'd messaged every few days, asking about Janet's records, questions about how CCTV worked, even requested copies of the police reports for Matthew and Stella's deaths. Sometimes he responded to say his superior wouldn't allow it, sometimes he told her he couldn't find anything, other times he just deleted her message.

'If it makes you feel any better, mine is envy. It's described as "rottenness of the bones".' Vivienne shudders. 'Perhaps the worst death is waiting for me.'

Melvin looks at Vivienne and, for the first time, sees fear in her face.

'You must try and forget about the numbers,' he says softly. 'It will drive you insane. The best thing to do is just live your life.'

'I know, but it's eating me up. My life feels richer than it ever has, which only makes me more afraid that it will be whipped away when I'm least expecting it,' she confesses.

Melvin rests his large hand on Vivienne's small one and smiles at her.

'The other part of my seven deadly-sins theory is that the party host – the killer – is the devil character in the pictures,' Vivienne babbles on.

'I'll humour you,' Melvin sighs. 'So, who's the devil?'

'Someone outside the group, someone who knows us all separately, who orchestrated the dinner party and the numbers, and is picking us off one-by-one,' says Vivienne. 'And I bet they weren't far away that night. Probably watching us all.'

'So…'

'Maybe properties around Serendipity's had CCTV and recorded someone lurking?' Vivienne says. 'Or it could even have been one of the waiters, or the chef?'

'OK, OK, Vivienne.' Melvin sighs. 'I'll speak to the landlord again. See what I can find out.'

'I'm going back to Salvation Road, going door-to-door and speaking to the neighbours,' Vivienne says.

Melvin leans back in his chair, a wave of exhaustion suddenly crashing over him.

'Are you ever going to let this go?' he says.

'No, I've got too much to live for,' she tells him. 'But Melvin, I've got to ask, what's going on? You look dreadful. Have you really come straight from a night out? Presumably Mary wasn't with you.'

'No, she wasn't,' Melvin sighs. Even his head nods forward, as if his neck is tired of holding it up, of facilitating all the lies that come from his mouth.

'You don't have to tell me,' Vivienne says, her blue eyes kind. 'People handle illness in different ways. Is Mary very poorly again?'

Melvin looks at her, weighs up his options and chooses to tell the truth. It will be a novel feeling for him.

'No, she's actually doing really well,' he admits, picturing her cheeks filling out again, turning pink when she laughs, which has been often lately. Those early months of Mary's treatment seem like a long-ago dream. Melvin looks back on his double life of comforting husband to Mary and inexperienced lover to Christian with a sort of nostalgia. He'd felt wanted and needed by them both. It had been exhausting and exhilarating in equal measure. And then something remarkable had happened. Mary's cancer had responded to the treatment, 'like magic', her consultant had said, setting Melvin's teeth on edge. The treatment had removed all trace of the cancer so that she didn't need to have more radiotherapy. The news had been a tonic to Mary. She had blossomed from that stooped, achingly thin person to a vision of life and vitality. She'd persuaded him to take up line-dancing at the town hall and was talking about them embarking on a three-month around-the-world cruise. Mary was constantly making plans, dinners, holidays, new hobbies, new ideas. He'd started to avoid going home for a whole new set of reasons. And Mary's recovery had led to Christian constantly asking, when would he tell her the truth? Christian had started to make changes to his flat in preparation for Melvin moving in. If he wasn't dealing with Mary's incessant plans, Melvin was batting away Christian's endless questions. His brain feels constantly under attack. All he wants is some quiet, some peace to process it all. But his life has other ideas.

'So, what is it?' Vivienne asks now.

'It's me. I've been … seeing someone else and it's got out of control, but I just don't know how to untangle it all.'

'It's Christian, isn't it?'

'How did you know?' Melvin is shocked.

'The makeover, the nights out, the way you smile when you talk about him,' she says. And Melvin sees how stupid he has been. He had thought he was so discreet, believing that his years as a police officer had taught him to hide his emotions, but they had found a way out. Had Mary seen it, too? Is she just pretending to befriend Christian while biding her time until she exposes the betrayal?

'I was going to tell her after Matthew's memorial, had it all planned out, but that night she told me the cancer had come back, so I couldn't do it to her,' he explains, suddenly desperate for Vivienne to see he wasn't such a bad person.

'Well good for you, Melvin,' Vivienne smiles. 'But now she's over the worst, perhaps it's time to come clean. She might take it better than you imagine. After all, you've been married all these years, she knows you better than you think.'

'The worst of it is, these last few months, Mary and Christian have become friends,' he admits. The 'we' Christian was referring to in his message was actually him and Mary. Melvin can hardly believe the situation he's got himself into. It's like a plot from some far-fetched American romcom that Mary used to watch. His wife and his lover have become friends. Really good friends. In fact, Melvin sometimes wonders if they prefer each other to him.

He is waiting for Vivienne's shocked response. But instead, he feels the bench start to shake. Puzzled, he opens his eyes and find that tears are streaking down Vivienne's cheeks. She's laughing, she's actually laughing at his pathetic life.

'Oh, I'm so sorry Melvin, I shouldn't laugh,' she chuckles. 'It's not you, it's just life. Someone, somewhere has a hell of a sense of humour.'

And with that, Melvin finds his despair is replaced with hysteria and he's laughing, too. Other customers look over at this large man and tiny woman roaring with laughter. Their shoulders are pressed together, supporting each other as their bodies become weak with humour. It *is* funny, tragically funny.

As part of Mary's new hobbies and revitalised social life, she'd suddenly decided they should have Christian over for dinner.

'I want to meet this colleague you keep talking about,' she'd said, and Melvin had searched her face for any signs she suspected something. But there had been nothing, just his wife's lovely innocent smile. So Mary had prepared salmon with new potatoes followed by apple crumble ('I know how you policemen can eat') and Christian had turned up at exactly 7.30 p.m., dressed in a pale denim shirt and smelling divine, armed with a bottle of his favourite red wine. Melvin had never sweated as much as he did during that meal. He'd been surprised that neither Mary nor Christian had noticed him dabbing his brow every few minutes, squeezing his arms close to his sides to hide the damp patches. But no, they'd had too good a time to spot Melvin's agony. Christian attentively kept Mary's glass topped up, Mary grilled Christian on the ballet training he'd done as a boy ('You didn't tell me your partner was a fellow dancer!'). By the end of the evening, they were hopping around the lounge as *The Nutcracker* boomed out of their ancient stereo, while Melvin had gloomily sipped his beer. Just after midnight, Mary had kissed Christian goodbye and practically swooned into Melvin's arms, 'If I was twenty years younger, you'd be in trouble,' she'd giggled. Actually giggled. Melvin had hoped that, with the introduction out of the way, there would be no reason to meet up again but, to his astonishment, Mary and Christian had swapped numbers when he wasn't looking and had agreed to go to the ballet together the following month.

'What are you thinking?' he'd fumed to Christian, but he hadn't shared Melvin's concerns.

'She's a lovely lady, Melvin,' he'd said. 'And now she won't mind when you tell her you're meeting me for a drink or whatever. It's just one trip to the ballet anyway.'

But it hadn't just been one trip to the ballet. There had been a dance exhibition at the V&A followed by lunch, wine-tasting at Borough Market and regular Sunday lunches at their house. Sometimes they didn't even consult Melvin on their plans, like today for instance. He'd thought he was meeting Christian, not both of them. Lately, he'd noticed them whispering together, then stopping abruptly when he appeared, and he'd overheard Mary talking to Christian on her mobile the other day, saying: 'Who shall we invite from the station?'. With a dull ache of dread in his stomach, it had dawned on Melvin that they must be planning a surprise birthday bash for his sixtieth next month.

'It's never too late for the truth, Melvin,' Vivienne is saying. But Melvin knows it is too late. It is years and years too late.

'I mean, where does she think you are on these nights?' Vivienne asks.

'Work parties, or training days.'

'If your number's coming, if we can't stop this person in time, you don't want to leave so much hurt behind. What Tristan says is true, sometimes not acting can cause the most harm,' she says.

'Is he OK? Tristan, I mean. He seemed pretty unhappy today,' Melvin asks.

'He's going through his own things,' she says, folding her arms across her chest. 'It's why I haven't told him about this seven-deadly-sins theory. Plus, he'd think I'd well and truly lost the plot.'

'Maybe we all have,' Melvin sighs.

'Why don't you open your envelope with me right now?' Vivienne suddenly suggests.

Melvin looks over at her, her vivid blue eyes staring intently into his. He shrugs and pulls the envelope from his pocket.

'Looks like Gordon had a little look before handing it over,' he says. The envelope seal had clearly been pulled back and resealed.

'No surprises there,' says Vivienne.

'You do it,' Melvin tells her.

Vivienne takes it from him. She turns it over and starts to peel open the envelope.

'Ready?'

He nods.

**You will die aged 61.**

'I'm nearly sixty,' he says.

Melvin stares at the number: 61. Two years away maximum, and actually, right now, the thought of two more years on this planet seems like two years too long. Melvin can't see how he can continue like this but also can't see a way out.

'Do you mind if I keep this?' Vivienne asks, holding up the envelope.

'A clue?' Melvin sighs.

'Perhaps,' she says, pushing the envelope into her bag.

Vivienne excuses herself to 'use the facilities', so Melvin takes the opportunity to switch his phone back on. He's had two more missed calls from Christian, a message from Mary listing out the options for starters at the restaurant. And there's a message from an unsaved number.

**Last night was fun. Let's do it again soon N x**

Melvin draws in a quick breath and pictures hefty, freckled shoulders, an endearing beer belly. N? Was it Nathan, or maybe Noel? What Melvin hadn't told Vivienne was that he wasn't with Christian last night. Christian had been working late and Mary was visiting friends, so Melvin had headed out into the night on his own. At one of the more low-key gay bars he'd got chatting to Nathan-or-Noel about rugby (not something that interests Christian). From beers, they'd moved to Jägermeister and Red

Bull and ended up at a lock-in at an Irish pub, where his new friend knew the landlord who shared out some cocaine. Before Melvin knew it, he was waking up the next morning in a strange house somewhere near Finchley, shame seeping from every pore. Leaving the man sleeping, Melvin had gathered his clothes and flagged down a taxi to take him straight to Janet's wake. As he sees Vivienne make her way back to the table, he deletes the new message. Maybe he should be giving his number more thought. But, right now, the tangled mess of his personal life is more than enough for Melvin to worry about.

'Another wine, Vivienne?' he asks.

# The Lecture
## *May 2017–*
## *eight months later*

**Vivienne**

The man blows his nose into a billowing white handkerchief and peers through wireless glasses at the menu.

'What to pick, what to pick?' he says, then sniffs twice.

'I think I'll go for the sea bass,' Vivienne decides, pushing a strand of glossy hair behind her ear. That morning, Cat had insisted on taking her to her own hairdresser where she'd endured three long hours of highlighting, a dramatic cut and various 'treatments' which, admittedly, had done the impossible and tamed her frizzy hair. Vivienne isn't convinced it will last one hair wash, but, at the minute, she can't stop touching it. Glancing over at her date, she tries to ignore the little voice in her head saying that her makeover is wasted on him. After all, she had promised Cat that she'd give this one a chance.

'I read an interesting article about mercury levels in sea bass recently,' he mutters, more to himself than Vivienne. 'I think I'll go for the tofu curry to be on the safe side.'

Tasteless tofu sums him up quite nicely, Vivienne thinks but just smiles and orders the sea bass, along with a large glass of wine. Then she lets out a little chuckle, which she quickly disguises as a cough, as she remembers Tristan had guessed her date would be vegetarian ('Just from what you've said about him. I bet he orders tofu.'). His insightfulness knows no bounds.

'So, I understand you're a journalist?' her date asks, then sniffs again.

'Yes, for years I worked on a women's magazine, but last year I launched my own website, thanks to my friend Tristan. It's been quite popular and covers some very interesting topics…' Vivienne says, always keen to talk about her 'baby'. She wonders if she should tell her date about the most recent, and most popular, articles on her site: 'How to Have Sizzling Sex in Your Sixties' and 'The Diary of a Granny Stripper…'

'Oh, I avoid the internet like the plague,' her date – Ian-something – says, cutting her short. 'Our office manager keeps trying to enrol me on a course, but I prefer the good old paper and pen and a trip to the library.'

'Right, then,' says Vivienne, unfolding her napkin and then refolding it. 'And where is it you work?'

She tries to listen, she really does, but finds she loses interest after ten minutes of him explaining the minutiae of what is basically book-keeping for an insurance company. Her eyes drift over to the next table where a young couple are clutching hands across the table, whispering excitedly, a diamond sparkling on her ring finger. They exude youth, love, confidence. A wedding, beautiful children, a charmed life lies ahead of them and Vivienne feels a malignant wave begin to rise from her tummy. *No!* She refuses to allow it to take over. *Go away envy, you're not welcome here.* The image of the eagle holding up scales from Vivienne's place setting often drifts into her mind. It has made her reflect on her past behaviour. Had she been an envious person? The answer, she'd concluded, could only be yes. She'd envied all those young male editors who had been promoted above her, envied Cat and her colleagues' youth, her friends with their marriages and children. She is still fighting her envious instincts every day, but she hopes that, in the two years since Serendipity's, she has let go of most of her old behaviour and changed her life for the better. The woman suddenly looks over at her and Vivienne smiles in her direction. Instinctively, she smiles in return but then quickly turns back to her fiancé.

*Focus on your own date, Vivienne...*

'Do you have children?' she asks, as the waiter delivers their meals and she realises that she'll have to stay in this man's company for as long as it takes to eat her seabass.

'Yes, a daughter.' He nods, a smile passing over his slim lips. 'She's quite the academic, currently studying for a PhD in economics along with Japanese business. She's hoping to move over there after she finishes.'

'Oh, you'll miss her, I'm sure,' says Vivienne.

'Yes well, she'll be back every Christmas, no doubt. We don't exactly see eye to eye, she took the divorce quite badly, so seeing her old dad once a year will probably be enough,' he says, concentrating on spearing a lump of tofu with his fork.

Vivienne had been ready to tell him all about Cat and Charlie – her surrogate daughter and grandson as she's come to see them – but now feels that her date would be even less interested than he'd been in her website. Perhaps as bored as she is right now. She's going to kill Cat when she gets home. Ever since she'd found that old picture of James and persuaded Vivienne to tell her the story, she'd been determined to get Vivienne 'back on the dating scene' as she'd put it. Although Vivienne isn't sure she's ever been on that particular scene. The expression makes her think of a play with the characters wearing exaggerated make-up and performing little song-and-dance routines, which she supposes is what dating is like.

Cat's initial suggestion had been to sign Vivienne up to a match-making website, which she had immediately rejected, so then she set about finding her dates. This Ian character had been cornered on the bus by Cat. 'He's tall and good-looking, reminds me a bit of Robert Redford,' she'd said excitedly. After two disastrous blind dates (Sidney with the hair implant and fake tan, who'd spent the whole date regaling Vivienne with every detail of the hotel in Turkey he visited three times a year; and then Vincent, who had flirted with the young waitress at dinner and constantly checked his phone, laughing uproariously at text messages and tapping away responses while Vivienne had tried to make small talk), Vivienne had vowed this would be the last one, and certainly isn't surprised to find that this man is as much like Robert Redford as she is like Demi Moore. He *is* tall and does have a decent head of hair, she has to admit, but she'd happily trade him in for a short bald man with a bit of charisma. Charisma was something James had had in spades.

When Vivienne had got her secretarial job at the age of eighteen (a source of joy and amazement, given her poor typing and shorthand speeds), her mother had taken her to buy some smart blouses and pencil skirts for the office, wagging a finger at her daughter in the mirror of the department store, lecturing her to 'stay away from the office boys, they'll give you *beaucoup de problèmes.*' Vivienne had rolled her eyes, her French mother had lived by the belief that Englishmen were only slightly removed from early man (which conclusion, Vivienne assumed, was based on her monosyllabic father who had spent his life in three different positions: standing on the production line at a plug factory; sitting in his armchair at home; and lying in bed, barely uttering twenty words in between), but all Vivienne had wanted was to earn a bit of money for herself and get some office experience so she could apply to work on a magazine. And yet, James had turned up on her third day in the office, called upon to fix her jammed typewriter. His strong fingers had the machine going again in minutes.

'There you go, Miss,' he'd smiled kindly, hazel eyes meeting hers for a split second. Vivienne had suddenly felt her mouth go dry and wished she'd washed her hair that morning.

'He's useful to have around, but I just feel for his wife. Fancy upping and leaving her after just two years of marriage,' the woman sitting next to Vivienne had tutted when James had gone.

Vivienne had taken no notice of the office gossip, she'd just been happy to have someone who'd asked how she was and listened to the answer. The much older women in the office only spoke to her to point out errors in her letters and to patronise her over her tea-making skills. One day, James had found her sobbing on the back stairs; he'd dashed off and then returned with a milky tea and a plate of ginger nuts. Then he'd kissed her. She'd been so taken aback, she'd burst out laughing before returning the kiss. Her very first. He'd taken her to the cinema, to a bar in Soho for champagne in delicate 1920s glasses and introduced her to all sorts of exotic foods. Her mother had been wrong … until she was right. Two months after they'd met, James had walked into the office looking pale and shaken.

'She suspects us,' he'd whispered. They'd managed to sneak out for a walk, and he'd broken the news that he'd quit his job that morning as his wife Sue had demanded they start afresh in Wolverhampton. Vivienne hadn't been able to take it all in. He'd told her he was separated, and she'd taken that to mean they were going to divorce, but apparently it had been a temporary arrangement. It had all been temporary, including Vivienne. Instead of bawling and making a scene, she had been struck by a sort of paralysis. She'd found herself nodding in agreement with James's plan, walking mechanically back to the office, sitting down at her typewriter and beginning her next letter. She hadn't wanted to show herself up as the eighteen-year-old she was. A part of her had hoped he'd change his mind, but, the next day, his chair stayed empty. And the next day, and the next. That's where, she'd told Cat, the story had ended. The traumatic, heartbreaking, life-altering conclusion was something Vivienne still hadn't felt ready to share.

'What a sleaze,' Cat had cried. 'A married man hitting on an innocent teenage girl like that.'

'I know it looks that way but it really wasn't. He was only a few years older than me, and we had so much fun together. More than that, I felt … *cherished* by him.' Vivienne had shrugged, unable to explain that feeling.

'And you haven't met anyone since, in all these years?' Cat had quizzed, making Vivienne quietly proud, a good journalist knows to keep probing until they get to the answer.

'Well, I haven't lived like a nun exactly…' She'd blushed, remembering that lost weekend in Corfu: glimmering brown back and a chipped front tooth; or the builder from Eastbourne with surprisingly gentle hands. 'But nothing like James again. And, believe me, I've looked. I've spent years and years looking, but in the end I decided that we all get one true love in our lives and he was mine. And Tristan agrees. He says the same about Ellie.'

'Tristan just wants you all to himself,' Cat had teased. Vivienne had rolled her eyes.

Ever since Vivienne's birthday meal, which Vivienne and Tristan had spent with their heads close together, deep in conversation, Cat had kept up this joke that Tristan was her 'toyboy'. As well as their Sunday meet-ups, they often saw each other midweek, too, for dinner in Soho or perhaps the cinema. They have surprisingly similar tastes in films. And TV shows. And books.

Vivienne and Tristan never seem to run out of things to say and Tristan is always so eager to hear her opinion on the world. Vivienne hasn't felt so 'seen' in a very long time. Tristan also opened up about his own life. He has such a talent for putting an amusing spin on excruciating moments, like the time he'd quoted 'those who can't, teach' to Ellie's teacher friends, or when he'd helped out at a trendy bloggers' event and been dismissed as an 'IT goblin'. What with Tristan, Cat, and Charlie in her life now, Vivienne feels that she doesn't need anyone else, but Cat isn't prepared to accept that.

'I'm not giving up on you. I'm finding you a man. Besides, none of us are getting any younger.'

'Fine, fine, what harm can it do?' Vivienne had sighed.

\* \* \*

Vivienne's new social life had kept her busy, but it couldn't totally block the fear of her impending number. In fact, as time went on, she'd found it was ringing louder than ever in her ears. So, two months ago, she'd arranged to meet Tristan at a café near Serendipity's.

**'I need your help with something,'** she'd messaged him.

He turned up armed with his laptop, presuming she'd meant help with her website.

Once they'd ordered their pot of tea and some cake to share, Vivienne had pulled out her notebook.

'What's that?' Tristan asked, pointing to a list of names going down one side of the page.

'Devils,' she'd told him, surprised to feel herself blush.

'What do you mean?'

'I've been thinking about possible suspects linked to the dinner guests,' she says.

'Lord Cooke, Gareth, Bill, Giles...' Tristan had read. 'So, Stella's father, Matthew's bully, Janet's husband ... and lover.'

'Just ideas, but I couldn't find a way to link any of them to the other dinner guests,' Vivienne had admitted.

Vivienne had initially been cautious about bringing up the topic of Serendipity's with Tristan, but lately it had crept into their conversations more and more. Tristan tended towards his original suggestion of self-fulfilling prophecy, believing that Janet had jumped in front of the taxi after becoming obsessed with her number. But Vivienne wasn't so sure.

'So I was hoping you could help with some investigating today.'

He was taken aback when she told him her plan.

'You're going to knock on every door on Salvation Road?' he cried.

'No, *we're* going to knock on every door,' she corrected him. 'I used to do this all the time as a junior reporter.'

'What are you hoping to find?'

'To see if anyone saw the 'devil' lurking around,' she told him. 'Or if they have any footage from the night of the dinner party.'

Vivienne had assigned Tristan the even-numbers side of the road and she'd taken the odds, including the Serendipity's building itself.

'Being back here gives me the creeps,' Tristan had shuddered, before plodding over to number two.

After an hour, they were no further forward. Most of the doors had been slammed in their faces, often accompanied by some choice language. The people who did listen couldn't remember a random winter's night from two years ago. As for CCTV, those that were working had had their tapes wiped after just a few weeks.

Finally, Vivienne had one more house to try: number thirteen.

Knocking on the heavy wooden door, she pictured herself standing there with Tristan two years before. Just two years, and yet so much had changed since then. The people who had come into her life and changed it beyond recognition: Cat, Charlie and Tristan. The people whom she'd met inside this building and who were now gone: Stella, Matthew and Janet.

To her surprise, the door had creaked open.

A short, stocky man with messy white hair, a worn tweed blazer and thick glasses peered up at her.

'What?' he'd snapped.

'Sorry to bother you,' Vivienne said. 'I think a police officer called Melvin Williams has spoken to you. I attended a dinner event here two years ago and I'm just trying to contact the host to … thank them. Do you happen to have their details?'

'I haven't heard from any police officers,' he said. 'We used to hire the place out but don't anymore. A company dealt with it all, the boss was a fella called Brookbanks or Brookham or something.'

With that, he'd slammed the door behind him. Suddenly, Tristan appeared next to her.

'What did he say?'

'He hasn't heard from a police officer, but Melvin told me he'd spoken to him,' Vivienne said, as they made their way to the tube station. 'He gave me the name Brookbanks or Brookham.'

They'd walked together in silence, both lost in thought.

'Why would Melvin say he'd spoken to the landlord when he hadn't?' Tristan wondered out loud.

'I don't know. To be honest, Melvin has disappointed me. He hasn't helped me investigate this at all. In fact, he's impeded the investigation if anything...' Vivienne said.

'His behaviour is certainly ... odd,' Tristan said. 'I tell you what, I'll look that name up for you. See what I can find.'

\* \* \*

A month after her trip to Salvation Road, Vivienne suddenly found herself sitting on the low wall outside her house. Her right hand was throbbing and she'd looked down to see blood pouring from a deep gash in her palm. The last thing she remembered was leaving her house early that morning to pick up the papers. Glancing at her watch, she saw it was after 4 p.m. She'd searched around for her handbag, which always contained a fresh pack of tissues, but it wasn't there. Another fugue state. This one had stolen her bag, about six hours of time and left her bleeding. She'd tried to stand but her head spun so aggressively that she'd been forced to sit straight back down on the wall, using the sleeve of her jumper to try and stop the blood pooling in her palm.

Finally, she managed to wobble her way to the front door, found her spare key under the red plant pot on the windowsill and stumbled her way to her settee, collapsing on to it. Thankfully, Cat had taken Charlie to the zoo for the day, so she'd slept it off without having to answer awkward questions.

But, the next morning, Cat had spotted Vivienne's still-bloody hand and had insisted on driving her to the nearest A&E for stitches. Vivienne explained it away with a story of a smashed glass and clumsy hands. Cat fussed over her for days afterwards, keeping up a constant stream of milky tea, hobnobs and chatter. But the incident cast a dark shadow over Vivienne for days, leaving her wondering if her increasingly troubling fugue states were a message that her number was catching up with her after all. The thought made her more determined than ever to solve the mystery of Serendipity's before it was too late.

\* \* \*

At the school gates, Cat glares at Vivienne.

'What are you doing here? I told you I'd pick Charlie up today, so you could relax and enjoy your date,' she cries, neglecting to even say hello.

'Robert Redford? You should get your eyes checked,' Vivienne snarls back, and then they both burst out laughing.

Charlie's face breaks into a huge smile when he sees her, and Vivienne's decision to leave her date early feels even more justified.

'Do you know, Cat, I think you need to stop worrying about me and sign yourself up for a dating service,' Vivienne says as they drive home.

'I've already told you, Charlie's the only man for me at the minute. Maybe once he's a bit older I'll think about it,' Cat says, her eyes not leaving the road.

Back at home they fall into their usual routine. Vivienne makes dinner for them while Cat sorts out the laundry.

'This one for tomorrow?' she asks, pulling a pale blue blouse from the laundry basket.

'Yes, I think so. I've never been to a university lecture before, but you can't go wrong with a blouse and smart trousers.'

'No, you can't,' Cat says, adjusting the iron so that Vivienne's delicate blouse isn't scorched. She might be haphazard with her cooking and patchy with her cleaning, but you couldn't fault the woman's ironing.

'Gordon's wife and daughter must be pleased they're commemorating his work given everything that happened afterwards,' Vivienne says, throwing some penne into the pan of bubbling water.

'Yes, the stuff in the papers was pretty awful,' Cat says.

Two days after Janet's wake, Vivienne had popped to the corner shop and picked up a pile of the red top newspapers. Of course, most of the news is online now, but she'd never got out of the habit of buying newspapers by the armful, enjoying the smell of the ink, how her fingers turned black after flicking through them. Opening the centre spread of one paper, an image had made her inhale sharply. It was Gordon, blue eyes peering from under his white hood and over his scarf, which was wrapped tightly around his mouth. He must have been caught unawares as his expression is one of fear, like a hunted white rabbit. The headline had screamed: '*TV Doctor's Devastating Decline*', showing this image alongside a freeze-frame of Gordon sitting on the burnt orange *The Morning Show* sofa, his navy-blue suit perfectly skimming his slim frame, a look of confidence-verging-on-arrogance on his face. Vivienne imagined he was explaining to the presenter in his typically patronising fashion exactly why the baby-food diet was not to be recommended. The article went on to talk about a 'worrying' (who was worried, Vivienne had wondered, certainly not the journalist writing the article) TV appearance before he disappeared from the spotlight and left his wife to live a 'hermit's existence' in his small studio flat near the university where he worked. An unnamed student is quoted as saying, 'We are all worried about Dr MacMillan. He looks ill lately, there are rumours going around that he's been doing weird experiments on himself.' A small note at the end stated that Gordon had refused to comment. Although Vivienne wasn't convinced by the content of the article, it did explain Gordon's strange behaviour on the day of Janet's wake.

Then, last week, Dr Gordon's name had been splashed across the same newspaper: *'Dr Gordon Dead from Allergic Reaction'*.

The article had listed all the important work he'd done in the field of nutrition, his 'insightful' TV appearances, and just a line referring to his 'controversial new research'. How he'd ended up eating something containing sesame seeds was unclear, the article had just stated that he'd been found dead in his flat and early reports had shown it was a result of his allergy.

With a heavy heart, Vivienne had opened her hummingbird notebook once again. She scoured the articles about Gordon's death, making notes as she went. He'd eaten an apple pie containing sesame seeds, but she could find no further details about where the pie had come from. An online search showed that sesame seeds weren't a usual ingredient for apple pie. So Vivienne had made her way to Gordon's street, had walked past the block of brand-new flats where Gordon had lived, past scores of baggy-trousered students. She wasn't sure what she was looking for until she spotted one student carrying a cardboard box bearing the name 'Happy Day Bakery'. She walked in the direction he'd come from and found a row of shops, including the bakery. The articles reporting Gordon's death hadn't named the bakery where the pie had come from but, on a hunch, Vivienne had stepped inside the busy shop. She'd got short shrift from the woman who worked there, who snapped that she'd 'told the police already' that her apple pies contained no sesame seeds so, 'God knows why it was inside one of my boxes.'

On the train home, Vivienne had pondered the woman's words. Tristan's self-fulfilling prophecy theory didn't work in this case. Presumably Gordon hadn't known the pie contained sesame seeds – surely there would have been a better way to go if that had been his intention. The only explanation was that someone who knew about Dr Gordon's allergy had baked the pie with the intent to kill him, and then put it in the bakery box. She'd typed out a message to Melvin, asking if what the woman had said was true. She went to press send, then stopped. She hadn't heard from him since Janet's memorial.

Vivienne had then flicked through her notes, from beginning to end. Her scribbled words, interspersed with some drawings, told their own story. Following Stella's death, she'd been sure that a trolling victim was responsible. After Matthew's death, she'd accused Janet. Then her mind had spun off on the notion of this eighth character, this watchful devil who was somehow connected to them all. Even her handwriting told a tale, starting neat at first, proper sentences and punctuation but gradually becoming messier, with crossings-out and random words. Vivienne's desperation clear to see. Her desperation to live. That's when she'd noticed something for the first time. A series of clues pointing towards a killer. And to one person in particular.

\* \* \*

Walking towards the black cast-iron gates of the university, Vivienne takes in Tristan's stooped frame. She'd made a few phone calls and found out that the university was holding a commemorative lecture in honour of Dr Gordon.

'I always wondered if my life would have been different if I'd gone to university,' she says to Tristan as they walk past students with giant headphones and even bigger trainers.

'It isn't everything it's cracked up to be,' Tristan mutters, eyeing the students warily, as if they might pounce on him at any moment and demand he hand over his wallet.

'You didn't enjoy it?' she asks. 'But you made some good friends here.'

Tristan just shrugs. He'd told Vivienne he'd been meeting up with his old university pals once a month for almost a year now. Apparently, they'd even been talking about embarking on a rail trip around Europe, as they'd done as teenagers. Tristan had beamed when he'd told her about this, yet now his mood is dark. He'd taken some persuading to come along today.

'Dr Gordon treated us all like idiots,' Tristan had snapped when she'd suggested attending the commemorative lecture.

'I know, but we saw him at his worst, and it sounds like he's done some important work before all of this. It's only right we go.'

'I'm sure you wouldn't be surprised to hear that I wasn't exactly the most popular kid on campus,' Tristan stuffs his hands in his pockets and marches ahead of her.

Vivienne sighs. She has another reason for attending the lecture but had decided not to confide in Tristan about it when he'd agreed to go along with her.

She has been wondering if his own number is playing on Tristan's mind. His fortieth birthday isn't far away. After that, he has five short years.

As they approach the wide marble staircase at the front of the building, Vivienne sees Melvin reclining on the stairs smoking a cigarette, apparently oblivious to the glares of several students who are forced to step around his large frame.

'Melvin, I didn't know you smoked?' Vivienne says.

'A new habit I've taken up.' He stands and puts his cigarette out under his shoe. 'So, it looks like the great doctor's formula didn't quite work out for him.'

'At least he tried,' mutters Tristan, marching past Melvin and up the stairs.

Vivienne shrugs at Melvin and they follow Tristan inside.

### Tristan

*You can do it, you can do it…*

Tristan looks down at his old, scuffed trainers and wills them to keep going, keep putting one in front of the other until he gets there. His head is bowed down, trying not to see the familiar curved staircase, the chipped pigeon-holes and dusty portraits of long-dead lecturers. But the smell of the place cannot be avoided, that mixture of teenage hormones, pencil shavings, and lemony wood polish. The last few weeks have been bad enough without having to come back *here*, but once again, he'd given in to Vivienne's nagging. He follows the paper signs for Dr Gordon's memorial lecture stuck on the wall with Sellotape. Behind him, he can hear Vivienne and Melvin chatting amiably. He arrives at the lecture hall where a young student hands him a piece of paper, instructing: 'sit anywhere'. He chooses a row three from the back, shuffles along to the end and then slips off his denim jacket, places it on his knees, and ducks his head to read the piece of paper. He doesn't look up but is aware of Vivienne and Melvin settling down next to him.

'OK, Tristan?' Vivienne asks, taking her own jacket off and placing it carefully over her knees. Had he copied that gesture from her or vice versa? He couldn't remember and tries to ignore the irritation that scuttles through him.

'Just didn't want to be late,' he whispers, pretending to be absorbed in the leaflet.

As Vivienne turns to Melvin to ask about his upcoming retirement from the force, Tristan looks down into the well of the lecture hall, where an image of Dr Gordon is projected on to the whiteboard. He is beaming into the camera, a patronising expression on his smug face.

'Good job we got here on time, the place is filling up,' Vivienne says, and Tristan finally looks up. She's right, all the seats in the lecture hall are now filled and there's a line of students standing at the back of the hall with more still streaming in. Tristan does a quick scan of the room and estimates there are 500 students, around seventy-three per cent are men, maybe forty-three per cent are wearing glasses and the average age would be twenty-one.

'Who'd have thought he was this popular?' says Melvin, breathing whisky fumes across Vivienne to Tristan, who wrinkles his nose and turns away.

'Maybe it's more to do with his recent fame,' says Vivienne, making quote marks with her two forefingers, causing Tristan to think of a song his mother sang to him: *'Peter Pointer, Peter Pointer, where are you? Here I am, here I am, how do you do?'*

A quiet falls across the room as a large man with a blond quiff strolls on to the stage. His body moves as if through water, more like he is swimming than walking, with a fluidity and grace not usually seen on a man of his size. He places a small red notebook on the lectern, buttons his pin-striped jacket over the matching waistcoat and takes in the body of people standing in front of him. Tristan would bet he's never seen the room so full and yet he seems totally unfazed.

'Good morning, I am Professor Linus Goodacre. Thank you for attending on this very sad day,' he says, with a slow and deliberate enunciation.

Tristan closes his eyes and suddenly it's twenty years ago and he's standing just where the professor is now, preparing to present to his fellow students. Studying his cue cards, he'd glanced up to see Dave amongst the faces, giving him a double thumbs-up.

Tristan had consistently been top of his class. He'd worked hard on his final-year project, knew it was something well above the capabilities of his fellow students. Sure enough, the room had fallen silent once Tristan had started talking, either as result of them being impressed – or simply confused. He'd trialed the project, which he'd called *Moralia*, with the help of unsuspecting classmates. Following further development, he'd felt sure it had the ability to transform the modern workplace, to give employers unique insight into their staff. In fact, Tristan had already been approached by a handful of IT companies, after a keen lecturer had sent round samples of the work. A sparkling career lay ahead of him, even worldwide fame... Then he'd heard it. A chuckle from the back row. A chuckle of disdain. Instantly, he'd known who the culprit was. Malcolm Hardy had been his closest rival. He'd never scored as highly as Tristan, but he'd made up for it with his confidence during classes, as well as his popularity amongst their peers. Tall, broad-shouldered, rugby-playing, with thick, wavy gold hair like a Romantic poet. In other words, he'd been everything Tristan was not. Any chance he got, he'd try to catch Tristan out, belittle him, make him question himself.

Taking a deep breath, Tristan had counted *two, three, five, seven* ... attempting to contain the heat rising through his body ... *eleven, thirteen, seventeen, nineteen*. He'd resumed his presentation, but then he'd heard another laugh. This time, there had been nothing he could do to contain the white-hot fury surging through him. Without conscious thought, he'd sprinted up the stairs of the lecture hall, dashed along the back row and grabbed Malcolm by his rugby-shirt collar. Despite being much smaller than Malcolm, Tristan had benefited from the element of surprise, and the taller man had fallen backwards on to the stairs, tumbling down. Landing in a heap at the bottom, Tristan saw Malcolm's ankle had twisted to an odd angle, blood poured from a cut on his eyebrow. As Tristan's anger had dissipated, so his apologies had come. Malcolm never played rugby again, and that incident marked the end of Tristan's university life, just a few months before he should have graduated. But, more importantly, it marked the end of his job prospects, too.

Suddenly he feels a sharp nudge in his side, and he forces his eyes open. He is almost surprised to see the professor in full swing to a quiet attentive audience.

'I thought you'd fallen asleep then,' Vivienne whispers. 'It's just getting interesting.'

'Worked late last night,' Tristan mutters and tries to tune back into the professor's words.

'Dr MacMillan had lately turned his attention to the topic of longevity. Now it is estimated that around twenty-five per cent of an individual's lifespan is determined by genetics. If your parents live into their eighties, the good news is that you probably will, too,' he says. A little murmur travels around the room. To these smooth-skinned students, death is still an imagined outcome, something that happens to really old people, even their parents are themselves probably still only in their forties. Tristan's parents are both in their sixties, and, apart from his dad's prostate cancer a while back, they are in very good health. And yet this fact doesn't have any impact on Tristan's own longevity, given that they're not actually his parents.

Tristan's mind flicks back to that day. Following the break-up with Ellie, he'd offered to leave their shared flat and ended up arriving at his childhood home bearing an old holdall and two black binbags. His mother had opened the door and then her arms, tears rolling down her cheeks, as if she'd been the one cast aside by life (that old adage had popped into his head 'a mother is only ever as happy as her least happy child' – which meant Tristan's poor mum didn't stand a chance). That night, as he'd lain in his old single bed, gazing up at the faded poster of Sonic the Hedgehog on the wall, he'd thought: *here I am again*. He'd quickly regressed back to his teenage existence, sleeping in until nearly noon when his mum had pulled open the curtains; eaten a plate of bacon and eggs as she'd fussed around him and then back to his room to work until late. The weekdays passed like this quite easily, but weekends stretched out in all their barren misery. On Saturdays, he'd prolong his lie-in as far into the afternoon as his mother would allow then had a leisurely lunch (couldn't reasonably still call it a 'brunch' at 3 p.m.) followed by a long soak in the bath. His mother would try and persuade him to 'pop into town' with her, which he'd refuse to do, and the evenings would be spent falling asleep on the sofa in front of whatever terrible programme his parents chose to pollute their minds with. Every Sunday without fail, his mum would dress in heels and tights no matter what the weather, his father would be freshly shaved and smelling of Tristan's childhood, and they'd head to church. Alone in the house, he'd taken to exploring the nooks and crannies that had held his attention as a child.

One day, he'd crawled under his parents' bed and pulled out an old shoebox. Easing the lid off, he'd found a series of photos of himself he'd never seen before. For some reason they hadn't made it into the dozens of photo albums on the bookshelf. Tiny Tristan lying on an ugly orange bedspread, naked apart from a cloth nappy; another shot of his mum proudly cradling him as she sits in the old rocking chair; then both parents standing together wearing their Sunday best as his father awkwardly holds him in both hands. As Tristan had lifted the photos one by one to place them carefully on the carpet, a piece of paper had suddenly been revealed. The words had been printed on an old typewriter, the letters not quite aligned, the 's' and the 't' not properly formed. It was clearly one page of a longer document but the content was clear, '... *hereby relinquish full custody of the child and agree to no further contact*'. Adoption papers. Tristan's adoption papers. He'd dropped the letter and searched through the rest of the box, but there had been no other papers like it. Then he'd looked again at the baby pictures. His mother's tummy is surprisingly flat in her yellow twin-set, given the fact she'd recently had a baby. His father's hold on him is unnatural, as though he is not a baby but an unexpected parcel he'd just discovered on the doorstep, a gift from someone…

Tristan grits his teeth and repeats his mantra.

*You can do it, you can do it.*

'The second factor that affects one's longevity is the environment in which they live. By that I mean access to clean water and sufficient food, good healthcare and living conditions. I'd like to think we all benefit equally from these things in 2017.'

Professor Goodacre nods amiably at the hundreds of eager faces smiling back at him.

'Dr MacMillan had turned his attentions to this environmental factor, specifically nutrition and exercise,' he continues.

Then Tristan had spotted a handwritten letter amongst the photos. It was addressed to his father, in confident looping script. In places, the words were blurred and smeared, but Tristan had been able to make out most of it. A woman had written to his dad to say she was pregnant with his baby. The date was February 1978 two years after his parents had married. The year Tristan was born.

'Dr MacMillan had presented me with his research. Some of it, to my traditionalist eyes, was indeed rather unconventional, but he certainly raised some interesting questions. What roles do calorie intake, exercise, and social interaction play in longevity? I'm sure that my accomplished colleague would have gone on to publish his findings. Tragically, his research was unexpectedly curtailed…'

A sob bursts from the front row, and Tristan's eyes are drawn to the two women sitting side by side, holding hands. He finds himself thinking back to the row of beautiful girls at Matthew's memorial. Yet there is nothing staged or insincere about the grief of these women, you can tell that from just the backs of their heads. One woman has brown hair streaked with white, her shoulders narrow and fragile-looking, her tiny frame leaning into the younger woman next to her. Taller and broader, Dr Gordon's daughter holds her reddish-blonde head high to listen to Professor Goodacre while clutching the other woman's left hand with both of hers. Tristan glances at Vivienne, whose terrier-like head is also raised as she takes in the two women and then turns sad eyes onto him. He tries to keep his face neutral as he looks back down at the leaflet, unable to conjure an expression of sorrow he does not feel.

'She had a lucky escape,' Tristan hears Melvin murmur, followed by a small chuckle from Vivienne and then a 'shh'.

Flicking through the leaflet again, Tristan forces himself to focus on each individual word and reads the line *'Dr MacMillan is survived by his wife Elizabeth and daughter Louisa.'* It strikes Tristan how odd that expression is, 'survived by'. As if the three of them had been clinging to an overturned boat. While Gordon had sunk beneath the waves, Elizabeth and Louisa had managed to swim to the shore. Professor Goodacre's words cut through Tristan's daydream.

'I want to leave you all with this thought. The longest ever study of human development, by my colleagues at Harvard University, concluded that the one factor which consistently increased longevity and happiness was not exercise, a certain diet or particular set of chromosomes,' he says, slowing his speech down to leave a full second between each word.

The room is totally silent as they wait for Professor Goodacre's big reveal.

'It is the quality of human contact,' he says and a treacly wave of 'ahh' travels through the lecture theatre. It makes Tristan think of those unbearable TV talent shows his mother loves so much, featuring young children with heart-wrenching backstories, all perfectly engineered to move the audience to tears. Tristan rolls his eye at the professor's self-satisfied expression. He has more in common with Dr Gordon than he probably realises.

'If we can learn anything from Dr MacMillan's tragic passing, it is that we must hold our loved ones close because they are the true secret to a long and happy life.' He glances over at Dr Gordon's wife and daughter with an expression that makes Tristan feel quite nauseated, yet they are nodding in unison. Clearly Dr Gordon hadn't agreed with this sentiment, given he'd moved out of the family home, Tristan thinks.

The white screen now flashes up a series of Gordon's book covers, followed by a picture of his smiling face. His lips are squeezed together as if his mouth is filled with honey. Tristan watches the professor walk over to Elizabeth and Louisa with an expression of just the right mixture of sympathy and sorrow, as if he's saying, 'I'm thirty per cent sad for the death of my colleague and seventy per cent sorry for your loss of a husband and father.' Tristan notices that the professor holds Elizabeth's hand for around three seconds too long. A blush lights up her pale face and a genuine smile creeps on her lips at something the man is saying to her. Tristan stands up quickly, reaching too late for his jacket, which slides to the floor.

'Refreshments in the lobby,' Melvin is telling Vivienne as Tristan bends over to retrieve his denim jacket from behind the chair in front of him. By the time he gets to the stairs, a number of students have pushed in between him and Vivienne, and he sees her frizzy head disappear amongst the crowd of identical floppy-tops with shaved sides. His feet feel heavy as he climbs the steps leading out to a large foyer. Where has Vivienne gone? He slows and stands on tiptoes to try and get a look above the mass of heads but then someone jostles him from behind and laughs right in his ear. He can feel his heart racing in his chest, like a fist punching against his ribcage. Stepping forward, he finds he's suddenly blinded by the light. Sunshine is streaming into the foyer from the large windows in a perfect obtuse triangle. He stumbles a few more steps and accidentally steps on the back of someone's flip-flops sending them lurching forwards.

'Watch it,' the man in front of him barks but Tristan propels himself forward until he's out of the sun's spotlight. He blinks several times and then he sees it. Sees her. A swish of blonde hair, a thick fringe over cat-like eyes, head tossed back, red lips open to throw out that distinctive laugh. It couldn't be. Janet? His heart is pounding now with two fists. He can't take his eyes off the woman sitting at the bar, taking a large drink from a glass of red wine.

'Tristan, what are you doing here?' a voice asks, and Dave is suddenly standing in front of him. He looks from the blonde woman to his old friend and fights an instinct to just run. Run away from this place and never see Dave, Vivienne, or Melvin again.

'Oh hi, Dave, how are you?' He puts out his hand and Dave's long fingers wrap around his own, a look of bewilderment on his face. Tristan remembers now that he's a lecturer. In their brief text message exchanges, he'd never asked where Dave worked. It would make perfect sense for him to have found employment back at their old university.

'I'm fine thanks, just surprised to see you here. Did you know Dr MacMillan?'

'Not very well but I wanted to … err … pay my respects,' Tristan says, eyes creeping back to the bar only to see that the woman has gone. He looks around the foyer but there's no sign of that blonde blow-dry.

'Tragic, isn't it?' Dave says, frowning and running his fingers over his short hair, a habit Tristan remembers from when Dave was still a teenager with hair down to his shoulders.

'Yes,' Tristan replies, nodding and then catching sight of the top of Vivienne's head, straining up to look for him. He turns his back and slouches slightly hoping that she won't spot him. Sweat is starting to drip down his forehead and he suddenly feels so hot in the foyer. The modern design and bright sunlight unwittingly creating a greenhouse effect.

'So what happened to you? I waited for an hour at The George,' Dave asks.

Before Tristan can think of an answer, Vivienne is standing next to him, beaming at Dave.

'I'm Vivienne,' she says, offering him her hand. 'Are you a friend of Tristan's?'

'Pleased to meet you,' Dave responds. 'I'm Dave. We went to uni together.'

'Oh yes, I've heard about you – and your travel plans,' she says.

'Dave's just heading off,' Tristan interrupts. 'I'll walk you to the door.'

He steers Dave through the now-dispersing crowd, mumbling about that 'confused old lady' and how she 'likes a drink or two'.

'So why didn't you turn up, Tristan?' Dave stops in front of the large glass doors. Tristan notices the crow's feet around his eyes, the slight paunch, but he hasn't changed that much. Same long-limbed awkwardness that had always reminded Tristan of a daddy longlegs.

'I'm so sorry. Something came up at work,' he says. 'Let's make another date and I'll be there. Drinks on me.'

Watching Dave make his loping way through the pedestrianised campus, Tristan wonders what to do next. He glances back across the foyer and sees Vivienne and Melvin perched on stools by the bar. Vivienne is clutching Melvin's hand with both of hers, nodding her head as she talks. Tristan knows they will be discussing the numbers. Her mystery number is on her mind more and more, especially as her health seems to be deteriorating (although she's never admitted that to him). Ever since he'd told her his number is forty-five, she regularly turns sorrowful eyes on him, often accompanied with the words: 'Forty-five is no age to die'. He can't bear to see and hear it again. Once he's sure that Dave is out of sight, he pushes through the door and runs.

### Melvin

Vivienne's dry hands feel strange in his. Her fingers are longer than Mary's and, rather than Mary's perfectly painted nails, Vivienne's are plain, cut in neat lines. Practical, no-nonsense hands.

'You've got to take this seriously now, Melvin,' she is saying, her blue eyes paler than ever, fixed intently on his so that it would feel impolite to look away. 'I know you said you weren't taking any notice of it, but that's four dinner guests gone now and your number's up next.'

'For all we know, *you* could be next,' Melvin says. Vivienne whips her hands from his. As she reaches for her notebook from her bag, he sees she's shaking.

'Is that so?' she snaps.

'Well, yes, unless you've found your envelope since I last saw you…' Melvin says, confused by her sudden frostiness

'Let me ask you, Melvin,' she says, glancing down at some notes in her book. 'Is it true that the pie that killed Gordon was put into a certain bakery's box but wasn't actually made by them?'

'How did you know that?' he asks.

'Another of my Miss Marple moments, I suppose you would say,' she tells him. 'So it's true?'

'From what I've heard,' he says, with a shrug. 'What does it matter, anyway?'

'What does it matter? You're a police officer, Melvin. It's the difference between murder and accidental death!'

'Don't tell me you still believe there's a killer out there?'

'How else would you explain it?' she snaps. 'Four deaths, all different but all made to look like accidents. All predicted two years ago.'

'Calm down, Vivienne,' Melvin says, sighing. 'You're right – I can't explain it.'

'So why won't you help me investigate, to try and stop it?' she cries. 'At first, I thought you genuinely believed the deaths were accidents, then I thought you just couldn't be bothered. But now I'm starting to wonder if—'

'Wonder if what?' Melvin says, suddenly understanding. 'If I'm the killer, is that it?'

'Well, are you?' she cries. 'Maybe a killing spree is the perfect way to end your police career!'

Melvin can't help laughter bursting from him. It is such a ridiculous notion.

'No, Vivienne,' he says eventually. 'And I can't believe you would think that. I thought we were friends. Besides, I spent the week Gordon died in Barcelona with Christian. I've even got pictures on my phone, look.'

He hands her his phone, and she quickly flicks through. There's Melvin grinning outside La Sagrada Familia, with Christian at Barcelona's football stadium, eating giant prawns by the sea.

'I'm sorry, Melvin,' sighs Vivienne. 'This mystery is clearly driving me mad.'

'That's OK. I'll confess, too, that Janet's comment about you being the only one who didn't know your number got me thinking at one point…'

'Me?' Vivienne gasps but then sees Melvin is stifling a laugh.

'I couldn't picture it, to be fair,' he says.

'When I found Janet's glove on that roof, I was convinced it was her,' she says. 'Then, I started to look outside the group but couldn't find anyone who linked us all together. And now we're down to three… I don't believe in psychics, as Janet suggested, but every number has come true, every death has been different. It all just feels so … inevitable.'

'Maybe you should take my approach. I feel like I've had a good life, I'm retiring soon, I can't complain,' he tells her.

She shakes her head.

'I've got too much to lose,' she says. 'I'm not ready to go yet.'

They hear a sob from further down the bar and look over at Gordon's wife and daughter, talking quietly.

'I do wonder, though, if the numbers were supposed to be a warning. Maybe there's still time to change them – if we change ourselves,' Vivienne says. 'Do you remember Gordon saying we should *learn from them*? Perhaps that's what he was getting at.'

'Viv, honestly, it doesn't matter to me if I've got one year, ten, or thirty…' He shrugs.

'I'd like to think we still have control over our own decisions, over our own lives, no matter what these numbers say,' Vivienne tells him.

Then Melvin feels his phone buzzing in the pocket of his tight trousers ('skinny' jeans Christian calls them, a word Melvin never thought would describe something he wore). Relieved to have an excuse to drop this intense conversation, he steps off the stool and pulls out the phone. Maybe it's Mary inviting him over for dinner. He'd give anything for one of her lamb roasts right now. He sighs when he sees the name flashing up.

'Where are you?' Christian demands before Melvin has even said hello. From those three words, Melvin can deduce that Christian is angry with him, also a little drunk, and that he is in the company of people he's desperate to impress. None of this is new to Melvin.

'I'm still at the lecture,' Melvin tells him, stepping towards the glass doors at the entrance. Looking out on to the campus, he's sure he can see Tristan's slim back racing away. Strange... 'Just catching up with Vivienne. She's quite upset about the doctor's death.' Melvin glances over at Vivienne, who grins back at him.

'Really? I thought she couldn't stand dull Doctor Gordon,' Christian snaps, and Melvin wonders if he'd ever said this to him. They drink so much lately that he often can't remember what he's told Christian about the dinner party and the numbers.

'Um, I don't think so,' mumbles Melvin, looking down at his bright red Toms, a gift from Christian. Who ever thought canvas was a good material for footwear? Ridiculous.

'I'm with Horatio and Bob at Bugo's. We've been waiting an hour for you,' Christian says now. Melvin can hear the restraint in his voice, the forced softening. Oh, so he's in Richmond with good old Horatio and Bob. Their names as ill-matched as they are.

'Sorry, time got away from me,' he says, glancing at his watch. Then he feels a fresh wave of guilt wash through him when he realises he isn't sorry and has no desire to be knocking back over-priced wine at Bugo's with London's most pretentious couple. 'You boys go ahead and eat. I'll catch up with you later.'

'Oh, Mel, I was looking forward to seeing you. We've been like ships in the night lately.' Christian is whispering now. Melvin knows Christian hates the thought of Horatio and Bob believing their relationship is anything but perfect. 'Melvin and I, we're like chips and gravy,' he likes to tell people, although Melvin would be astonished if Christian had ever sampled that northern delicacy. But he's right, in the last few weeks Melvin has worked late and made excuses each time Christian invited him out with his friends.

'We've got the whole weekend together,' Melvin reassures him now, trying to ignore the tightness squeezing his stomach at the thought of yet another weekend with Christian in his Brixton flat. Because, really, the flat will always be Christian's. Yet that's not where the trouble lies. If only it was.

After promising Christian he'll take him 'somewhere nice' (i.e. expensive) for lunch the next day, Melvin hangs up the phone and goes back to Vivienne. Despite her intensity, Melvin finds her easy to talk to, easy to confide in. She raises one eyebrow at him now and waits to hear the latest from the drama that is Melvin's life.

'That was Christian,' Melvin says, feeling his jeans squeeze his thighs (and everything else in that region) as he sits back up on the stool. 'We live together now. It all came out in the end. Mary knows everything.'

If Vivienne is shocked, she doesn't let on. She nods slowly, inviting Melvin to continue his tale. He takes a deep breath. It's hardly a story that covers him in glory, it must be said.

'You know I told you that Mary and Christian had become friends,' he says. 'Well, they ended up organising a surprise party for my sixtieth birthday last September. I'm not one for a lot of fuss, but they got a bit carried away. They hired the upstairs of a bar in Battersea, filled it with balloons and laid on a ton of party food. Invited half of London, most of my colleagues were there, Mary's family, rugby pals I hadn't seen in years...'

Melvin remembers the moment when Christian had led him up the stairs of the bar, having promised him a quiet birthday drink – and then they'd been greeted by a wall of noise, of gruesome grinning faces, including his wife's. He'd just about stayed on his feet, dizzily pinballing from one old friend to another. Nausea rising in his body, behind his rigor mortis smile, and repeated exclamation of: 'I had no idea.' The evening had been an endurance test, which he thought he'd passed until the end of the night. Most of the guests had gone, most of the food eaten, Melvin had been chatting with a retired copper, the man's rheumy eyes reminiscing about long-dead police colleagues, when he'd heard two (very familiar) raised voices. He'd hurriedly excused himself and rushed over to the banquet where Mary and Christian were squaring up to each other, each clutching a half-eaten plate of cheese cubes.

'They were both three sheets to the wind and you won't believe what they were arguing about,' Melvin tells Vivienne.

'What?' she asks, her eyes wide as if she's watching a Christmas special of her favourite soap.

'Well, Mary was adamant that I only ever ate mild cheddar and wouldn't even touch medium cheddar let alone anything stronger, while Christian was just as confident that my rule was "the smellier the better" and Camembert was my number one,' he says.

'So, who was right? Do you prefer mild cheddar or smelly Camembert?' Vivienne asks, her face serious enough to quiz Michael Gove on *Question Time*.

'That's the funny thing, Viv, they were both right. I only ever ate mild cheddar with Mary and Camembert with Christian, so I didn't know what to say,' says Melvin, picturing the look of abject betrayal on Christian's face when he had hesitated.

'What happened then?'

'Well, of course, Christian couldn't help making a sarcastic comment, something about my tastes changing since he came along, and then Mary burst into tears. It turned out she'd suspected something ever since I'd started talking about Christian and embarked on those 'ridiculous waxes' but hadn't known how to broach it with me,' says Melvin, his hands moving from his eyes to his temples as he brings back that night. Thankfully, there hadn't been many guests left to witness this extraordinary scene.

'Oh, poor Mary,' Vivienne says, sighing and Melvin is pleasantly surprised to hear no blame in her tone.

'I know. We talked it through, and, in the end, decided I should move out. I stayed in a grim B&B for a bit. Now I'm living with Christian,' says Melvin. His hands touch the silver phoenix he wears around his neck, another gift from Christian ('you've risen from the ashes of your marriage, now we'll fly together').

'So are you and Mary getting a divorce?' Vivienne asks. 'You and Christian could get married.'

Melvin sighs. Of course, he'd seen the stories in the papers, pictures of happy gay couples – and Christian hadn't stopped going on about it. But Melvin didn't feel ready to divorce Mary, let alone consider entering into a second marriage. With anyone.

'Not gonna lie to you, Viv, I haven't thought about that yet,' Melvin says, hoping that his number will save him from that conversation at least.  He orders another two glasses of red wine from the bar. Student standards, so not the best, but Melvin isn't fussy. It is one of Christian's (many) complaints about him.

As Melvin waits for his drinks to be poured, he marvels once again at the craving we all have to hear happy endings, to tie stories up in a neat little bow. He'd managed to present his mess of a life into an almost fairy-tale story, with an impossibly happy ending. *Mary had suspected all along, she's upset but she'll get over it, and Christian and Melvin will live happily ever after in their Brixton flat. The End.* But of course, that's not quite the truth. Real life is never tied up in a neat little bow. As he looks down at the pale line on his finger where his wedding band used to sit, Melvin remembers that night. That dreadful night. Thinking of it feels like touching a recent wound, so fresh it's still aching and itchy, getting used to the stitches keeping it together.

People talk about time standing still in those big moments, when a crime is committed, when an accident happens, when a baby is born. Well on that night, it wasn't so much that time stood still, it was as if it disappeared altogether; they entered a vacuum where there existed only them and their memories. As if they were in a darkened cinema watching a show reel of their life together and Mary had control of what was shown. She'd bring up one 'clip' and then slow it down, rewind and fast-forward, searching in the background for clues.

'What about our wedding day? You and the best man went out for a smoke, you were gone for over an hour…' she'd said. 'Those Six Nations rugby trips with your mates, you always came back looking so guilty… And when we went to Crete and stayed at that spa hotel, you were always chatting with that bloke by the pool, what was his name, was something going on with him?'

Mary had thrown accusation after accusation at him, like poisoned darts. Sitting at their old, stained dining table, tiny elbows propping up her moon-shaped face up as tears freely rolled down without being caught in a tissue or pushed away. She'd wanted Melvin to see those tears, to take responsibility for them.

'Of course not. I loved you. I still love you. I was so happy to be marrying you.' It didn't matter how many times he'd told her that there were no other men, no previous indiscretions, her anger and hurt only escalated.

'Did you only stay with me because of the cancer?' she'd asked him at around 5 a.m., the rising sun pushing a sliver of light through a gap in the curtains. Melvin had stood, walked over to the window, pulled the drapes together and was silent.

'You were going to tell me that night, weren't you?' she'd screamed, in a surge of energy that had shocked Melvin. 'You made lasagne and bought some nice wine, as if you were trying to seduce me. I thought you were just being nice, but you were going to tell me about Christian then, weren't you? Well, I'm sorry my cancer got in the way of your good time.' Bitter words that seemed so strange coming out of Mary's mouth.

Finally, at 7 a.m., exhaustion had won them over and Mary plodded to bed as if she was sleepwalking, while Melvin had let his eyes close as he sat on the sofa. When he'd come round, he'd glanced at his watch and saw it was 11 a.m. A mug of hot coffee had been placed on the table in front of him and he'd looked up to see Mary standing by the window in her old, fluffy purple dressing gown.

'You should move out,' she'd said, her voice cold. 'I'm sure Christian will find room for you at his place. There's only one bedroom, but that won't be a problem.'

'Mary, please,' were the words that had shot out of Melvin's mouth. He hadn't even known what he was pleading for, what he'd wanted her to say, but it wasn't this. Not this coldness, not this rejection.

\* \* \*

'Here you go,' the student gives him his change as Melvin shakes his head and hands Vivienne her glass.

'So how's Mary doing now?' Vivienne asks, taking the glass from him.

'Thriving without me,' he admits. 'She's still line-dancing, planning a girls' holiday to Ibiza, got a cracking new haircut.'

Despite everything that has gone ahead, Melvin is proud that he and Mary have managed to piece together a tentative friendship. They talk once a week on the phone and about once a month they meet for a Sunday roast, sometimes back at the old house.

'New haircut for a new man perhaps?' Vivienne wonders aloud.

Melvin starts. Yes of course, that's it. Mary has a new man. He hadn't been able to put his finger on what had changed lately. Her spark was back.

'Well, congratulations,' Vivienne says, holding her glass up.

'For what?'

'You've done it. You've told the truth and you've found the man of your dreams.' She smiles. 'Surely, if any of us have managed to change our destiny, it's you.'

Melvin smiles, too, and takes a big sip from his glass. When he was with Mary, and fighting his passion for Christian, he'd pictured this alternate life they would lead. Melvin free at last from the shackles of his suburban heterosexual marriage. He'd soar through the sky with Christian by his side, enjoying new experiences every day, exploring a world he hadn't known existed. But in practice, it felt like he'd just swapped one marriage for another. He'd swapped the 1930s semi he'd shared with Mary for Christian's cool Brixton flat at the top of a town house. Instead of a roast beef at the dining table on Sundays, he had sushi from a conveyer belt. Where he'd watched *Midsomer Murders* with Mary, now he watched foreign films at the Everyman with Christian. Yet, just three nights ago, when he and Christian were at a club, Christian had stepped outside for a cigarette and Melvin had found himself having sex with a stranger in a toilet cubicle. Bareback too. Afterwards, still smelling the man's floral aftershave on his skin, mixed with his own guilt, Melvin had asked himself *why?* Because the stranger had offered himself up and Melvin had needed to feel his heart race, his senses alight. Or because he couldn't bring himself to say no. And it wasn't like that was a one-off, these moments of betrayal were becoming more and more frequent.

'You know, I'm sure I saw Tristan running away just now,' he says, keen to move the conversation away from him and his 'happy ever after'.

'Running away? He was just walking his friend out, he'll be back in a minute. We're supposed to be going out for dinner.' Vivienne frowns, turning her head in the direction of the glass doors.

'Strange,' Melvin sighs.

Distracted now, Vivienne pulls her phone from her bag and starts to type a message. Melvin finishes his drink and is about to make his excuses, when a shout from further down the bar makes him turn.

'No, Mum,' the girl cries, followed by a panicked 'shush' from the older woman next to her. Vivienne looks up from her phone, glances over and then meets Melvin's eye. It's Dr Gordon's wife and daughter. The mother's face is flushed and streaked with tears, her head shaking and shaking. 'No'.

'Louisa, please. You can't say that about your father,' Elizabeth sobs, her voice low but trembling with desperation.

'But it's the truth. He was a self-centred bore, a hypocrite and an embarrassment by the end. It's better that he's gone,' Louisa fumes, anger magnifying her voice so that the bar is totally silent as her words sink in.

'That's not fair, Louisa. He was your father and he loved you. He'd just lost his way, he wasn't well,' says her mother.

'It's his fault I'm the way I am about my body. He just wouldn't stop going on about empty calories and cellulite,' she says. 'He got worse after he moved out. As if he had licence to be an even bigger idiot than he was before.'

'Louisa, I really think we should carry on this conversation at home,' Elizabeth mutters weakly.

'Don't worry, I'm going anyway,' Louisa says. She hops down from the barstool and marches away from her mother, without a backward glance.

The ten-or-so people left at the bar are all watching Louisa as she pushes through the glass doors and marches up the hill, in the same direction Melvin had seen Tristan running. Behind them, Elizabeth's slim body slumps over even more, her shoulders moving up and down in rhythm with her silent tears.

'Oh love, don't take it too seriously. Her dad's just died. She's clearly hurting. I'm sure she'll come around,' Melvin says, standing from his stool and resting his hand on her slim shoulder.

'Thank you,' Elizabeth mumbles, lifting her head to reveal streaks of mascara down her face. 'But I don't think so. They've never got on. She blames her dad for her body issues, he was very forceful with his advice. It didn't make for an easy home life.'

'Yes, he was quite the preacher,' Vivienne mutters, and Melvin shoots her a frown.

'But he was fighting his own demons,' Elizabeth says, instinctively defending her husband. 'He had an eating disorder, you know. Bulimia. It's what sparked off our separation. He refused to get help. He seemed to think it was normal.'

'None of us are perfect,' Melvin says, suddenly aware of the three empty wine glasses in front of the woman, her slim frame.

'Mrs MacMillan,' a confident voice calls over and they look up to see Professor Goodacre strolling easily towards them. 'Let me escort you to the college brasserie for a bite to eat.'

The man nods at Melvin and Vivienne and then sweeps Elizabeth away. She is dabbing at her face with a tissue and looking up at the professor as if he's just saved her life. Perhaps he has, ponders Melvin as he watches them walk away, their legs perfectly in sync like runners in a three-legged race.

'Dr Gordon was bulimic?' Vivienne whispers.

'Remember how strange he was with his *foie gras* at Serendipity's,' Melvin says, picturing him snatching back his plate when Janet had offered to take it.

'You're right,' Vivienne says. 'And it explains why he ate a whole pie in one sitting.'

Melvin sighs, he's had enough of Vivienne's theories, her prodding, her accusations, her desperation for the truth. He's tired of it all.

'I think I'll head off now, I'm already late to meet Christian,' he says, finishing off the last of his red wine, standing up and performing an exaggerated bow for Vivienne.

'Oh, to be young and in love,' Vivienne laughs, slipping off her own stool, a pained grimace briefly crossing her face. 'I think I'll stick around and see if Tristan shows up. Just promise me you'll think about what I said? There are only three of us left and we need to watch out for each other.'

Melvin nods and walks away from Vivienne, her words 'young and in love' echoing in his mind. He reaches into his pocket, pulls out his mobile to check for the next train into town. Then he switches his phone off and wonders what tonight will bring.

# The Bridge
## *November 2018 –*
## *eighteen months later*

**Vivienne**

Vivienne hears bells ringing from far away. Sunday morning, she's on her way to church. Her mother is clutching her hand, walking a little too fast. She's cross that Vivienne took too long to fasten the tiny gold buckles of her 'Sunday shoes'. Her fingers had felt fat and clumsy under her mother's impatient scrutiny. Vivienne is trying to keep up with her mama's marching legs, while also avoiding the muddy patches on the lane…

She blinks, stares around. She is not a child anymore. She's not trotting alongside her mother on the way to church. The church bells are not far away, they're coming from the church she's sitting outside. Vivienne is suddenly cold, shaking. She glances at her watch. It's just gone 5.30 a.m. Where is she? How did she get here? Patting her hands over her arms, her stomach, her thighs, she reassures herself that she isn't injured. She also still has her bag on her shoulder, which is a relief. Searching inside for clues, she finds her mobile. Her fingers are numb as she unlocks the screen, goes to her messages. The most recent one, sent at 11.02 p.m. last night, is from the friend she'd had dinner with at 8 p.m.

**Thanks for a lovely evening, Vivienne, get home safe! Xx**

She digs her hand into her bag again. There's her hairbrush, her lipstick, her purse, some tissues. Then she finds a crumpled-up piece of paper. It's a receipt from a bar called Unit, timestamped 2.32 a.m. The amount is for £12.62. Expensive for one drink. Who had she been with? There are no other clues in the bag.

Once she's sure that her legs will hold her, Vivienne stands and walks slowly towards the sign in the churchyard. With every step, her legs feel heavier. 'Our Lady of the Assumption and St Gregory Church' the sign announces. She knows this church. It's just off Regent Street. Her old office is walking distance away. She used to come here sometimes, walk around the edge, admire the building. Vivienne takes tentative steps towards the nearest tube station.

\* \* \*

Pulling her laptop on to her knee, Vivienne types 'fugue states' into the search engine. She takes a deep breath and imagines cogs inside her old laptop spinning and whirring as it collates the required information. Tristan had once tried to explain how search engines work, but she'd struggled to concentrate when he'd started using expressions like 'uniform resource locator'. Finally, some definitions appears on her screen. Vivienne clicks on one: *A rare phenomenon characterised by reversible amnesia in conjunction with unexpected wandering or travel*. Vivienne clicks on 'possible causes'. *Can be caused by physical trauma, a medical condition or dementia*. Then she searches for cures of fugue states. All she can find is: *treatment involves helping the person process the trauma causing the condition*.

Sighing, Vivienne puts her laptop to one side. It isn't just the fugue states that are worrying her. The shooting pains in her back and hips have definitely got worse over the last few months and regularly keep her awake at night. She's been too scared to go to her doctor, though. Too fearful of  discovering the worst.

Is this it, has she finally run out of time? Is her number coming for her? And with her investigation no closer to uncovering the truth.

Following Gordon's memorial lecture, and her chat with Melvin, Vivienne had hit a dead-end. Despite her pleas for help, Melvin had 'ghosted' her – as the young people say – in the last eighteen months. Perhaps she'd offended him with her suspicions, though he'd seemed characteristically unfazed at the time. Vivienne had read through her notes over and again, even gone back to Salvation Road, knocked again on the door of Serendipity's, but had no reply this time. Tristan hadn't found anything about a Mr Brookbanks or Brookham, either. Then, as the months had gone by without any bad news, she'd forced herself to push her missing envelope from her mind and instead focus on finding happiness in the present day, on savouring the time she had.

'Vavi, look at this,' Charlie says, bouncing on to the sofa next to her. He's holding out a complicated-looking vehicle he's fashioned from Lego. There are wings, four large wheels and two tusks.

'Oh wow, that is really something,' she says and Charlie beams at her.

Vivienne hears keys in the front door and immediately closes her laptop.

'Mummy!' Charlie says, jumping up from the sofa.

Thankfully, Cat and Charlie were still sleeping when Vivienne had crept in that morning. Over breakfast, Cat had asked if Vivienne could watch Charlie whilst she did some jobs. Vivienne was still exhausted for her night-time adventure, but she'd never say no to a morning with Charlie and his beloved Lego.

'Hiya,' Cat calls, shouting over the pile of boxes balancing precariously in her arms and towering over her head.

'Let me help,' Vivienne says, putting her laptop to one side and standing up as quickly as she can manage. She takes two of the empty boxes off Cat and lays them on the living room floor.

'Thanks,' Cat says, tossing the other boxes haphazardly on to the rug and then dashing straight to the downstairs toilet. She emerges minutes later with flushed cheeks and a relieved expression.

'The baby still tap-dancing on your bladder?' Vivienne smiles. 'You really shouldn't be doing all this in your state.'

'Oh, it's just a few empty boxes. I've got to finish off packing or I'll be bringing the baby home here,' she says.

'I've told you I wouldn't mind,' Vivienne replies, stepping into the kitchen to put the kettle on whilst Cat sits cross-legged in the armchair, knees forming a nest around her bump.

'You wouldn't be saying that when she wakes up every hour screaming the place down,' Cat says. 'What's that you're building there, Charlie Boy?'

As Vivienne waits for the kettle to boil, half-listening to Cat and Charlie's chat, she wonders if it's time to come clean about her health concerns. She'd already told Cat about Serendipity's, the numbers and the sins. God knows, Cat's helped Vivienne search the house numerous times for her missing envelope. She even knows about James – and has finally given up on finding Vivienne a new man ('too fussy, that's your trouble!'), something Vivienne couldn't be more thrilled about. Since meeting Ziggy, busking outside a tube station near her work, Cat has become a hostage of her own happiness. It was the last thing she'd expected when she'd tossed a pound coin into the open guitar case every Friday as she'd passed the man with shaggy hair and large brown eyes, bringing to mind a friendly chocolate Labrador. One day, she'd stayed a little late at work and he was packing up as she'd passed. 'Any special requests?' he'd asked. 'You don't have to pay me this time.'

'I thought, *what a cheesy line*, so I decided to challenge him and asked for Beethoven's "Fur Elise". Well, he didn't skip a beat and gave a perfect rendition. In fact, he kept going for a good ten minutes. My cheeks must have been burning by the end, I was mortified,' Cat had told Vivienne that night. He'd persuaded her to join him for a drink the following afternoon and three months later she'd fallen pregnant.

'I know I swore I wouldn't rush in again, but…' she'd blushingly told Vivienne, who could only reflect her smile and pull Cat into a huge hug. Vivienne had had her doubts – as any surrogate mother would – but when she'd met Ziggy, watched the easy chemistry between them, Ziggy padding after Cat like a loyal puppy, she knew that Cat had done it, she'd found the one who had been looking for her.

Glancing from the open kitchen door to Cat leaning back in the old armchair, Charlie's ear pressed against the bump now, Vivienne smiles to herself. As the pregnancy had progressed, Cat had despaired at how quickly her new addition had made itself known, how soon she'd had to give up her old skinny jeans and give in to 'maternity tents' (her words), but Vivienne herself had relished watching Cat's body change, grinning until her cheeks hurt as she spread her palm across Cat's tummy waiting for the baby to kick. That wonderful spark of life, safely cradled inside its mother's body, with no idea of the love that awaits. Just like a proud grandma, she'd taken to picking up little Babygros and impractical wooden toys whenever she went shopping, batting away Cat's complaints about 'the world's most spoilt unborn baby'.

It was one evening, as Cat had gushed over the cuddly octopus that Vivienne had bought in a chic little gift shop in Richmond, that the ending of her own story had burst from her. She hadn't planned to tell Cat, hadn't even been consciously thinking of him in the moment, but out it came regardless.

'I had a baby when I was eighteen,' she'd said. 'It was James's. I didn't know what was happening until I was about six months along. My mother was horrified, took me to a hospital for unmarried mothers…'

'Oh, Vivienne,' Cat gasped, clutching the octopus to her bump. 'What happened?'

'I went into labour early, had a baby boy, but he didn't survive,' Vivienne had told her, remembering her one and only cuddle with her son, her mother delivering the dreadful news before everything went black.

Tears soaked her cheeks, but Vivienne hadn't pushed them away this time.

'I'm so sorry,' Cat cried, matching Vivienne, tear for tear. 'You were so young to go through that.'

It had felt good to release those words out into the world, to free all the sadness she'd bottled up for so many years. Afterwards, they'd sipped hot chocolate and watched *Look Who's Talking* on Netflix, Cat howling as John Travolta and Kirstie Alley celebrated their son's potty-training success with the song 'Pee-pee on the potty!'.

That night, lying in bed, Vivienne had pictured herself holding Cat's baby, that first clutch from tiny hands, that first smile, that first word. So much to look forward to. She'd crossed her fingers, *please don't let my number come before I meet the baby…* Vivienne had made a silent promise with herself that, after the baby came, she would make an appointment to see her GP about her aches and pains, even mention the fugue states and, if it was nothing serious, then of course she'd tell Cat. But until then, she saw no reason to put a blot on Cat's happiness – or her own. Her doctor would no doubt dismiss her symptoms as the usual aches that ageing brings, she tells herself. Vivienne had eventually drifted off to sleep, having still not shaken the creeping fear that her number was close.

Inevitably Ziggy's gain had become Vivienne's loss and six months into the pregnancy Cat had gently broken it to her that she and Charlie were moving into his place in Blackheath (turned out Ziggy has a very successful logistics business and busking is just a hobby – with all proceeds going to charity). Over the last few weeks, Cat had incrementally deleted herself from Vivienne's cottage. The colourful boxes of Charlie's toys, Cat's endless supply of shoes, cosmetics, and various animal-print accessories had been paraded through Vivienne's house and out of the front door.

Today, Cat and Charlie's last few things would fill these boxes and they'd be saying goodbye tomorrow. Not for good, of course. They'd already arranged to take Charlie to watch a film the following weekend and planned a trip to a health spa next month. But still. Vivienne would never wake up to the feeling of Charlie climbing into her bed, snuggling into her back, and telling her about his dreams of wolves, dark forests, and Peppa Pig. Or to the smell of coffee, emanating from her own mug plonked on her bedside table by a harassed Cat, despite Vivienne insisting she doesn't need to. Or wake up at 2 a.m. on the sofa, head to head with Cat after they'd dozed off whilst drinking their 'one for the road'. But she could never deny Cat the hard-won unexpected happiness that has knocked at her door. And it's not like Vivienne would be plunged back into her lonely life before they'd moved in. She has family now, even if they live on the other side of London. And she has Tristan, too.

Splashing milk into the mugs, a needle of sadness pierces Vivienne's heart at the thought of her friend. After he'd run off following Gordon's tribute lecture, he'd avoided her calls for a week. Finally, she'd managed to coax him back to life and he'd opened up about his struggles at work and about the previous string of bad luck he'd endured in his professional life, bosses who'd refused to pay him, a start-up company he'd put everything into that was sold from under his feet. Then she'd got him talking about his university days and his eyes had shone as he'd spoken about some software he'd worked on back then. He'd called it *Moralia*, a clever-sounding program that helped employers create profiles of their staff members. Vivienne had encouraged him to go back to it and that had led to some interest from a company in Silicon Valley, which they'd cautiously celebrated over champagne cocktails in Covent Garden. But, over the last few months he'd retreated once more. Last week, he'd failed to show up at Vivienne's birthday lunch, leaving Cat fuming and Vivienne concerned.

'You know, I'm worried about Tristan,' she says now, carefully handing Cat her tea. 'He was so excited about the software. When the company declined in the end, he seemed to take it well, but he's gone quiet on me again. I haven't seen him in weeks. He hasn't answered my last three phone calls, or my umpteen text messages and emails.'

'He's probably just licking his wounds,' Cat says, with a shrug. 'You know what he's like when he gets in one of his moods.'

Vivienne slowly lowers herself back on to the settee and considers how Cat has never really warmed to Tristan. To Cat, his quiet thoughtfulness translates as moody, and his occasional directness is 'bloody rude'. She just doesn't understand him, and Vivienne no longer tries to explain. In her mind, they've become her bickering children.

'Well, I'm not giving up. Without Tristan's advice, I wouldn't have you, or Charlie, or my website. I *can't* let his fortieth birthday pass by without a celebration,' Vivienne insists, sounding more confident than she feels.

'Tristan is lucky to have you – as we all are.' Cat smiles and Vivienne unexpectedly feels the prickle of tears itching her eyeballs.

'So did you hear back from the caterer?' she asks. Oh, and Cat's engaged. Six months after the baby comes, she and Ziggy are planning to tie the knot in Richmond Park.

Cat opens her mouth to answer, when Vivienne's mobile starts to ring.

'Who can that be?' she says, picking it up and seeing an unsaved number flashing up. She answers.

'Vivienne?'

'Yes, speaking.' She doesn't recognise the voice.

'I'm so sorry to ring you like this. It's Mary, Melvin's wife … ex-wife. I found your card, and Melvin always talks about you. I didn't know who else to call.'

'Mary, hello. So nice to hear from you. I've heard so much about you, too.'

'Melvin is…' Mary starts, then Vivienne hears her stop and take a breath. 'He's in hospital. They said he took some drugs, which I can hardly believe. He's on a life-support machine.'

Vivienne's legs fail her and she drops down on the sofa. The familiar fingers of doom clutch her stomach once again. Melvin's number has come for him, just as she'd known it would.

'Oh, Mary. I'm so sorry,' she finally splutters as Cat watches her, her tea frozen halfway to her mouth.

'Melvin?' she mouths, and Vivienne nods.

'It was his sixty-first birthday yesterday, and I'd dropped a present off at his,' Mary explains. 'He was so excited, had all these plans to go out celebrating with Christian and that lot.' Vivienne hears her spit out the name, as if it tastes rotten in her mouth.

'Which hospital are you at?' Vivienne asks.

'St George's,' Mary says. 'But you don't need to—'

'I'll be there in thirty minutes,' Vivienne says and then hangs up.

\* \* \*

Twenty-eight minutes later, Vivienne marches through the revolving doors of St George's Hospital. She'd said a hurried goodbye to Cat and Charlie, hardly the heart-wrenching, protracted moment she'd been picturing, but she knew she had to get to the hospital.

'You've never even met her,' Cat had spluttered, but Vivienne had just shaken her head, like a duck brushing off rain from its feathers. She hadn't met Mary, but she *knew* her.

'I'll see you at the weekend, send my love to Ziggy,' she'd shouted, heading quickly for the train station. Cat had suggested calling a taxi, but, on a Saturday night, Vivienne knew the train and tube would be the quickest way. And she knew she had to get there quickly. Before heading down to the Underground, she'd typed a message out for Tristan.

**Mary rang, Melvin's at St George's Hospital, heading there now.**

When she came up the escalator at Tooting Broadway, she'd pulled her phone from her bag to see if he'd responded. She'd watched her phone find the signal, then stay silent. Vivienne hadn't been surprised. Ever since she'd told Tristan about Melvin's affair with Christian – and then how Mary had found out about it – he'd been cold whenever she mentioned him, mumbling something about 'lies teaching him the degradation of the world'.

Vivienne walks into the hospital foyer and stops in front of a large sign listing the different departments. Then she spots a petite woman with an elfin haircut and the tiniest wrists she's ever seen. Her dainty ankles disappear into pink ballet pumps. Graceful is the word her mother would have used, or rather the French version '*gracieuse*'. Vivienne is amazed how French translations pop into her mind, all these years after her mother's death. In fact, she finds she thinks of her mum more as she gets older. And out of nowhere, she misses her.

'Mary,' Vivienne says, and the woman turns to face her. Small herself, Vivienne is unused to looking down at another person, unless it's Charlie. Against her six-foot-five husband, Mary must feel tiny. And yet there's a strength behind her eyes.

'You didn't need to come, but thank you,' Mary says. 'Since the separation, our mutual friends have fallen away, and I'm afraid my own friends and family have no time for Melvin now.'

'Shall we go and find a cup of tea?' Vivienne suggests.

Minutes later, the two women sit opposite each other in the hospital café, stirring sugar into their teas.

'What happened?' Vivienne asks.

'I only know bits. Christian isn't saying much, unsurprisingly. They'd been to a late club in Chelsea and then back to his flat. He called an ambulance when he found Melvin lying on the floor. God knows how long he'd been there. Christian admitted they took Ecstasy pills but claims he doesn't know where they came from.'

'Must have been from a dodgy batch,' says Vivienne. 'Did the doctor say it contained PMA?'

Mary gives her a strange look. 'Yes, she said something like that,' she says.

'Will he be OK?' asks Vivienne, fearing she already knows the answer.

'I don't think so. They say his body isn't responding. If there's no change in the next few days, I think they'll suggest switching off his life-support machine.'

Vivienne looks at Mary's pale face and it dawns on her that, since she's still married to Melvin, it is she who must sign the forms and agree to let her husband die. This woman who has overcome cancer, accepted a cheating husband, found the strength to keep him in her life and support him no matter what. And suddenly Vivienne is furious. Furious at this Christian chap for handing Melvin the drug that killed him, furious at Melvin himself for his lackadaisical attitude towards his number, and furious at whoever – or whatever – invited them all to

Serendipity's in the first place and handed them each their death sentence.

'I'm so sorry,' is all Vivienne can think to say. And it's so inadequate.

'I'm sorry I've dragged you here,' Mary says, now looking up into Vivienne's eyes. 'But I thought you might be able to answer my question.'

Vivienne holds Mary's gaze, trying to keep her breathing even, to give nothing away. But with Melvin unlikely to survive, and after everything she has been through, surely Mary deserves an honest answer to whatever her question is.

'Something happened around three years ago that changed him,' she says. 'He went to a work dinner party and came back different. I couldn't put my finger on it, it was so subtle at first, but it escalated and then everything unravelled. Christian suddenly appeared in his life – in our lives – and then Melvin finally admitted he was gay. But even after he'd left and was living with Christian, he seemed to still be losing himself. I just didn't imagine he'd ever touch drugs, not at his age and having been a police officer for all those years.'

So Melvin hadn't told Mary about the numbers. How much should Vivienne say? She's only just met Mary, doesn't know how she will react, doesn't even know if she'll believe her. But she's right, since the dinner party, Vivienne, too, had watched Melvin gradually lose his grip on his own life. His betrayal of his wife, his affair with Christian, the all-night partying. Every time Vivienne had seen him, he'd drifted further out to sea, allowing the increasingly wild waves to throw him here and there. The last time they'd spoken, at Gordon's memorial lecture, he'd told her a story of 'happy ever after' and yet he'd still seemed unsettled, unconvinced of the words he was saying. He'd tried to act like his number hadn't bothered him, but Vivienne suspected that the opposite had been true. She'd tried to warn him, tried to give him a chance to change things, but it hadn't been enough. He'd kept running from his number and, in the end, he'd been caught.

Taking a deep breath, Vivienne explains to Mary about the numbers, the sins and the deaths.

'Now, there are only three of us from the dinner party still alive,' says Vivienne. She lifts up her tea and takes a sip, her mouth suddenly so dry.

Mary looks down at her cup, wraps both hands around it and shivers.

'So Melvin's number is sixty-one?' she asks and Vivienne nods.

'I know it sounds so far-fetched…' she says, then stops herself from saying more. Mary stays quiet, sips her tea and looks out of the window, at the busy car park. It's Saturday night, but try and tell that to the people who own those cars: patients, hospital staff, visitors.

'If I didn't know for sure that Christian is responsible for what's happened to Melvin, I'd be wondering which guest was the murderer,' Mary says, her voice with a dreamy timbre. 'The way you described the restaurant brings to mind the Agatha Christie novels I read during chemo.'

'Yes – it's just like my favourite book, *And Then There Were None*,' Vivienne says. 'I had the same thought at first…'

'And what's your number, if you don't mind me asking?'

'Oh, I don't know. I lost my envelope not long after the dinner party,' Vivienne splutters, noticing the nervousness soaking her words.

Mary raises her eyebrows and blows on her tea. 'That's … strange,' she says.

'I don't think—' Vivienne starts to reply but isn't sure what she doesn't think. Anyhow, Mary's mobile goes off. She answers it and Vivienne watches her face drain of any colour. It's over.

'I've got to go,' she says, standing up quickly.

'Yes, of course. Ring me if you want to talk again,' Vivienne calls, but Mary is already out of earshot, her tiny, elegant feet barely making a noise as she races down the corridor to her dying husband. Vivienne knows how this will end. She breathes out and continues to sip her tea, taking in Mary's words: '*which guest was the murderer*'… Vivienne thinks back through her investigations, the red herrings, the dead-ends. The glove she'd found on Matthew's office roof, Janet slicking on her lipstick as Vivienne accused her of murder. Then discovering the seven-deadly-sins link, her list of devils, her return to Salvation Road with Tristan, the Happy Day bakery. Gordon's parting words '*learn from them*'. Tristan's self-fulfilling-prophecy theory. Melvin's refusal to help her and his laughter when she'd accused him.

Then her phone rings.

'Hello, stranger,' she says. 'Where have you been hiding?'

'Sorry, I've just been busy with work,' Tristan says. 'How's Melvin?'

'Not good. I've spoken to Mary. She says he took a dodgy pill on a night out with Christian. He's on life-support and not responding.'

She hears Tristan breathe out.

'Poor Mary,' he sighs.

'And then there were two,' Vivienne says.

\* \* \*

Vivienne is emptying her big black handbag ready to take to Melvin's police memorial drinks the following day. A piece of black paper drops on to her bed and she gasps. For a second, she thinks she's finally found her missing envelope but then she sees Melvin's name on the front and remembers taking his empty envelope following Gordon's lecture. At the time, she'd noticed a little symbol on the back, tucked away in the corner. Now finally, she puts on her reading glasses and takes a close look at it. The symbol is lightly embossed and seems to show the letters EMB in decorative scroll. Grabbing her laptop, she types the letters into Google, but thousands of responses come up, everything from insurance companies to the European Milk Board. So she adds 'printing' to the search, and 'London'. That narrows the list down and she works her way through. One catches her eye, in central London. She clicks on the website and her blood runs cold.

'Just popping out,' she shouts to Cat and quickly pulls the front door closed.

Twenty minutes later, she's walking up the tube steps, arriving on an all-too-familiar road. A young woman overtakes her impatiently, her large bag knocking against Vivienne's side, leaving a loud sigh in her wake. Vivienne remembers feeling frustrated with all the slow walkers around the city, back when she was rushing around herself. *When did she become one of the slow walkers?*

She stops outside the printers' shopfront, catches her breath before stepping inside.

'Vivienne! So lovely to see you!' the woman greets her.

* * *

*Where is he?* Vivienne glances around the room and looks at her watch again. It's not like Tristan to be late. In fact, he's usually several minutes early. The tardiness of other people is one of their pet topics. 'Since when did the whole world start running ten minutes late?' he'd say, and that would set them off for a good half-hour comparing stories of colleagues and friends who regularly turned up twelve to fifteen minutes late without an apology or explanation. More than seven minutes earned an apology and more than ten minutes earned an explanation, and not just 'I don't know where time went,' which was highly ridiculous in Vivienne's opinion because time is one of life's few constants. Every minute, every hour is always the same length, it is not a moveable feast, thank God. Tristan always agrees wholeheartedly with Vivienne about this, so why is he now running late? He'd promised he'd come and support Vivienne and Mary. Vivienne had recently read an article linking panic attacks with suicide and now she worries about Tristan whenever he doesn't respond to her.

'Tristan will be here soon,' she says to Mary, for the third time. Mary nods and continues to watch the police officers moving around the working men's club. Every few minutes, one ambles over to offer his condolences. These men (it is mostly men here) are professionals when it comes to speaking to the grief-stricken. You don't hear the go-to 'I'm sorry for your loss' from them. Oh no, their words are considered, personalised, heartfelt you might say. 'He was a fantastic copper, one of our best.' 'He taught me everything I know.' And, somewhat unexpectedly, 'I felt his presence this morning when I was shaving.' And yet Vivienne has noticed how they are keeping their distance. There is something unsaid in this room, perhaps it's the unexpected manner in which Melvin died, or perhaps it's something else. She wonders if Mary can feel it, too.

'My friends were always jealous of our marriage, you know,' Mary suddenly says, looking down at her perfectly pink nails.

'Oh, yes?' Vivienne prompts. Like being a parent or living with a deadly disease, Vivienne always thinks that marriage is something that remains a mystery to you until you do it. She has friends who have married the most unlikely of men, who grow to seemingly hate each other through the course of their marriage, and yet they stay together. Vivienne had once made the mistake of blurting out to her friend, Celia – who'd been mid-rant about her vile husband, Harry – 'Maybe it's time to speak to a divorce lawyer?' and Celia had been so horrified, so offended that Vivienne spent the rest of their lunch apologising and then ordered a bouquet from Interflora the next day. Even now, years later, she's not sure Celia has fully forgiven her. Perhaps it was a generational thing. Cat always seems to be talking about friends of hers who are getting divorced just a few short years after she'd danced at their weddings.

'They would say, "Melvin is so devoted to you",' Mary continues. 'He always held my hand, never forgot a birthday or anniversary, he kept the garden immaculate, he was a fantastic cook, he wasn't a slob or a drunk like some of their husbands.'

'He loved you, Mary.'

'Yes, I suppose he did, in his own way,' she whispers. 'I've been thinking about what you said about sins, Melvin's being sloth. I suppose there have been times when he's looked the other way for an easy life. I remember one occasion, when he came back from a night out and told me he'd stopped a gang attacking someone in the street. He'd taken the poor chap to hospital to be patched up and promised to write up a report at the station. A week or so later I asked him about it and he just shrugged, said he'd forgotten and that the lads probably would never have been charged anyway.'

Vivienne takes in Mary's words and gazes out of the window at the busy Londoners marching down Bishopsgate. She thinks back to her last conversation with Melvin. How he'd told her that he and Christian had moved in together after their secret had been spectacularly exposed and Vivienne had congratulated him on his 'happy ever after', been impressed that he was no longer living a lie. But now she sees that he'd just followed the tide once again. This time, into Christian's arms. Yet he would have drifted in any direction, depending on the strongest current.

As she watches, she sees Tristan crossing the road and walking slowly towards the club. His head is down, his brow furrowed, his right hand gripping the leather satchel he wears across his body, as if he's protecting his heart. Vivienne shivers: she hates to see her friend looking so sad.

'Here's Tristan,' Vivienne says as he pushes open the door and walks towards their small table. He gives Vivienne a quick kiss on the cheek and then crouches down low next to Mary, taking her hand and speaking in a whisper, his words out of Vivienne's earshot.

As Tristan moves to sit on the stool beside Mary, she is beaming, nodding, tears rolling down her face. This is what Cat doesn't see about Tristan, Vivienne thinks. Moments like these, when he knows just what to say, just what that person needs to hear. Tristan insists on ordering them more drinks and heads to the bar, just as another police officer walks towards their table.

'Mary, I'm so pleased you came,' the familiar man says. He's tall and slim with angular cheekbones jutting against flawless skin, putting Vivienne in mind of a long-distance runner. Not an ounce of fat on him. He's objectively handsome, but Vivienne herself prefers a chunkier chap, hates the idea of feeling large when compared to your other half.

'Oh, hello, Christian,' Mary snaps, then Vivienne remembers where she'd seen him before – in the holiday pictures Melvin had proudly shown her eighteen months ago.

The temperature at the table suddenly drops by about ten degrees. Mary picks up her empty wine glass and pretends to take a small sip.

'I know we can never be friends after everything that has happened. But I want you to know that I am heartbroken, too. Like I told my colleagues, I have no idea where that pill came from, but I take full responsibility for Melvin's … passing…'

Christian delivers the words looking down at the table, takes a breath and finally looks up at Mary. His eyes are haunted, it's the only way Vivienne can describe them. He is telling the truth, his heart *is* broken and, even worse, he believes it's his own fault. Vivienne's stomach spins.

'Thank you, Christian. I'm sure Melvin would have been *touched* to hear that,' Mary spits back at him. Her voice is low, and each word is like a bullet in Christian's side. Visibly wounded, the man scuttles away from them, nearly knocking into Tristan who is carrying their drinks over.

'Mary…' Vivienne says, reaching for her hand. Tristan sits down quickly and raises his eyebrows at Vivienne.

'The cheek of the man,' Mary mutters through clenched teeth. 'He pretended to be my friend while all the time he was sleeping with my husband. And then he does this. I can't – I won't – ever forgive him.'

Vivienne remembers Melvin telling her how Christian and Mary had got on famously before the truth came out. How they'd enjoyed theatre trips, art exhibitions and talked endlessly about their shared passion for dance. All of that had been blown apart when Christian had told her about his affair with Melvin. And now, here they are, Melvin is dead, with both Christian and Mary grieving for him; two hearts broken, but unable to find comfort together. *Melvin – by doing nothing, you created one hell of a mess,* thinks Vivienne.

'Oh, Mary,' she sighs.

'You know, Melvin was going to tell me at one point and then the cancer came back, and he had no choice but to stay with me,' she says.

'He had a choice,' Tristan says gently. 'We always have a choice. Some are just harder than others.'

'You're right, and I'm choosing to leave right now.' Mary stands, picks up her handbag and marches towards the door. Her chin is pushed forward in indignation.

Vivienne opens her mouth to call after her and then closes it again. She can't blame her for leaving. She can't blame her for any reaction, really.

'Should we follow her?' she asks Tristan.

'I didn't hear it all, but I saw Christian's face afterwards. I think Mary has said her piece and probably needs some time alone now,' Tristan says. 'Let's go somewhere else.'

Vivienne nods. They quickly polish off their drinks and then head outside. Without discussing it, Vivienne flags down a black cab and ten minutes later they're sitting down at their favourite Italian restaurant on the Strand. In fact, they don't speak again until Tristan has a bottle of Peroni in front of him and Vivienne a red wine.

Finally, Vivienne looks over at her friend and takes a big drink of her wine.

'I think I'm the killer,' she tells him.

## Tristan

It isn't until Tristan has taken a sip of his beer that he registers what Vivienne has just said.

'What?' he cries, putting his bottle down a little abruptly, sending a clanging sound through the restaurant. The tourists on the table next to them look over, eyebrows raised, perhaps hoping for a lovers' tiff.

'*I think I'm the killer,*' she whispers once they've looked away.

'I think you've finally lost the plot,' he splutters. 'Why on earth would you say that?'

'Ever since Serendipity's, I've been having these fugue states,' she explains.

'What are they?' Tristan asks.

'Periods of time when I'm awake and doing things but my brain sort of checks out. I lose hours and come to with no idea where I've been, what I've done,' she babbles, holding her head with both hands.

'You didn't tell me about this,' Tristan says, reaching across to hold her hand. For the first time ever, Vivienne snatches hers back, her eyes on the table. She's ashamed, Tristan realises.

'I didn't want you or Cat to worry about me,' she says. 'I had my first one years ago, aged eighteen, when something very traumatic happened to me. Then, after Serendipity's, they came back, and I've had one before every death.'

'Well, that must be a coincidence,' Tristan says. 'Just a response to the stressful situation.'

'That's what I thought, but then I spoke to Mary at the hospital. She asked about my number and I suddenly felt so guilty. It got me thinking, I *am* a likely suspect. I love crime novels and detective TV shows, could have picked up ideas from there. Both Janet and Melvin have pointed out that I'm the only one who doesn't know my number. And these black-outs. Who knows what I was doing during those missing hours!

'I had one before Melvin died and found a receipt from a bar near where he'd been that night,' she cries. 'Another time, I came to, and I'd badly hurt my hand. If I can hurt myself without knowing, I could just as easily have hurt someone else.'

'Vivienne, it just doesn't add up,' Tristan says gently. 'Take Melvin, for example: there's no way you could have sourced a dodgy pill and then somehow encouraged him to take it, in the space of a few hours during one of these fugue states.'

Vivienne takes a deep breath, out and in.

'I suppose you're right,' she says. 'And, with Gordon, I'd have had to bake a pie filled with sesame seeds and deliver it to him without being spotted.'

Tristan nods, passes her a napkin.

'Besides, you're not capable of murder,' he tells her. 'You just don't have it in you.'

'Do you think?' she cries, finally looking up at him.

'I really think.'

Vivienne takes another big gulp of her wine. Tristan notices that her hand is still shaking but she seems a little calmer.

'There's one more thing that's bothering me,' says Vivienne.

'What's that?'

'I looked into the dinner-party invitations. It turns out they were made in a printing shop near my old office,' she says.

'OK...'

'I used to go there quite regularly with jobs for the magazine. They know me well. I hadn't been in years, but they remembered me when I called in the other day...' she explains, getting worked up again.

'That doesn't mean anything,' Tristan tells her. 'It's central London, half of the city could be using that printers.'

'You're right, Tristan,' murmurs Vivienne, polishing off her glass of wine. 'I'm sorry to get so upset – especially on your birthday.'

'To be honest, I hoped this one might pass by without a celebration...' he said.

Vivienne pulls a tissue from her bag, blows her nose loudly and then reaches inside her bag again, pulling out a little black gift bag.

'Happy fortieth,' she says, placing the bag on the table between them.

'You didn't need to get me anything.' Tristan blushes. His parents had given up on buying him presents years ago, instead just emailing him online vouchers so he could choose what he wanted. He had forgotten that other people actually wrapped up gifts for birthdays.

He reaches inside the bag and finds a brown leather cube, worn in the corners. Squeezing it open, a pearlescent watch face is revealed, with two fine gold hands, pointing to 8.10 p.m.

'Oh,' he murmurs.

'It was my father's,' says Vivienne quietly, looking down at Tristan's hands. 'I notice you always wear that old plastic one, so I thought you might like it.'

He opens the small card inside the bag and reads what Vivienne has written.

*To my dear friend Tristan, time is on your side.*

'Thank you,' is all Tristan can say. It's quiet in the restaurant, but all of a sudden his ears are ringing, as if waves are crashing into his brain.

'It's not a big deal.' Vivienne turns her attention to the menu. 'It was only gathering dust in my drawer.'

Vivienne orders spaghetti carbonara for herself and a pepperoni pizza for Tristan while he silently stares at the watch face. Fighting his instinct to close the box and push it aside, Tristan slowly removes his Casio, pushing it into his pocket and carefully puts the watch on his wrist. It's clear he is a smaller man than Vivienne's father had been as the buckle pushes through a pristine hole two above the one he'd used. The watch's brown leather strap is ridiculously large on his arm. He feels like a schoolboy playing dress-up. He looks at it and breathes in through his nose… *Two, three, five,* and out through his mouth… *Seven, eleven, thirteen.* It's no good; he can't escape the feeling of a handcuff tightening around his wrist. Vivienne starts talking and Tristan forces himself to listen.

'Well, Mary wasn't pulling any punches,' she says. 'Can't say I blame her, though. The way Christian befriended her, took her to the ballet, the theatre, all the while having an affair with her husband…'

As he lets Vivienne's words wash over him, Tristan stares at the watch on his wrist. The leather around the hole that Vivienne's father had used is slightly split. He wonders what sort of man he had been.

'Before you arrived,' Vivienne babbles on, 'she was talking about Melvin, how he'd been targeted by racists during rugby games as a young man.'

'Really?' murmurs Tristan, only half listening.

'She thinks that's what made him so laidback about things, just lived his life under the radar, not wanting to make a fuss, not wanting to draw attention to himself...'

A waiter appears with their meals and carelessly plonks them down on the table.

Tristan lets out a long world-weary sigh.

'So, what's been going on with you? You've been quiet these last few weeks. Are you disappointed about your *Moralia* project?' Vivienne asks.

'It's not that.' He shakes his head, picking up his cutlery.

When he'd told Vivienne about *Moralia*, in the most basic terms, she'd jumped on it and encouraged him to revisit the program. So he'd spent a couple of weeks working on it then had emailed Raymond, a graduate from his class who had gone on to work for a successful company in California, telling him about the software. Expecting to be ignored or quickly rebuffed, Tristan had been astounded when Raymond had replied within hours eager to hear more. That weekend Vivienne had insisted on buying champagne and toasting him, despite Tristan's protests.

'So, what's troubling you?' Vivienne asks, resting her serviette on her knee without taking her eyes off him.

'I ... met up with Ellie last month,' he admits, cutting his pizza into ten even slices.

'Really?' she asks, letting the spaghetti on her fork plop back down onto her plate. He'd told her about Ellie, about how she had broken his heart when she'd abruptly ended their relationship. Vivienne had often suggested he get in touch with her, to try and 'get closure', an American term that makes him cringe when she uses it.

He takes a big bite from his pizza and chews it slowly, trying not to give away the twist in his stomach when he remembers that evening. That same night, after he and Vivienne had got through two bottles of champagne, Tristan had been buzzing from the bubbles – and the sniff of success – and had pulled up Ellie's Facebook page once again. For the hundredth time, he'd opened the messenger screen. But this time, he'd started to write.

**Hi Ellie, this is Tristan. I've been thinking about you lately and wondered if you would like to meet for a catch-up?**

Then he'd deleted 'I've been thinking about you lately' (too creepy). His heart had raced as the arrow hovered over 'send'. He'd swallowed and pressed it. Somehow, he'd managed to get to sleep quite quickly after that and, on switching his computer on the next morning, only remembered the message when he saw a notification of a reply from Ellie.

**Hi Tristan, Yes let's catch up! How about next Wednesday in town, 7ish?**

A chuckle had shot involuntarily out of Tristan's mouth, as he'd taken in Ellie's familiar style, the exclamation mark, how she referred to central London as 'town' and the 'ish' that followed any time suggestion. Time to Ellie had always been a fluid concept. When they were together, it had infuriated Tristan that she'd presumed the whole world ran fifteen minutes late, like her. Perhaps she hadn't changed as much as he'd thought.

And true to form, she'd arrived at the pub Tristan had chosen seventeen minutes late, stumbling through the door with her curly brown hair down to her shoulders and a second baby bump poking out of her open coat, dark circles under her eyes. Then her lovely smile had broken out when she'd spotted Tristan.

'Tris, how are you?' she'd said, pulling him in for a hug, her curls tickling his nose as he'd leaned in and they'd bumped pot bellies. For the next twenty minutes, she'd talked non-stop about her husband Dale, her son Alfie, nearly two, and her soon-to-be second son. She'd even shown pictures of them on her phone while Tristan nodded and smiled in the right places. By her second glass of lemonade, she'd moved on to every detail of her teaching job, their Easter production, her latest classroom display, a little boy in her class called Henry who never left her side.

'Don't keep me in suspense, Tristan. How did it go?' Vivienne asks now.

'It was nice to see her,' he shrugs. 'She's still working as a teacher, has a little boy and is pregnant with her second. Happily married.'

Vivienne snorts. He knows she always finds it hard to believe anyone can be happily married ('an oxymoron if ever there was one,' she likes to say).

'Oh well, good for her,' Vivienne says, not even pretending to eat her meal. 'Did you tell her what you've been up to?'

'What *have* I been up to, Vivienne?' It comes out harsher than he'd intended.

'Your software, your flat...'

Tristan finishes off his bottle and waves at the waiter to bring another. Once Ellie had run out of steam, she'd asked about Tristan's life; well actually, she'd asked if he'd met anyone. He might even flatter himself to think she'd seemed nervous about his response and, once he'd confirmed that he was still single, she'd visibly relaxed. Then there had been silence. As if anything outside that was meaningless. Perhaps it was. The ticking of a grandfather clock had swelled from the depths of the pub, accompanied by the low chatter of the two old fellas sitting at the bar. And all Tristan had thought was how empty his life had become, how very little. Ellie had still been looking expectantly at him, so he'd spluttered out something about his work and his flat in Manor House.

'Sounds like you're doing well for yourself,' she said. Then she'd asked the question: 'Do you ever think about the day we broke up?' and Tristan's heart had soared. He'd nodded, ready to tell her how much he thought about her, how much he regretted. But she carried on talking.

'I just wanted to let you know that I forgive you,' she said, reaching up to hug him.

'Thank you,' he muttered into her curls.

She'd bent over to pick up her large bag from the floor, and he'd noticed her hands were trembling. One last wave and she was gone. In that instant, Tristan had realised that they'd made no plans to meet again.

Then he'd stared at his barely touched pint and thought back to the day they'd split up, the day that Ellie had irreparably broken his heart. After their make-or-break holiday, he'd felt like things were back on track. It was a Sunday morning. He'd made her breakfast in bed, asked about her plans for the day and she'd blurted out: 'Tristan, I'm moving out. It's not working.' She'd been so cold. It was so sudden, he'd felt like he was standing on a tall building and the ground had just disappeared from under him. Then she'd calmly started to pack her things up. Yes, he'd lost his temper at the sight of her clothes, books, jewellery, piled in boxes by the front door. But who could blame him, really?

The week after meeting up with Ellie, Tristan's fledgling hopes for *Moralia* had also come crumbling down. Raymond had arranged a video meeting and Tristan has been asked to present the idea to the company's board. The presentation had gone well, right up until one young upstart had queried the ethics of his program. His words had created a wave of fear through the board and they'd unanimously agreed, a resounding no.

'Let us know if you come up with something less … controversial,' Raymond had told him, and Tristan had said he would, doing his best to contain his frustration at the thousands of hours of wasted time. Tristan had quietly put the folders away and deleted the file on his laptop. He'd reverted back to spending his days on his freelance jobs followed by evenings slumped on the sofa playing *Grand Theft Auto*, or just staring up at the damp patch in the corner of his bedroom. Curled up in his bed for around eighteen hours a day, he'd only move when his hunger had become unbearable, wolf down some crisps or toast, and then climb back under his still-warm covers. Every few days, he'd force himself to take long walks around the city, usually in the early hours of the morning when he was more likely to avoid the annoying masses. Last month, he'd cancelled on Vivienne three times in a row and then didn't show up for her birthday lunch. He'd had every intention of going, had showered, got himself dressed and was standing by his front door but hadn't found the strength to open it. Afterwards, Cat had left a shouty voicemail on his phone. 'Selfish' was the word she'd used and 'you've let Vivienne down again'. So, when Vivienne had messaged to tell him Melvin was in hospital, he'd called her and, a few days later, guilt had led him to agree to meet her at the working men's club.

'And how did you feel after seeing Ellie?' Vivienne asks, finally returning to her presumably cold carbonara.

'Fine,' he says, shrugging, and Vivienne gives him a sharp look. 'Well, not great but … I'll be all right.'

Vivienne nods at her dinner and makes a half-hearted attempt to finish it off. Tristan suddenly has no appetite for his pizza and finishes off his beer in three big gulps. They both know he's lying. After Ellie left the pub, Tristan had waited for fifteen minutes – to be sure she was gone – and then made his own way home. He'd been stupid to contact her, he sees that now. What had he been thinking? That she'd confess she'd never loved her husband and offer to leave her son and move into Tristan's studio flat with him? He'd had his chance and he'd blown it all those years ago.

Today, on his way to meet Vivienne and Mary, all he'd seen was couples. London was crawling with them: an elderly pair strolling slowly along the pavement hand in hand, as annoyed pedestrians frowningly overtake them; two teenagers enjoying a passionate embrace outside Boots, their matching Dr Marten boots pushed together, hands disappearing under their leather jackets; tired-looking parents each clutching a bawling toddler, both wearing the same 'why did we bother?' expression. All different stages of life, but all with something in common: they all had someone else to share it with, the reckless passion of youth, the exhaustion of parenting young children, the aches and pains of old age. Tristan would probably never know that feeling.

'I'm so full. Shall we get going?' Vivienne asks now, tapping the small bulge at her middle. Stepping back outside, Tristan is surprised by how light it is. Looking up, he sees why – the moon is full and proud. He's always preferred the moon to the sun; it is often his only companion during his early-morning meanderings. Right now, it gives him strength.

'How about a walk?' Tristan suggests. He sees Vivienne hesitate, and has noticed how tired she gets lately after walking only short distances, how she sometimes grimaces and clutches her hip, but she nods anyway. Tristan steers them down the steps by Waterloo Bridge, onto the pavement along Embankment.

'I know it's not pretty, but Hungerford Bridge is my favourite bridge in London,' Vivienne says as they look across the inky water of the Thames at the white pylons, like the masts of a row of ships. 'Do you know it first opened in 1845?'

'Albert Bridge is the best bridge in London,' Tristan murmurs, keeping his eyes locked on the river. 'No contest.'

'I think that's the first time we've disagreed about something,' she says, weaving her hand into the crook of his elbow, something she had started to do when they walked together. Sometimes Tristan finds it comforting, bringing to mind a long-ago time when ladies were 'escorted', and gentlemen instinctively walking on the road-side of the pavement so that their female companions weren't splashed by the carts and horses. But this time, as Vivienne's fingers curl around Tristan's arm, he has to marshal all his concentration, hold his whole upper body tense, to stop himself from knocking her hand away. It feels like a lead weight, dragging him down. Every one of her fingers seems to be digging into his skin, like talons.

'Sorry, I've got pins and needles,' he mumbles, his arm shooting up as he clenches and unclenches his fist. Blissfully, Vivienne's hand falls back down to her side.

They stay quiet as they make their way along the river. The uncanny light gives the impression of daytime, but it's deadly quiet and their footsteps echo as they walk, Vivienne's kitten-heeled *clip-clopping* alongside Tristan's squeaky trainers. A brightly lit boat chugs by, happy voices float towards them, and a man waves from the deck, one hand high in the air, the other clutching a bottle of beer. And the words 'not waving but drowning' pop into Tristan's head. It was a poem he'd studied at school, hadn't thought about it for years. Vivienne gives a small wave back, but Tristan looks down at his trainers. He'd got them after Vivienne's endless digs about his ancient Converse high tops. They'd looked so smart in the shop, but now they seem ridiculous, illuminous in the moonlit night, far too flashy for a forty-year-old computer programmer.

'Last night, Cat came over and we had another search for my envelope,' Vivienne prattles. 'Now that her room is cleared out, we thought we'd stand a chance of finding it, but no luck. I think I just need to accept I'll never know my number.'

Vivienne's lost envelope is something she has spoken about often over the last three years. Tristan sees through her light tone: she has a deep, urgent need to know what the little black envelope holds. Vivienne is looking at him, and he realises she's expecting a reply.

'Perhaps it's better you don't know,' he murmurs, the phrase so familiar to him, it spills from his mouth without thought, giving an oddly robotic tone.

'You're right. I suppose everyone has a number, they just don't know it. But it would be nice to be able to plan, what with Cat having a baby and then getting married next year…' Vivienne's words peter out and she shakes her head. She's not listening to Tristan, lost in her own worries.

'Just make your plans, Vivienne.'

'I'm sorry, I shouldn't go on like this. I know your number is forty-five, which is so young…'

'Really, it isn't,' he snaps, then forces his voice to soften. 'Well, it doesn't feel like it to me.'

'Listen, Tristan, I've done my best to investigate these numbers. I've pointed the finger at Janet, Melvin and even myself. And still I've got no idea who's behind this. I'm starting to think the best we can do is to take the numbers as a warning. If we carry on in the same way, then they might come true. If we change, then perhaps the numbers can change, too,' she says.

'Vivienne, there's just no—' Tristan starts.

'After Gordon's lecture, I told Melvin that his sin was sloth and tried to warn him,' she says. 'He laughed it off, but look what happened.'

'I can just imagine it,' Tristan says, shaking his head.

'We still don't know what my number is, but I believe I'm less … envious these days and maybe that's why I'm still here,' Vivienne babbles on. 'I know it sounds far-fetched but, if I'm right, and the numbers are a warning, then perhaps you have time to change yours. I don't see you as angry but perhaps it refers to your inner anger, how critical you are of yourself.'

'It doesn't make any sense. What about Stella? She died two weeks after the party. She had no time to change.'

'No, that's true,' she says quietly, shrugging her shoulders in defeat.

Another silence settles between them.

'I remember when I turned forty, I cried myself to sleep, feeling that I'd missed my chance of marriage and kids,' she says. 'But now I see that forty is young. There's still time for you to meet someone, have children…'

'Who would want *me?* Never mind another five years of this living hell, I'm ready now.'

With that, he dashes away from Vivienne, his new trainers bouncing him up the steps of the bridge. At the top, his muscles start to ache with the effort, and he slows to a fast walk. He keeps going until he is approximately halfway across the bridge. Taking a deep breath, he lifts one leg over the railing, pausing as a gust of wind takes him by surprise, making him wobble. He steadies himself then swings his second leg over and perches on the edge of the railing. Looking down, the dark water seems suddenly smooth and inviting, like a soft silk duvet. He closes his eyes, and the image of the water is replaced with a busy pavement in Canary Wharf. He thinks of Matthew and feels his nerve waver.

'Tristan!' Vivienne is standing right next to him, breathless from the effort of her run.

'Please, leave me alone,' he sighs, leaning his body slowly forward so that his arms are stretched out, his eyes fixed on the water below.

'I won't,' she says, her shoulder almost touching his, albeit from opposite sides of the railing. She seems oddly calm, just looking down at the water as Tristan is doing.

'I won't let you do this. I can't, Tristan. I can't bear hearing you talk like that. You're a beautiful, intelligent, kind person. You have so much to give. This world needs people like you, *I* need you.'

She's crying. Tristan's heart gives an involuntary ache, but he forces himself to turn away and focus his attention back on the river. He must concentrate.

'What's got into you? I thought things were going better, Tristan.' Her hand is on his arm, those long fingers curling around his wrist, just above her father's watch. She's surprisingly strong, he thinks, but not strong enough.

'That's just what you wanted to believe. The truth is, it'll never get better. Not for me.'

'Listen, come back over here and let's go and get a coffee somewhere. We need to talk this through properly,' she says, and he hears the fear in her voice.

'I'm so sorry,' he says, tears now falling down his own cheeks.

'You have nothing to apologise for—'

Tristan swings his body around to face her, stumbles, grabs at her elbows, and pulls her over the barrier with him as he plummets off the edge.

He stares into her shocked eyes as they fall together. He hopes they will lose consciousness before they hit the water. His ears are filled with Vivienne's terrified scream and then he feels pain shooting through his feet. Cold envelopes them as the Thames opens its icy arms to welcome them inside. And then nothing. Blissful nothing.

# The Funeral
## *May 2019 –*
## *six months later*

**Vivienne**

Opening her eyes, Vivienne gasps as she sees Tristan standing in the corner of her bedroom, leaning lazily against her wardrobe. *Deep breath, deep breath.* Blinking several times, she scoops up her glasses from the bedside table, puts them on and looks again. It's just her old blue cardigan, draped haphazardly over the wardrobe door. Tristan is gone, she reminds herself. *He's gone.* And yet she sees him in her bedroom all the time, feels him sitting on her floral duvet, her dreams are filled with him. Standing in the rain when they met for the first time; sobbing into his hands when he spoke of his panic attacks; looking into her eyes as they dropped together into the water.

Sleep overcomes Vivienne once again and she allows herself to be tossed around by her dreams. Now she is stroking her own pregnant belly; now she's shoulder-to-shoulder laughing with Melvin; now she is feeling Tristan's hand squeeze her elbows on the bridge…

'Are you awake, Vivienne?' Cat whispers, her head peeping around the bedroom door.

'Yes, just about,' she croaks and then smiles as Cat walks in with baby Angharad on her hip and a cup of tea in her other hand.

'Drink this and then we should start to get ready. Ziggy's coming to pick up Angharad at nine,' Cat says, sitting on the bed and handing the baby over to Vivienne. 'If you're sure you're up to it.'

'I am. A cuddle with this one and I'm ready for anything,' says Vivienne, with a confidence that she does not feel.

'Did you sleep much?'

'A little bit,' she says, bouncing the baby on her knee, who giggles with delight. 'Still having those dreams, but the doctor said that's normal.'

Cat nods and smiles distractedly at them. Vivienne takes in the dark circles under her eyes, the look of worry that hasn't left her face in the last six months. She hates that she put Cat through all of that when she was heavily pregnant. Vivienne can't remember much at all from that night. She remembers holding on to Tristan on the bridge. But that's it. Cat has since told her that someone walking along the embankment had seen them go under and alerted the Thames Coastguard. Vivienne had been found quickly and rushed to St Thomas' Hospital where she'd been treated for brain hypoxia and pneumonia. That week in hospital had passed in a haze of delirium: lucid dreams and brief moments of wakefulness slugging it out, with dreams usually emerging victorious. When she'd finally been awake long enough for a conversation, Cat had informed her that the Coastguard hadn't found Tristan that night, but they'd seen him struggle and slip beneath the water.

'The doctor said you might suffer memory loss, but can you remember anything about what happened?' Cat had asked.

'Tristan had a panic attack and wanted to jump off the bridge … I tried to stop him…' Then Vivienne had turned her head away from Cat, falling silent, and soon pretended to fall asleep. It was only once Cat's visit had ended that she'd let the tears come. Tristan was gone and she'd failed to save him.

Towards the end of her hospital stay, a woman had appeared by Vivienne's bed.

'Your doctor has suggested that you experienced a dissociative fugue state on the bridge,' she'd carefully explained, her fingers playing with the wooden beads around her neck. 'As if you travelled out of your body for a while. I wondered if this was something you'd experienced before in moments of extreme stress?'

Vivienne's heart had hammered against her chest ... *mur-der-er* ... *mur-der-er*... *No!* She might have suffered a fugue state afterwards but she'd remembered what had happened with Tristan that night. She'd tried to save him. So she'd shaken her head and reassured the woman that it had been a one-off, unwilling to go into all of that. Once the woman had left, Vivienne's mind had drifted back to her very first fugue state, aged eighteen and pregnant.

Cat takes Angharad off her now, and Vivienne sips her sugary tea, still feeling an ache in her elbows where Tristan had gripped her, all those months ago. If only she'd been strong enough to save him. Six months after they went into the water, Tristan's death certificate had been issued and his mother Susan had set the date for his funeral.

'You don't have to go, you know, if it's going to be too hard,' Cat says, tears already rising in her eyes. 'Ole waterworks' as Vivienne sometimes still calls her, once critically, now affectionately. Back on the magazine, she'd seen Cat's regular tears as a weakness, as a means to show her (male) colleagues she couldn't cope, a signal that she was bowing down to their superiority. Now Vivienne sees those assumptions as signs of weakness in herself. Cat is one of the strongest women, no – people, she knows. Her tears show her empathy, her heightened sense of the pain of others. What is weak about that?

Once Vivienne had been released from hospital, Cat had insisted on coming back and staying in the loft room, right up until she'd gone into labour. Vivienne will never forget the night when Cat had woken her, actually relieved her from a terrible nightmare, to say that she had to get to hospital. They'd called a taxi and met Ziggy there. Just two hours later, a baby girl with a thick head of brown curly hair arrived. They named her Angharad (Welsh for 'much loved' which had been Vivienne's suggestion, and made her think of Melvin). Since the birth, Cat, Charlie and Angharad regularly stayed over, utilising the cot that Vivienne had had set up in the loft room.

'I love you, Cat, but I do have to go. You don't, though. Why don't you stay at home, have a quiet day with your family?' She touches Cat's wet cheek with the pad of her thumb, not wiping her tears, just touching them, letting them soak into her own body, hoping Cat's strength will help her through the day.

'You're my family. Drink your tea and I'll make some breakfast,' she says.

* * *

'I didn't know Tristan was religious,' Cat whispers as she and Vivienne walk slowly towards the church. Vivienne is wearing her long-sleeved woollen dress, black tights, boots and her warm coat and already she's sweating. This Spring has been unseasonably cold, but the sun has come out today, just when Vivienne would welcome dark clouds and drizzle. Maybe Cat was right, maybe she wasn't up to this. But how could she have missed Tristan's funeral?

'No, Tristan wasn't, but his mother is,' Vivienne replies, remembering him laughing about his parents dressing in their 'Sunday best' every week, 'as if God cares if Dad had stubble on his chin, or Mum had a set and blow-dry'.

The village is oddly familiar, perhaps because it's just like something from the front of a charity Christmas card. The low stone wall lining the road, the modest little church with its proud steeple, ancient, mist-covered gravestones on one side, like soldiers waiting for battle. A small group of people are gathered under the arched doorway (where Vivienne pictures giddy newly-weds posing for the camera). But this group are not here to celebrate new love.

'Let's just wait here for a minute,' Vivienne mutters, pulling Cat back from the church entrance.

'You've got nothing to be ashamed of,' Cat tells her. 'You have every right to be here.'

But Cat does as Vivienne asks and they stand together at the churchyard entrance, allowing mourners to pass them and file into the church.

'Did you reply to Ian's message?' Cat asks, not one to allow a funeral to get in the way of matchmaking.

'No, but I will. He wants to cook me a vegan curry,' she says, trying to keep a smile off her face.

'Well, I think you should let him,' Cat tells her, meeting her eyes.

'Maybe I will,' Vivienne says, with a shrug. 'Time to go in.'

She can't let on to Cat, but she has been wondering if she'd dismissed Ian too quickly. He'd been so kind since the accident, sending flowers and regularly calling to check on her.

'Vivienne, thank you for coming.' Tristan's mother is suddenly in front of them, like a castle guard or nightclub bouncer. Her sand-coloured hair forms a perfectly permed helmet, the deep purple arch of her eyeshadow matching the large flowers on her busy floral dress.

'Susan,' Vivienne stumbles, words spilling out. 'I-I'm so sorry for your loss. It was such a tragic accident.'

'Yes, it was,' Susan says, nodding and avoiding Vivienne's eye.

During that hazy week in hospital, Susan had regularly appeared at Vivienne's bedside, desperate for answers. Some days, she'd been dripping in tears, a vision of grief; other days she'd been dry-eyed and quarrelsome, bearing an arsenal of questions. Vivienne and her muddled mind had done their best, but so often Susan had left dissatisfied with her vague responses. A panic attack, a cry for help, a struggle, and a fall.

'He's never had a panic attack in his life,' she'd snapped at Vivienne several times, and Vivienne had thought how sad it was that Susan didn't really know her son at all.

Stepping inside the church, Vivienne's body temperature cranks up another few notches. The overwhelming scent of lilies hits her as they walk down the aisle to the third row. White lilies and peonies are bunched together at the end of each row, making Vivienne think of a wedding for the second time. Neither Vivienne nor Tristan had been married, had never known that feeling of being joined to another person by law, teammates for life – well that's how it's supposed to go. Yet, in their own way, they'd been joined to each other. Joined by their matching loneliness at first and still now by secrets that Tristan did – and Vivienne would – take to the grave.

Vivienne unzips her coat and drapes it over her lap, trying to ignore the dampness under her arms, on her lower back, behind her knees.

'It's a nice church,' Cat whispers as they gaze up at the towering marble altar, which is guarded by two large displays of yet more lilies and peonies, out-performed only by the crucifix on the back wall. Vivienne's eyes are drawn to Jesus's hip bone poking from his skin, such an unexpectedly human detail.

'It's beautiful,' she replies, because really, it is: no matter what your thoughts about religion, there is beauty here. The ornate, yellow-gold tabernacle behind the altar, the intricate stained glass arching high above them. But more than that, the comforting, reassuring atmosphere of the place is beautiful. Here, sadness is welcome, grief is safe.

Looking around, Vivienne is surprised by how full the church is. In the row in front, she sees three men around Tristan's age, his university friends she presumes. A pale woman with dark curly hair falling over her shoulders walks in alone and stands at the back, keeping her head down and hugging her long black coat tight around her, despite the rising heat in the church. Then Vivienne watches as Susan, and Tristan's dad, Jim, make their way to the front. Jim wears an old suit which must have fit him once but is now too large at the shoulders and too tight at the waist. As they walk down the aisle, Susan's hand is tucked into her husband's elbow. They could be any couple on their way to church, but instead they're here to bury their only child.

The organ starts its low moan, and Vivienne picks up the sheet of paper that someone has left on her pew. *'Order of service'* is typed on the front, underneath the words *Tristan James Jones* and the dates *23rd November 1978 – 23rd November 2018*. She opens the order of service and sees the first hymn is called 'Be Not Afraid', not one that Vivienne is familiar with. In fact, it has been years since she's stepped inside a church, and not much is familiar to her. Suddenly, a lovely clear voice starts up from the back. She spins around but can't see anyone with a microphone, so she closes her eyes and listens.

*'You shall see the face of God and live…'*

Vivienne wonders what – or who – Tristan saw as he slipped away beneath the cold Thames water. She hoped he'd seen a face he'd loved in those final moments. Perhaps his mother, perhaps Ellie, perhaps a kindly grandmother.

*'Come follow me and I will give you rest…'*

She thinks about how unlucky Tristan had been in his life. Brought up by parents who didn't understand him, plagued by panic attacks, a relationship breakdown he never recovered from, scarred for life in a random attack and continually exploited in his job by employers who didn't seem to think he was worth paying. Wherever Tristan is, and whoever he is with, Vivienne hopes against hope that he has found some respite, as he certainly never got it in life.

A silence falls over the congregation. Vivienne is still stuck in her thoughts when Cat turns to the back of the church.

'It's here,' she whispers.

For a second, Vivienne isn't sure what she's talking about. She turns and follows Cat's gaze and sees it – Tristan's casket. Without a body, Tristan's mother had explained that they would be burying some 'meaningful items' inside, although she didn't state exactly what. Vivienne imagines childhood photos, clothes (his rock band T-shirts?), perhaps favourite books. Vivienne thinks that perhaps *she* should have had that job, sure that she knew Tristan better than his mother. The priest is walking slowly down the aisle, leading the dark wood coffin into the church. Vivienne isn't sure of the etiquette. She knows you're supposed to watch a bride come down the aisle (weddings again!) but are you supposed to watch a coffin? Or do you bow your head, not looking directly at it, like it's a vampire or Medusa? Cat meets her eye, seemingly having the same dilemma. Quickly scanning other members of the congregation, Vivienne turns to face the altar, clutching her hands together as if in prayer. As the coffin is brought forward, an 'Oh' echoes out from the front row. Vivienne lifts her eyes to see Jim pulling Susan into his chest. His own back lifts and falls with controlled effort as he whispers into his wife's ear. She hears the name Tristan whispered over and over. As if they are trying to bring back their son with the force of their love.

One memory that had been unexpectedly brought back to life following that night was the feeling – not just the memory, it was more visceral than that – of being a mother. Vivienne had buried the memory for so many years that the details had faded over time. But something about that night had stirred it up, infused it with colour and texture once more, as if it had happened just last week and not decades ago. When James had abruptly ended their relationship, Vivienne had put her daily nausea down to heartbreak, but then she'd noticed a hard lump in her otherwise concave stomach. Her doctor had confirmed the pregnancy and been taken aback by Vivienne's joyful reaction. As soon as she'd got home, Vivienne had pulled out some of her special kitten-themed writing paper from her drawer and written to James, delivering the news with a flourish of lots of hearts and kisses, expecting him to jump in his car and drive straight over, perhaps stopping off to pick up some flowers for the mum-to-be. But his response was silence and, as the weeks passed, Vivienne's tummy grew along with her panic, and she'd had no option but to tell her mother everything. What followed was a traumatic five months of tears, pain (mostly of the heart), and screaming arguments, culminating in a lengthy hospital stay, strong sedatives and the death of Vivienne's baby boy after only seven months in her belly. Much of this had been relayed to Vivienne by her mother afterwards, as she'd experienced the first of her fugue states. During her weeks in hospital, her fitful sleep had been haunted by vivid dreams that merged the fall with her ill-fated pregnancy. She'd had to force herself awake in the middle of the night to escape the nightmares.

Vivienne breathes deeply and allows her eyes to rest on the coffin, now positioned in front of the altar. The priest sprinkles holy water on the wooden lid and she watches the drops roll down the side and make dark circles on the carpet. The priest then carefully places a white cloth over the coffin and slowly grazes the tips of his fingers across the top. It's a surprisingly gentle, tender gesture. She knows that Tristan's body isn't inside the casket, rather it is lying at the bottom of the Thames – somewhere in amongst the mud and old coins – and yet she still pictures him inside. Then she thinks of Stella, of Matthew, Janet, Gordon and Melvin, too. All of them reduced to husks, empty bodies, now rotting in the ground, or reduced further to ashes of dust. And Vivienne thinks again of the seven of them gathered around that table at Serendipity's. Janet's wine-stained lips and raucous laugh, Matthew's perfect cheekbones and darker-than-dark eyes, Melvin's strong handshake, and Tristan, silent and watchful, his wonderful qualities ignored by the others, Vivienne included.

Vivienne finds she can't look away from the coffin, specifically the spot where the priest's fingers touched the cloth. The priest's prayers are washing over her, and though she's not listening to the words, the rhythm of his speech is having a soothing effect on her, as if the words are bypassing her brain and speaking directly to her soul. There's silence and then Cat is whispering her name.

'Vivienne, you're up,' she says, and Vivienne drags her eyes away from the coffin and looks over at the priest, who has stepped down from his podium and is nodding at her.

Cat pushes a piece of paper into her hands, and Vivienne unsteadily gets to her feet. Vivienne had been as surprised as anyone to receive the letter from Susan asking her to do a reading at Tristan's funeral, especially given their difficult moments at the hospital. But Susan had written that he'd spoken about her often and she'd been the last person to see him alive. Something in this had felt like an accusation, but Vivienne had written back, agreeing to Susan's wishes. Her cheeks burn as she picks up her stick and leans heavily on it. The hot thick smell of incense fills her nostrils, confusing her as she can't remember seeing the priest waving one of those silver balls around. Her knees and hips cry out, but she breathes out slowly and focuses on the rhythm of stick, foot, foot, stick, foot, foot. Stepping up to the podium, she unfolds the paper and clears her throat, jumping slightly as the sound echoes around the church through the speakers.

*'There is a time for everything, and a season for every activity under the heavens: a time to be born and a time to die…'*

Susan lets out a muffled cry and Vivienne lifts her head to see Jim tenderly stroking his wife's hair. Vivienne searches the congregation for Cat, who nods encouragingly at her.

'... *a time to plant and a time to uproot, a time to kill and a time to heal, a time to tear down and a time to build, a time to weep and a time to laugh, a time to mourn and a time to dance...*'

Vivienne makes her way back to her pew, where Cat takes her hand. More readings follow, but Vivienne doesn't listen. She focuses on Cat's cool hand in hers and the sight of the rough cloth on top of Tristan's coffin. When the priest steps up to speak, he has a tone of familiarity as he says Tristan's name, which jolts Vivienne from her reverie. He talks of Tristan's baptism, first communion and confirmation, and then on to his interest in the Old Testament and other ancient texts, one in particular called *Moralia*, in *Job*, a commentary on the *Bible*. The priest goes on to talk about how *Moralia's* ancient teachings about human morals are still relevant today.

'In fact, *Moralia* holds the first known reference to the seven deadly sins,' he says, and Vivienne lifts her head as she takes the words in.

'We spent many a happy hour debating the merits of reading these texts literally,' the priest continues, with a smile, and Vivienne sees Susan nodding her head. When Cat had asked if Tristan was religious, Vivienne had answered 'no' with some authority, but it seems that she was wrong about this and wonders why he'd never thought to share this with her. Finally, the service comes to an end and the priest invites the congregation to the front to say their goodbyes to Tristan. Vivienne stands up, walks towards the end of the pew and feels her feet turning, not right towards the coffin, but left, out of the church. Outside, she takes deep breaths, filling her lungs with the cool country air, and looks out across the churchyard. A figure appears to move from behind a gravestone but then disappears. She shakes her head – her mind playing more tricks on her – and walks out of the church grounds.

\* \* \*

'Are you sure you don't want me to stay?' Cat asks, concern crossing her face.

'No, you get back to Ziggy, Charlie and the baby.' Vivienne tells her. 'I want to pay my respects to Tristan's parents. It's an easy train ride home.'

Vivienne can see that Cat isn't happy, but she knows by now when there's no point trying to change Vivienne's mind, so she gives her a big squeeze and climbs into the car. Glancing back towards the church, Vivienne sees that the mourners have now followed Tristan's coffin outside and are gathered around his grave. Even from 400 metres away, she makes out Susan's bent frame, Jim's solid arm around her, glued together in grief, in their enduring love for their son who left too soon.

Turning her back on the church, Vivienne walks slowly down the quiet country road. For once, she is grateful for her stick; her body feels useless today, her joints like jelly, her muscles turned to mush. Thankfully, it doesn't take her long to see the sign for The Ship. It is the only pub in the village after all, nestled between the post office and a corner shop. In the letter that Susan had sent her, she'd explained that the pub landlord was an old family friend and had offered up The Ship for Tristan's wake. Toasting a person's death is called a wake, as it is Irish tradition for the family of the departed to keep the body at home for three days and stay with them to be sure that they are definitely dead. Actually, now Vivienne thinks of it, it was Tristan who had told her this. He has a fantastic memory for useless facts. *Had* a fantastic memory...

She pushes open the heavy door and sees that no one else has arrived yet. Of course, they're still at the graveside. Vivienne wonders what the other mourners thought of her hasty departure. She supposes it is terrible etiquette to leave a funeral before the casket is put into the ground, but she just couldn't do it. Even though she knows he's not inside, she couldn't watch the coffin being lowered into the ground, soil being tossed on to the wooden lid. It would all feel so final. The door creaks shut but still no one appears, so she makes her way to a table in the corner nearest the ladies' and lowers herself onto a cushioned bar stool. It is comfier than it looks. Taking in her surroundings, Vivienne sees that The Ship is like any other cosy country pub. Roaring log fire – tick. Worn red-patterned carpet – tick. Beers on tap with saucy names ('Breathy Blonde' makes her think of Janet) – tick. Then she sees the framed photo of Tristan on the bar. She stands and steps towards it for a better look. The picture had been taken before Vivienne met him. Tristan's hair is thicker on top, he's not wearing glasses, and his face is clear of spots and the large scar she'd got used to. Freckles speckle his nose and he's sitting up straight in his chair, not slightly bowed like she'd always known him. He's wearing a brightly coloured T-shirt with swirls of red, orange and blue. His head is cocked backwards, a wide smile on his face, as if he's just about to roar with laughter. Vivienne steps closer again and sees that Tristan's right arm is stretched across the back of the chair next to him. She can just about make out a few strands of curly hair. *Ellie…*

'Well, you're early,' a voice suddenly booms from behind the picture. Then a giant of a man with a bushy auburn beard is facing Vivienne from the other side of the bar.

'Oh, sorry, yes,' she splutters. 'I've come from Tristan's funeral. I … didn't feel so well so I came away before the …erm … burial.'

'Can't blame you, my sweet, I couldn't even face the service. I'm Billy, the landlord. What can I get you?'

Vivienne isn't sure what he means, and then remembers where she is. 'Whisky?' she hears coming from her mouth. Although she's doesn't think she's had one since tasting her father's as a teenager, but it seems the right answer.

'No money crossing this bar today,' Billy tells her, handing over her large drink in a heavy-bottomed glass.

Vivienne thanks him and returns to her table. Sitting down, she counts the six empty chairs and lists them off in order: Stella, Matthew, Janet, Gordon, Melvin and Tristan. How has it come to pass that she is the last one? The only one left. The oldest one of the group. By rights, she should have been the first to go. They'd all died just as their numbers had predicted. All except Tristan, who had gone five years early. He'd always suggested that the numbers were meant to push the dinner guests into their deaths, so perhaps he'd decided to take control of the situation and shape his own destiny. Perhaps Vivienne's murder theory had been just that – a theory, a result of reading too many murder-mystery novels. From nowhere, her head starts to throb. She reaches up and clutches her temples. After everything that's happened, she feels like someone has taken hold of her by the ears and given her a good shake. Nothing seems to make sense anymore. Tristan's death, the numbers, that dinner party that had started it all. She can remember the other guests in vivid detail, how they all died, but the images are floating loosely around her brain. All lost threads and red herrings. The one concrete fact she knows is that she is the only one left. Could she possibly be responsible for all those deaths? It doesn't seem right and yet…

Vivienne takes a small sip of her whisky and is shocked by the strong taste of peat, by the burning inside her throat. Instantly she feels light-headed and yet somehow a sense of lucid clarity washes over her. If Tristan were here, he'd be watching her closely, his light blue eyes warning her not to lose control, worrying about her. And the pain of missing him hits her again; she knows deep inside that she'll never meet anyone who understood her like he did.

Suddenly, the door of the pub is pushed open and the curly-haired woman from the funeral tentatively steps inside. Vivienne watches as she notices the picture of Tristan and is drawn forward as Vivienne had been, a shadow of a smile crossing her face and then disappearing just as quickly.

'You must be Ellie?' Vivienne says, making her jump.

'Oh yes, sorry, have we met?' she asks, taking a glass of white wine from Billy and stepping towards Vivienne.

'No, I'm Vivienne, a friend of Tristan's, and he spoke about you. Quite a bit, actually.'

'Really? I saw him a while ago, we had a quick catch-up in the pub, but then I never heard from him again...' She looks down at her hands, chipped purple nail varnish on her fingernails. Her curls are streaked with grey. She'd attempted to hide the dark circles under her eyes with make-up but there is no disguising her sorrow.

'Sit with me?' Vivienne asks.

Ellie nods, still hugging her coat tightly, looking down at the table, not at her wine but past it. Her grief is huge and suffocating, as if she's walked into the pub with a hippo by her side.

'I wish I'd been kinder to him when we met up. I feel like I didn't ask enough questions, just spent the whole time jabbering about my children and my job...'

'I'm sure Tristan wouldn't have seen it that way,' Vivienne says, remembering his sad eyes as he'd relayed his meeting with Ellie.

Ellie shakes her curls and lets out a long breath. Glancing back up at the picture again, she allows herself a smile, flashing a wide gap between her front teeth. ('From kissing too many boys,' Vivienne's mother used to say.)

'That was taken on holiday in Crete,' says Ellie, tilting her head towards the picture. 'I'd asked a waiter to take our photo and Tristan was convinced he had the hots for me...'

'Sounds like Tristan.' Vivienne mirrors her smile.

'He treated me like a princess. Showered me with gifts and attention. We had so much in common, loved the same books, the same music...'

Vivienne nods and smiles. It feels wonderful to be talking about her friend with someone who loved him, too.

'It always seemed like he knew what I was going to say before I said it. I've never found that since. I mean my husband looks after us, don't get me wrong, but it was different with Tristan.'

'Yes, I know just what you mean,' Vivienne says.

'Do you know what happened the night he died?' Ellie asks in a low voice, and Vivienne realises that Susan probably hadn't broadcast the details of Tristan's death.

'We were walking along Hungerford Bridge, and he had one of his panic attacks, ended up falling in,' Vivienne says. 'It was an accident.'

'Panic attacks?' says Ellie. 'I didn't know he had those. When we were together, he never seemed anxious. There were other things, but not that.'

'What do you mean?' Vivienne asks.

'He could be … angry sometimes. He hid it well most of the time, but occasionally it burst out of him, like on the day we split up,' she says.

'What did he do?' Vivienne asks and then, seeing the sorrowful expression on Ellie's face, wonders if she really wants to know.

'He … well, he destroyed something very precious to me,' Ellie says, haltingly. 'We'd been on holiday in a desperate attempt to salvage our relationship, but it was obvious it was over. Afterwards, he became really controlling, not wanting me to go out without him, insisting we do everything together. So I told him it was over and started packing my things. He was furious and ripped up a book that my mother gave me when I was little, *Charlotte's Web*. It was falling apart anyway, but he knew what it meant to me.'

Vivienne looks at her in open amazement. Tristan, who had always talked passionately about the novels he loved, destroying a treasured book like that.

'I think he must have changed after you broke up. That doesn't sound like the Tristan I knew at all,' Vivienne says but can't help picturing that black-and-white image from the dinner party, the two dogs fighting, depicting wrath.

'That's good to hear,' Ellie says, pushing a tear away from her eye. 'Actually, I once suggested he should get checked out for a personality disorder, but he point-blank refused.'

'Oh?' Vivienne murmurs. 'He never told me that.'

'I should go and speak to his parents,' Ellie says, standing up and smiling stiffly at Vivienne.

'Ellie,' Vivienne asks, a thought suddenly coming to her. 'Did Tristan wear contact lenses when you were together?'

'No, he had perfect vision.' She shrugs and gives a small wave goodbye.

As Ellie shuffles away, Vivienne gets the distinct impression that Ellie had deliberately cut their conversation short, perhaps feeling that she's said too much to a stranger. Looking around the pub, Vivienne is surprised to see that the place is now half-filled with mourners. Susan and Jim are standing at the bar, nodding gravely at Billy. Vivienne watches Ellie take small steps towards them. As soon as Susan sees Ellie, Vivienne notices her eyes narrow. Poor Ellie is greeted with a brief 'Thank you for coming,' before the couple turn back to Billy. Vivienne watches Ellie wrap her coat tight around herself once more and walk out of the pub.

'Do you mind if we sit here?' Vivienne looks up to see the three young men from the church. 'Young' has a whole new meaning to her these days, she realises. The trio are balding and/or grey-haired – and yet to Vivienne, they're barely adults.

'I'm Dave.' The taller one of the group reaches across to shake Vivienne's hand.

'Vivienne. I think we met briefly at the university a while ago,' she says, taking his large soft hand. 'Are you all Tristan's university friends?'

Dave nods and introduces Fergus and Eddie, who give Vivienne small waves. They carefully set down their drinks on the table.

'Is it so obvious that we're computer scientists?' Fergus says, raising an eyebrow at Vivienne, who simply shrugs.

'Snakebite and black,' Eddie says, noticing Vivienne eyeing his drink. 'It was always Tristan's favourite.'

'He made us all try it on our first Student Union night out, do you remember?' he says, turning to his friends. 'I'll never forget my hangover the next day, but I think Tristan's was worse.'

Laughter spurts out of Dave's mouth – along with some purple fluid – and a group of elderly ladies behind them turn around and stare. He covers his mouth and ducks his head down.

'I remember. He wouldn't speak to us for days. Barely opened his bedroom door. I think it was his first hangover and he was convinced we'd spiked his drinks. We hadn't, he just couldn't handle his booze, and never did learn to,' he says.

While the boys chat about their university days, Vivienne scans the pub and notices Susan and Jim facing each other by the bar. Susan's head is bowed over her floral bosom as Jim dabs at her face with a tissue, inadvertently smearing her purple eyeshadow, but she doesn't notice – or care – as she sobs and clutches at his hand.

'He'd found out Emilia liked Jane Austen, walking holidays, and sparkly shoes so, for her birthday, he got her a first edition *Pride and Prejudice*, a subscription to the Ramblers Association, and some pink glittery wellies,' Fergus is saying. 'He went into his overdraft for the gifts, thought he'd cracked it, but she freaked out, accused him of spying on her and ditched him.'

'It was a good idea, but he should have been more subtle about it,' Eddie laughs, wiping tears from his eyes.

'Sorry, what are you talking about?' Vivienne asks, tuning back into their conversation.

'Oh, did he tell you about the spy software he developed?' says Dave.

'I know about Moralia, but it wasn't spy software, it was for employee profiling,' Vivienne says, thinking of the priest's comment about *Moralia*, an old religious text.

'Well, however he explained it, he started work on it at uni. In its early versions, he used it to spy on girls he liked. He'd offer to help with their laptop, secretly install it, and find out everything he could about them before making his move. Things like their shopping habits, their music tastes, everything they'd searched online,' explains Fergus, and Vivienne feels suddenly uneasy.

'The software worked perfectly; it was Tristan's flirting style that let him down in the end,' says Eddie.

'Well at least you all got together over the last few years,' Vivienne says.

'I think Dave bumped into him once, exchanged a few messages, but I hadn't seen him since uni,' Fergus says.

'Me neither,' says Eddie. 'And because he'd been kicked out after that fight, we didn't even see him at the graduation.'

Vivienne looks at all three of them, one by one, and sees they're telling the truth. Why had Tristan told her they'd been meeting every week, even planned to go on holiday together? And how come he'd never once mentioned that he'd been kicked out of university for fighting, of all things?

'Could I ask you something?' Vivienne says. 'Did Tristan wear glasses at university?'

'Yep, couldn't see a thing without them,' Dave replies.

After draining their pints, the three boys (no, men) stand up and make their excuses. They explain to Vivienne their plan to get the train back into London and toast their friend at all their old university haunts. As she watches them go, she smiles to herself at the thought of three bad heads tomorrow and then of Tristan's first – desperately sad – hangover.

Reaching for her stick, Vivienne stands up and is a little shocked by the sway of her legs. How had her dad managed to polish off a whole bottle of whisky on Saturday nights and remain proudly sober? A quick loo stop and then she would head home, Vivienne decides. Standing in front of the mirror of the ladies', she fishes out her lipstick from her handbag and carefully applies it. Giving her reflection one last look—

Vivienne gasps at the sight of Tristan standing just over her shoulder.

'Oh!' She spins but sees she's alone. Looking back in the mirror, there's nothing but a hand dryer next to her shoulder.

Her hands clutch the sink as she wills her pounding heart to slow down. The doctor had warned her that hallucinations were a side effect of the hypoxia and should eventually ease off. Most likely, drinking whisky in the afternoon has left her a little squiffy.

'Thank you for your reading,' a voice says, making Vivienne jump again. But this time it's no hallucination. Susan is stepping out from a cubicle, her eyeshadow now fully smudged on one side, giving the impression of a black eye.

'I'm so sorry for the way I behaved when you were in hospital,' she says, looking at Vivienne's reflection in the mirror.

'Don't even think of it, you were in shock.' Vivienne waves away the apology. 'What do you suppose Tristan would have made of all of this?'

Susan doesn't miss a beat.

'Oh, he'd hate all the fuss,' she says. 'Never liked parties, even as a child.'

'Is that right? What was he like as a child?'

'He was an unusual little boy really. Jim and I worried about him all his life. The two of us, we're not ones to talk about our emotions much, we just get on with things. But Tristan was always having one emotional outburst or another. One minute he'd hate me, the next he'd be clinging to me. I found it embarrassing sometimes,' says Susan, looking at Vivienne's reflection in the mirror. It seems like she finds it easier to look there than straight at Vivienne.

'I can imagine that would be difficult,' Vivienne says, keeping her voice low, mindful of not breaking this strange spell that the alcohol and mirrors have created, willing the door not to swing open.

'You know, he wasn't ours. Jim and I had tried for a baby for years. I suffered miscarriage after miscarriage, and it nearly ended our marriage. Jim even moved out for a few months. In those days no one talked about these things. Jim said he'd be happy just us, we didn't need a child, but I did. I ached to hold a baby in my arms, it was all I could think about,' she says.

'I'm so sorry,' whispers Vivienne, thinking of her own baby, snatched away before it was strong enough to live, followed by those unspoken years of wanting and wishing for another child to love.

'Then, one night over dinner, Jim told me about a friend of his who was a hospital porter and had found a baby boy just left in the foyer. The mother had given birth to him and then scarpered. Can you imagine? Jim was talking about it like a bit of office gossip I might be interested in, but I couldn't stop thinking about the baby, motherless and abandoned,' says Susan, her eyes now wet, her chest rising and falling with the weight of her words.

'What happened?' Though Vivienne could guess the rest, she wants to hear the words from Susan.

'I begged Jim to get us that baby, told him I needed to have it. I'm so ashamed now, but I even said our marriage was over if he couldn't do this for me.'

Her head is now bowed, mortified by her past desperate self.

'And he did it, don't ask me how. Two weeks later, the baby was in my arms, and we called him Tristan.'

There's silence as Vivienne is lost in Susan's world and can practically feel the joy – the relief – of the weight of a baby in her arms.

'You clearly loved him very much,' says Vivienne.

'I did, I hope he knew that. He suffered badly from colic as a baby, but I never minded him crying through the night. I was just so happy holding him for hours on end until he was ready to sleep. If only he'd been so easy to comfort as he got older.'

'How did he get on at school?' Vivienne asks.

'Oh, he was academically brilliant, but a bit of a loner. He did find his way in the end and made some friends, in fact he'd be with a different group practically every week. One minute he dressed in all black like the heavy metal kids, then it was baggy jeans and asking for a skateboard.' She chuckles. Then her smile disappears as another memory pops up.

'I don't know if he told you, but a few years ago – when he moved home for a while – he found out about the adoption. It was the worst day of my life. I've never seen him so angry. He moved back into his own flat soon after. We eventually made peace, but I'm not sure he ever got over it.'

'He didn't say anything to me,' Vivienne admits.

'One night, he rang the house very late, sounded like he'd had a few drinks and started rambling about how he'd found his real mother and didn't need me anymore. I was devastated, but the next day he denied it all, tried to laugh it off as a joke.'

'I know he had some difficult moments, Susan, I wouldn't read anything into that,' Vivienne says, giving the woman's hand a squeeze.

'Thank you,' she says. 'Oh, dear, I think I've had too much port. Please don't repeat what I've said. No one else knows. I know I can trust you, you looked after my boy when I wasn't around.'

'Of course I won't say a thing.'

Susan turns to leave and then stops, reaching into her bag. 'Oh, I have this for you. I found it in Tristan's flat,' she says, handing Vivienne a small white package with her name on the front. With a shaking hand, Vivienne takes it off her and pushes it straight into her own bag. She watches Susan disappear out of the door, back into the fray of the mourners, waits a few minutes, and walks out of the toilets, and straight out of the pub door.

'Hold up, will you?' a voice calls behind her, just after she hears the door swish closed.

'Just walking to the station,' she says over her shoulder, but that doesn't stop the man from dashing after her. She curses her old bones for preventing any kind of swift exit.

'Are you getting the train?' the man asks. 'I'll walk you there.'

Vivienne looks to her left and sees it's Tristan's dad, Jim, his top button now undone above his tie, cheeks and large bulbous nose bearing the telltale, ruddy glow of a regular whisky drinker.

'In the hospital, I thought you looked familiar,' he says, his words coming in short, breathless bursts.

'Really?' Vivienne responds, wishing she'd managed to get away before well-meaning Jim had seen her.

'Yes, and then Susan started talking about Tristan's friend Vivienne and it clicked,' he says. 'Do you remember me? It's been many years, but I hope I haven't changed that much.'

Vivienne stops and stares at Jim. Or rather James. How had she not recognised him before now? Her James, the love of her life, the man who had left her pregnant and heartbroken.

'It's you,' she splutters. Really, he had changed. Gone is the wavy, dark-blond hair that had endearingly stuck out in all directions, replaced by bald, mottled pink skin on top with very short grey coating on the back and sides, like a greyhound's fur. His lean athletic body has given way to a more portly frame. Then she looks a little closer and spots some hints of the man he used to be. Green eyes with brown flecks, the habit of raising one eyebrow every few words like he was permanently suspicious.

'What a coincidence,' he says, grinning. 'After all these years you end up befriending my son.' He shakes his head at the strangeness of the universe.

'A coincidence,' Vivienne replies. Her brain seems to have stalled, only capable of repeating the word he'd said.

'I doubt the adoption issue came up with Tristan, did it?' he says, more a statement than a question.

'No. Sorry, I just need to catch my train,' she mutters, desperate to get away from him. Once she's sure he's no longer following, she turns back and sees he's gone, already back inside the pub with his floral-bosomed wife and sympathetic friends. Vivienne looks at the closed door of the pub and feels like that abandoned eighteen-year-old all over again.

Then she turns and marches as fast as she can to find the first train out of there.

* * *

As Vivienne's train trundles its way back into London, she looks out of the window but doesn't see the houses, the fields or the trees passing by. Her mind is playing out today's events. The priest describing long talks about religious texts with Tristan, her atheist friend. His ex-girlfriend Ellie talking about anxious, sensitive Tristan's angry moments. His friends describing Moralia as spyware, developed to help him stalk prospective girlfriends. His mother talking about Tristan's adoption, him drunkenly telling her he'd found his 'real mother'. And then James, suddenly back in her life, in the role of Tristan's father, standing in front of her talking of coincidences.

She'd planned to wait until she was home but is overwhelmed by the need for answers. For that crucial piece of the puzzle that will make the whole picture make sense. Pulling the white package out of her bag, she cradles it in two hands. Her name is written on the front in Tristan's small precise handwriting, each letter sitting separately to the others. Taking a shaky breath, she carefully peels back the flap, reaches inside and pulls out a sheet of paper she hadn't seen for more than forty years. Tiny tortoiseshell kittens frame the writing paper. Exclamation marks and love hearts are dotted around the page and the handwriting is undeniably her own.

Vivienne's eyes scan the words:

*I have wonderful news, Jamesy – I'm pregnant!!! I don't know if it's 'mother's intuition' or what, but I feel sure it's going to be a boy, just like you've always wanted. I really like the name Kieran, what do you think?*

The letter a pregnant Vivienne had written to her married lover. She cringes at the naïvety that drips off the page. A tear falls down her cheek as she remembers the agony of James's silence. She had wondered back then if the letter had even made it to her intended: perhaps there had been a mix-up at the post office, or an intervention from his furious wife. Gradually she'd come to accept the most likely outcome: he'd read it and chose to forget about her.

But how had the letter come to be in Tristan's possession?

Vivienne's head drops back against the seat. She closes her eyes, remembers those terrible weeks in hospital, the pain of childbirth, the brief moment of holding a bundle in her arms, her mother delivering the news that her baby boy hadn't survived. Then, the first of her fugue states crashing into her brain to protect her. Vivienne squeezes her eyes, trying to wring some detail from the hazy decades-old memory. She folds her arms together as she remembers the weight of the baby. He'd been light but substantial, his feet had wriggled, he'd let out a cry…

Her eyes spring open and the truth is suddenly in front of her. Her baby survived and her baby was Tristan.

\* \* \*

Back at home, Vivienne stumbles through the front door and drops heavily onto the sofa, sinking back into the familiar cuddle of the worn tweed fabric. The adrenaline which had carried her home starts to seep away and exhaustion throbs through her body and mind. Before she allows her eyes to close, she reaches for the white package once more, turns it over and gives it a shake. A little black envelope drops to the floor. With her last shred of energy, Vivienne bends down and picks it up. She turns it over in her hands, taking in her name on the front. How many times had she pictured finding it? How many times had she imagined the number inside? Her hands shaking, she peels open the envelope and pulls the card out.

**You will die aged 63.**

With a yelp, she drops it to the floor, her whole body trembling. Sixty-three is her current age.

Forcing her exhausted brain to rally, Vivienne thinks back over today's events, searching for the clues she'd missed during her four-year friendship with Tristan. And slowly, like a film developing, she starts to see the whole picture.

*Moralia.* 'The earliest reference to the seven deadly sins,' the priest had said. The strange quotes Tristan would recite… 'a man's life does not consist of the abundance of his possessions' at Stella's funeral. He'd told Melvin 'evil exists where good people fail to act' after Gordon's death. Vivienne had taken them as signs of

Tristan's extensive reading, but now she sees they're ancient references to the seven sins.

She remembers her conversation with Susan, pictures of Tristan living back with his parents, heartbroken after his break-up... 'He'd found out about the adoption ... worst day of my life...' Vivienne sees him plan the dinner party, collecting his doomed dinner guests. During her investigations, she'd searched for a link between them – and that link had been Tristan all along. Each of them must have wronged him in some way, thanks to their sins. She guesses he'd used his clever spy software – named after the text – to find out about them all: hence how he'd known Vivienne's favourite books, TV shows and so on. Vivienne imagines that it also helped him track all of their movements.

One by one, he'd come for them. Until there was only Vivienne left.

That's how he'd planned it. She'd been the focus all along. Tristan's 'envious' mother, whom he believed had abandoned him at birth.

Then she thinks of the moment they'd fallen into the Thames together. Or rather, the moment he'd dragged her into the water, intent on murder.

'Oh Tristan, no!' she sobs.

# Before the Dinner Party
## *November 2015 -*
## *four years earlier*

**Tristan**

Tristan's shoulders ache as he makes his way carefully down the wooden staircase clutching the heavy box in front of him. With every step, the bottles make a cheerful jingly sound as they knock together and he grimaces, willing them not to smash. The last thing he needs is red-wine stains all over his T-shirt tonight, of all nights. At the bottom, he attempts to nudge the door open with his shoulder, but it's too heavy so he puts the box carefully down on the first step. As he does so, the rolled-up print tucked under his arm drops to the floor. He stands too quickly and a head-rush sweeps over him. *You can do this, you can do this...* Taking a deep breath, he uses both hands to push at the door and it reluctantly creaks open. The heat from the fire hits him right away, and sweat is suddenly trickling down his temples. He exhales as he rests the box on the floor and stretches up to look around the room.

'Wow,' he murmurs to himself. The chandelier wrapped in ivy, the beautiful table with its pristine linen tablecloth and sparkling silverware, the place settings, the dramatic fireplace surrounded by framed paintings. It's all just as he'd pictured it when he'd dreamed it up from his old bedroom in his parents' house. All that's missing are the other six guests. He glances at his watch. They'll be here in an hour. He just needs to make the final few preparations.

In the dark weeks after his break-up from Ellie and then the discovery that his parents had lied to him his whole life, he'd searched the old shoebox again and found a letter that teenage Vivienne had written to his father 'James', declaring her pregnancy just seven months before his own date of birth. It hadn't taken him long to track down Vivienne and to discover the sort of person she was. He'd even contacted some of her ex-colleagues, pretending to ask for a reference, and the same comments had cropped up each time, 'bitter', 'nasty', 'hated me because I was young/pretty/married'. Every story, every comment portrayed an envious woman. Even her letter to his father had expressed envy towards his wife. Vivienne, he'd decided, wasn't fit to be anybody's mother.

Soon after, he'd rediscovered the *Moralia* texts that he'd been obsessed with as a teenager and which laid out the seven sins that plague humanity. At university, he'd named his experimental computer program after it, imagining it as something that employers could use to ensure their staff are who they say they are, flagging up any unsavoury secrets, any unpalatable sins. But skimming the books again all these years later, he'd felt a clarity sharpen his mind. The book had contained a bookplate illustration of the sins, represented by different animals dressed as humans. The images had imprinted on his brain, crept into his dreams at night and swam behind his eyes during the day. He'd started to look back on his own experiences and pinpointed the moments – the people – that had changed the course of his life, from its promising trajectory to plummeting down into the doldrums. And each of those people had been ruled by one of the seven sins. Starting off with Vivienne.

And so he'd hatched his plan, a plan that he'd instantly known would be his greatest work, his F-you to the world, his lasting legacy. With his seven sinners already chosen, he'd set about finding the perfect 'stage' for this particular piece of theatre.

Firstly, he needed to find a nondescript road in central London, with a hidden and elegant dining room. He didn't want his guests having to travel too far to the venue, but also he wanted somewhere instantly forgettable. It couldn't be part of a chain or larger company, as he'd wanted to pay cash and leave no digital or paper trail. From all his hours of night-time wandering, much of London was engraved in Tristan's brain and, with some help from Google Earth, he'd tracked down that particularly miserable street, which held a classy little underground room. As it turned out, the venue had been used for period dramas years before but had mostly stayed empty since it had been sold to a local (questionable) businessman who was listed as director for a series of failed enterprises. All Tristan had to do was put in a call from a payphone, and a week later he dropped off an envelope of cash at the venue. Posing as an indie director, eager to create a 'convincing space for a period drama with a post-modern twist', he'd approached a set decorator. She hadn't come cheap, but he'd taken out a loan to cover all the expenses. Usually, just the thought of getting into debt set his teeth on edge but he'd kept telling himself it didn't matter as he wouldn't be around to pay it off. He'd nearly blown the rest of his budget on a high-end catering company that promised the very best in food and service. Hopefully it would be worth it.

He retrieves the rolled-up print from the floor and carefully, with great deference, unravels it and walks back to the fireplace. He chooses a similar-sized image on the right-hand side, pulls out the poster glue from his pocket and carefully covers the back of the image before smoothing it on to the front of the portrait. Luckily, in the dim light of the room, the new picture blends in quite well with the others. He glances at the seven monochrome images and allows excitement to bubble up from his tummy.

Then he picks up the box again, takes it through to the dining room and stands in front of the door where the makeshift kitchen has been set up. He leans his shoulder gently into it so that it opens a few centimetres. Peering through, he can see that the room is alive with activity, bow-tied waiters scuttling around with purpose. If he's seen, he will pose as a courier delivering the wine, but he's hoping to get in and out without being spotted. So he places the box next to the door and lifts out the large brown envelope he'd tucked inside, balancing it on top. Inside the envelope is a list of instructions for the evening: each guest must be poured at least one glass of the red wine, with no alternatives except water; the seven small black envelopes must be discreetly distributed after the dessert course; the waiters must engage with the guests only minimally. He reminds the caterer this is a very high-end murder-mystery party and it must be a night none of them will forget.

He looks once more at the special wine before tiptoeing away. It is lightly dosed with Rohypnol, key to the evening's success. He needs his guests to be relaxed, their senses slightly dulled, their experience adopting a dream-like quality.

He walks back through the dining room, giving it one last check over. Then he makes his way back upstairs, puts his glasses on and takes his place in the doorway of a boarded-up shop opposite.

First to arrive is Melvin. Sloth. As Tristan watches his bulky frame amble along the pavement, he thinks how Melvin had been in the right place at the right time on the night they'd met – or should that be wrong place at the wrong time? That terrible night when Ellie had dumped him, Tristan had walked and walked for hours along the mostly quiet streets of the city. Finally, his exhausted legs had called him home and he'd hopped on a night bus, hoping it would take him somewhere north of the city. He'd walked to the back of the quiet bus, put his headphones on and leaned against the cool window, watching the world fly by. His eyelids drooping, he'd fought sleep and hadn't noticed the group of young men get on the bus. He'd felt something hit him in the back of the head. Without thinking, he'd turned and shouted, 'What the hell?' The three men had jumped up and were on him before he could respond. One pinned him to the ground while the others kicked him in the side and the head. The bus driver had ordered all four of them off and, watching the bus pull away, blood dripping from a cut on his head, Tristan had been convinced he was going to die. He was pushed to the ground once again and then the biggest of the group swung his foot back to kick him.

'Police – stop right there!' a deep voice had suddenly yelled, sending the boys scattering. He'd felt himself being lifted up by strong arms and a large man peered into his eyes. 'Are you OK, bud?' the man asked. He'd found a taxi and escorted him to the nearest hospital. 'Are you really a police officer?' Tristan asked the man, who'd introduced himself as Melvin. 'Yes, but off-duty,' he'd told him, taking his details and assuring him he'd be in touch the following day to take a statement. 'We won't let those cowards get away with it,' he'd said. After having seven stitches in his face and an X-ray that showed his cheekbone was broken, Tristan made his way home. Over the next few days, he'd watched the bruises flourish all over his aching body, scrutinising his scarred and dented face in the mirror, as it dawned on him that Ellie would never take him back now, not looking like this. He'd relentlessly monitored her social media as he'd waited for Melvin to ring. He'd never called. Some research had confirmed Tristan's suspicions: the man is sloth personified. Calls unanswered, cases pushed to the back of his drawer, a poorly wife neglected.

Now as he watches, Melvin quickly locates the restaurant door and walks in without any apparent trepidation.

It has started to rain. As he waits, Tristan hopes the rest of his guests arrive soon. He doesn't want it to be obvious that he's been standing outside the restaurant. He wants them to believe he's just another guest, invited to this very mysterious dinner party. Then a car screeches to a halt outside the restaurant. The sweating driver quickly jumps out with an umbrella and legs it around the car to open the back door. Janet ducks out and marches impatiently along the pavement as the driver struggles to keep up and hold the umbrella above her head. Tristan watches on, taking in the red soles of her heels, remembering how her insatiable gluttony had nearly ruined him. He'd been unemployed for a few weeks when he'd agreed to help design the technology behind a new vintage-clothing app, for one Janet Tilsbury. At the time, he and Ellie had been looking for a place to buy together. She'd inherited some money when her grandmother passed away, so Tristan had been desperately saving up to match her deposit. Soon after he'd started working with Janet, she'd booked in a video call with the four other staff members, who'd all worked remotely. Janet's lipsticked smile had filled the screen as she'd explained excitedly that she had a fantastic opportunity for them. She'd had interest from a large company who wanted to buy the app at the end of the financial year. It would be a unique opportunity to make some serious money for them all if they invested in the company now, with the sale of the app guaranteeing to 'return their investment ten-fold'. Janet had even screenshared the email from the company to prove their interest. When he'd told Ellie about it that night, she'd immediately suggested they invest all of her inheritance plus the bit he'd saved. So all their money had gone into the app, plus hours and hours of Tristan's time.

That summer, Ellie had come home bursting with excitement, she'd seen the 'perfect flat' in East Finchley; it needed some work but nothing major and it was located right next to the tube station and a lovely park. They'd put an offer in, relying on getting the money from the company sale in the autumn. But, in late August, his emails to Janet had gone unanswered. His colleagues couldn't get hold of her, either. In the end, they'd found out via an online business news site that the app had been sold for 'a record seven-million pounds' to an American blue-chip company, with a clear plan to fire the existing staff and bring in their own people. They'd all been on casual contracts, so Janet hadn't even paid her freelancers for the work done, let alone repaid their investments, never mind the ten-fold return. The article had also mentioned that the set-up had been originally bankrolled by her 'millionaire husband'. Tristan guessed that she'd blown it all by her excessive spending on entertaining clients, gifts to celebrities who deigned to wear the products, as well as spending on her own wardrobe. So that's why she'd turned to her own staff to top up the funds. Ellie had been inconsolable. She'd promised him she didn't blame him, but things between them were never the same after that. All thanks to Janet's voracity.

Janet and her driver pace back and forth on the pavement three times, then she rudely snaps at the driver until finally they spot the door. Janet steps back to let the driver open it but then struts through without a word or backward glance.

The rain doubles down and Tristan huddles in a shop door, eyes not leaving the restaurant opposite. His denim jacket is now drenched, his glasses speckled with rain drops. Then he sees a figure walking along his side of the road. He turns to hide his face, pretends to be typing a message on his phone. He feels sure that Matthew will hear his racing heart as he nearly knocks him over in his confident march along the pavement, his giant black umbrella obnoxiously bearing the name of his investment bank. Although Tristan desperately doesn't want to be spotted yet, he finds himself irritated that Matthew doesn't apologise for barging into him, or register his existence in any way.

Matthew's sin is lust. He'd popped up on Ellie's Facebook page just six weeks after they'd split. From what he'd seen on her emails (thanks to Moralia), she'd still been upset by the break-up, perhaps even considering taking Tristan back, wondering if she should finally answer the phone to him, respond to one of his many emails. But then Matthew had scooped her up at a night-club, taken advantage of her upset state. He'd wooed her with fancy restaurants and theatre trips, shown her that she was capable of finding happiness with someone else. And then, once he'd had his way with her, he'd cruelly cut all ties and moved on to the next girl.

From his spot across the road, Tristan sees Matthew briefly pause at the door of Serendipity's and pull the invitation from his pocket before taking down his umbrella and stepping inside.

He hears Gordon's self-righteous voice booming out before he sees him. Speed-walking along, with the hood of his raincoat pulled tightly over his head, he keeps his conversation going even as he stops and looks around to find the door.

Pride is known to be the worst of the sins. He'd never forgiven Gordon for what he'd done back in his university days. Admittedly, shoving his fellow student Malcolm down the stairs in an angry outburst, leaving him with an irreparably broken leg, hadn't been Tristan's finest hour but – while Malcolm had deserved the shove – Tristan certainly hadn't deserved what happened to *him*. His case had gone to the university panel, which included Dr Gordon. Since he'd been so close to graduating, they'd had the option of letting him finish, but Gordon had argued fiercely against this outcome, swaying a few other board members, and so he'd been kicked out, after almost three years of studying, without a degree to his name. And without any references to help him find work or apply to another university. He'd never been in any of Gordon's classes, but they'd had one encounter that he's sure Gordon had remembered. One afternoon, as he'd raced to a lecture, Tristan was caught short. The only toilets nearby were designated teacher restrooms, but it had been an emergency, so he'd ducked inside. From inside his cubicle, Tristan had heard the bathroom door creak open, and then he'd heard someone throwing up. When it went quiet, he'd stepped out of the cubicle to see Dr Gordon staring at him in horror. Tristan had mumbled something about 'feeling better soon' and legged it. It had struck him at the time how odd that look was that Gordon had given him, filled with guilt, as if the sickness wasn't the result of a stomach bug, but had been self-induced. Tristan had been aware of the rumours that swirled the campus of the doctor's strange behaviour and terrible breath. Afterwards, he'd convinced himself that that moment had knocked Gordon's pride to the extent that the doctor had grabbed his chance to get rid of him.

'I'll expect an email from you shortly, in that case.' He hears Gordon snap down the phone now before pushing open the door to Serendipity's.

Tristan glances at his watch. 8.06 p.m. His last two guests are running a little late. Then a black cab pulls up and Stella steps out. She glances up and down the road with a look of such disgust that he starts to worry that she'll hop back in the taxi and drive off. Seeing her hungry eyes scan the road, his memories of her greed come pulsing back. Following his ejection from university, he'd set up his freelance company but, with no degree to his name, or references from previous work, he'd struggled to get going. Around that time, he'd met Ellie working at a bookshop and was amazed when she'd agreed to meet him for coffee. She'd been so impressed when he'd told her he worked for himself, he'd crossed his fingers that he'd get some clients soon. Days later, on a freelance forum, he'd seen a post from a fashion vlogger called StellaStylez who was looking for IT support to help produce videos for her YouTube channel. The pay she was offering was pitiful but, with no other options, he'd sent her a message. She'd rung him right away, ranting about how rival fashion vloggers had 'trillions of subscribers' and sponsorship deals despite their videos being below par (not exactly the language she'd used).

A quick look at Stella's page and Tristan had seen the problem: her amateurish videos were posted sporadically, sometimes weeks apart, she rarely responded to her followers' comments and, when she did, her replies were dismissive and unhelpful. But despite his better judgement, he'd agreed to work with her.

It had been hell. Stella had slept most of the day and stayed up all night messaging him with endless complaints, links to her rival vlogger's latest posts, always ending with the current number of subscribers next to a frowny-faced emoji. She'd send him rough videos giving him sometimes a matter of minutes to edit and post for her. Every single date with Ellie was interrupted by countless messages from Stella, usually ending in him having to rush home to edit her videos. As the weeks went by, the views and subscription numbers for StellaStylez rose exponentially thanks to his help. He'd installed Moralia on Stella's laptop so he could keep tabs on her emails and saw with satisfaction that her inbox had started to fill with interview requests from journalists, offers of free clothes, dinners out, invitations to fashion events. Yet not once did she thank him, increase his wage or ever show any satisfaction about the phenomenal success of her page. He'd comforted himself with the thought that his association to her YouTube page would secure his reputation in the world of vloggers and bring him more work.

Then, Tristan logged on one morning to see her subscription numbers had jumped from 121k to 252k overnight. He couldn't understand it and messaged Stella. Hours later, she'd responded letting him know his 'services were no longer required' and promptly ghosted him. Through her emails, he'd found out that her barrister father had paid for the extra subscribers, which in turn had brought in two sponsorship deals. A close look at the casual contract she'd had him sign had included a non-disclosure clause that he never work for any rival company to StellaStylez, including any online company. It had all been for nothing. He had barely any money to his name and no means to get more commissions in the area he knew best. Ellie had been understanding and paid for their next few dates as he'd scrambled for work, but all he could think about was Stella's rich, barrister father, her paid-for flat in Kensington, her barely-used Porsche in the underground car park. Stella had everything and yet demanded more. Greed. The only insurance policy he'd had was evidence of Stella's shocking trolling of her rival vloggers. He'd had an inkling that it might come in useful one day.

He holds his breath now as Stella appears to debate staying but something draws her towards Serendipity's and, holding her large bag above her head as a makeshift umbrella, she hops and skips towards the door.

Now it is only Vivienne left to arrive. As he waits for her, the rain starts to come down more heavily. He looks up, allowing the drops to soak his face and hair. *This* is the moment he's been planning for all these months. And he wants to escort her inside personally. He watches her taxi arrive and sees her step onto the pavement. Quickly, he crosses the road and sees her curse as the taxi drives off.

'Looking for Serendipity's?' he asks.

# The Graveyard
## *May 2025*

**Kieran**

He watches the sobbing woman walk slowly through the graveyard. A lanky teenage lad – tie askew – throws an arm around her on one side and a younger girl clutches her other hand while carelessly carrying a bunch of white flowers by their stalks. Loose petals flutter unnoticed onto the grass behind the sad group, making him think of a funeral flower girl. Following them are two men, one middle-aged with dark curly hair streaked with grey, the other older but very straight and tall with a full head of silver hair (lucky sod, he thinks, scratching at his own bald head). The older man pats at his cheeks with a large white hand-kerchief, while the younger man keeps glancing over to check on the crying woman, who is now by the graveside, crouching down next to the girl and holding the battered bouquet close to her chest. She suddenly looks up and frowns in his direction. Instinctively, he pulls his collar up and bows his head. But he's worrying over nothing, the bench he's sitting on is a good fifty metres away from her and is hidden by a sprawling magnolia tree. It's a large graveyard, he could be here to pay respects to any of the hundreds buried here. But he isn't. He's here for the same person as that woman. He just has to stay hidden.

'Do you mind if I sit here?' a female voice asks, and he has to stop himself from jumping up and running away.

'Erm… no, it's fine,' he mumbles, putting his hands together and lowering his eyes to give the impression he's praying for the departed so that the woman won't engage him in conversation. She doesn't get the hint.

'Who are you here for?' she asks, the wooden bench shaking as she plonks herself down. He keeps his head bowed but sees a purple coat in his peripheral vision.

'My grandfather, he was buried last week,' he responds, gesturing vaguely to the gravestones closest to them.

'Oh, I'm sorry to hear that,' she says, in the same tone as she might have used to comment on the inclement weather or the latest hopeless prime minister.

'He was in his nineties,' he finds himself saying.

'I'm Sally. That's my old colleague being buried over there,' she says, pointing towards the group he had been watching. More mourners have joined them.

'Kieran,' he mutters, still not turning towards her or offering his hand.

'Hadn't seen her in years, but, when I heard she'd died, I felt I should come along. She was quite a lonely woman, never married or had children, not much going on in her life,' she says. 'Plus, I heard they'd hired out that fancy bistro around the corner for afterwards. It does the best prawn satay you've ever tasted.' As she speaks, the trickle of mourners keeps coming, then a large group of grey-haired ladies appears, bringing a chorus of chatter and even some laughs.

'Are they all here for her?' he asks, more to himself than the woman sitting next to him.

'They must be,' she says, her eyes widening. 'Here was me thinking that no one would turn up. There already looks to be more than twenty people here, and still more arriving.'

Six years ago, he'd watched a smaller group of mourners gather at a different churchyard. Sure, it had been a risk to go but he hadn't been able to resist the temptation of turning up at his own funeral. How many people get the chance to do that? He'd pulled on a tweed flat cap and a baggy beige suit he'd picked up in a charity shop. To complete the look, he'd clutched a wooden walking stick and adopted a stooped shuffle when he'd taken his spot on a stone bench on the farthest side of the yard, the perfect place to see the comings and goings that morning. It was the first time he'd seen Vivienne since they'd 'fallen' off the bridge together and he'd been shocked by how much older she'd looked in a matter of only six months. She had her own NHS-issued metal walking stick and she was frailer than he'd ever seen her. He'd watched her lean heavily on Cat's arm as she spoke briefly to Susan before making her way inside.

Ellie had arrived shortly after, with no muscular husband holding her hand, as he'd pictured following Matthew's death. He'd been gratified to see her wipe tears from her eyes, take a deep breath before walking inside. Clearly, she'd been shaken by his 'passing'. Maybe she'd finally regretted ending their relationship, he'd wondered. And then he'd watched his old uni pals arrive, their happy chatter quickly curtailed by his mother's sobering presence. He had imagined them comparing old stories about their student days, no doubt that first hellish hangover getting a mention. His toes had wriggled in the second-hand boots; he'd never quite forgiven them for spiking his drink that night.

Unfortunately, he hadn't been able to go inside but he'd enjoyed listening to the hymns and then had stood to leave but had been caught unawares by Vivienne hobbling out of the church, alone and clearly agitated. She'd glanced around the churchyard and so he'd abruptly sat back down, gripped with fear that she'd somehow worked out what had happened and would march straight over to confront him. But, no, she'd turned away from the church and made her slow way down the road, towards the village pub. After that scare, he decided he'd overstayed his welcome. Leaving his stick propped up on the stone bench, he hopped over the wall from where he'd recovered his old bike and backpack from the lane behind the church. Without looking back, he'd set out on the long cycle to the nearest big town where he'd caught a train to take him to his new life.

'I suppose I should go over,' Sally says, finally standing up. 'Gosh, I hope I get this many people at *my* funeral. She wasn't even a nice woman!'

He watches her thick ankles and voluminous coat totter across the grass towards the still-growing group. He exhales through an ironic smile. In that brief conversation, this woman had shown envy, pride and greed. Three out of the seven deadly sins. If you looked hard enough, they were everywhere.

As he watches the large group at Vivienne's grave, they gradually fall silent and the priest in his long white robes makes his slow procession to the makeshift lectern at the head of the grave, bows his head and clutches his hands together. He cannot hear what the priest is saying but he murmurs his own prayer for Vivienne. Things hadn't turned out quite as he'd expected, not in the end, anyway, not when it came to Vivienne's death.

The dinner party itself had gone perfectly and the guests had shown themselves to be worthy of their sins – as well as their deaths. He'd been nervous as he'd waited for Stella at the tube station. She'd been his first, after all. But he'd done his research, so he knew she'd be at the press party and that she'd get the tube back as it was only a few stops to her place. He'd found a 'no entry' sign, waited for Stella to walk by, and then placed it in front of the stairs so that no one else could come down that way. He'd pulled his black hood tight around his face and waited in the shadows until he felt the warm air of an approaching train. Stella, tapping on her phone with one hand and holding an armful of gift bags in the other, stepped forward when she heard the train approaching. Just a little push had sent her head-first under that train, still clutching her beloved phone.

Matthew's death is the one that he is most proud of. It wasn't as simple as pushing him in front of a taxi or tube train. It had involved some creative thinking, some serious engineering. His research had shown that Matthew had suffered from depression in the past. No doubt a result of his dreadful upbringing, his cruel mother. In fact, Matthew had still been taking antidepressants. So, he'd decided to remind Matthew of where he'd come from, remind him who he was, underneath the well-cut suits and expensive dental work. He'd used one of his Facebook alter-egos and joined Matthew's old school group, had pretended that he'd attended the school in Matthew's year and soon pinpointed the worst of the bullies – Gareth Atkinson, now living in London. He'd contacted him, got chatting about 'poor old Matthew', told the bloke that he was in touch with him and suggested they all go out for a drink, at the same spot where he knew Matthew would be taking his latest date. *That* had certainly shaken him up. Then he'd created a bogus profile for Gareth and sent a few threatening messages. In the end, Matthew had agreed to meet 'Gareth' at work, and then he had turned up himself, pretending to be just passing and offering to help Matthew out. They'd gone to the top floor to get some air and, well, Matthew hadn't needed much persuading in the end. Afterwards, he'd made sure to drop Janet's glove up on the roof. He'd kept it in his pocket since picking it up at Serendipity's, had hoped someone might find it. It had taken everything he had not to laugh out loud when Vivienne had pulled it out at Matthew's memorial and accused Janet of murder.

Once Janet had accepted that her number was soon to be up, she'd allowed her sin to overtake her completely, the eating, the drinking, the shopping, and also the sex. He'd taken to following her after work, and most nights she was at her brother-in-law's flat. She'd emerge around 2 a.m, drunk and unstable as her feet swelled more every day thanks to her ever-increasing weight. It had been so easy – almost laughably so – to give her a little nudge off the pavement right into the path of a taxi. He'd made sure it happened on a road with no CCTV and had arranged for a taxi to be driving along at just the right moment.

Gordon's death had been quite straightforward in the end, and arguably his own fault, as the man had eaten the pie of his own volition. He had, however, gone to the trouble of buying an apple pie from Gordon's local bakery, thrown it away and then baked his own, with enough sesame seeds to do the job. He'd known about Gordon's binge eating and purging and felt sure that he wouldn't be able to resist the apple pie, and that he wouldn't stop until it was all gone.

He'd watched with interest as Melvin's life had fallen apart thanks to his inability to act. In the end, it had been so easy to get rid of him. Melvin had done most of the work himself, he'd just needed a gentle steer. He'd pulled on his baseball cap, left his glasses at home, followed Melvin and Christian as they'd hopped from bar to bar that night. He'd seen them argue outside one club, a devastated Christian questioning Melvin about whether he had in fact slept with a man they'd just bumped into. Melvin had laughed it off with the line, 'Isn't that what gay men do?' to which a horrified Christian had responded, 'Not this gay man.' By the time they'd got to a late bar in Soho, Melvin could barely walk straight. It had been so easy to approach him, slip him the little bag of pills and whisper, 'Sex on ecstasy is amazing.' Melvin had just grinned inanely at him, too far gone to recognise Tristan, or realise that he hadn't paid his 'drug dealer'. The following evening, he'd seen the message pop up from Vivienne that Melvin was in hospital, and he'd known right away that the poisoned drugs had worked their magic.

And then there had been Vivienne. In the three years following the dinner party, she hadn't acted as he'd expected her to. He'd watched in amazement as she'd slowly changed her ways, letting her envy drop away from her. She'd invited Cat and Charlie to come and live with her, learning to love them both; she'd embraced technology and grown an army of online fans thanks to the empathetic and considered content on her website. Their own friendship had sprung from nowhere, surprising him at every turn. No matter how much he'd tried to push her away, claiming panic attacks, heartbreak, depression, and rudely ignoring her messages and boycotting her birthday parties, she'd clung to their friendship, turning up for him again and again. That's why that night on the bridge had been so hard for him. He'd known what he had to do and yet a part of him had hated himself. And, even after he'd gone through with it, she'd surprised him once more.

He'd planned out the bridge fall with the utmost precision, spent weeks watching the tide, even practised the 'fall' a few times, working out the best point he'd be able to get out of the river and even studied how people look when they're drowning. It had all gone perfectly to plan – except the part where Vivienne was supposed to die. She'd told him that she hadn't swum since she was a teenager, when her parents had taken her to the French Riviera. She told a very long-winded story about struggling in the deep water and a handsome Frenchman rescuing her. Her health had been fading at the time, she'd had a busy day and he'd made sure she was tired after a long walk when they'd gone into the water. He'd been convinced she wouldn't stand a chance.

He stands and casts his eyes across the mourners one last time. This number far exceeds his expectations. It is a tribute to the extent to which Vivienne turned her life around in the last ten years. He looks at Cat, Charlie, and Angharad and sees a family mourning a woman they'd come to love like a mother and grand-mother. Vivienne's fiancé Ian, his face also drawn, had tears openly rolling down his cheeks. She'd found love in the end, real love rather than a teenager's infatuation. After their first disastrous date, Ian wouldn't take no for an answer and eventually pulled

Vivienne into a six-year love affair involving cruises and ballroom dancing lessons. Vivienne's website had continued to flourish, and she'd earned herself a devoted following of 'free-thinking women'. In the end, she'd sold it for an excellent nest-egg to pass on to Cat. She'd mourned him, though, and carried unnecessary guilt that she was the only survivor of Serendipity's.

Or at least, that's what she'd thought. That's what he'd led her – and everyone else – to believe. That night, he'd seen the Thames guard patrolling for him. Made sure they saw him slip under the waves. Six months later – though they'd never found his body – they'd concluded he'd died, and then he was safe to live his next life. As Kieran, the quiet chap who works at a tiny village library hidden away in the Yorkshire Dales.

As he watches Vivienne's casket being lowered into the ground, he allows a tear to fall down his cheek.

It's fair to say that Vivienne did well with her extra years. He hadn't expected her to get her hands on the package he'd left in his old bedroom but presumes that Susan would have passed it on, probably at his funeral. Straight after the dinner at Serendipity's, he'd had a stroke of luck when Vivienne had spilled the contents of her handbag, including the envelope, onto the pavement. He'd quickly stuffed it in his pocket, having the instinct that her not-knowing might be more damaging to her in the long run. On his first visit to Vivienne's cottage, as he'd 'spring-cleaned' her laptop, he'd also installed Moralia to keep an eye on her internet searches and correspondence.

He can't be certain if Vivienne ever opened her envelope, although he guesses she wouldn't have been able to resist. If she had, she'd have seen her number was sixty-three, the age she'd been on the bridge that night. She would have known that the 'fall' had in fact been a push, intended to end her life. Well, she'd had another seven years until death caught up with her. Perhaps she never did open it and lived out her days still wondering about the mysterious party-planner. The woman had always surprised him. He supposes he's inherited her tenacity. He would have given anything to be there when she found that old letter she'd written to James. The letter that proved that he was her son, the son she'd given away all those years ago. When he'd found the adoption papers and Vivienne's letter hidden under his parents' bed, he'd found other letters, too, a series between Vivienne's mother and his own father, at first accusatory then negotiating and finally acceptance and a plan. From further letters after the adoption, he'd understood that Vivienne hadn't remembered handing him over and signing the papers. She had been confused and convinced herself that her baby hadn't survived, but he had. He'd survived again and again.

He walks away from the graveyard. As he goes, he thinks how Vivienne had been right about a lot but wrong about one thing: he hadn't planned to allow the guests the chance to change their ways. And yet look how well Vivienne had done. Because of him.

\* \* \*

He approaches the letterbox and pulls the six envelopes from his bag then drops them one by one through the slot. An invitation to a fancy dinner party no one would refuse. He smiles to himself, and then walks along the street. His pace quickens; it's time to go home and get to work.

# ACKNOWLEDGEMENTS

Thank you to every reader who has picked up this book, enjoyed it and recommended it to someone else.

Thank you to my agent Samantha Brace from Peters Fraser + Dunlop whose enthusiasm bounced off the screen on our first Zoom chat – and, later, in real-life. Your effervescent confidence in my work has made all my dreams come true.

This book wouldn't be what it is without HarperNorth publisher Genevieve Pegg and editor extraordinaire MJ Johnson from Source Books. Your brilliant and insightful advice, along with Liv Turner's keen eye, really made it fly. I can't thank you all enough.

I'm incredibly grateful for the work done by the publicity and marketing gurus at HarperNorth: Alice Murphy-Pyle and Jess Haycox, and at Source Books: Cristina Arreloa, Hartley Christensen and team. Your faith in *Seven Reasons* has blown me away.

Thank you to Rebecca Wearmouth, Head of International Rights at PFD, for your ice cool foreign rights representation.

Thank you to Claire Ward for this eye-catching cover.

Big thanks to my little group of Curtis Brown Creative alumni, for your unwavering encouragement, gold-dust feedback on my work and several willing shoulders to cry on when things weren't going to plan. Fabulous authors all of you: Nicola Masters, Zoe Rankin and Susie Lovelock.

Thanks especially to Linda O'Sullivan for your invaluable reading of my work, constructive and kind feedback and your wise words.

And to Rebecca Hilton: our regular phonecalls-slash-counselling sessions saw me through the writing of this book and inevitably ended with the words: 'just keep going.' Still great advice!

To my partner-in-crime Samantha Wilcox for years of magazine-based fun and now joining me as we get to know the publishing world together. Here's to many more Harrogate trips, always finishing with a trip to Betty's!

To my friend Dr Sonja Vujovic for your gentle encouragement of my writing and particularly your clever advice on elements of Dr Gordon's research.

To my sister Jenna Grealish, my first reader and original cheerleader for this book. You gave me the confidence to believe that I had something and your suggestions of actors to play the seven roles "when it gets made into a film" really brought my characters to life.

Thank you to my parents Christine and Charlie Harden for a lifetime of love and support and for encouraging my love of reading from a young age, facilitating my tastes right through Roald Dahl, Judy Blume, Point Horror and Dean Koontz, making sure that every birthday and Christmas saw my TBR pile increase.

A special mention of my gorgeous sons Luca and Tommy who are a constant source of joy, laughter and inspiration. I'm so proud of you both!

Finally, the biggest thanks goes to my husband Antony. You always believed I could do this. You supported me at every stage, in every way, providing an invaluable voice of reason, humour and encouragement. I feel very lucky to have met you all those years ago at London's most salubrious night spot.

**Harper North**

would like to thank the following staff and contributors for
their involvement in making this book a reality:

Fionnuala Barrett
Sarah Burke
Alan Cracknell
Jonathan de Peyer
Anna Derkacz
Tom Dunstan
Kate Elton
Sarah Emsley
Simon Gerratt
Monica Green
Natassa Hadjinicolaou
Emma Hatlen
Jess Haycox
Taslima Khatun
Megan Jones

Rachel McCarron
Alice Murphy-Pyle
Genevieve Pegg
Laura Amos
Bobbie Slade
Eleanor Slater
Hilary Stein
Katrina Troy
C J Harter
Claire Ward
Dean Russell
Amanda Percival
Lydia Grange
Imogen Gordon Clark
Millie Morton

For more unmissable reads,
sign up to the HarperNorth newsletter at
**www.harpernorth.co.uk**

or find us online at
**@HarperNorthUK**

Harper
North